BY

SCARLET WILSON

HIS GIRL
FROM NOWHERE

BY

TINA BECKETT

first story aged eight and ...ped. Her family have fond memories of *Shirley and the Magic Purse*, with its army of mice, all with names beginning with the letter 'M'. An avid reader, Scarlet started with every Enid Blyton book, moved on to the *Chalet School* series and many years later found Mills & Boon®.

She trained and worked as a nurse and health visitor, and currently works in Public Health. For her, finding Medical Romance™ was a match made in heaven. She is delighted to find herself among the authors she has read for many years.

Scarlet lives on the West Coast of Scotland with her fiancé and their two sons.

Born to a family that was always on the move, **Tina Beckett** learned to pack a suitcase almost before she knew how to tie her shoes. Fortunately she met a man who also loved to travel, and she snapped him right up. Married for over twenty years, Tina has three wonderful children and has lived in gorgeous places such as Portugal and Brazil.

Living where English reading material is difficult to find has its drawbacks, however. Tina had to come up with creative ways to satisfy her love for romance novels, so she picked up her pen and tried writing one. After her tenth book she realised she was hooked. She was officially a writer.

A three-times Golden Heart finalist, and fluent in Portuguese, Tina now divides her time between the United States and Brazil. She loves to use exotic locales as the backdrop for many of her stories. When she's not writing you can find her either on horseback or soldering stained glass panels for her home.

Tina loves to hear from readers. You can contact her through her website or 'friend' her on Facebook.

TEMPTED
BY HER BOSS.

BY
SCARLET WILSON

Publis   d in Great Britain 2014
by Mi   & Boon, an imprint of Harlequin (UK) Limited,
Eton House, 18–24 Paradise Road, Richmond, Surrey, TW9 1SR

© 2014 Scarlet Wilson

ISBN: 978-0-263-90781-0

Printed and bound in Spain
by Blackprint CPI, Barcelona

Dear Reader

This is the third story I've set in my fictional Disease Prevention Agency. You might have guessed by now that I love everything about infectious diseases and immunisation campaigns—which is probably why I've ended up working in Public Health for the last nine years.

This story is about Donovan Reid, the resident hunk at the DPA, who was briefly mentioned in THE MAVERICK DOCTOR AND MISS PRIM and noted for his ambition and drive.

Grace Barclay has only been at the DPA for seven months. She's finished her residency and is trying to gain a coveted place on one of the fieldwork teams. Then one day she opens an envelope at work and everything changes…

For this story I've used the Marburg Virus. You might not have heard of it, but it's the disease they based the film *Outbreak* on. I watched that film again recently, and was very amused to see the resident hunk of *Grey's Anatomy*, Patrick Dempsey, looking very young and being bitten by a monkey. I had totally forgotten he was in it!

The most fun I had with this book was trying to write a sexy, emotional kind of scene with two people dressed in the equivalent of space suits!

I love to hear from readers. You can contact me via my website, www.scarlet-wilson.com, follow me on Twitter @scarlet_wilson, or find me on Facebook at the Scarlet Wilson Author Page.

Hope you enjoy Grace and Donovan's story!

Scarlet Wilson

Dedication

This book is dedicated to my dad, John Niven Wilson,
who tells me that everything I write is wonderful and
encourages me to do the best I can. I challenge anyone
to find a man with as much integrity as my dad.

This book is also dedicated to my mum,
Joanne Barrie Wilson, the woman with the best singing voice
I know, who has spent her life putting her family first.
There aren't enough words for how much
my sisters and I love you!

**Recent Mills & Boon® Medical Romance™ titles
by Scarlet Wilson:**

**Recent Mills & Boon® Cherish™ titles
by Scarlet Wilson:**

**These books are also available in eBook format
from www.millsandboon.co.uk**

**Praise for
Scarlet Wilson:**

'HER CHRISTMAS EVE DIAMOND is a fun and
interesting read. If you like a sweet romance with just a
touch of the holiday season you'll like this one.'
—*harlequinjunkie.com*

CHAPTER ONE

'DONOVAN REID IS sex on legs,' sighed Grace as she gathered up the remains of her lunch. Her two colleagues mumbled in agreement, too busy watching the object of their admiration through the glass window to the workout room.

It really wasn't fair. How was anyone supposed to concentrate on their lunch when they had a view like that?

His light brown curly hair was wet with perspiration, his running vest and shorts allowing every sculpted muscle to be on display as his legs pounded on the running machine. The look on his was face intense, as if every single thing on this planet depended on him reaching his goal. The machine started to slow and he blinked in recognition, decreasing his pace and picking up the towel on the handrail to dry around his face and neck.

This was their Friday lunchtime ritual. Come down to the staffroom and goggle at Donovan Reid. Their local Matthew McConaughey lookalike.

Lara dumped her half-eaten sandwich in the trash, her eyes flickering between Grace and Dr Gorgeous. 'How long is it since you've had a date, Grace?'

'Don't start.'

Lara folded her arms across her chest. 'No, really. What happened to the computer guy?'

Grace shook her head; she could feel the hackles going up at the back of her neck. 'Leave it, Lara.' She wasn't about to tell her friends that dating just freaked her out. Everything was fine in a busy, crowded restaurant. But take her out of that situation and into a one on one and a whole pile of irrational fears raised their heads.

'Are you going to tell me what happened?'

'Nothing happened. We went on a few dates but that was it. Nothing.' It was simpler not to date. She just didn't want to say that out loud. They would be rushing her down the corridor to the nearest counsellor and that she could do without. She just needed a little time. She would be fine. She would.

Lara nodded her head at the glistening muscles of Donovan Reid, who was towelling himself off before heading to the showers. 'So, have you considered any other options?'

Grace rolled her eyes. 'Oh, get real, Lara. The guy doesn't even know I exist. Have you seen the kind of women he normally dates?'

Anna piped in, 'Oh, yeah, blondes, big Amazonian types.'

They turned to look at her.

She shrugged. 'What? I saw him out at dinner the other week.'

'And you never mentioned it?' Lara seemed annoyed.

'Why would I? He never even recognised me. Believe me, he was otherwise occupied.'

Grace looked down at her own curvy body, visions of Donovan Reid wrapped around some lithe blonde model plaguing her mind, then back through the glass towards him. 'Well, I guess that rules me out, then.' She tossed her water bottle in the recycling bin, but her eyes were drawn straight back to Donovan like a magnet. She just couldn't stop staring. Maybe it was the safety aspect. Donovan Reid was in the 'unattainable' category for her. Plus there was the fact she already knew how he'd reacted in a similar situation to hers. He'd come out of it unscathed. It kind of helped with his hero persona. 'The DPA should have one of those calendars. You know, the charity kind with a naked man for every month? Think of the money we could raise for charity.'

Lara laughed. 'And apart from Donovan, who are we going to get to model for it? We're kind of short of handsome men around here.'

Anna smiled. 'That's okay. I could easily look at a different picture of Donovan every month.' She tilted her head to the side as the three of them turned to appreciate their prey once more.

He'd finished in the gym and was grabbing his gear and heading to the showers.

Grace sighed. It was official. His butt was her favourite part of him.

It had been seven months since they'd finished their residencies and started at the Disease Prevention Agency. The DPA had over one thousand five hundred employees in Atlanta alone, with another ten thousand across the US and fifty other countries worldwide. Grace and her colleagues were currently part of the two-year training programme within the Emerging Disease branch of the DPA. Two years to learn everything they needed to know about preventing disease, disability and death from infectious diseases.

Placements included lab work, epidemiology, contact tracing, public health statistics and fieldwork. Some of the placements were exciting, some mundane, but the glimpse of Donovan Reid's butt was often the highlight of Grace's long twelve-hour-shift day.

'Where are you covering this afternoon?' she asked Anna.

'I'm down in the labs. What about you?'

She shook her head. 'I'm on the phones. Crazy bat lady, here I come.'

Lara hadn't moved. She was still watching Donovan's retreating back. 'You know there's a place going on his team, don't you?'

'What?' Both heads turned in unison.

Lara nodded. 'Yeah, Mhairi Spencer's pregnant. She won't be covering fieldwork any more.'

It made sense. A few years before, one of the DPA staff had died from an ectopic pregnancy in a far-off land. That was the trouble with working for the Disease Prevention Agency. A field assignment could mean staff would be miles from the nearest hospital. The weird and wonderful diseases they covered didn't often appear in built-up areas. Regulations had been reviewed and it had been decided that as soon as any member of staff discovered they were pregnant, fieldwork was a no-no.

The tiny hairs on Grace's arms stood on end. This was it. The chance she'd been waiting for. Seven months she'd been at the DPA, desperately waiting for the opportunity to get on one of the field teams. And to be on a team with the resident hunk? Wow.

The trouble was, the same thought was mirrored on her friends' faces. She could almost hear the sound of whirring as their brains started frantically calculating the best way to make the team.

She held out her fist. They'd all started here together. They were friends. And this was their little show of unity. 'May the best girl win.' Lara and Anna held out their fists so that all three were one on top of the other.

Lara gave a wink. 'Time to fight dirty, girls.'

Grace was trying to appear casual, trying to appear calm. But it wasn't working. Since she'd arrived back at her seat she'd been making frantic notes. Things she could put on her résumé if they asked for one. Conversations she could try and have with Donovan Reid to let him know she would be the best person for his team.

She blew her bangs out of her eyes and leaned back in her chair. Who was she trying to kid? Donovan Reid had never had a conversation with her. He barely knew she existed. Her eyes focused on the sign above the phone. 'NORMAL PEOPLE DON'T PHONE THE DPA.' Didn't she know it?

Ten calls in the last hour. Six from people who had rashes that they thought ranged from bubonic plague to scarlet fever. The other four from healthcare professionals who had patients they couldn't diagnose. The internet was a wonderful thing. These days she could ask callers to take a picture and send it to her, giving them a diagnosis or reassurance in a matter of seconds.

She glanced at her watch. Crazy bat lady was late today. She'd usually phoned in by now. It was always the same conversation. Could the bats nestling in the nearby woods and caves be rabid? What kind of diseases could they carry? What would happen if she came in contact with bat droppings? All the doctors who manned the phones at the DPA knew crazy bat lady, she even greeted some of them by their first names.

Grace turned to the pile of incoming mail. The admin support was off sick. The irony of a sickness and diarrhoea bug sweeping around the DPA headquarters wasn't lost on her. She started opening the brown envelopes and sorting the mail into piles. Lots were lab reports, some queries about different infectious diseases, some journal articles and a few requests from reporters. Nothing too difficult.

The last letter was stuck in the envelope. More difficult to get out than the rest. She gave it a little tug and it finally released, along with a plume of white dust.

The powder flew everywhere like a waft of white smoke, clouding her vision and catching in her throat.

And just like that, everything around her halted.

Donovan heard the collective gasps around him. The office was usually noisy, with a chatter of voices constantly in the background, along with mumbled telephone conversations and the rattle of keyboards.

Every sense went on alert.

He stood up, looking over the top of his pod, his eyes automatically scanning in the direction in which all the heads were pointing.

Was that smoke? No one was allowed to smoke in here. Realisation struck him like a blow to the chest.

That girl. That curvy, gorgeous brunette he'd been meaning to ask a few people about. She was standing stock still with a look of terror on her face. Dust was settling around her, covering her hair, face and clothes with a hazy white powder. If it had been any other setting, and any other season, she might have looked like she'd just been dusted with the first fall of snow.

But this was the DPA in the middle of autumn. And that was no snow.

Donovan was used to dealing with emergency situations, but they didn't normally occur in his office space. He went into autopilot.

He was the most senior member of staff in the room and the responsibility of implementing safety procedures fell to him. All staff were trained about biohazard risks in the field. But he was already aware by the panicked faces that not everyone would have the quick thinking adaptability to apply them to their own workplace. He had to take the lead.

His long strides took him to the wall where he thumped the red button and the alarm started sounding. 'Everybody, this is not a drill.' His words brought the few people who hadn't already noticed what was happening to their feet. 'Biohazard containment procedures, *now*!'

He kept walking, straight towards his frozen coworker, racking his brain for her name. Darn it. He should have asked days ago. She was on his list of possibilities for a replacement for Mhairi Spencer. He might not know her name, but he'd noticed her capabilities. Smart. Switched on. And focused. Three essential components.

The last remnant of dust was settling around her. He was walking straight into a potential disaster. But it was far more dangerous to leave her in an office space with circulating air-conditioning. She looked shocked and needed a push in the right direction. He took a breath before he reached her and clamped his mouth shut tight, putting both hands on her shoulders, spinning her round and marching her towards the door.

He didn't speak. He couldn't speak. The risk of inhaling or ingesting the substance was too great. He could only hope she was sensible enough to have stopped breathing.

He glanced sideways at a colleague who pressed the automatic door release, letting the door swing open and Donovan keep his hands in place.

He steered her to the left, nudging another button on the wall with his elbow and heading into the showers he'd just left. The door sealed behind him with a suck of air.

He could hear the motors above him stop. Perfect. The air-conditioning had been switched off. This whole building was designed for a possible disaster—the laboratories downstairs handled a whole range of potentially lethal toxins and pathogens. But this was the first time to his knowledge that there ever been a biohazard via the mail system.

The showers started automatically around them. Steam started to fill the room. 'Strip.'

The word sounded harsh and there was a fleeting second of hesitation in her face before she started to comply, tearing off her shirt and sliding her trousers down over her thighs.

He took the same actions. Pulling off the shirt and tie he'd only replaced ten minutes ago and kicking off his brand-new Italian leather shoes. His designer trousers lay crumpled at his feet. All of these clothes would be incinerated.

It wasn't just her at risk any more, it was him too. And everyone else in the building.

As soon as they were both naked he pulled her into

the showers, grabbing antibacterial scrub and starting to lather it into both their skins.

There was a glazed look in her eyes. She was following instructions but didn't seem to have quite clicked about what had just happened.

There was no room for shyness, no room for subtlety. Everyone in this department knew what to do in the event of exposure to a potential biological threat. Evacuate. Decontaminate staff and area. Isolate any threats. Identify agent. Act accordingly.

He looked at a clock hanging on a nearby wall. 'Fifteen minutes.' The minimum scrub time after exposure.

They had to try and remove every tiny particle from any part of their skin, face, hair and nails. No trace should remain. They couldn't do anything about the particles they might already have inhaled, but further exposure should be eliminated.

Her eyes met his. Caramel brown in this steam-filled room. Her skin was glistening. Her hair was glistening. What was that stuff?

Water was coursing over both their bodies, the showers set at maximum. He poured some of the antibacterial soap into his hands. 'Come here.' He didn't wait for her to reply, just dumped the soap onto her head and started scrubbing furiously. It was probably some special product she'd deliberately put there and not the mystery powder but he couldn't take that chance.

'What are you doing?' she shrieked. It was the first thing she'd said. It was as if she'd snapped out of her trance. Things were about to get interesting.

The emergency procedures ordered all staff to scrub following exposure, but they certainly didn't imply they should scrub each other. Donovan was improvising. Grace couldn't see the stuff currently glimmering in her hair.

'What do you think I'm doing? I'm trying to get this stuff off you.'

The water and soap ran into her eyes and she spluttered. 'Stop it.' She slapped his hands away. 'I'll do it myself.' She turned her back to him, her first hint of shyness, leaving him with a great view of her curved backside.

'Darn it,' she muttered. 'This stuff will play havoc with my hair.'

He tipped his head back, sloshing water over his face and shampooing his head fiercely. He knew the protocols here. He'd been involved in reviewing them for the last five years. He'd just never expected to have to use them in this set of circumstances.

He started work on his shoulders and arms, rubbing the antibacterial soap over all his body. 'What's your name?' he shouted under the blasting water.

He'd never been naked with a woman whose name he didn't know.

Her head turned and she glowered at him over her shoulder. 'Grace. Grace Barclay.'

He smiled. So that was her name. In a building with one thousand five hundred employees he couldn't possibly know everyone's name. He held his hand out towards her—it was time for official introductions. 'Pleased to meet you, Grace. I'm Donovan Reid.'

She scowled and glared at his hand, making no attempt to take it. 'Oh, don't worry. I know who you are. I've been here for more than seven months.' The water was running over her face and she tilted her head to take it out of the direct stream. 'It would be nice if you could take the trouble to remember your colleagues' names.' She turned her back to him again and started scrubbing her skin.

Feisty. He liked it.

Her long brown hair fell halfway down her back, water streaming down it. He pushed it to one side. 'Let me do your back.' It made sense. She couldn't reach those parts herself and the decontamination protocol was clear. There was no room for shyness at this point in a crisis.

His hand touched her shoulder and he felt her sharp intake of breath under his touch. He started moving his hands, circulating the soap. Her skin was lightly tanned, with white bits in all the right places. And smooth. There was nothing like being naked in the shower with a woman you barely knew. It kind of cut through all the crap.

His hand felt something else and she flinched. He blinked. Steam was circulating around them. What was that bump in her skin?

It didn't really matter. But the doctor in him—or the man in him—was curious enough to look.

So he did. This time it was his turn to suck in a breath. His fingers moved over the mark—over the scar on her skin. This was no neat surgical scar, this was a rough-edged, deep penetrating wound. A stab wound.

Why would a girl like Grace Barclay have a stab wound? She spun round in the shower. His eyes went automatically to her breasts. He couldn't help it. They were right in front of him. Crying out to be touched. Bigger than he'd noticed, matching the rest of her soft curves.

She could see exactly where he was looking. She folded her arms across her breasts and turned back round.

Caught. Like a kid with his hand in the candy jar. This was getting more interesting by the minute.

Grace was in shock. Naked in a shower with Donovan Reid shock. She couldn't stop her slightly snarky responses. It was as if her automatic defence mechanisms had dropped into place. She couldn't actually believe this was happening.

Because this wasn't real. This *couldn't* be real.

Any fantasies about Donovan Reid having his hands on her body in a shower hadn't been anything like this. Not even close.

No. In those scenarios he'd had her pinned up against a nice glass door with lots of raspberry-smelling bubbles winding their way between their two bodies.

It hadn't resembled anything like this. And for a dream this was pretty awful.

Surely her imagination knew better than to give her a horrible work-related incident?

The hands streaking up and down her back didn't feel sensual, didn't feel gentle. The hands massaging her hair weren't doing it with loving care. They had a purpose. A function.

She cringed as his hands touched her neck and she squeezed her eyes shut. Mr Washboard Abs had a prime view of her big backside and occasionally dimpled thighs right now. Bet none of his Amazonian girlfriends looked like this in the shower. As if they'd just had a battle between a cupcake and a candy bar.

Then they moved. His fingers. And she could almost

hear his intake of breath over the pummelling water stream. She couldn't help the natural flinch of her shoulder, pulling her scar away from his fingers. It was inbuilt into her. The permanent reminder of that hideous night.

It didn't matter that this was far removed from that situation. Just the touch of his fingers next to her skin sent her spinning back there. Back to a dark night and an unlit parking lot. The unknown assailant and the struggle for the bag that had been on her shoulder. Why hadn't he just cut the strap? Why did he have to stab her?

Her heart fluttered in her chest. Just what she needed. A run of SVT in the shower with Donovan Reid. Any minute now she'd hit the floor and there would a whole different emergency going on.

She breathed slowly. Controlled breaths. In through her nose and out through her mouth in a long steady stream. The rapid heart rhythm—super ventricular tachycardia—had only occurred a few times since her attack and was always stress induced. Her two fingers reached up to the side of her neck and massaged gently for a few seconds. It didn't take long.

Her heart rate settled, her breathing eased. The tight feeling in her throat released.

Phew. She kept her eyes closed for a few seconds. She had her back to Donovan so he couldn't see her and wouldn't have noticed her manoeuvre.

But he had noticed her scar.

And now she was even more conscious of his touch. Conscious of the fact that the man she dreamed about was inches away from her in a shower. If she leaned back, just a little, she would lean right into his...

Her eyes started open as she felt her body drift backwards. No! She cringed. What must he think of her anyway? First introductions and she'd snapped at him. There was something kind of brutal about a man revealing he'd no idea what your name was. Particularly when you were naked right next to him. Kind of made you realise exactly where you were on his importance scale. Right where you thought—lower than the belly of a snake.

There was no way she was going to be moony eyed around Donovan Reid. She had to remain short, sharp and professional. Just maybe not *quite* so snappy.

It was the shock of the situation. That was all.

Her palms were tingling. Reacting to the feel of his hands on her back, shoulders and neck. If they reached a little lower…

No. Stop it. Anyway, two could play at that game. She was quite sure the protocol hadn't said anything about scrubbing each other's backs. But it did seem practical.

For the first time since she'd got in the shower a smile played around the edges of her lips As she pictured her hands all over Donovan Reid's body. What was it the girls had agreed to earlier? Fight dirty? The thought raced across her mind and quickly back out again.

She'd never do that. She just couldn't even contemplate it. Even with her active imagination. Deep down, that just wasn't her.

She wanted to win her place on his team fair and square. She'd probably have to be interviewed along with another ten members of staff. But she could do that.

No matter how much he was making her skin tingle, or how much her imagination went into overdrive. Donovan Reid was always professional at work. The last thing he'd be doing right now was having any erotic thoughts about her. Up until a few minutes ago he hadn't even known she existed.

No. Donovan would be contemplating whatever substance the mystery powder was. Just like she should be doing.

Guilt flooded her. Where was her professional responsibility? What about her colleagues out there? It wasn't just her that had been potentially exposed—it had been all of them. Her fingers clawed into her hair, scrubbing for all they were worth. What was the powder? Was it really something dangerous? Could it be an act of terrorism?

The DPA worked worldwide, often leading to some difficult conversations on a global level about their findings. Governments could often take offence when suggestions were made about their contribution to a disease outbreak. Her brain was going into overdrive. The DPA was a US institution. Everyone knew about the work that they did. Maybe someone had decided to make an example of them and hit them with one of the diseases they fought against.

She shuddered. She couldn't help it. The seriousness of the situation was really coming home to her now.

'Grace, are you okay?' The voice came from behind her. Donovan had leaned forward, his head almost resting on her shoulder. The concern on his face made her catch her breath.

If she had to be exposed to something nasty, at least she had one of the best in her corner. No matter what he looked like, as a doctor he was brilliant.

She was in safe hands. Figuratively and literally.

'Turn around,' she said briskly to him. He snapped to attention, meeting her glare. There was no point in trying to pretend he hadn't been staring.

'What?'

She spun her index figures in circles. 'Turn around, so I can do *your* back.' Of course. She'd spoken to him as if he was an idiot. Which at this point he was.

Her eyes were fixed firmly on his. He could almost see the determination in her glare that she wouldn't make the same mistake he just had and look in places she shouldn't. That sent an immediate rush of blood through his system and he pivoted on his heels quickly.

No. This was work. This was an emergency situation. His body might be reacting with a rush of hormones but his brain wouldn't let him go there.

Her hands scrubbed his back a little more roughly than required. He so wanted to lighten the moment, so wanted to quip, *Wanna go lower?* But Grace Barclay wouldn't find it funny.

He started scrubbing his face to try and take his mind off the fact there was a very gorgeous, very curvaceous, naked brunette inches away from him. All his fantasies about a woman in the shower with him hadn't started like this.

What could they just have been exposed to?

His brain flooded with possibilities. Anthrax, botulism, cholera, smallpox, bubonic plague. The list was pretty long. All high-priority agents that could be used in a bioterrorism attack. Easily spread and transmitted from person to person, with high death rates and the potential for spreading panic.

Some of his colleagues called him Worst-Case Don. And it was true. He always imagined the worst-case scenario in any situation. It was his mantra. *Plan for the worst, hope for the best.* It was what any doctor working at the DPA should do.

He looked back over to the wall. Steam was clouding the clock's face so he strode across the tiled floor and wiped it clean with a towel.

'Time's up, Grace,' he called, reaching for the switch to the showers. But she hadn't heard. The showers around here didn't halt automatically. No, they had some weird anomaly that meant for the final few seconds they turned icy cold. Everyone around here knew about it.

Half the fun of new recruits was letting them find out for themselves.

He picked up a towel and started rough-drying his legs, smiling as he heard the yelp behind him.

'Yaoow!'

There was the padding of wet feet behind him and the noise of someone whipping a towel from the top of the pile on the bench.

'You did that deliberately!'

He looked over his shoulder, vaguely aware that right now Grace Barclay had a prime time view of his bare backside. 'I did not. I shouted to warn you. You obviously didn't hear above the noise from the showers.'

'Obviously.' The word dripped with sarcasm.

He wrapped a towel around his waist. The immediate crisis was over; it was time to start handling a whole new one. He turned to face her.

Grace was holding the towel directly in front of her bare body. She hadn't even had time to wrap it around herself. If someone came in the door behind her they would get an unholy view of Grace Barclay.

He pointed to the scrubs in the corner. 'Get dressed. Someone should be along to let us know if the isolation room is ready.'

He pulled a set of navy scrubs over his head. Already

the room seemed too small. Donovan didn't do well in small spaces. Maybe it was the steam? Clouding his vision and taking up space. If the air-con had been working, this would have been gone in seconds.

There was a knock at the door. Through the glass he could see the outline of a hazmat suit. A face appeared at the door.

He breathed a sigh of relief. Frank, from the lab. He already spent most of his day in one of these suits. They'd probably just unplugged him, fastened him to an oxygen cylinder and sent him upstairs.

He signalled a thumbs-up. 'Ready, Grace?' She'd wound her hair in a wet knot at the nape of her neck and was wearing a pale green set of scrubs.

There. That was better. That was the sight he was used to—a colleague in a set of scrubs. Now he didn't need to worry about his eyes wandering to places they shouldn't.

She gave the slightest of nods. He paused for a second. He might be known as a brilliant doctor with an encyclopaedic knowledge, but his people skills were sometimes lacking. Should he have sat her down and given her a pep talk? She looked a little pale. Her hand was pressed against the wall as if to stop her body swaying.

But there was no time for pep talks. Donovan needed to be surrounded by colleagues who conducted themselves in a professional manner. There were things to do. Tests to be ordered. Clean-up precautions to be taken. Risk assessments made on the exposure of others. Chances were he'd be stuck in an isolation room with Grace for hours—maybe days. There'd be plenty of time for pep talks later.

Her gaze met his. 'Let's go.' Was she trying to convince herself or him?

He didn't really have time to think about it, and if Grace Barclay was a potential member of his team she was going to have to be ready for anything.

He pulled open the door and gestured towards space-suited Frank. 'Then let's go.'

Ninety minutes later Grace had been X-rayed and her bloods were being analysed in the lab. She was still in shock.

The negative pressure room was used frequently for training scenarios at the DPA. She'd been in it countless times—she'd just never expected to be a patient in one.

The glass walls reached from ceiling to floor, leaving every aspect of them on view to outside observers. The only part of the room that had any modicum of privacy was the screened-off bathroom and shower area. In the meantime, she and Donovan were prime viewing material to the rest of the department, who all seemed to be staring at them from outside.

People were scurrying around, huddled in conversations, talking on phones. All busy. All doing their jobs. Grace just wished she could be out there with them.

It was like being a goldfish in a bowl. A big bowl, with a shark circling inside.

Donovan didn't seem to like being in isolation either. He hadn't stopped talking since he'd got in here—talking about everything and anything. If she didn't know better she'd have thought he was nervous or a bit agitated. But that didn't fit with what she knew about Donovan Reid. The guy was practically a legend around here.

Last year he'd led work on an outbreak of West Nile

virus, saving the lives of over a hundred people because of his rapid diagnostic skills. Then there had been the incident that had made the news the year before. Donovan had shown complete and utter self-control when dealing with a gunman who'd entered a hospital where the DPA was working. He'd managed to persuade the gunman to release some hostages and had eventually tackled and disarmed the guy himself. Donovan Reid was every schoolgirl's hero. But it wasn't helping her head. She pressed her fingers to her temples and started rotating them in small circles.

'Has Frank been able to isolate anything in the lab yet? What about the blood tests? Have they shown anything? Is Bill Cutler from the FBI here yet?'

Grace swung her legs up onto one of the two beds in the room and leaned back against the pillows. Her wet hair was really beginning to annoy her. She'd never be able to sleep. She closed her eyes for a second. 'Donovan, any chance of some quiet? I have a killer headache.' The words were out before she'd even thought about them.

'What?' He spun around, his forehead creased with lines. He crossed the room in a few strides, putting his hand on her head.

A prickling sensation swept over her skin. The expression on his face was serious. Maybe this wasn't the start of a migraine. Could this be a symptom of something? She hadn't even considered that.

But she didn't need to. Because Donovan was considering it all for her. Out loud. 'When did your headache start? Is this normal for you? How is your vision—are you having any problems?'

She reached her hand up and put it over his, squeezing her eyes closed and trying to ignore the instant tingle that shot up her arm like a pulse.

Just like when he'd touched her in the shower.

Could this day get any worse?

She swallowed. Her mouth was dry, she was desperate for something to drink. Was there even water in this fishbowl?

She removed Donovan's hand from her head. 'Stop it. You're not helping. I suffer from migraines but I haven't had one for the last four years.' She didn't even want to open her eyes, the spotlights around them were just too bright.

He sighed with relief. 'Thank goodness. What can I do to help?'

'Stop talking?' She squinted out the corner of one eye.

He smiled. The first time he'd smiled since they'd got in the isolation room.

'Never gonna happen.'

Her stomach rumbled loudly and she pressed her hands over it in embarrassment.

'Would some food help? Or some meds?'

She nodded. Having a migraine around Dr Handsome was bad enough. Having it under the spotlight of just around every member of staff was even worse.

She mumbled the name of the meds she normally used. The normally brisk manner he used around others had vanished. 'Can you put the lights down?' she asked.

He hesitated for a second. 'Sure, I'll keep you under my watchful eye.' He walked over to the wall. Every word they said in here, every noise they made could be heard by the outside world.

'Can we get some migraine meds for Grace, please? And can someone put the lights down around here?'

There were a few nods and some words exchanged by members of staff. Anna walked over to the glass. 'Grace, are your meds in your locker? I can get them from your bag.'

Grace nodded. Donovan was back at her side. 'What do you want to eat? We need to plan on being in here for the next few hours—maybe even the next few days.' He gave her a cheeky grin. 'We can order in—what's your favourite?'

She laughed and shook her head. 'You're joking, right?'

'Why?' He held up his hands. 'Anything that comes into this room goes through the cross-contamination system. We can ask for anything. It's only our air that can't get out.' He raised his eyebrows, 'Personally, I'm going to order a pepperoni pizza and a pastrami on rye for later.'

She smiled as her stomach growled again. 'Well, there is something that helps my migraines.'

'What?'

She named a coffee house a few minutes away from the DPA. 'I've used it for years. They have the best skinny sugar-free caramel lattes and banana and toffee muffins I've ever tasted.'

He frowned, as if his brain was trying to process her female logic. 'The skinny latte counteracts the banana and toffee muffin?'

She grinned. 'Exactly. You get it. It's all about the calories, Donovan.' She pointed at his washboard stomach. 'Though I'm sure you'd spontaneously combust if you ate anything like that. You probably don't even know what a banana muffin looks like.'

He leaned forward and lowered his voice, just as the lights flickered off around them. His eyebrows arched as a dim glow of pale blue appeared, giving their skin a strange pallor. 'It's only work-related things that make me spontaneously combust, Grace. I can assure you I'm well acquainted with the muffin family.' He gave her a wicked smile. 'And from where I was standing you certainly don't need to worry about calories.'

She felt her cheeks burn. How would they look in this strange light? Had she just imagined it, or had Donovan Reid just given her a backhanded compliment?

There was no hiding her curves. She was never going to look like one of the gym bunnies he normally dated. But maybe that wasn't his preference.

There hadn't been time to think earlier. No time to be shy. He'd seen every single part of her—scars and all.

The thought of his fingers brushing over her shoulder scar sent shivers down her spine. He must have noticed it, but he certainly hadn't mentioned it.

He'd seen her ample breasts, rounded stomach and curved hips and thighs. Her backside didn't even feature in her thoughts. In her head it was her best feature— round enough to rival J-Lo's. If only she had J-Lo's matching height…

There was a hiss of air, doors were opening, items left to be decompressed before the second set of doors opened. Her migraine tablets were pressed into her hands, along with a glass of water, and she swallowed them gratefully.

Donovan Reid had never struck her as the kind of man to have a good bedside manner. He wasn't much of a people person—his mind was always focused on the job. He'd been the youngest team leader around here for the last four years.

And the last few years had been tough. A potential outbreak of smallpox, discovered by an ex-employee, followed by one of the biggest operations the DPA had ever been involved in. Donovan had missed that call by a matter of minutes. She could only imagine how much he'd smarted about that.

And now another member of his team was pregnant. Jokes had been circulating the office for the last year about a certain swivel chair. Callie Sawyer, Violet Hunter and now Mhairi Spencer had all sat in that chair at some point. Grace and her friends had vowed not to sit in it for the next five years.

She swallowed her tablets and sighed, leaning back against the pillows. They were softer than she'd thought; she could almost forget about her still damp hair. If she closed her eyes just for a minute, she might feel a little better. She sank down into the comfort zone, tugging the soft blanket up around her shoulders. She could day-dream for a few seconds.

Daydream about what she really would have liked to have happened in that shower. Donovan to give her a cheeky wink and sexy smile, loving her curves and having a look of pure lust in his eyes for her. Donovan, with his light brown curls, chiselled jaw and sculpted body. For her eyes only. Ah, well, a girl could dream.

She could hear mumbling. Donovan was in deep talks through the glass with Frank. He gave a sigh and walked over to her.

She sat up. 'What is it?'

'Oh, good. You're awake.'

She rubbed her eyes and looked around. 'Was I sleeping?'

He nodded. 'Just for the last thirty minutes.'

Great. In the middle of a crisis with the man she wanted to impress and she'd fallen asleep. 'What have I missed? Has something happened?'

'Yes, well, no. It's good,' actually. Frank couldn't screen the sample until it had been irradiated. At first glance it's not anthrax and it's not any form of plague.'

She let out the breath she hadn't even realised she'd been holding. 'Well, that's good, isn't it? Maybe it's something stupid. Maybe it's flour or talcum powder—something like that? Something that means we'll be okay.'

He ran his fingers through his already mussed-up hair. 'It'll take a few hours before we know anything for sure.'

She could read in his eyes exactly how he felt about that, he was watching everyone outside rush around. 'And you can't stand the thought of being stuck in here? You're wandering about like a caged animal. Don't you know the meaning of the word "chill"?'

As soon as the words were out of her mouth she knew she'd made a big mistake. He whipped around to face her, his eyes as black as coal. His expression matched.

'How can I chill, Grace? The DPA has just received a potential biological hazard through the mail system. No note. No explanation Nothing. Just an Arkansas postmark. Hundreds of people in our department could have been exposed. Hundreds of mail workers could have come into contact with that letter. If this *is* a biological contagion, this could be a disaster. And you want me to chill? This is my watch, Grace, these people are my responsibility.'

She gulped. Oh, no. She'd just killed any chance of impressing Donovan Reid. He probably thought she was a dumb-ass schoolkid. All thoughts of powerful thighs and six-packs were flying out of the window, although she reserved the right to conjure them back up in her dreams. She stammered, 'A-and it's m-my f-fault—because I opened the package?'

His eyes widened. 'Is that what you think? Why on earth would I blame you, Grace? You only did what any-one would do—you opened the envelope.'

She held out her hands. Her migraine really wasn't improving. The thirty-minute nap hadn't helped. The meds hadn't even touched the edge of her pain. 'But look at the effect it's had on the whole department.'

He shook his head. 'Don't read too much into my ranting, Grace. I hate that I can't be out there, doing more. It doesn't matter who opened that envelope today, the effect was always going to be the same.'

He moved over next to her and lifted an electronic BP cuff from the wall, switching on the monitor with his thumb.

'What are you doing?'

'Your migraine isn't any better, is it?'

She shook her head as he wrapped the cuff around her arm. 'I'm doing what any good doctor should. I'm checking your BP. Maybe it's not a migraine. Maybe it's something else entirely.'

Her stomach gave a little flip. Back to the whole 'you've breathed in a contagion and are going to die' scenario. She was trying to keep that one from her head right now. If this was a tension headache it was only going to get a whole lot worse.

She felt the cuff inflate, cutting off the circulation to her arm. These darned things always felt as if they overinflated and any minute now her fingers would fall off. After what seemed like for ever it gave a gentle hiss and started to go down.

Donovan's eyes stayed on the monitor, watching the figures. He leaned over and pulled the cuff free. 'Perfect. Your blood pressure is fine.'

A few minutes later the food appeared and was placed in the decompression section between the doors. After the obligatory number of minutes the second set of doors hissed open and smell of pepperoni pizza and caramel latte wafted into the room.

Their stomachs grumbled in unison and they both laughed. Donovan opened the pizza box and grabbed a slice. 'Mmm, delicious. I hadn't got round to having lunch earlier. I was just about to eat at my desk when someone…' he gave her the eye '…decided to brighten up my day.'

She should be feeling guilty that she'd managed to eat some of her sandwich while Donovan Reid had worked out at the gym. But as his muscled body had proved too much of a distraction, most of her sandwich had ended up in the trash. And the smell surrounding her was just what she needed.

Grace took a long sip of her latte, letting the smooth, sweet caramel hit the spot. It was just the perfect temperature. Someone had obviously had to spend ten minutes walking it back from the coffee house. She took a bite of the muffin. Perfect. 'Fabulous. I love these. I could eat them all day.'

'Wouldn't you get sick of them?' He was watching her. As if he was curious about her.

'Are you crazy? Of course I wouldn't. I limit myself to one a week because there's about a billion calories in each one.' She licked some toffee from her finger. 'But you know what? I love every single one of them.'

He was watching her appreciatively. Apart from being naked in the shower, it was the first time she'd noticed him run his eyes up and down her body, although right now he was focused entirely on her fingers. She tried not to smile.

It hadn't even crossed her mind that her actions could seem provocative. She'd been too busy enjoying her muffin. But somehow the thought of Donovan Reid having those kinds of thoughts about her was sending shivers down her spine. He'd never even noticed her before. He hadn't even known her name.

Her gaze met his and he looked away hurriedly. But not before she'd caught the expression in his eyes. One of pure lust. Wow.

He glanced at his watch, cursed and pulled his phone out of his pocket.

'What's wrong?' She looked over at the clock. It was just after six. Chances were they would be stuck in here all night. Was Dr Handsome going to have to break a date?

He took a couple of steps away from her—as if that made any difference in an isolation room. There was no privacy in here.

His voice was deliberately low as he left a message on a machine, 'Hi, Hannah, sorry I couldn't catch you. I've got a problem at work. I could be here a while. Possibly even overnight.'

She could almost imagine the lithe blonde model of the moment weeping into the salad she was about to miss at her cancelled dinner date. But then things took a strange turn.

'So, if you don't mind, could you check on Casey for me? Do what needs to be done? You've got the keys to my apartment. Thanks. I'll be in touch.'

Now Grace was confused. That hadn't seemed like a broken dinner date. 'Who's Casey?' The words were out before she could stop them. Being confined with Donovan Reid was giving her a confidence that had been missing for a long time.

He shot her a look. Would he tell her it was none of her business? No, he was scrolling through something on his phone. He turned it around. 'Casey's my dog. He's a bit old and temperamental.'

'Wonder where he gets that from?' She leaned forward to look at the photo, which had obviously been snapped in a park somewhere, of a black and white terrier-type dog. She looked at Donovan and wrinkled her nose. 'I didn't take you for a dog person.'

'Really? Why not?' Was he offended?

She shrugged. 'You're too intense. Always totally focused on the job. I always imagined you live in one of those sparkling white apartments that you're hardly ever in. A dog's a commitment. You just didn't strike me as a commitment sort of guy.'

He folded him arms across his chest and looked amused. 'Well, there's a character assassination if I've ever heard one.'

'What?' Her heart beat started to quicken. 'No, I didn't mean it like that.'

'Yes, you did. And that's what I like about you, Grace

Barclay, you say what's on your mind. You don't spend six hours trying to think of how to word it.'

She let out a little laugh. 'Okay, guilty as charged. I sometimes speak without thinking.' She shook her head. 'But I'd never, ever deliberately offend someone.' She raised her chin, 'I happen to think Casey looks like a great little character.'

Donovan wagged his finger at her, 'Oh, no, don't ever let him hear you call him little.'

'He won't like it?'

'He definitely won't like it.' The atmosphere between them was changing. It was almost as if he was *flirting* with her. Did Donovan Reid even do that? Maybe she *was* under the effect of some weird disease and it was playing havoc with her brain cells.

'Will your dogsitter be able to help out?'

He gave a brief nod. 'Always. Hannah's very reliable. She'll go around as soon as she gets the message and make sure Casey's walked, fed and watered.'

Her imagination immediately started whipping up pictures of what Hannah looked like. A woman with a key to Donovan's apartment? But something distracted her. There was a huddle of people outside the glass. But she was far more interested in the conversation that seemed to be happening outside. Six of her colleagues were gesticulating and arguing about something.

'Donovan…' She pointed her finger. Her heart sank. Please don't let them have discovered it was some weird, deadly disease. They were obviously drawing lots to see who would tell them.

Donovan looked over his shoulder and his gaze narrowed. 'What's going on?' He strode over to the glass. 'Has something happened?'

There were a few mumbles, before one of the staff members was finally selected to answer the question. He walked over and spoke in a low tone to Donovan. Questions were fired backwards and forwards.

After a few seconds Donovan turned to face her. But it wasn't fear on his face. His brow was furrowed and the tiny lines around his blue eyes had deepened. It was total confusion. He ran his fingers through his hair and shook his head as he took a few steps towards her, 'Grace, what do you know about the Marburg virus?'

CHAPTER TWO

WOW. TOTALLY OUT of left field. So *not* what she had been expecting him to say.

It took a few seconds for her scrambled brain to get itself in order. Then her professional mode switched into play. Donovan Reid wasn't the only one around here with an encyclopaedic knowledge—she just hadn't had much opportunity to show hers off.

She swung her legs off the bed and walked towards him. 'What's going on? The Marburg virus? Is that what we've got?' Because from what she could remember, she certainly wouldn't want to have it.

He shook his head. 'No. It's not what we've got. But someone else has it—down in Florida. First case in the US in years.' He started pacing around; she could tell he was agitated. Desperate to get out of this glass box and start dealing with another infectious disease. Donovan Reid was permanently looking for the next disaster to deal with. And this would be the biggest disaster since the suspected smallpox outbreak. How on earth could an African disease be in the US?

She screwed up her face. The migraine was still there, but the dimmed blue lights were definitely helping—as was the fact she'd had something to eat. Along with the meds and the quick thirty-minute nap she might actually shake this off.

The blue glow was doing strange things to Donovan Reid's skin. It was almost like being in a nightclub. She didn't even want to think how pale it was currently making her look.

She reeled off the first thing that came into her head. 'Marburg haemorrhagic fever. First discovered in Germany in the 1960s where workers were exposed to infected tissues from monkeys. Now it's usually passed to humans by bats. Previous cases have mainly been in Africa, or in travellers who'd just visited. There's no vaccine, no real cure, just treatment of symptoms.'

Donovan spun around to face her, his eyebrows lifting appreciatively. 'Well, well, I'm impressed. All that with no computer in front of you.'

She folded her arms across her chest. This was it. This was her chance. A chance to make up for her earlier blunder and try and find a foothold into his team.

Everyone wanted to get a permanent place on one of the fieldwork teams. It was the cutting edge of disease detective work. The front line in dealing with patients and making the biggest difference to the prevention of infectious disease.

She'd made an agreement with girls earlier to fight dirty for a place on his team. It was time to show him just how encyclopaedic her brain was.

'Actually, that's the just the summary. Would you like me to tell you the rest of the details? The fact that the last known case was in Uganda? It's got an incubation period of five to ten days. And it's got between a twenty-three to ninety per cent fatality rate.'

Oh, yeah. She was batting big style now. Being

trapped in here hadn't been much fun. Getting naked in front of Donovan Reid had been nothing short of humiliating.

There had to be at least one bonus in this lousy day.

Her mouth was running away with her now. 'Under the microscope it has a really distinctive shape—like a shepherd's crook, which means it's rarely mistaken for anything else.'

She saw the flicker of amusement in his blue eyes. 'That's okay, Grace, that's more than enough.'

Just as well. The light in here was doing distracting things to his blue eyes. Enhancing the colour and making them look a movie-star bright shade of blue. She was fast losing all concentration.

David, one of the other doctors, was reading a whole host of information through the glass to Donovan about the lab tests. 'Frank just got phoned about these. He's confirming the results.'

It was standard procedure. Most labs weren't equipped to do the specialist tests that the DPA carried out. Anomalies were noted, along with patient's symptoms and if there was any query of infectious disease, the samples were forwarded to the DPA.

'Do we know anything about the victim?'

Victim. Not patient. It only meant one thing.

'They're dead?'

David nodded. 'They died an hour ago. But they've had a child admitted with similar symptoms, so we've got a rush on to try and get a diagnosis.'

It made sense. Once they had a diagnosis they could find the best possible treatment for the patient.

David was still reading from the paper in his hand. 'Jessie Tanner, sixty-seven, from Florida. Admitted four days ago with diarrhoea, vomiting, maculopapular rash and jaundice.'

That name.

Grace's skin prickled, every hair on her arms standing on end. There was no air movement in the isolation room but she could almost swear a cold breeze had just blasted her. No. It couldn't be. It just couldn't.

David was still talking, 'Deteriorated rapidly. Didn't respond to IV or oxygen support.'

'Oh, no.' Her hand covered her mouth. She was trying frantically to remember. When was the last time she'd spoken to her? Had she said anything different? 'Oh, no. I've missed something. I didn't take her seriously.'

Donovan frowned. 'What on earth are you talking about. Grace? How on earth would you know someone in Florida?' His face paled, 'Is it family?' There was an edge to his voice, a real concern.

Grace shook her head fiercely, her heart beating furiously in her chest. 'You don't get it, Donovan. It's her. Jessie Tanner phones here every day.'

'What for?' He didn't get it. It was clear he had no idea what she was talking about.

She took a deep breath, 'Donovan, Jessie Tanner is crazy bat lady.'

'What?' All the heads outside the isolation room shot round at the rise in pitch in Donovan's voice.

Grace jerked back as if she'd just been stung by a wasp.

He couldn't believe his ears. This wasn't happening. It just wasn't. This was one of those crazy, muddled dreams you had, with totally random things happening all around.

Nothing about today seemed real.

Least of all being naked in a shower with Grace.

He put his hand on her shoulder, trying to make sense of what she'd just said. 'How can you be sure?' He had a bad feeling about this.

She took a deep breath. 'Because I remember things. I remember details. That's her name. That's where she lives.' Grace put her head in her hands and groaned. 'She hasn't phoned the last few days. I wondered what was wrong with her.'

Donovan looked at David. 'Get the call log. Find out the last time she called and who spoke to her. Find out what her query was.' David walked away swiftly.

Grace lifted her hands. 'But it's the same thing every day. It's always questions about the bats. There are some in the caves near her, and in the forest next to her.'

She screwed up her face. 'But how could African fruit bats get to a cave in Florida?'

David shook his head. 'African fruit bats probably couldn't, but Jamaican fruit bats could. I'll get someone from environmental health or the fish and wildlife service.'

There was a movement to their side. Frank from the lab. This time he wasn't wearing the hazmat suit and he had something in his hands. He pushed the button outside the isolation room's pressurised doors, not waiting for the second set to close before he walked in.

He was laughing, holding up the sample bottle with a tiny bit of powder in the bottom.

Donovan caught the shout in his throat. Frank had been here longer than him. He knew more about biohazards than Donovan ever would. It must be safe. *They* must be safe.

'What is it?'

Frank smiled, he was shaking his head. 'You'll never believe it.'

'Try me.' He wasn't in the mood for jokes. The sooner he knew that the staff around him hadn't been exposed to anything dangerous the better.

'It's honey dust.'

'What?' Of all the things in the world he'd expected to hear, that hadn't featured at all. No wonder Grace's skin and hair had glistened.

Frank kept laughing. 'I know. I can't believe it either. Must have been some high-school kids playing a prank.'

Now he knew his staff were safe Donovan felt his blood pressure rising. 'Some prank. They shut down our agency for the last few hours.' He waved his hands around the isolation room. 'Look at the procedures we had to put in place. I don't even want to guess how much this has cost us.'

Frank shrugged. 'I'm just glad we don't have a full-scale incident on our hands. This could have been our worst nightmare.' He lifted his hands. 'I'll take a high-school prank over a real-life disaster any day.'

'What's honey dust?' Her voice was quiet, timid. He'd almost forgotten she was standing behind him.

He and Frank exchanged a glance. Grace Barclay didn't know what honey dust was. Who was going to tell her?

Frank pressed the sample bottle into Donovan's hand with a glint in his eye. 'I'll leave this with you, Don. I've let the lead investigator from the FBI know we'll be standing down. I take it they'll fingerprint the letter and try and track it.' He was still smiling, his gaze flicking back towards Grace. 'I have some more tests to run on another possible outbreak. Come and see me in an hour.'

The Marburg virus. He'd need to deal with that as soon as possible.

Frank left, chuckling away to himself as Grace continued to stare at Donovan.

She stepped towards him, fixing her green eyes on his. 'I don't get it. What's going on? What's honey dust? I take it's not dangerous?'

He shook his head and tried to hide his smile. 'Dangerous—no.'

'And?'

There was no way out of this. He was just going to have to spell it out. 'It's a type of body powder, it makes the skin glow and…it tastes like honey.'

'Why on earth would it taste like—? Oh.' Her eyes widened as realisation struck home. Her cheeks flushed with colour and she instantly looked down at the floor. 'Someone sent that as a prank? Wow.'

She was embarrassed. And he liked it. Her feet shuffled nervously on the floor, her hand twiddling a still-damp strand of her hair.

He really ought to put her out of her misery and change the conversation, but this was kind of cute.

The more he was around her, the more she piqued his curiosity. He rubbed his finger and thumb together. He could almost still feel the smoothness of her skin, along with the angry, ragged stab wound. There was more to Grace Barclay than met the eye.

He cleared his throat. 'We'll need to do a debrief about this later. The Director will expect one.' He looked around him, 'We've only ever done drills in here before. This time we had a real life chance to see how things could work out.' He picked up some notes that he'd scribbled earlier. 'Maybe this wasn't such a bad thing after all. I can think of a few areas for improvement. How about you?'

She sighed and leaned against the glass wall. 'I don't ever want to be in here again—drill or no drill.'

He smiled. He knew exactly how she felt. 'Me neither. I'm sort of hoping that my suit and shoes haven't already been incinerated.'

She cringed. 'I'd forgotten about that. Darn it. That was my favourite shirt.'

'Mine too. It brings out the colour of your eyes.'

Their gazes locked together for a second, ignoring the movements around them as the news spread and their colleagues realised the crisis had ended.

He'd meant it. And the words had come out before he'd had a chance to think about them. Being in close quarters with someone did that to you. Made you say things you really shouldn't.

She shot him a sarcastic smile, 'Yeah, right, Donovan. This from the guy who a few hours ago didn't even know my name.'

He shrugged. 'I know you lunch every Friday in the staffroom opposite the gym.'

Her mouth gaped a little. Did she really think he hadn't noticed her? His cool act was working way better than he thought.

Grace Barclay was smart. She'd been able to tell him about Marburg virus off the top of her head. She'd connected the dots and realised who Jessie Tanner was. It could have taken them days to find that connection. She was gorgeous. And had a body to die for.

What more could a man want?

His focus shifted. He could think about the last few hours later. Right now he had another priority—one in which it seemed the DPA was already implicated.

'How do you feel about fieldwork, Grace?'

She shuffled her feet. It seemed to be her 'thing'. The trait that revealed her nerves. But the gaze she met his with was steady. She was doing her best to give the impression of someone with confidence.

'I'd really like to get some experience. I've been here for the last seven months. Apart from a few practical assignments with Callum Ferguson, I've not had much experience.'

Callum Ferguson, the longest-serving member of the DPA. They even called him the Granddad of Disease. If she'd done a few practical assignments with Callum then she'd learned from the master. He hadn't heard anyone complain about her.

It secured the thoughts he'd already been toying with. He had a vacancy in his team that needed to be filled. In everyday circumstances he'd ask for all the files of his junior colleagues and look for a suitable replacement. He'd ask around for recommendations—find out who was ready for the next step.

But he didn't need to do that now. And he didn't want to waste time. If Marburg virus was the next big outbreak he wanted a full team available to investigate.

They were free now. Free to get out of this isolation room and get back to work. And he knew exactly who he wanted to work with.

He held out his hand towards her. 'Grace Barclay, welcome to the team.'

CHAPTER THREE

GRACE WAS FROZEN. She wanted to jump up and down and let out a scream. But professionalism stopped her.

Instead, she reached out her hand to take Donovan's. Zing. The current shot straight up her arm. She couldn't acknowledge it. She was watching his eyes for any hint that he might have felt it too. But Donovan Reid was as cool as the proverbial cucumber.

'Are you sure? You don't need to do an interview or an evaluation?'

He shook his head. 'My team. My choice. I'd only need to go to internal interviews if I didn't have a candidate.' He gave her a smile. 'But I do. Do you want to be part of the team, Grace?'

Did she want to be part of the team? Did teenage girls dream of being Mrs Beiber? Did every medical student dream of meeting their own Dr McDreamy or McSteamy?

She shot him her best beaming smile. 'I'd love to be part of the team, Donovan. What do you want me to do first?'

'Why didn't I open the envelope?' groaned Anna as she flopped down on Grace's bed.

Lara was much more pragmatic as she poured wine into three glasses. 'Well, even if I had opened the envelope, I would never have remembered all the stuff about Marburg virus off the top of my head.' She raised her glass, 'So, here's to you, Grace. The best girl won.'

Grace's stomach gave a little flip as she reached for her glass and clinked it against her friends'. She knew they were happy for her, even though there was deep-rooted envy. It was normal in their profession. They all wanted to do their best.

Lara walked over to her wardrobe and started pulling out clothes. 'Yes, yes, no, no, definitely no.' Clothes were littered over the room like coloured fluttering butterflies.

'What do you think you're doing?'

'We're helping you pack. You're going to Florida with the best-looking guy for miles around. I want to make sure you look your best.'

She held up a bright orange bikini. 'Oh, yes!'

'Oh, no.' Grace grabbed it from the bed and stuffed it in a drawer. 'I won't have cause to wear a bikini. It's the last thing I'll need.' She looked at the other things on the bed, picking up one of her black skirts. 'What's wrong with this? Why did it get a no?'

Anna giggled. 'I can tell you. It's too old-fashioned. It doesn't enhance your best bits.'

'And what are they, if I have them?'

She rolled her eyes and picked up an alternative, pencil skirt. 'Your ass!' both girls said in unison.

Lara pulled out a couple of dresses and fitted shirts. 'These are the same style, pencil skirts that show off your shape and fitted dresses that make us all jealous of your boobs.'

She wrinkled her nose at the bright blue dress and similar styled black and white polka-dot one. 'Aren't they a bit *too* fitted for work? I'm not sure that's what I should be wearing.'

Anna shook her head and held one up. 'What's wrong? They cover all the bits that should be covered, they're a perfectly respectable length and—look—no sleeves. It's going to be hot down in Florida. You need to be comfortable.'

Lara nodded, holding up a red and then a bright pink shirt. 'And these will look great with your black pencil skirt. You need to wear more colour, Grace. It suits you.'

'Why do I feel as if you're giving me a secret makeover?'

Anna and Lara exchanged knowing glances, before sitting on either side of her on the bed. Lara tapped her thigh. 'We just don't want you to waste a valuable opportunity.'

Anna had started lifting her hair and was looking at it as if she was imagining taking a pair of scissors to it. 'Stop that!' Grace batted her hand away. 'My valuable opportunity is my chance to prove myself as a capable fieldwork team member.' Maybe if she kept saying it loudly enough she might start believing it herself.

The thought of being stuck on a flight between Atlanta and Northwest Florida Beaches with Donovan Reid was more than a little daunting. Now the crisis was over and a new investigation was starting, she was sure he would have lost all interest in her.

Maybe rethinking her wardrobe wasn't such a bad idea at all?

Lara tapped her shoulder and dumped a set of straighteners in her suitcase. 'Watch out for the frizz down there, it's very humid.' She lifted a strand of Grace's hair too. 'You should maybe think about a deep conditioning treatment.'

Grace stood up, 'What is the obsession with my hair? Is something wrong with it?'

She stood in front of the mirror looking at her reflection. She'd had long brown hair for as long as she could remember. On the odd occasion she might get some highlights or the odd hair dye job when she got it trimmed, but apart from that she usually tied it up for work. She frowned, taking a look at her ends. Maybe it was a bit straggly. Maybe it could do with a tidy up?

'Do you think I should get it cut?'

Anna stood behind her, putting her hands around either shoulder and resting them on her shoulder bones. 'What about a few inches? It might be easier to handle. Give it a bit more volume.'

Grace took a deep breath. She'd never had her hair that short before. She looked at the several straggly inches that hung beneath the position of Anna's hands. Maybe it wasn't such a bad idea.

She looked at the clock. 'I don't have time. I need to be at the airport in five hours. I'll never be able to get my hair cut before then.'

Lara swung her legs off the bed. 'Yes, you can. There's a salon in the mall that stays open really late. I'll call them now.'

'But what about my packing?'

Anna shrugged. 'I'll do it. Look out some toiletries and some underwear. I'll just throw in everything we've got on the bed, along with shoes and some casual gear for under the hazmat suit.'

She'd forgotten about that. Wearing the hazmat suits

in a hot climate was going to be really uncomfortable. Thank goodness her friends could keep her right.

She looked at the clothes on the bed. Truth was, if her friends left right now, she'd probably pack a whole load of bland clothes that she wouldn't even think about. Having their expertise was actually quite exciting after all, Donovan had commented how much he liked her green shirt…

'Come on, slowcoach!' yelled Lara. 'I've just spoken to the salon. They can take you in twenty minutes. Let's go.'

Grace grabbed her bag. A new haircut. A revamped wardrobe. And a chance to prove herself to her team leader. What more could a girl want?

Donovan stuffed things into his carryon bag. He hated luggage with a passion and had no intention of standing around while a conveyer belt of multicoloured suitcases filed past at two miles per hour. He only hoped the rest of team were as prepared as he was.

He folded one suit and a couple of shirts and ties. The rest of his clothes were casual. He was going to be on the ground investigating or in the local lab. He wouldn't need a lot of professional clothes. Just as well, as his latest suit and handmade shoes had just been incinerated. He winced when he remembered how much those shoes had cost. It had seemed like such a good idea at the time—spend a little extra, shoes that were measured and moulded to fit. It had been like wearing a pair of comfortable slippers, the Italian leather had been so pliable. Too bad they were gone for ever.

He flung his shaving gear and toiletries into a wash bag and stuffed that inside his bag. His last item was his most essential. His tablet. He'd stored all the information that the DPA had on Marburg virus, along with incidences and procedures manuals. He liked to have everything he needed at the touch of a button.

He smiled. Or maybe he should just have Grace Barclay at his side. Her knowledge seemed to rival his own and he liked it. He liked it a lot.

He glanced around his apartment. White, clean lines everywhere. She'd pretty much nailed the place with her description. Not that it bothered him. He wasn't fixated on soft furnishings and curtains. He was much more interested in the glass around him. The view of open space.

As long as he had a window with a view outdoors he was fine. Put him in a room with no windows and within a few minutes he started to get antsy. It wasn't a big deal. Because he didn't let it be. He'd never used the elevators at the DPA. The stairs were the healthier option anyway, and there were windows in the stairwell. It didn't matter that they were small, they were still there. And that's what was important.

Up until now the only place in the DPA that had really made him uncomfortable was Frank's lab. A totally enclosed environment. It needed to be. There were too many potential toxins in that lab. Any of them escaping into the natural environment would be a disaster.

He'd just about held it together today in the isolation room. There had been lots of practice drills involving the room before but he'd always had a timescale. He'd always known he'd only be in there for a few hours. Today the timescale had been indeterminable, and it had almost given him away.

At one point he'd noticed Grace's green eyes fixed

on him, watching the slight tremor in his hands with a question in her eyes. He'd ignored them. Had focused on one of the many other things that he'd had to be concerned about. It had helped. It had helped him stop visualising the walls of the elevator he'd been trapped in as a child. Six long hours in an elevator by himself. It had seemed like fun for a six-year-old to jump in the elevator and press the button, watching the doors slide closed on his horrified mother's face. Typical mischievous little-boy behaviour. Only it hadn't been so much fun when the lift had ground to a halt.

It hadn't been fun at all when the alarm hadn't sounded when he'd pressed the button and it had felt as if no one could hear him shout.

It had taken him a long time to finally hear the distant voices of adults calling to him.

Six hours, staring at four walls, was a long, lonely time for a little boy. It had felt like for ever. His imagination had run riot and left him with a permanent, and no doubt irrational, fear of being trapped again.

So windows were his friends. If he could see out of a window he was fine. Anything else he kept brief and to the point. Enclosed spaces were definitely time limited for Donovan Reid.

There was a nuzzle of something wet and soft at his feet. Casey. He bent down and picked up the little terrier, giving him a hug. 'Hey, boy. You're getting collected any time. You're going to stay with Auntie Hannah for a few days.' He was lucky. Not only did Hannah dog-walk for him, she was also able to take Casey for a few days at a time when he was on assignment. Dog-walking and dog-sitting services weren't cheap in Atlanta, but he would have hated to leave Casey in kennels.

He'd never actively looked for a dog. A pet had been the last thing on his mind. But Casey had kind of found him. One night when he'd been out running he'd noticed Casey lying by the side of the road. He'd hesitated for a few seconds—what did he know about dogs?—but as soon as he'd looked into the big black eyes he'd been sucked in. A few hundred dollars' worth of vet bills later he had become the proud owner of a terrier of unknown origin.

And it was an interesting partnership. Casey was more temperamental than most women he'd known. Snarky some days, loving on others, and absolutely determined to get his own way. On more than one occasion he'd grabbed hold of Donovan's trouser leg and dragged him towards the door when he wanted to be walked.

Hannah rang the doorbell and walked in. Her immediate attention went to the dog and she dropped to her knees and started tickling Casey behind the ears. 'Hey, boy. You're going to come with me for a while.' She picked up the plastic bag sitting on the counter, filled with Casey's favourite dog food. Donovan only merited a mere wave. 'Give me a call when you're due back, Donovan. Casey and I will be fine,' she clipped his lead onto his red collar and walked him out the door.

Donovan took a quick glance around the apartment, set his alarm and headed for the airport. It was a late flight and check-in wasn't until eleven p.m. but a few members of his team were already there when he arrived, checking in their specialised equipment. He could travel light, but the equipment required by the team was a logistical nightmare.

He was going through one of the check lists when the voices around him stopped. He looked up. Dave and

John were totally ignoring him, their attention focused elsewhere. Dave lifted his hand and waved. 'Over here, Grace,' his shout came out as something resembling a squeak, and the two other men smiled in amusement.

Donovan glanced across the concourse. And blinked. Twice. He could hear movie theme music playing in his head. What the hell?

It seemed like Grace was moving in slow motion—one shapely leg striding in front of the other—with every eye in the building on her. Her hair had been cut shorter by a few inches and a red wrap dress enhanced every curve. Her black jacket was clutched in one hand, and her suitcase dragged behind her.

Dave murmured, 'If that's what she looks like with her clothes *on*...'

Both sets of male eyes turned to face Donovan, their question apparent.

'Stop it, guys,' he said brusquely. 'Let's keep it professional.'

He kept repeating those words in his head because not one of his thoughts about Grace right now could be described as professional.

Why had she cut inches from her hair? He'd liked watching the way it had streamed down her back, finishing at the base of her spine, in the shower. But it bounced as she walked across the concourse in her stiletto heels. It was just touching her shoulders now, the colour more vibrant and a few little curls appearing. Darn it—it was sexier than before.

As she neared, his gaze was drawn to her green eyes. Now her face wasn't clouded by the expanse of hair, they stood out even more. Fixing on him with that deep colour.

Grace Barclay had attracted his attention before. But the Grace Barclay standing in front of him now was stunning.

Her case trundled to a stop and her face fell as she glanced at her companions. 'Are you ready to go?'

Donovan could sense her discomfort. It was just after eleven at night and she was dressed as if she were going to a power meeting in the office. He and the rest of the guys were dressed in jeans and baseball hats. He could curse. He should have given her a heads up about what dress code was expected on field assignments. He only hoped her heavy-duty case—that looked as if it held three weeks' worth of clothes—wasn't filled with suits and stiletto heels. They wouldn't be any use where they were going.

He was normally so good at this sort of thing. When he'd recruited anyone to his team in the past he'd always had a meeting with them, giving them a printed list of essential equipment for field assignments and some basic instructions about wherever they were travelling.

What was wrong with him? Why hadn't he done the same for Grace?

The little voice in his head wasted no time in telling him. *None of the other recruits were naked in the shower with you.*

He took a deep breath and swung his rucksack over his shoulder. 'We like to travel light, Grace, so there's no waiting around at the other side.' He gestured towards her case. 'Sorry, I should have given you a heads up. We'll spend most of our time in scrubs and they've been sent on with the rest of the equipment.'

She looked down at the huge case. 'Oh, I didn't realise.' She glanced at the rest of team's rucksacks. 'It's okay, guys. When we land you go on ahead. I'll wait for my case and meet you there.'

Dave shook his head. 'Oh, no, we don't mind waiting for you, Grace.' His voice was almost a drawl. Donovan shot him a look as the check-in girl gave him a nod.

'Hand over your passports. We'll get our seats allocated and head to the departure gate.' He signed a few forms about their other equipment, as Grace rustled through her leather bag for her passport.

Her scent was drifting up around his nostrils. Something new. Not like the perfume she'd been wearing as they'd hit the shower. This smelt like vanilla. The kind of cupcakes his mother had baked when he was a boy. She smelt good enough to eat.

She finally found her passport and pulled it from her bag. 'Sorry, Donovan.' She looked down at her clothes. 'I just assumed that because we were on business for the DPA it would still be office wear.' She tilted her head to the side, giving him a view of her smooth skin and a rueful smile. 'No matter what time of the day or night. But, hey, I guess we learn something new every day.'

She heaved her case up onto the check-in conveyer belt. There was no way this could be mistaken for carryon luggage.

He handed over the passports to the beautiful blonde desk clerk, who didn't look too impressed that she was being ignored. 'I guess we do,' he replied.

She had no idea how true those words were. He was trying to work out why he hadn't got a handle on Grace Barclay seven months ago. He'd noticed her, and had meant to find out more. But Donovan was a work first kind of guy. He didn't like things to interfere.

Still, seeing the reactions of Dave and John had sent

the hackles up at the back of his neck. He'd wanted to rip their eyes from their sockets—not exactly rational behaviour, particularly around a woman he barely knew.

Grace Barclay was an adult and a professional. She was perfectly capable of looking after herself. She didn't need him to protect her, so why was that the way he felt around her?

He was trying not to stare at her curves. He'd already seen her naked—what more was there? But Grace wasn't just wearing this red dress, she *va-va-voomed* it. It covered every inch that it should. But its coverage was just great. It clung to the full curve of her breasts, the swing of her hips and the smooth swell of her backside. As for the tanned legs and black stiletto heels…

'Donovan, is something wrong? Did I forget something?'

She was staring at him, twiddling one strand of her shorter hair between her finger and thumb. Another 'tell' when she was nervous. It was cute. It was sexy.

He shook his head, trying to get his mind back on the job. 'Nice hairdo.' The words were out before he thought about them and her cheeks flushed in an instant.

'Thanks.' Her fingers were working overtime on that strand of hair. Any more and she would pull it clean from her head. 'My friends thought it would be more practical for a first field assignment.'

He raised his eyebrows and couldn't help but smile. 'Did they think the dress would be more practical too?'

He knew it. He knew there had been a makeover team involved. Grace looked fabulous, but he kind of preferred her the way she'd appeared twenty-four hours ago. When he'd been the only one who had noticed her.

Her shoulders sagged. 'Like I said, I wanted to look professional.'

The blonde behind the desk cleared her throat and handed over the boarding cards, her eyes drifting up and down the length of Grace's body with disapproval. Her gaze was so blatant he cringed.

But Grace didn't. She laughed. Out loud. And reached over and took the boarding cards from her hand. 'Thanks honey,' she quipped. 'I'll take care of these guys now.'

With a confidence Donovan hadn't seen before she swung her bag over her shoulder and started to walk towards Security. 'Come on, guys, let's go.' All eyes followed the swing of her hips and the rest of the team grabbed their bags and hurried after her.

By the time they reached Security Grace had emptied the contents of her bag, removed her gold necklace and put her shoes in the tray. She beeped as she walked through the scanner and stood patiently while the female security team scanned her with the wand. The scanner paused around her shoulder blade and she said a few quiet words to the staff member.

The woman reached up and pulled the stretchy red material out where indicated by Grace. It wasn't enough. A few seconds later she was asked to stand in the full-body scanner. What on earth was going on?

It took less than thirty seconds. The female guard viewed the scan and had a quick discussion with her counterpart. He nodded and she indicated to Grace to come out and handed her her shoes, talking away as if they were old friends. Grace was shrugging her shoulders and smiling. Donovan was concentrating so hard on what was happening between them he felt a sharp

nudge at his back. 'Hurry up, buddy. The guard has signalled you through twice now.'

Donovan had already removed his belt, shoes,
money and watch. There was no reason for him to
beep. He hurried through and caught the last few words
of the conversation. 'No problem, it happens every
time...'

It had to be her scar. Questions were firing in his
brain. There were lots of reasons people could beep at
the airport. Metal plates in their bodies, other kinds of
implants or devices. But the only scar he'd seen on her
entire smooth skin had been the angry–looking one on
her shoulder.

It just made him all the more curious. Grace didn't
seem like the kind of girl to have had a knife wound.
Maybe he was wrong? Maybe it was from a car wreck?
A sports accident? A skiing mishap?

But it didn't matter how many 'what ifs' he planted
in his brain. Donovan knew a knife wound when he saw
one. He just wasn't sure he wanted to ask the question.

She was sliding her painted red toes into her black
stiletto. 'What next? Can we all go for a coffee somewhere and make some plans?'

Her voice jolted him. It was embarrassing. She wasn't
having any problems focusing on the job. It was only
him. Why hadn't he noticed the painted toes earlier?

'Sure. Let's go to the coffee shop. I'll recheck my
emails and see if we've got any new information.'

She moved away and started chatting with John. He
noticed the glances from passers-by as they walked
through the terminal. Grace seemed to chat easily with
people. She had a nice friendly nature, a killer smile
and she appeared to be a good listener, all things that

would make her an asset to the team. It would make her good with patients and give her the ability to integrate well with staff they might meet wherever they travelled.

They joined the queue and Grace frowned at the coffee selection.

'What's wrong? No skinny, caramel lattes?'

She wrinkled her nose. 'Oh, yeah, they've got them. They just don't have any sugar-free caramel.'

'Is it important?'

'My hips seem to think so. And my thighs.'

'Not from where I'm standing.'

She met his gaze. It was only the briefest of seconds. Everything else around her seemed to fade into the background. All she could see was the cheeky twinkle in his eyes.

It panicked her. What did that mean? Was he joking with her or was he flirting with her?

Her friends may have given her a physical makeover but they hadn't done anything to sort out her woolly brain. Academically she could rival most of her colleagues but as for being street smart or worldly wise, she was neither. Never had been—never would be.

Her shoulder was a permanent reminder of that. The tiny tip of the knife still embedded in her tissues caused havoc every time she was near an airport scanner. The ER doc had done the best he could. It had been bad night in the ER and a surgeon hadn't been available. The tip was apparently right next to some nerves and unskilled removal could have resulted in damage. The scar was already going to be ugly, so she'd decided just to take the patch-up job, the antibiotics and go.

She tore her gaze away from Donovan's as she felt heat spread into her cheeks. She'd already used up her day's supply of sassiness on the desk clerk. As they moved along the line and grabbed coffee her eyes fixed on his well-worn jeans and slouchy T-shirt. Her fingers itched to touch it. It looked so soft, so comfortable— the kind of material that her pyjamas were normally made from.

She shifted on her heels. She'd felt a million dollars walking out the door tonight. It hadn't even occurred to her that the team would travel casual. Her heart had sunk like a stone when she'd realised how inappropriately dressed she looked in comparison to everyone else. This was going to be a long flight.

They settled at a table in the airport lounge, Donovan pulling out his laptop.

'This is what we know.' He gave Grace a little nod. 'Jessie Tanner, sixty-seven, reported to her physician five days ago. She had a whole range of symptoms that she claimed to have had for around three days. She was physically and mentally unwell. Dehydration, confusion, diarrhoea, and her skin was described as red and covered in bumps. Their initial diagnosis ranged from scarlet fever to measles then rubella. Her condition deteriorated very rapidly and she didn't respond to treatment.'

'Did we miss something with Ms Tanner? I don't ever remember her reporting symptoms like those.'

Donovan shook his head. 'She didn't. Not in any of the phone calls to the DPA. We checked our records— she's phoned us over four hundred times, for a whole variety of reasons.'

David and John let out simultaneous groans. John ran his fingers through his hair. 'Why do we get all the crazies?'

Donovan didn't acknowledge the comment, keeping focused on the facts. 'Our last call from Jessie Tanner was actually seven days ago. She never reported any symptoms then, just asked a range of questions about the bats that were near her home.' He lifted his eyes from the screen. 'That seems to have been the norm for Ms Tanner. Unfortunately, it looks like she might not have been as crazy as it seems.'

Grace leaned forward. 'What about the other patient—the child?'

Donovan paused, 'Actually, as of one hour ago, it's two patients. Since the provisional diagnosis by Frank, we sent an alert out to all medical centres. It seems that a maculopapular rash is appearing all over Northwest District in Florida. We still have the first child, an eight-year-old boy, but we also have a thirty-five-year-old woman.'

John took a deep breath. 'An epidemic? Are we prepared for that?'

'We'd better be.'

There was silence at the table as they all contemplated the words. It didn't matter how much experience he had, it didn't matter how many times he'd circled the globe to investigate some weird and deadly disease—in the DPA you were only as good as your last case. The truth here was he was investigating a disease he hadn't encountered before, none of the team had. There was no magic cure or vaccination against Marburg virus. The sad fact was that surviving the virus could almost be down to luck. And Donovan hated it when things were left to unscientific rationales. He didn't work like that.

Their flight number was called and Donovan stood

up, grabbing his bag. The casual atmosphere in his team was gone. They were all too concerned about what they might face when they arrived.

Grace's face was serious. He had to keep reminding himself this was her first fieldwork assignment. He had to stop thinking about what she'd looked like in the shower when the water had streamed down her soft skin and they'd been surrounded by steam...

No. Stop it. Be professional. Lots of new doctors thought they would love the fieldwork aspect of the DPA then quickly found out they hated every second. Things could be tough. Equipment wasn't always available, local staff might not be sufficiently trained and communications back to the DPA could be sketchy.

He'd have to remember that. Once Donovan arrived on the job he tended to shut out everyone around him. His drive, single vision and extreme focus were the aspects of his character he relied on. Trouble was, he forgot about supporting those around him. He expected everyone just to do their jobs. He didn't hand-hold. He didn't have time for that. So Grace had better not expect it. He needed her to hit the ground running and concentrate on the task.

The flight took off smoothly. Grace sat next to John and spent the forty-five-minute flight time talking about the virus and reading up notes on her tablet. It was just as well she wasn't next to him. He was conscious of every time she crossed and uncrossed her shapely tanned legs. At one point a black stiletto dangled from her painted toes. He had to drag his gaze away and concentrate on the strong black coffee served by the stewardess.

It was just before midnight by the time they arrived. The night was dark, hot and humid. The guys were ready to go straight off but found themselves hanging around the luggage conveyor belt, waiting for Grace's oversized case to arrive. It would be unkind to go on without her, Donovan kept telling himself as he paced around the airport.

The finally exited the arrivals hall and he looked around for their transport. 'Anyone see a card with DPA on it?'

John and David shook their heads. 'What about that guy on the phone over there? Doesn't his card say DPA?'

Grace pointed to a guy who was talking frantically on the phone, the crumpled sign in his hand. He must have thought he had missed them.

Donovan hurried over and tapped him on the shoulder. 'I think you're waiting for us.'

The guy cut his call. 'Donovan Reid, from the DPA?'

He nodded. 'Can you give us an update and take us straight to the hospital? Is it still two patients?'

The guy shook his head. He was unusually pale for a Florida local. Or maybe he was just feeling the lateness of the hour, like the rest of them. He gave a wave to couple of police officers near the doors.

'Two? You're joking? We're going to need a police escort. Latest count is thirty-five.'

He started walking towards the doors, not waiting for them to follow.

Donovan's strides lengthened. 'What do you mean, thirty-five? Where did they come from?'

The guy sighed as he pulled open the door of the police car. 'It seems that a kindergarten trip was at the state park caves five days ago.' His gaze swept around the team. 'I hope one of you guys is a paediatrician.'

Donovan felt his heart sink like a stone. Grace's face was a picture. It looked like her first assignment was going to be a baptism of fire.

CHAPTER FOUR

THE HOSPITAL WAS pure and utter chaos. People wandered everywhere, staff looked bewildered and hospital security seemed to have no idea what they were supposed to be doing.

Last time Grace had seen anything like this had been a nightmare shift in the ER as a resident during a major incident when there had been a pile-up on the nearby highway.

Three ambulances were in the bay outside, currently unloading patients. Hysterical parents were talking on mobile phones and one kid seemed in danger of wandering outside.

Grace grabbed the little hand in hers, thought about it for two seconds then lifted the toddler into her arms. The child looked around two and a half and wasn't in the least bit worried about being in the arms of a perfect stranger.

Donovan had moved into full team-leader mode. The chaos didn't seem to worry him at all—in fact, he might even be thriving on it.

'John, I want you to find who is in charge of finding our primary source and co-ordinate with them. We need environmental controls in place to stop the spread of disease.' John nodded as if this were an everyday request and disappeared into the melee of people. 'David, set up communications with our labs and find out who is charge of the lab facilities here. I need you to start doing some provisional testing to move things along.' He spun round and caught sight of Grace, who had perched the toddler on the reception desk. 'Grace, what are you doing?'

'It seems like I'm looking after a lost child.'

He wrinkled his nose and shook his head. 'Hold on.' He walked over to the desk and grabbed the Tannoy system. 'Anyone lost a little boy, around two years old? Brown hair, red T-shirt.' His voice boomed around the waiting room and crowded ER. Heads turned from every direction. Donovan's wasn't a voice to ignore.

There was a shriek from the corner, where a woman was waiting with another child in her arms. 'Mason!' she yelled, as she pushed her way through the crowd with one arm outstretched and the other clamped around the other child. 'I'm sorry, I didn't even notice he'd vanished.' She promptly burst into tears as Grace handed the little boy over.

'Don't worry, he's fine and it's bedlam in here.' She squinted at the other child, who was older but whimpering and lethargic in his mother's arms, with a distinct tinge of yellow to his skin.

She glanced at Donovan but didn't wait for his response and bent down, 'Are you waiting for someone to see your son?

The woman nodded. 'We've been waiting for three hours.'

Grace did the sums in her head. It was after midnight. This woman had been here since nine p.m. with a sick kid. Not good.

She smiled. 'Okay, I'm going to show you to a cubicle then have a look at your son. Does he attend kindergarten? Was he on the trip the other day?'

Donovan seemed to be talking to three people at once, but he gave her a little nod and pointed her in the direction of an empty cubicle. Grace didn't need to take instruction from him; she knew exactly what she should be doing. The staff around here obviously couldn't cope with the influx of patients and would need the assistance of the DPA staff. She might not be a paediatrician but she was an experienced doctor and could do a basic assessment on a kid.

She dragged her suitcase behind her and dumped it in a corner. She could retrieve it later. Right now, she had a job to do.

The assessment took minutes. She charted the little boy's obs, took some bloods, set up an IV line and ordered some further tests.

By the time she joined Donovan a few minutes later he'd managed to acquire himself a clipboard, which he handed to her.

'Everything okay?'

She nodded. 'I'm pretty sure he's going to be another case. He's five and was on the cave trip with the kindergarten class and is clinically dehydrated and showing signs of jaundice.'

She looked around. 'Is there somewhere we can admit him?'

Donovan held up his hands. 'Right now, that's the million-dollar question. I've just spoken to the hospital director. He looks as if he's ready to have a heart attack.

They are reorganising some patient areas to try and give us two ward areas for patients who are affected.'

'Do you have a number?'

The lines in his forehead seemed to have deepened in the last few minutes. 'Yeah, around thirty-seven. Thirty-eight if we count your latest. I've contacted the DPA for another team with some specialist paediatric staff. It'll be around twelve hours before they can get here, though.'

Grace understood. Until the rest of the team arrived, they were it. 'I'll manage,' she said swiftly. 'I can do a basic assessment and prescribe drugs and put in IVs for kids.'

Donovan was looking at her with those blue eyes. He should look tired because it was late. But he didn't. Instead, he looked invigorated. She'd heard that about him. About how he thrived on his job. Thrived on the pressure of it all.

She had to admit to feeling a little buzz herself on this first field assignment. But was the buzz from the job or from being around Donovan? The man was infectious. She liked the way that energy radiated from him. She liked the way his brain never seemed to stop thinking about the next task. Did he even have an off switch?

She looked at the list of names he'd given her. 'What do you want me to do with these?'

His voice was serious. 'I realise this is your first assignment, but I really need you to hit the ground running. You don't need to work up backgrounds or histories on any of the patients—John will be doing that. I need to check they've had all the bloodwork they should have, make sure the samples get sent to David at the lab, and keep an overall note on the condition

of the patients. We need to keep on top of things here.
The situation could become very volatile. Paediatric
patients can deteriorate very quickly—we've already
lost one older patient—and I'm assuming most people
don't know that. If they did, we'd have a whole host of
hysterical parents to deal with.'

His eyes swept around the room. 'This hospital only
has sixty beds. It's usually only used for basic surgeries and medical complaints. Up until today there were
only five paediatric beds. Anything major usually gets
transferred to Panama City. If we have any kids that
need ITU facilities, we'll need to transfer them.'

Grace nodded. She understood how serious the situation was, and how easily it could get out of control. For
the next twelve hours Donovan needed a team he could
rely on. It didn't matter that her stomach was currently
churning. It didn't matter that she'd doubted for a few
seconds if she could actually get the IV into the five-
year-old's tiny vein. One look at that mother's face had
given her all the determination she needed.

It was strange. Around twenty minutes ago all she'd
wanted to do was drag her case somewhere, find her
pyjamas and lie down for half an hour. She'd hit that
point—the one that usually hit medics in the early hours,
when it seemed as if everyone in the world was sleeping
but them and they would kill for a bed. But the adrenaline surge had hit since then. Things were looking up.
Maybe if she could grab some food she would get her
second wind.

She took the clipboard and swallowed hard. So many
names, so much information to gather. She gave him her
best smile. 'This will be fine, Donovan. I'll give you a
shout if I run into any problems.'

He gave her a tight-lipped smile. Maybe not. Looked like she'd better deal with any problems herself. She pressed the clipboard to her chest. 'See you soon.' She kept the smile plastered on her face as she walked down the corridor. She could almost feel his eyes drilling a hole into her back.

She could do this. She could. Sleep was for amateurs.

He was watching her again. Watching the swing of her hips in that red dress. Darn it. He needed to tell her to change into a pair of scrubs. That way most of her curves would be hidden beneath the pale green material and he could concentrate on the things he needed to.

The Marburg Virus outbreak was much worse than first expected. One fatality already and a whole host of possibilities with a class of kindergarten kids all exposed. He'd already reported to Callum Ferguson, who was organising another team to come and assist. In the meantime, he had to try and get a handle on how to treat these patients and stop the spread of the virus. This place was a logistical nightmare. The lab facilities were basic. The staff were already run off their feet. Judging by the number of people in the ER they were going to run out of beds soon. The hospital facilities were fair, but there were no specialist facilities for any of the kids if their conditions deteriorated quickly.

Above all, he needed to communicate with the staff who were here. And he needed to do it quickly to make sure everyone was working from the same page.

John appeared at his side. 'We need to have a briefing for staff. Can you collect all the available staff on duty and we'll give them an overview of what we're dealing with and how they can contain the risk and stay safe?'

John moved quickly. He was used to this, and he was a professional. Donovan could rely on him.

In around ten minutes the staff were gathered in one of the large nearby treatment rooms. There were around twenty of them—some nurses, some care assistants, two onsite doctors, admin staff and the hospital director. Most of them looked anxious and at least one woman was heavily pregnant.

Donovan stood in the doorway. 'Hi, folks. Thanks for stopping for a few moments. I'm Donovan Reid, a team leader at the Disease Prevention Agency. David Coles is working in your lab, John here will be doing case histories and Grace Barclay, one of our doctors, will be reviewing the patients and looking at symptom control.

'Most of you already know that we suspect we're dealing with the Marburg virus. We've had two confirmed laboratory cases and we're waiting for the results of others. Marburg virus can also be called **Marburg haemorrhagic fever**. We treat it the same way we treat other viral haemorrhagic fevers. Most patients are infected at source.' He glanced over at John. 'We're still establishing where that it is, but at the moment we suspect it's some bat caves in the local state park. Previous sources of infection for this virus have been African fruit bats.' All eyes in the room were watching him. He wanted to make this brief but comprehensible.

'The incubation period is between three and ten days, followed by a sudden onset of symptoms. These can include a rash over the trunk, nausea, vomiting, diarrhoea, chest pain and abdominal pain. More severe symptoms include jaundice, delirium, haemorrhaging, inflammation of the pancreas and liver failure.' He ran his hands through his hair. It didn't matter that there were over twenty people crammed into this room. Right now you could have heard a pin drop. Everyone was hanging on his every word.

'There is no magic cure for the virus. We don't have a vaccine against it. We can only treat the symptoms. Maintain fluid balances, give oxygen therapy, replace lost blood and clotting factors and treat any complications.' He looked around the staff. 'For everyone here, barrier nursing techniques have to be used in all cases. Any staff member exposed to body fluids is at risk. Protective gowns, gloves and masks have to be worn at all times. Take care with the disposal of needles, equipment and patient excretions.

'Patients who are worst affected should be placed in isolation if possible.' He held up his hands. 'I realise facilities here aren't ideal. But the people with the worst symptoms should be nursed in side rooms if possible. Parents have to be warned about the spread of disease. They have to be gowned, gloved and masked if they want to stay with their kids.'

The questions flew at him from all corners of the room.

'What if we've already been exposed?'

'How many people die from Marburg's?'

'Is this the only outbreak?'

'How long do the lab tests take?'

Donovan was calm, cool and collected. He answered everyone as best he could. The death rate could be terrifying. But he didn't want people running scared. There had already been a death here. Jessie Tanner hadn't been old. But the death of a sixty-seven-year-old was a lot less terrifying than the death of a kindergarten-aged kid. He had to try and keep things in perspective.

He kept everything brief and to the point. After around fifteen minutes most of the staff had returned to their stations.

Lucy Kirk, the head nurse, appeared at his side. 'I've got a couple of kids that need to be reviewed. Their symptoms are getting worse and they're not responding to their IV fluids. They can't stop vomiting and the fluids are coming out quicker than they're going in.' Her face was flushed and her hair had escaped from the elastic band at the nape of her neck.

Donovan looked up. 'Can't you ask Grace? She's supposed to be reviewing the patients.' He felt a little surge of annoyance. He'd just been asked to take part in a press conference for the local TV and radio stations. He'd done many of these in the past but knew he was supposed to run things by the communications department of the DPA first. Trouble was, he hadn't worked out what he was going to say yet—let alone put pen to paper.

Lucy shook her head. 'Grace is caught up with a kid with breathing difficulties. We've got six adults and thirty-four children as patients now. Grace hasn't stopped for a second. We've already nicknamed her Superwoman. But she's only one person. Our regular doctor is spending most of his time trying to move the rest of our patients to other facilities.'

Donovan nodded quickly, running his hand through his hair. 'Okay, thank you. I'll be with you in two minutes.'

Lucy disappeared back to the ER while Donovan scribbled some quick notes for the press conference. He was being unreasonable. He couldn't really expect Grace, on her first assignment, to look after more than forty patients. Trouble was, things frequently worked out like that on DPA fieldwork trips.

He gowned, gloved and masked. It only took him a few minutes to review the kids and agree with Lucy's assessments. He wrote up some orders but, after looking around him, decided just to administer the anti-emetic IV shots to the kids himself. It didn't take long and he quickly disposed of his equipment and clothes.

He walked past an office where John was buried up to his neck in paperwork with two open laptops next to him. 'Okay? How are you getting on?'

John stood up. 'Exactly like we first suspected. The common denominator in everyone's story is the caves in the State Park. But they don't contain African fruit bats—they have Jamaican ones. What I can't work out is why Jamaican fruit bats have made it this far up state. They've been spotted in Key West before, but never this far northwest.'

'Have any of the state park staff reported being unwell?'

John pointed to the notes. 'I'm tracking down as many as I can. Two have already been admitted as patients. David's checking their blood results as we speak.' He gave a little smile, 'Grace seems to be taking samples quicker than he can analyse them.'

He mentally ticked the little box in his head. Another plus point for Grace. That reminded him. 'John, do you know where the supplies are? I'd like to get changed into a set of scrubs.' His voice drifted off. 'I need to tell Grace to get changed too.'

John shrugged. 'I think the boxes might be down at the lab.' He gave a little smile. 'I kinda like what Grace is wearing now.'

Donovan could feel his blood pressure start to rise. But John was watching him with a smirk on his face. He was playing him. Were his thoughts about Grace so apparent?

Darn it. He'd thought he was being cool. Romantic interludes between team members were never encouraged in the DPA. Team members were supposed to be focused and professional. Letting anything happen between him and Grace would be the quickest way to get her transferred off his team. And it would do nothing for her reputation.

Grace needed to establish herself as a solid fieldwork team member first. A year or two of experience in the field would cement her place in the agency and open a whole host of other opportunities for her.

And no matter how she looked in a red dress or how sexy her new haircut was, he had to keep his mind on the job.

The phone rang and John answered it. 'Yes, yes, he's with me.' He glanced over at Donovan and started taking a few notes, which he passed over. Donovan read quickly. David had the lab tests running already. Out of twenty new samples—Grace really had worked quickly—the first few were already confirmed as Marburg virus. It would be another few hours before the rest were ready.

One of the admin staff appeared at his side. 'We've got problems.'

'What?'

'We're running out of IVs.'

'You're what?' He'd heard it all now. What kind of a hospital didn't have enough IV supplies?

'Most of the patients are really dehydrated. We're

going through the infusion bags at a much quicker rate than normal and so far every single patient has an IV in place. We're going to have to send for some more equipment from one of the other local hospitals.'

'How quickly can it get here?'

She shrugged. 'Hopefully within a few hours.' She turned to leave, then spun back. 'Oh, and the other thing, the nurse supervisor said to let you know that she can't get enough extra nurses to cover all the shifts.'

Could this night get any worse? He took a deep breath. 'There will be some nursing staff coming down from Atlanta. Hopefully they'll be able to fill any gaps.'

She gave a nod. 'I'll let Lucy know, thanks.'

His stomach growled loudly and John smiled. Food. When was the last time they'd eaten? Probably in the airport before they'd left Atlanta.

'There must be a canteen around here. Can I get you something to eat, John?'

He nodded. 'Anything. And coffee. Black and lots of it.'

'No problem, see you in five.'

He walked along the corridor, his eyes looking through all the open doors in the hope of a glimpse of red. Finally, he heard the click-clack of her stiletto heels on the floor to his right. Her feet must be killing her by now.

He could hear her talking to one of the mothers, offering some reassurance about the condition of her child. 'Grace, can I borrow you for a second?'

She spun around and gave him a smile. At first glance she still looked as fresh as she had at the airport. But that had been hours ago now. And on closer inspection he could see the fatigue hiding behind the glaze in her eyes.

He put his arm through hers. 'Walk with me for a second.'

'Why, where are we going?'

Her legs kept pace with his as they turned the corner. 'Any place that serves food.'

She stopped walking and frowned. 'The hospital kitchen only serves the patients. Staff have to eat elsewhere.' She pressed a hand to her stomach. 'I already asked.'

'Is there someplace close by?'

'There's apparently a coffee stand across the street, some vending machines in the ER and a twenty-four-hour diner on the corner.'

'But nothing on site?' His brain was working overtime. They had a potential deadly virus with patients needing round-the-clock care and staff needing round-the-clock facilities.

She shook her head and he smiled. 'Well, things are about to change around here. Do you know where the kitchen is?'

She nodded and pointed down the hall. 'What are you going to do, Donovan?' She followed as he marched towards the kitchen door. 'We just got here—don't go upsetting people.'

He shot her a smile—she was really cute when she was worried. 'Don't worry, Grace. I'm just going to get us some food.'

The kitchen door opened with a crash and a formidable woman scowled at him and started talking in rapid Spanish. He walked over, his arm extended firmly in front of him. Donovan Reid knew exactly how to use his charm to full effect.

'Hi, there. I'm Donovan Reid from the DPA. I understand you're in charge of the kitchen?'

The woman nodded, still scowling. 'I'm Mara.' She waved her other hand, 'And staff aren't allowed in here.'

He kept smiling and didn't let go of her handshake, instead wrapping his other hand over hers. 'It's a real pleasure to meet you. I'm sure you're aware we've got some really sick patients. And I'm expecting a whole host of other staff to arrive to help us take care of them.' He gave her his best smile. 'I absolutely don't want to give you any extra work.' He pointed over towards some empty workspace. 'So, if it's okay with you, I'll just get my staff to come in and fend for themselves.'

He could see her taking a deep breath, ready to tell him exactly where to go. So he spoke as quickly as he could.

'Obviously, at this time it's really important that my staff don't leave the premises while they are on duty. I don't want an emergency situation when all my staff are at the diner across the street. Can you imagine how dangerous that could be?'

He could see her eyes widen and her brain start to digest his words.

He dropped her hand and moved over to the workspace. 'You just tell me exactly where we won't interfere with your routine and I'll make sure my staff stay clear. I mean, some of us have been up all night travelling, and won't be getting any help for another...' he glanced at his watch '...six hours. It's important I keep my staff hydrated, don't you think?'

He could see Grace watching him out of the corner

of his eye. Her arms were folded across her chest and she was leaning against the wall with her eyebrows partially raised. The bamboozling seemed to have worked. Mara looked lost for words.

Time to keep the momentum going. He started opening a few cupboards. 'Do you have coffee, Mara? I'd like to make some for my staff.'

He kept moving, looking through cupboards. Everything he'd just said was true. He didn't want his staff leaving the premises when they were on duty, and it didn't seem too much to ask to let the staff use the kitchen to prepare food. But Mara looked like the kind of woman not to be tangled with. He only hoped she didn't notice he was holding his breath.

Mara moved, her round body almost at odds with her lightning feet. She pulled open a door and thumped a tin of coffee down on the counter, pulling a glass coffee pot from another cupboard. 'I don't want anyone touching my range.' She eyed him for a few seconds before adding, 'I have bagels. And I can make some eggs.'

He walked over and slid an arm around her shoulders. 'Mara, that would be wonderful. Thank you so much.'

She moved sideways. 'Make your own coffee,' she muttered as she started cracking some eggs into a pan.

Donovan breathed a sigh of relief as he filled up the coffee pot with water. Grace appeared at his side with a grin on her face. 'Oh, very smooth,' she murmured quietly.

'I was, wasn't I?' With the coffee on and percolating he moved to the refrigerator and grabbed some milk.

His phone beeped and he pulled it from his pocket, half smiled and gave a little shake of his head.

She arched her eyebrows at him and he shrugged, 'It was Hannah.'

'How is Casey?'

'Apparently pining for me.'

She gave a little laugh. 'Well, somebody's got to.'

Grace picked up some mugs, plates and cutlery. Mara was slicing and toasting bagels now with ruthless efficiency. No wonder she didn't like people in her kitchen.

'There's a staffroom down the hall. I'll go and find David and John and meet you there.' She glanced over at Mara and gave him a wink as she disappeared out of the door.

Donovan smiled. He couldn't help it. Just when he least expected it, Grace did something like that. It was like at the airport, when the check-in girl had looked at her as if she had been something on the bottom of her shoe. Grace had just lifted her chin and acted as though she owned the world. He liked it. He liked it a lot.

There was a thump on the counter in front of him. Toasted bagels and a large bowl filled with scrambled eggs. His stomach growled loudly again. It smelled delicious—he hadn't realised just how hungry he was.

That seemed to be the way Mara worked. Thumping. He gave her the playboy smile again. 'Thank you so much, Mara, that was really good of you.' He grabbed the plates and the coffee pot and juggled them in his hands as he backed out the door.

Grace was handing over a five-dollar bill to John as he reached the staffroom. 'What's going on?'

Grace rolled her eyes and pulled up a chair. 'I lost a bet.'

'What bet?' He handed out the bagels and filled his with scrambled egg.

John grabbed the coffee pot and started pouring the tantalising liquid into mugs. 'I bet Grace as soon as we arrived that you would commandeer the kitchen, some way or another.'

She laughed, her head going back and revealing the paler skin of her neck. 'I'd already run into Mara when I was looking for a bottle of water. I thought you didn't have a hope of getting in there.'

David and John clinked their coffee cups conspiratorially. 'Let me tell you, Grace, you lucked out with this team. Donovan *always* manages to find us food. Rae Jenkins's team? Last time they were out in the field they ate granola bars for three days.'

Donovan laughed as he took a bite of his bagel. Delicious. Mara could thump around all day if she gave him access to food that tasted like this. 'It's true, you know. The other team complained about it for weeks.'

Grace was looking around the table, obviously trying to figure out if they were playing her or not.

David rolled his eyes. 'I can't do without food. I get all cranky these days if I don't eat. It's not pretty.' With his white shock of hair, David was the oldest member of the team. He was worth his weight in gold.

'How are things in the lab?'

'Don't worry about the lab. I'll be fine. Worry about staff on the floor—there aren't enough.'

Donovan frowned. 'I know. I spoke to the hospital director. They're just not set up for a major incident like this. Trouble is, to move all these patients elsewhere would probably take the National Guard. We have to manage as best we can.' He looked over at Grace. She'd finished eating and was sipping her coffee quietly. 'How about you, Grace?'

Her tongue ran along her lips. She was thinking before she spoke. Was that because she was unsure of herself or because he'd snapped at her earlier? She still hadn't managed to get changed into scrubs and the high humidity in Florida was making her hair start to frizz. But even he knew better than to point that out to a woman who'd had a makeover less than twenty-four hours ago.

She spoke quietly. 'I've got three kids I'm quite worried about. How long until the other team arrives?'

His brain was ticking rapidly as he tried to remember what was in her file. Grace didn't have much experience in paediatrics apart from a stint in the ER as an attending. She was obviously anxious for the team of more specialist staff to arrive. He should have thought of that.

'I'll come and review them with you before I go to the press conference.'

She let out her breath, her shoulders relaxing and rigid fingers loosening around the mug in her hands. She gave a grateful little nod of her head.

Their eyes met. It was a moment. A flicker. A connection.

Something about that shade of green, not pale and insipid, not deep enough to be emerald, but something in the middle. More like the colour of the ocean on a bright summer's day. It was holding him. It was dragging him in.

She blinked. Now he was looking at her long dark eyelashes and the way they framed her eyes perfectly. She was tired—he could see the faint lines around her eyes, the little furrows across her brow. She'd tried to capture her silky curls back in a ponytail. But its new shorter style didn't want to comply. A few random strands were still bouncing around her shoulders.

He dragged his gaze away. His brain should be computing what he was going to say at the press conference, not being distracted by the woman opposite.

John helped himself to a second toasted bagel. 'Are you ready for the onslaught?'

He focused. It was time to keep all his attention on the job. 'What onslaught?'

'The five hundred and fifty questions you're going to get about the bats. Maybe we should start calling you Dr Doolittle?'

Donovan shifted in his chair. 'Where are we with the bats? Do we have confirmation of the primary site yet? When can we collect samples?'

John shook his head. 'The state parks are giving me the runaround right now. I think they've been inundated by calls from frantic parents. About the only thing I've managed to accomplish so far is to get them to put a temporary closure notice on the caves. What I haven't managed to do yet is secure us entry to collect samples.'

Donovan sat back in his chair. 'You are joking, right? I'm going to a press conference, and I've got to tell the world we have an outbreak of Marburg virus but we haven't even managed to collect samples yet?'

John lifted his hands. 'Doing the best I can, Donovan. These things take time—whether we like it or not. And Marburg virus is tricky. Most people have never heard of it. It's not like smallpox, with a six-hundred-page plan ready to download from our website *if* there was ever an outbreak anywhere. Our trouble is we didn't really plan for this.'

John was right. Donovan knew he was right. But it didn't make things any easier.

He pulled a piece of paper from his pocket. 'Okay, guys, keep me posted on any changes and I'll let you know how things go once I've been thrown to the lions. Here are the details of our accommodation. No doubt it will be a luxury five-star, all-inclusive resort.'

There was a collective groan around the table. The DPA didn't like to waste money on staff accommodation. They were lucky they hadn't been expected to pitch tents.

He lifted up his coffee mug, 'To teamwork.'

'To teamwork.' The mugs clinked together. 'Here's hoping the rest of the staff arrive soon.'

CHAPTER FIVE

GRACE CHECKED THE list again. The words were beginning to swim in front of her eyes. She still had two children to check over then another review of the three she was worried about.

She felt a warm hand at the base of her spine. Not low enough to be cheeky but something familiar. Donovan's head rested on her shoulder for a second. 'Are we still awake?' he groaned.

'Barely.' She turned round to face him, dislodging his chin from its resting place. If he wasn't getting to sleep, neither was he. She was still worried about these kids.

'Spoilsport.' He arched his back and it gave a loud crack.

'Yeurgh.' She raised her eyebrows. 'You should see a doctor about that.'

He wagged his finger at her. 'Don't even go there.' He rested his elbows on the nurses' station. 'I'm sorry I've been so long. The good news is I've found another four nurses, the equipment and supplies have been sorted and it's only two hours until the other team arrives. The bad news is I've got the press conference in twenty minutes.'

She let out a long slow breath. It was difficult to be patient when all she wanted to do was grab the nearest bed and lie down. But that was the thing—there *were* no empty beds now. All sixty beds were filled. All with patients with suspected Marburg virus.

There were a few cases she suspected were false alarms, but nonetheless all samples were currently lined up and waiting for David to test them in the lab.

She pushed her clipboard towards him. 'Well, my bad news is we're full. No beds. The last two were filled as soon as the previous patients were transferred to another local hospital.'

'The hospital director managed to get all the other patients transferred?'

She nodded. 'He's been great—even though he looks as if he's about to have a heart attack.' She lifted her hands and let out a sigh. 'We are now officially the Marburg hospital.'

He bent over the list. 'You've got through all these patients?' His voice rose and she felt a little tingle across her skin. Was that a note of admiration in his voice?

She tried not to smile. 'Yes, by the time I get to them John has done the patient history and background. I've been taking care of all the clinical components.'

'Show me the children you're worried about.'

She nodded and grabbed the sets of notes she'd put aside. The admiration for her hard work would only take her so far. She started down the corridor. 'I've done some moving around. The three patients I'm concerned about are all in single rooms down here. All children.' She lowered her voice. 'All on the kindergarten trip.'

She heard him suck in a breath. She knew exactly where his mind was going. They really needed access to those caves. They needed to identify where the virus had originated and get plans in place to help stop the spread.

She stopped at the entrance to one of the rooms. Donovan was concentrating so hard that he wasn't paying attention and walked straight into the back of her.

Her body shot forward, her hands still clutching the clipboard, with no time to try and break her fall as her feet started to disconnect from the floor. The green rubber flooring loomed beneath her eyes.

A warm arm grabbed around her waist with such intensity that her breath was taken clean away from her. She was yanked back hard, straight into the chest of Donovan Reid.

'Grace, I'm sorry. I wasn't paying attention.'

She couldn't speak for a few seconds. All the air had shot out of her lungs. When she finally managed to suck in a breath and relax back against him, all she could do was laugh.

It was a nervous laugh. An I'm-feeling-something-I-shouldn't kind of laugh.

Like the heat of someone else's warm skin seeping straight through her thin scrubs. The feel of the rise and fall of his chest muscles against her shoulder blades. She should have kept her dress and her heels on. The thicker material and little more height wouldn't have left her quite so exposed. She could feel the outline of other parts of his body too.

His hand was still locked around her waist, holding her close to him. It didn't matter that he'd already seen every part of her. It didn't matter she'd been naked in a shower with him. This was up close and personal. This felt even more intimate than that.

This was the kind of position you assumed with a lover when you were looking out at a setting sun and glorious landscape. This was how you stood before he murmured in your ear and started to nuzzle around your neck. This wasn't a position for a public setting.

She jumped forward, pushing her hair out of her eyes. The shorter style was beginning to annoy her. It was at that in-between stage. Not quite long enough to stay in a ponytail band and not quite short enough to go without.

Donovan was looking at her with a strange expression on his face. His brow was furrowed but his blue eyes were fixed completely on her. Was he about to say something?

Then she got it. He felt it too.

It wasn't just her. She wasn't going crazy.

All those mad midnight dreams about Donovan Reid in a semi-naked state weren't as wasted as she'd thought. In her head he'd always been miles out of her league. The man hadn't even noticed her, let alone spoken to her. But things were definitely changing. He looked just as confused as she felt.

She broke the gaze, staring at the clipboard. Patients. Let's talk about patients.

'Okay Donovan, there's three kids I'm worried about—and you already reviewed them earlier. All aged five, all on the kindergarten trip. David has just confirmed that all three have Marburg virus. Jacob and Sophia are both showing signs of jaundice. Both are now having bloody diarrhoea. Breathing is becoming laboured and I'd really recommend that we transfer both these kids to the ICU in Panama City. Ryan is also deteriorating rapidly. Pulse is rising, blood pressure dropping and oxygenation rate is decreasing. Although all of these kids have had anti-emetics, they've had limited effect. All three kids are still vomiting and severely dehydrated.'

She took a deep breath. The words had just rattled out. She hadn't been able to stop them. She had real concerns about these three kids. Donovan was watching her carefully. The last thing she wanted was for him to think she couldn't cope. Because she could.

But every instinct in her body told her that these kids needed specialist treatment. She knew the death rate for Marburg could be as high as ninety per cent, but those rates were based on Marburg in countries that weren't as developed as the US. With all the facilities available, these kids had to have a better chance than that.

He reached out his hand and took the charts from her hands. 'Let's not waste time. Go, and try and arrange to get these kids airlifted out of here. You'll have a fight on your hands—first, with ICU at Panama City to accept three kids with an infectious disease and, second, with the air crew.' His hand rested on her back. 'It won't be the first fight you'll have like this, Grace, but I have confidence you'll make the case.'

His eyebrows were raised. It was almost like drawing a line in the sand. Setting her a challenge. Her stomach flipped over.

His eyes were serious, but the corners of his mouth were edging upwards. He was trying not to smile. And she was trying not to react to the feel of his hand on her back.

His fingers were inches from her scar and the heat emanating from his hand through her thin scrub top was making her skin tingle and the scar area itch.

The wound never bothered her, never caused her any problems—except, of course, at airports. While it had been healing the itch had driven her mad. Probably because that tiny part of her shoulder blade seemed like the most inaccessible part of her body. No matter how she twisted and turned, her hands just couldn't reach the spot. She'd ended up rubbing her shoulder blade up and down a wall instead.

The fingers moved, shifting their position on her back. 'Grace, are you okay?'

Heat rushed into her cheeks, Donovan had given her some clear instructions. She didn't have time to dither. She had to get on and do the job, prove herself as a responsible member of the team.

His fingers were still in contact with her body so she took a step forward to get out of reach.

'No problem, I'll get on the phone straight away.' She started to walk down the corridor. She'd no idea where she was going. There was a perfectly good desk, chair and phone at the nurses' station where they'd been standing but she needed some space. She needed some distance.

She could almost feel his eyes burning a hole into her back. As she rounded the corner she glanced back just in time to see him pull his eyes away and look down at the files in his hands.

She swallowed. She hadn't missed anything with these kids. She knew she hadn't. But she was worried. Their condition was deteriorating and they needed more support. So why was her stomach doing flip-flops?

She was nervous. She couldn't help it. She wanted Donovan to think she was a capable member of the team. It seemed so important that he respect her work abilities above anything else.

She had to prove to him she was a worthy member of his team. She wanted his respect. There had been a moment in the isolation room, when she'd told him what she remembered about Marburg virus, that he'd looked at her—*really* looked at her for a few seconds. It had almost been as if he was seeing her for the first time.

And there had been something. Whether it had been admiration, respect or just downright curiosity, she'd liked it.

She wanted it to happen again.

Even now, from the second she'd set foot in the airport, she had sensed something else. She wasn't as street smart as some. Her wound was proof positive of that.

But she didn't use the art of flirtation as a means to anything else. She wasn't skilled at those techniques and sometimes she wondered if she even read things the way she should.

In any other world, if she were any other person, she could swear that Donovan Reid had been flirting with her sometimes. Had been looking at her in a way that hadn't been entirely professional. And she liked it. She liked it a lot.

Up until yesterday she hadn't featured on this guy's radar at all. She may have admired him from afar. He may have said a few things that had hinted he had noticed her. But that had probably been just to soothe her ego, keep her sweet while she was on his team.

She wasn't a blonde supermodel. Not like the last girl he'd dated. Or anything like any of the others he'd been rumoured to wine and dine. She was just Grace Barclay, doctor at the DPA.

But when he'd held her gaze a few times and looked at her, it had felt like so much more. It had made her skin tingle and the blood race through her veins. He'd looked at her in the shower when they'd both been naked. He'd looked at her at the airport when she'd had her mini-makeover. The first time she'd barely been able to meet his gaze. The second time she'd felt more confident, more ready to deal with it.

Donovan Reid interested in her? She couldn't wipe the smile from her face or the tingles that were sweeping over her skin.

She picked up the phone. Now it was time to be charm personified. Now it was time to develop some of her persuasive skills to get these kids somewhere appropriate.

And maybe she could use those persuasive skills later...

The room was stifling and it was packed. It was Florida in the middle of summer and the air-conditioning wasn't working. Sweat was starting to run down his back, he only hoped his shirt wasn't sticking to his back.

Worse still, there were no windows. No outside view to escape from. Two doors, both surrounded by people and both closed. It made his skin prickle. Maybe he wasn't sweating because of the temperature, maybe he was sweating because he couldn't see the outside. His mind was retreating into the six-year-old-boy space again and he pressed his lips tightly together, willing it back to the present.

He wasn't a six-year-old boy. He was an adult. And all his rational sensibilities were telling him he was fine. The room wasn't entirely comfortable but there was a clear exit, *two* clear exits. Well, not entirely clear. But visible.

That should be enough. That should be enough to allow him to continue through this. The last thing he wanted to do in the middle of a packed room full of reporters was have a panic attack.

He'd always managed to stave them off. He'd always managed to talk himself out of them, even when all the symptoms and sensations had been there, he'd recognised them and tried to rationalise things in his brain.

A team leader with panic attacks in enclosed spaces would be no use in the DPA. You never knew what situation or set of environmental circumstances you could end up in. Doctors in the DPA had to be able to deal with everything. Team leaders? They had to deal with the impossible.

He couldn't let his childhood traumas interfere with his present-day life. He had no time for this. It didn't make sense. Not even to him. Sure, six hours trapped in an elevator was terrifying for a child. But it didn't really feature as traumatic. In his experience he'd met lots of people who'd had a million experiences more terrifying than his. It almost had him feeling embarrassed that his body reacted this way—in a way he couldn't control.

He took a few long deep breaths, letting the air hiss out slowly through his lips. He'd read his DPA-agreed statement around thirty minutes ago. It had been hastily written on an unused chart then faxed to the department. He'd thought he could be in and out of here in ten minutes. But he should have known better. The reporters had other ideas. They were out for blood. And by the look of it—his.

The questions were coming thick and fast. 'Have you identified the source?'

'Marburg virus has been known in the past to come from the African fruit bat. While we've identified bats before in Key West, that type of bat has never been found here. We have, however, identified Jamaican fruit bats in the area. Further investigations are taking place.'

'But weren't all the kids that were affected on a kindergarten trip to the national park? Should the park be closed?'

He shifted in his seat. This was where things got difficult. 'Our investigators are taking detailed histories from all people who have contracted the virus. We are looking at any and all commonalities. Until the investigation is complete I can't make any further comment.'

What I really mean is the park authorities still haven't let us in there. It was beyond frustrating. All establishments had their own protocols but nothing was supposed to get in the way of a DPA investigation. Federal law stated they had jurisdiction. It just didn't seem apparent right now. For some agencies the wheels of time seemed to move slower than shifting sands.

'What can you tell us about the first victim? The woman who died? We heard she called the DPA on a regular basis.'

How on earth did they know that? He did his best to smile sweetly, while racking his brains. Someone from the DPA must have leaked the information. There would have to be an investigation.

'The first confirmed case of Marburg virus was Jessie Tanner, age sixty-seven, from Northwest District in Florida. She has phoned the DPA in the past, but I can confirm she never reported any clinical signs that were related to Marburg virus.'

This was a nightmare. The sooner he could get out of here and on the phone to the Director of the DPA the better.

'Is it true that there was another kindergarten trip at the same site the day after this one?'

His skin started to prickle as a chill swept across his body. That was the absolute last thing he wanted to hear. He kept his face as bland as possible. 'We've not yet been notified of that possibility.'

He wanted out of there. He wanted out of there as soon as possible to check those facts. He wanted to make sure another thirty kids weren't at risk.

The door at the side of the room burst open. 'Donovan! I need you, now!'

In any other set of circumstances he might have been grateful for the interruption, relieved even. But Grace's face was as white as a sheet. The head of every reporter in the room turned to her and in one action the whole crowd seemed to surge towards her.

Donovan couldn't take his eyes off her. Her previously coiffed hair was sticking out in all directions, her scrubs were rumpled, but the thing he noticed most was her unwavering focus.

He stood up and pushed his way through the crowd. 'Out of my way!'

It was only seconds until he reached her, but it felt like for ever. The reporters were too busy chasing the story, rather than thinking of the emergency situation. Grace's hands and legs were spread at the doorway, firmly stopping any of the reporters getting through. Her chin was set determinedly, but her eyes were scanning the crowd frantically, looking for Donovan.

He placed his hand over hers in the doorway and she grabbed it quickly and pulled him through with a force he underestimated, kicking the door closed behind her.

He felt the first flush of fresh air surround his skin.

'Now,' she said, her feet running a few steps down the corridor, giving him no time to think. As soon as the door had closed behind him he was instantly aware of the cardiac-arrest alarm sounding in this part of the hospital. It had been years since Donovan had heard one. It had been years since Donovan had responded to one in this kind of environment, but all his automatic medical senses kicked into place.

He was right behind her as she ran into a room, dragging an emergency trolley from the corridor behind her. There was one nurse, with a knee on the bed, counting out loud as she did chest compressions on the small boy.

Donovan did a double take. 'Where is everyone?' In all his years he'd never seen this. Whenever a cardiac arrest alarm sounded in a hospital setting, everyone responded. It was an unwritten rule. Only one nurse and Grace? It was unheard of.

The little body had two IVs running, one with fluids, one with bloods, and from the signs on the bed he'd already been haemorrhaging.

Donovan moved to the top of the bed, taking the most obvious position of airway support. He released the brake on the bed, pushing it forward and lifted the headrest out of place. He grabbed the Ambu bag from the top of the trolley, connected the oxygen and inserted a child-sized airway to maintain the little boy's respiratory status. This was a temporary measure. The child should be intubated but he couldn't see the equipment he needed right now.

Grace was connecting the monitoring equipment and defibrillator around the nurse's hands. 'Sorry, Donovan, I needed urgent assistance.'

'Where on earth is the rest of the staff?'

'There are four of them outside, transferring one of the kids onto a helicopter.'

'You arranged the transfers?' He was surprised she'd managed to pull it off. Grace was rising in his estimation all the time.

'Yeah, with a few conditions.' She waved her hand. 'We'll get to them later?'

As for getting him out the press conference? It wasn't ideal. The press would be all over this like a rash. But patients always came first. And Grace had looked as if she couldn't care less about the members of the press. She'd just known she'd needed help.

He couldn't even begin to let himself acknowledge how panicked he'd begun to feel in that room. Right now it felt safer to recognise that Grace had interrupted the conference to get help. Safer for him at least.

She finished connecting the electrodes to the little boy's body. 'There's a sick adult on the other side of the ward. Two staff are inserting a chest tube.' She gave her head a little shake. 'We just don't have enough staff for the poor condition of these patients, Donovan.' She opened up the IV nearest her, quickly moving back to the patient. 'This blood isn't going in quickly enough.'

Donovan nodded in agreement. Tyler Bates. Five years old. He'd reviewed him with Grace a few hours ago and recommended he be transferred as soon as possible to ICU. The little boy was deathly pale. It was clear he'd started to haemorrhage. Rapid fluid replacement, both blood and clotting factors, would be needed to help him survive.

'Hands off.' The nurse stopped what she was doing and immediately started running the cryoprecipitate to aid blood clotting through another IV.

Donovan turned his eyes to the monitor. His hand was routinely squeezing the Ambu bag to push air into his lungs. He identified the heart rhythm immediately. 'VF. Shock him, Grace.'

She didn't hesitate and set the level on the machine. 'Stand clear.' He'd no idea how long it had been since Grace had resuscitated someone—let alone if she'd ever resuscitated a child before—but she made it look as if she did this every day. Now she had the additional support she'd needed for his airway, she was the coolest person in the room. He lifted his hands away from the little boy's face.

The little boy's body shuddered and they watched the flickering blue line for a few seconds. The unruly squiggle, ventricular fibrillation, had shown them his heart wasn't beating properly—just quivering in his chest. There was few seconds of hesitation then the squiggle changed. One little blip, slowly followed by another.

'Give him some adrenaline.' The child's heart rate was still too low but at least he had one. In another minute Donovan would have needed to intubate, but now the little boy gave an involuntary cough and his temporary airway was expelled. Donovan turned the oxygen supply up full and pulled a mask over his face, keeping the Ambu bag close by in case he needed it again.

The slow heartbeat took a few minutes to gradually pick up its rate. Their biggest concern now would be helping this little boy maintain his pulse and blood pressure while they tried to replace his lost blood products.

Two other nurses appeared at the door. 'What happened?' one of them asked.

Grace gestured to the bed. 'Tyler arrested.' She looked up. 'Did Jacob get transferred?'

They nodded. One of the nurses moved over towards the bed and started clearing away the used supplies, while the other checked Tyler's blood pressure. 'The medevac team did mention something about other doctor and nurses.' She raised her eyebrows in question at Grace.

Donovan caught the glance between them. Tyler's breathing was becoming steadier. 'Grace?'

A little colour flushed her cheeks as she checked the rate on the IV delivering blood to Tyler. 'I might have agreed to a few conditions for the transfer,' she mumbled.

Donovan felt his ears prick up and cool wave wash over his skin. 'And what might they be?'

He couldn't even begin to imagine how Grace had managed to arrange the transfers so quickly. He had visions of the DPA budget being blown out of the window, with his name attached to it.

He straightened up, because she hadn't answered. 'Grace, what did you agree to?'

She was checking Tyler's heart rate again. Her eyes glanced quickly over at him then skittered away. 'I might have agreed to put a team into the hospital at Panama City.'

He sucked in a breath. They already had another team headed here. Three teams? Working on the same outbreak? Well, that would make DPA history.

'You phoned the request in?'

She licked her lips. 'Yes.' She still wasn't looking at him.

'And they agreed?' He could see how nervous she was, how edgy.

And he wasn't mad at her. He wasn't. Patient care

came first. And if this was the only way to get the kids transferred to the facilities they needed, then so be it.

He could make the argument in the director's office later.

She took a deep breath and finally looked him in the eye. Her words tumbled out. 'I'm sorry, Donovan. I said you insisted. I said you authorised it. I didn't know what else to do. They didn't have the expertise at Panama city ICU and said the only way they could accept the kids was if they had specialist help. They made the case that they had other patients to protect. I couldn't think of a way around it. So I just said yes. And I gave your name.'

She'd moved, and was standing in front of him now. She was breathing quickly; he could see the little pulse throbbing at the base of her neck. She looked as if she might cry. The nurses looked up, both with amused expressions on their faces. Tyler heart rate was steady now. 'I'm going to talk with Tyler's mom,' said one. 'I'm going to get some sheets to change the bed,' said the other, and they both exited the room at top speed.

Another doctor appeared at the door. He was one of the regular hospital staff. He looked at the equipment. 'Sorry, I couldn't respond to the arrest call. The chest drain is in now and my patient is stabilised. Can I take over in here? The second medevac phoned to say they'll be here in ten minutes. Can you write up Tyler's notes about what just happened?'

Grace hadn't moved. She was still standing in front of Donovan. Looking at him with those big green, trembling eyes. 'Of course,' he said quickly, picking up Tyler's case notes and grabbing her hand to pull her from the room.

The corridor was quiet. There was only him and her.

But it seemed too open, too exposed. He pulled her towards the nearest on-call room and closed the door behind them.

Now it was definitely just him and her. He hadn't even flicked the light on in the room. He could almost sense that she wouldn't want him to.

He put his hands on her shoulders. 'Grace, are you okay?'

It wasn't just her eyes that were trembling, it was her whole body. Did she really think he'd be annoyed about her decision?

Then it hit him. And he didn't hesitate. He wrapped his arms around her and pulled her close against his chest.

'You've never resuscitated a child before, have you?'

The stifled sobs told him all he needed to know. His free hand stroked the top of her head. A waft of fruit came in his direction, she obviously used citrus-scented shampoo. 'You did good, Grace. Real good. Tyler's back.'

She shook her head against him. Her words were muffled, 'But I panicked, Donovan. I panicked. No one responded to the call and I knew I couldn't do everything with just one nurse. I didn't mean to interrupt the conference. I know I should have checked about the other team. But I didn't want you to think I was incapable.' Her voice was even quieter, 'I panicked.'

He walked her backwards towards the single bed against the wall, letting her sit down on it. He kneeled in front of her, taking his hands and putting them on her cheeks, tilting her head up.

He knew all about panic.

Her eyelashes were damp, her cheeks flushed. He

could feel the slight perspiration at the base of her neck. 'Grace, I don't care about the promise of the other team. I don't care about the interrupted press conference. All I care about is that Tyler Bates's heart is beating again and he's about to get transferred to an ICU.'

She was trying to draw a breath, but her whole body was shuddering. 'I should have been able to handle an arrest on my own. I'm a doctor. I shouldn't need any assistance. I should have managed.' Her eyes were fixed on the floor.

He shook his head. 'Grace, look at me. *Look* at me.'

Her eyes finally lifted again. 'I don't know how I would have managed a paediatric arrest on my own.'

Her lips tightened. 'You're just saying that. You're just saying that to make me feel better.'

'No. No, I'm not. I'm your team leader, Grace. I'm not here to make you feel better. I'm here to assess your work and make sure you're a good fit for the team.'

She bit her lip. She was waiting. Waiting for him to say she should go. He couldn't stand how upset she looked.

Grace Barclay really had no idea just how good she was.

He did something he probably shouldn't. He stroked a finger down her cheek. The lightest, gentlest touch against her soft, silky skin. It was a much more intimate gesture than before. 'Grace, I think you are very capable. You were in a situation that was unusual for you. You recognised that you hadn't handled a paediatric arrest and asked for assistance. Some people might not have done that. One of the biggest faults a doctor can have is not to recognise their own shortcomings. But you did brilliantly in there, Grace. You have no reason to doubt your abilities.'

Her lips were still quivering. Tears were shimmering in her eyes.

He lowered his lips to her ear. 'I don't.' It was a whisper. But he said it with the intensity he thought she was due.

He felt her suck in a breath and hold it. He straightened up and dropped a kiss on her head, pulling her close again. It felt natural. It felt like a completely natural response.

But they weren't the actions of a team leader. And he knew that.

She relaxed against him for a few seconds, her hands reaching down and touching the sides of his waist.

Then he moved and did something he absolutely shouldn't. He sat on the bed next to her and lay back, pulling her with him so she rested against his chest. His arms were encircling her warm body. He could still feel the shudders going through her. And he didn't say a single word.

What was he doing?

He'd never had a relationship with anyone in his team before. He'd never got this close to anyone in his team before.

But Grace was different. From those first few moments in the shower he'd known things were different.

Keeping her at arm's length was becoming more tricky. And he certainly didn't have her at arm's length right now. As soon as he'd realised how upset she was, he'd been unable to stop himself from putting his arms around her. He'd comforted lots of colleagues in the past by giving them a quick hug, but this was different.

Everything about Grace Barclay confused him. And part of him was hoping she was just as confused as he was.

The shuddering came to a peaceful end. He had one hand wrapped around her body and the other gently stroking her hair. It had seemed natural. He hadn't even thought to stop. Their breathing had slowly synched and he could almost feel the gradual change in the air around them.

The time for comforting had passed. He really didn't have an excuse to be lying on a bed with Grace Barclay now. But he didn't really want to move.

And it seemed that neither did she.

He could sense the change in her breathing again. The awareness.

Electricity seemed to be forming in the air above them.

He squeezed his eyes closed. What was he thinking? They had young patients to prepare for transfer out there. Grace had notes to write up. And his mind was somewhere else entirely. He felt another sensation, a rush of blood and a stirring awareness elsewhere.

Enough.

He sat up rapidly, pushing Grace up along with him. For a second she looked a little flustered and he prayed she hadn't noticed anything going on in his body.

He took a deep breath and tried to sound as professional as he could. 'Better?'

He stood up and made a grab for Tyler's notes, which he'd abandoned on a nearby chair.

She lifted her chin. She looked calmer now. More like herself. She licked her lips. 'Better.'

Neither of them were going to acknowledge what had just happened.

He tried to keep it all business. 'We need to write up Tyler's notes to prepare him for the transfer.'

She nodded. He had no idea what was going on in her head right now.

She reached out her hand. 'I'll do it. You wait for the medevac team.'

It was back to business. She took the notes and pushed open the door. It let in a gust of fresh air that cooled the body parts that had been reacting and he watched her walk down the corridor to the nurses' station and start writing.

He smiled. She'd just given him an order.

And, team leader or not, he kind of liked it.

CHAPTER SIX

GRACE'S PHONE BEEPED as she turned on the shower in the slightly rundown motel room. The only saving grace of this place, with its old-fashioned décor and rough towels, was the fact it looked directly onto the beach.

She was trying to calculate in her head how long she'd been awake, but her brain was currently mush, so she'd reverted to using her fingers. She had been up since six-thirty yesterday morning, then a late-night flight, arrival in the Florida hospital after midnight, followed by a full eleven-hour shift. Callum Ferguson had arrived just under an hour ago and taken a full handover from every member of staff, then he had promptly sent them all to go and sleep.

Donovan hadn't wanted to leave. He'd been hanging around Callum like a moth to a flame. It was only natural. It had only been two years ago that Callum had experienced a heart attack on a DPA mission. Everyone was naturally protective of the man they all admired. But Grace had noticed there was an extra doctor in Callum's team. She could only guess he'd been placed there by the director to ensure Callum had enough support.

Eventually, Donovan had agreed to leave but only

with a guarantee that if there was an influx of patients
he be called back in.

She put her hand under the shower, shrieked and
pulled it back. The water was icy cold. A bit like the
water at the DPA when Donovan had turned the showers off.

She looked out of her window at the beach. Maybe
there was an alternative? The sun wasn't even close to
setting and there were still lots of people in the water.
She opened her mammoth case and pulled out the orange bikini. Her friends must have had a sixth sense.
She could put this to some use.

The phone beeped again and she picked it up. A text
message from Lara.

Love you, honey, but you need to check out your Twitter feed.

She screwed up her face. What on earth did that
mean? She tapped the app open and started to scroll
down the last few hours of tweets. Her heart stopped
and she held the phone closer to her face. Did it really
say that?

Best way to get on a team? Get naked with the boss in
a shower! #whosentthatmysteriouspackage?

Her legs felt like wobbly jelly and she sagged onto
the corner of the bed. She recognised who had sent the
tweet. It was another member of staff at the DPA. Frank
Parker had always been obnoxious in the extreme but
this was a whole other level.

Her hands started to shake. The first part was hurtful. Sexist. Something that wasn't entirely unusual for Frank, whose ambition emanated from his very pores. He was obviously furious that she'd got the place on a team that he would have likely killed for.

But it was the hashtag that killed her. She took a deep breath. The upset shaking was stopping. It was being rapidly overtaken by trembling rage.

How dared he? He was implying that she'd had something to do with the package. That she had somehow manipulated things to trick her way onto a team.

It was pathetic. Truly and utterly pathetic. There was no conceivable way she could have predicted she would be opening mail that day—who on earth could switch on their telepathic powers to know someone else would be off sick? And who on earth could know that Donovan would have been the nearest team leader at that moment of time?

It was insulting, but it was also manipulative. Other members of staff at the DPA would have seen this. Why else would Lara have given her a heads-up?

She sent a quick text back, thanking Lara but containing a few expletives about Frank. She couldn't help it. If he'd appeared in her room right now she could have killed him with her bare hands.

She started pulling her clothes over her head, leaving them scattered over the floor. Normally Grace was a neat freak. But all those compulsions had left her. She switched off the still-cold shower. There was no way she was getting in there.

Her shoulder gave a little twinge as she fastened her bikini top. It was odd, almost as if her body occasionally came out in sympathy with her. She grabbed her flip-flops and slammed the door behind her.

She wasn't normally a beach bunny. She didn't have the figure or the inclination for it. But today the beach had never looked so good. She was sticky. She was uncomfortable. And maybe a quick dip in the ocean would wash away the horrible sensation that was creeping over her skin.

Or maybe it would help her plan her revenge…

Donovan was fretting. It didn't matter that Callum appeared to be back to full health and was working as a team leader again. It didn't matter that someone had decided to put an extra member on his team.

He was still worried. He loved the big guy. He admired him. He wanted to *be* him when he grew up. Most of the doctors at the DPA felt like about the Granddad of Disease. He couldn't imagine how sick to her stomach Callie Turner must have felt two years ago when Callum had had an MI on a flight with her. Which was why he had a horrible sinking feeling that he shouldn't have left the hospital.

That was the trouble with admiring someone so much. He didn't want Callum to think he was being disrespectful by hanging around. So now he would just have to make sure his phone was permanently charged in case of a call.

He heard a little yelp next door and gave a smile. He'd recognise that noise anywhere. Grace had obviously discovered the showers came from a mysterious underground water pump flowing directly from the Arctic. He'd tried to speak to the guy on the front desk about the cold water but he'd been on the phone and had just shrugged and gestured Donovan away.

He looked out at the blue ocean. Unsurprisingly there

was no gym or workout room at this low-cost motel and Donovan thrived on his daily run. A jog along the beach would be perfect.

Even though he had an ocean view the walls in this smaller-than-average room felt as if they were pressing in around him. A sensation that didn't sit well with him. It didn't matter that it would be warmer outside than in. The air-conditioning in the room was clawing at his skin.

It was still light and the beach wasn't too busy at this time of the day. There were only a few die-hard surfers and some families that hadn't yet packed up for the day. He pulled on his running shorts and vest, tucking his cellphone in one pocket and his music player in the other. He could brave the cold shower later or, if the beach was quieter, he might even go for a swim.

It had been a long time since Donovan had run on sand. It didn't matter that he'd moved onto the firmer sand next to the shoreline. He could still feel his muscles burn. The late afternoon sun felt good on his shoulders, relaxing even. The sounds of Dire Straits pounded in his ears.

Atlanta was so different from here. No beaches. No view of the never-ending ocean. There were a few parks but none close to where Donovan lived. Just miles and miles of apartments and buildings. Street running just wasn't the same.

He could get used to this.

He glanced at his watch and slowed his speed. He averaged around three miles back home, listening to the same tracks. The beach was a little emptier now and he could feel the rivulets of sweat run down his back and chest. It had been years since he had gone swimming.

Some of his friends had pools but they weren't designed for serious exercise—not like the kind Donovan craved. Time for a swim in the ocean.

There were no warning flags. No lifeguards either. But Donovan wasn't worried. He just wanted a chance to sluice off.

He ditched his running shoes and vest, putting his phone and MP3 player underneath the pile on the sand. It only took a few strides to reach the edge of the water.

He placed his hands on his hips and took a few deep breaths, arching his back to stretch out any lingering sore muscles. The water was chilly but not as cold as the shower.

As he took another few steps he could see a few people around him. A few hundred yards up the beach some surfers had gathered, half in the water and half out, watching the waves from under their hands as they shielded out the glare from the lowering sun.

A swimmer was coming back in, their smooth over-head strokes barely causing a ripple in the water around them. It was a woman and she slowed, obviously catching her feet on the seabed.

She moved closer as the water cascaded around her. Dark shoulder-length hair, a bright orange bikini and a curvaceous figure. Hadn't there been a scene like this in a James Bond movie?

His breath tightened in his throat as he realised who it was. Grace. Somehow he hadn't figured she'd prefer a dip in the ocean to the cold shower. Grace didn't seem like the type.

He walked towards her, the waves surrounding his hips and chest. The water was streaming down her face and she rubbed her eyes as she took the tough strides forward against the tide.

Her hands froze as Donovan came into focus. He didn't know where to put his gaze. It was automatically drawn to her breasts and hips in the orange bikini against her lightly tanned skin.

He'd already seen every part of Grace. But that didn't matter. That had been work. That had been professional—and it had been a clinical emergency.

Seeing Grace Barclay gliding out of the water towards him, barely dressed, with the gradually dipping sun glinting off her tanned skin, was a whole other ball game.

'Donovan.' The word came out a little breathless. A little throaty. She might just have been swimming towards him—it might have been entirely natural for her to be out of breath—but the timbre of her voice had a direct effect on his senses.

He moved towards her, drawn like a magnet. Walking against the tide until only a few inches of ocean water held them apart.

Their gazes met in open acknowledgement of the sexual attraction between them. He could see the glimmer of nerves and uncertainty in her eyes. Why would Grace doubt he was attracted to her?

'Hey,' he murmured. He couldn't stop his eyes devouring her body. Looking made his hands tingle to reach and touch all parts of her. This close he could see a few tiny freckles scattered across the bridge of her nose. Had they just appeared?

He had a new appreciation of her shorter hairstyle. Now none of her body was shielded from his gaze.

Everything was there for his appreciation. And, boy, did he appreciate it.

Grace wasn't acting too shy herself. 'Hey,' she replied, as her gaze focused on his broad chest. Donovan was used to working out. He liked to be fit. He liked to stay healthy. There was no spare fat on his body, just toned muscle. Her gaze followed the scattering of hair across his chest that darkened and increased as it drew her eyes downwards. It was almost teasing her to keep following its line across his flat abdomen and beyond.

No one else was near them. His peripheral vision was shutting out any movement or colour around them. All of his focus was on Grace. His internal monologue was trying to talk sense to him but right now he wasn't thinking about the fact she was a member of his team. Right now he was doing his best to forget it. Right now he was concentrating on the fact that every time he was near Grace his senses were scrambled. All he could think about was acting on the unspoken acknowledgement between them.

He smiled. He couldn't help it. It was a smile of expectation about what could happen next.

The sun was getting lower in the sky behind her, lighting up every curve of her body, every drop of water on her skin. He couldn't have pictured her any more perfectly.

The tidal surges were strong. They were hit by one wave and dragged back towards the ocean by another. His reactions were automatic and his hands were on her waist in an instant. Her palms landed on his chest and they both lowered their gazes, staring at them there.

Her eyes lifted to meet his. The green almost hidden next to her wide dark pupils. He could see the pulse throbbing at the base of her neck and it willed him to lean a little closer. To touch it with his mouth.

'Great minds think alike,' he murmured. He was talking about the fact they'd both headed for the ocean. But it didn't quite come out like that. Not while they were standing so close and their bodies were touching. It was as if the words danced across her skin, edging her closer until their hips met underwater. The cool water was doing nothing to dull the fire in his blood. Nothing to dampen his desire for her. If things heated up any more the ocean around them would start to sizzle.

His fingers around her waist pulled her even closer, leaving her in no shadow of a doubt about his reaction to her bikini-clad body.

Her body reacted too, her nipples hardening against his chest.

This was it. This was the outcome of the electricity that had been around them right from the start. If Donovan stuck his hand into a socket right now he could light up the national grid.

He felt her take a deep breath. It was as if she were calming herself. Steadying herself for the next step. She relaxed her head and neck, letting her head tip back to reveal the pale skin of her throat. Her hands moved, sliding slowly up his chest onto his shoulders, and he let out an involuntary groan. She raised herself on tiptoe under the water, bringing her head into closer alignment to his. He tipped his downwards until their noses almost touched.

Neither had really spoken. Only those few words. But the air around them was charged with electricity. Every time she breathed her barely covered breasts came into contact with the planes of his chest.

Donovan didn't want to waste another second. He dipped his head and claimed her lips as his own, tasting the salt, mixed with some lip balm. Her arms curled around his neck as she pressed her body into his. Grace wasn't shy. She was more than a match for his kisses.

Their mouths parted and the kiss deepened. His hands moved from her waist, sliding down the curve of her firm backside. Her breasts were pressed against his chest. Grace Barclay was all woman. And, boy, did it turn him on.

There was a little noise. A little whimper as their kiss deepened. Heat was coursing through his body. He moved from her full lips, turning his attention to the soft skin of her neck and throat. Finding the throbbing pulse at the nape of her neck and luxuriating in her sighs as he worked his way round.

His hand moved in one movement from outside of her bikini bottom to the inside, cupping the bare skin of her backside. No one was close enough to see a thing, and even if they had been, the ocean was covering the lower halves of their bodies.

Her fingers were gliding across his back, pulling him even closer as they were buffeted by the waves. Then they changed direction, following his lead downwards. The movement made his stomach muscles twitch as they skirted past the hairs on his lower abdomen and headed even lower. They skirted around the edges of his shorts, tentatively making their way beneath.

Suddenly this seemed like a much more private party.

He let out a growl and pulled back. Her eyes widened at his release and the water swept between them. He lifted his feet from the sea bed, leaning back a little and letting the water take his weight. Grace was breathing heavily, trying to compose herself after what had just happened. Donovan was hoping the cool water would soothe the fire in his groin. Thank goodness for baggy running shorts. Leaving the water could give someone an eyeful.

Her breathing started to slow. He could see the hesitation flickering in her eyes. There it was again. That doubt.

Why did she think he'd stopped? He'd had to. They were on a public beach. It was the first time he'd touched her. The time in the DPA shower had been entirely different. He wasn't even sure what he was doing here. He'd never made a move on a colleague before.

Relationships in the DPA had consequences.

He moved in the water, catching her hand in his. 'Grace? We're out in the open. Anyone could see us.'

'I know.' Her voice was quiet. She straightened as her feet connected with the sea bed again and she took a couple of steps closer to the shore. Her eyes were averted, focusing on the motel next to the beach. 'This wasn't meant to happen.'

The words jolted him from the current euphoria his body was feeling. It was one thing for him to have doubts about what he was doing. It was another for Grace. Was he really that arrogant? He planted his feet down. A wave of disquiet started to crowd his senses. Maybe he'd misread this situation completely. 'What do you mean?'

Her voice had the tiniest tremble, but her tone was determined. 'I mean that you're my boss. This is my first assignment.'

She was saying the words, but the conviction in her eyes just wasn't there. His head started to swim. What was he doing? Law suits and legal terms started to circulate in his brain. Would Grace claim some kind of harassment? The cool breeze prickled his skin, every hair on his arms standing on end. He had no idea how to play this. He'd never been involved with someone at work before. Had never wanted to cross that line. Maybe this was why.

'Are you trying to deny what's happening between us, Grace? Tell me I'm not imagining this. Tell me I'm not reading this wrong.' He was feeling panicked. Was all of this in his head? He'd never had any problems reading signals from the opposite sex before. The thought that he'd misread Grace was alarming in more ways than one.

But Grace shook her head. There was a sheen in her eyes. Was she going to cry?

He reached over before he could stop himself, putting his hands on her shoulders. 'Then what is it, Grace? Tell me what's wrong.'

He could see her gulp, licking her lips and flinching from the taste of salt that must be on them. The tremble in her voice had increased. 'Go online, Donovan. Read Twitter. See what my colleagues have to say about me.' She pressed her hand to her chest. 'I want people to think I earned my place on the team not by getting naked with the boss. I want to be here because I deserve to be here. Not because you've decided I'm flavour of the month.'

'What on earth are you talking about?' She was moving away. Striding back towards the shoreline.

He couldn't figure out what was going on here. One minute she had been kissing him like her life depended on it, the next she'd been looking at him as if he'd just crossed some unspeakable line. Which he had. And which he didn't want to think about.

The semantics of should he/shouldn't he kiss a team member couldn't even figure in his brain right now. What was front and centre was the way Grace had just looked at him. As if she'd been disgusted with both him and herself. As if they'd just done something terrible.

That was the expression that was going to keep him awake tonight.

'Grace! Come back. Talk to me.' His voice verged on desperation. He almost didn't recognise the sound. None of this was familiar to him.

But his words fell on deaf ears. Her strides were becoming longer as she neared the shore and the pull of the water lessened.

Should he go after her?

If she'd been wearing anything else when she'd come down here it was clear she was abandoning it. As she hit the beach she didn't stop, walking as swiftly as possible across the sand and back to the motel.

He had a clear view of her body, but his eyes were drawn to the ragged scar on her shoulder. In this fading light it stood out angry and red. A clear reminder of something that had happened in Grace's past. Something he didn't know about. Something he wanted to ask her about.

Every bone in his body wanted to go after her. But every brain cell told him not to.

He had to stop. He had to think this through. What on earth did she mean about Twitter—and why would that have any impact on what was happening between them?

Donovan couldn't remember the last time he'd logged onto his account. Social media wasn't really his thing.

He liked the internet, he liked the opportunity of access to information and facts whenever he needed it. But did he really want to know what someone else had for dinner? No. Not at all.

A wave rolled over his head and shoulders, pushing him towards the shore. The momentum gave him some motivation to move. Slowly.

It would be so easy to power up the beach after her. But Donovan was normally known for his self-control. The incident with the gun had proved that. He walked out of the water, grabbing his vest in his hands and checking his phone.

No messages. No calls from Callum.

He was about to look away when he remembered the app. He clicked on the Twitter button. The last time he'd looked had been thirty-five days ago. Showed how often he paid attention to it.

The phone almost shook in protest and the data downloaded. He started scrolling, letting his still-wet fingers drip water onto the screen. Nothing. Nothing. Nothing.

He followed a number of colleagues at work, some national Twitter feeds about public health, and some official organisations. His feed wasn't exactly overrun with celebrity small talk.

Then his finger froze and he squinted at the screen. He expanded the words with his fingers. No way. Frank Parker. That little no-good stinking rat.

Donovan had never liked him. Too cocky. Too confident. That would be fine if he had the kudos to go along with it. But he didn't. Donovan had picked him up a few times on clinical errors and not following protocols.

He could feel the heat surge into his cheeks. Fury

building in his chest. He'd kill him. He'd kill him and drag his body off to some dark forest somewhere.

He could hide a body. He could do that. He'd watched *CSI* enough times to know about forensic evidence. Or maybe he could poison the creep. Better still, he could just wring his neck with his bare hands.

He couldn't remember the last time he'd felt rage like this.

He stopped on the sand, hand on his hip, and took a few deep breaths, trying to still the fury and uncontrollable thoughts. No wonder Grace was upset. No wonder the last thing she wanted to be seen doing was kissing the boss.

The implications were clear.

But Frank Parker couldn't be more wrong if he'd tried. He and Grace had never had a conversation before the incident. They had no relationship. And Grace was incapable of anything he'd accused her of.

As for the implied slur on him—that he'd selected Grace for anything other than her expertise—that did make him mad.

The caveman urges started to dissipate and the DPA team leader's mind started to reappear. This was unprofessional conduct without a shadow of a doubt. A phone call to the director was called for. His legs started covering the beach in long strides.

He had worked hard for this position. He wasn't about to let some trouble-making colleague call his professionalism into question.

Yes. He had given Grace the job without application or interview, but that wasn't unusual in the DPA. As soon as a team member revealed she was pregnant she was immediately pulled from fieldwork. It was a necessity.

If it had been a few weeks before the team was called out again, he would have time to interview from the pool of potential candidates already within the DPA. Their recruitment for fieldwork teams was always done internally.

But because they had been called out straight away he'd had to make the decision to select a new team member or leave with a member down. People had been recruited like this before. Grace had impressed him with her knowledge and expertise. She was ready. She was ready for a fieldwork assignment.

Frank Parker was not. His skills were best suited to the lab.

His phone buzzed. A text. From Callum Ferguson.

Just heard about the social media debacle. Frank Parker will never have a place on my team or yours. Tell Grace I think she's done a stellar job so far. As for you, keep calm. The damage is done. Talk to the Director. Tell him if Frank Parker is still in the office when I return I'll deal with him myself.

A smile spread across his face. It wasn't just him that was about to blow a gasket. There was reassurance from the Granddad of Disease that he thought Frank's actions were inappropriate too. The big Scotsman always spoke his mind and took no prisoners. Donovan shook his head. He would speak to the director. And he would pass on Callum's warning. Neither he, nor the director, would want to see Callum's reaction.

He scrolled down for the number of the director's PA. The phone answered after two rings. 'DPA, Director Kane's office.'

'Julie? It's Donovan Reid. Can I speak to the director?'

There was a long pause. 'Yes, Donovan. We were expecting your call. Unfortunately Director Kane is unavailable.'

'I need to talk to him as soon as possible.'

He could almost hear the smile in her voice. 'He's dealing with a member of staff who is being transferred to another office immediately. I'm doing the paperwork now.'

Donovan pulled back his shoulders. The inference was there. 'Is it who I think it is?'

Julie cleared her throat, 'Let's just say the same individual will have a permanent note regarding unprofessional conduct and bringing the organisation into disrepute on their file.'

'I don't need to call back, do I, Julie?'

'I wouldn't think so. The director is keen for his fieldwork teams to be able to concentrate on the job in hand.'

'No problem.' He cut the call. It was strange what a surge of pleasure he felt at hearing those few words. Someone had obviously alerted the director to the comment in the social media and he'd acted immediately. Just the way he should.

He reached the entrance to the motel. He had to let Grace know things had been dealt with. She didn't need to think about Frank Parker's comments. She didn't need to think about what had just happened on the beach. She could just concentrate on being Grace Barclay, doctor on her first fieldwork assignment.

He was outside her door a few moments later, his hand hesitating for a second before he knocked on the door. He had to keep this professional. He had to keep this above board.

He stood in silence for a few moments. Was Grace not going to answer the door? Maybe she'd looked through the peephole and decided not to answer? He didn't even want to admit how much those thoughts bothered him. How very uncomfortable they made him.

The door inched open, Grace's face appearing in the narrow gap. Her hair was bundled up on her head and one of the thin motel towels was wrapped around her body.

'You braved the ice-cold shower?' He said the first thing that came to mind and wanted to grab the words back as soon as he'd said them. Of course she'd had a shower. Anything to cool the heat that had been in their bodies.

She adjusted the towel, trying to cover her boobs a little more. 'I didn't have much choice.' She said the words quietly. 'What do you want, Donovan?'

He glanced over his shoulder. He really didn't want to have this conversation in the corridor. 'Can I come in?' When her face didn't change he added, 'It's about work.'

It felt strange, having to talk his way into a woman's room. He'd never had to do that in his life before. He'd never wanted to do it before. But this was different. This was important.

She gave a brief nod then opened the door, allowing him to edge inside.

The room felt oppressive. Dark and closed in. He almost didn't want her to close the door behind him. He was conscious of how close he was to her and kept his arms firmly by his sides. Resisting the urge to reach out and touch her.

'Grace, I called the office.'

Her eyes were huge in the dim room. Her pupils dark

and wide. She was biting her bottom lip, obviously nervous. 'What did they say?'

'I didn't even get to speak to the director. I suspect he had Frank in his office and was tearing a few strips off him. He's being transferred to another office.'

Her eyes widened. 'Really? Just like that?' She took a few seconds then stared down at the floor. Her voice was quiet. 'All because of one tweet?'

'Don't you dare feel sorry for him, Grace.' He kept his voice low. He hated the way she looked right now. Hated it that she'd been hurt. Grace had no idea what people really thought of her. Her confidence had been shattered by Frank Parker's one selfish act. He pulled his phone from his pocket and held it out towards her. 'Read this.'

'What is it?' Her hand reached out hesitantly before she took the phone and pressed the button to light up the screen. It only took her a few seconds to read the message. Her hand came up to her mouth. 'Oh. Wow. Callum Ferguson said that about me?'

He nodded. There was an edge of disbelief to her voice and her expression was changing. All in an instant. Her shoulders and back straightened, making her two inches taller. Her eyes lit up and the corners of her lips curved upwards. It was like she'd just been given a shot of confidence. And the transformation was startling.

'Yes, Callum Ferguson said that about you.' It would be so easy to cross the small space between them and put his arms around her. But he wouldn't do it. Not again.

Not unless she asked him to.

He had to keep this on a professional footing. For both their sakes.

He put his hand on the doorhandle. Even with Grace

lit up he still didn't like this small space. At this rate he would spend the night sleeping with the doors in his room open to the beach.

'Why do you think I picked you for the team, Grace? Do you think for a single second it had anything to do with us ending up in the shower together?'

Her eyes widened slightly, probably in shock at the directness of his question.

She didn't answer straight away. Did that mean she was even considering it? Or that she was trying to conjure up another answer?'

Finally, she shook her head. 'I hope not.' Her voice was quiet, almost whispered. Her chin tilted upwards as she adjusted her towel again, drawing his gaze. 'I hope you picked me because I impressed you with my knowledge of the disease and not with my breast size.'

Her cheeks were flushed, as if she was embarrassed by the very thought of that.

He looked her straight in the eye. 'I'd already pulled your file, Grace, along with ten other candidates who would be suitable replacements for Mhairi Spencer on the team. You had glowing references from several of your previous placements in the DPA. Being exposed to the powder just brought us together a little quicker. We would have crossed paths soon.'

He folded his arms across his chest.

She stayed silent for a few seconds then sat on edge of the thin mattress on her bed. 'Thank you, Donovan. That means a lot. When I saw what had been written about me...it just made me doubt the reasons I was here.' She gave a rueful kind of smile. 'But I should have known better. After all, let's face it, I'm not exactly your type, am I?'

Her tone had changed. They were back to the informal, almost playful mood that bounced between them.

He tilted his head to the side. 'My type? What is that?'

He was amused.

She looked down at her body covered in the thin towel. 'I'm hardly your usual. Don't you usually date tall, blonde, willowy types?'

'Do I?'

'Apparently.'

'And are they my type?' He was still amused. He wasn't aware that he only dated one kind of woman.

She shrugged. 'So I've heard.'

'I had no idea my love life was of interest to my colleagues at the DPA. That's why I never date at work. Too many complications. I don't like anything interfering with the job.'

Her brow furrowed. 'Why is that?' Straight to the point. He was getting to learn that this was a trait of Grace's. And, to be honest, it was part of her appeal. He'd never liked tiptoeing around people before. It was much better to be up front. Yeah, well. About most things.

'I like my work to be about work. I don't like distractions at work. I had a colleague who once got distracted when his wife was taken ill. It played havoc with our work.'

It was almost like a cold chill passed over her body, even though she knew the air temperature hadn't changed. 'You're talking about Matt Sawyer's first wife, aren't you? She died on a mission a few years ago.'

His feet shifted uncomfortably and his tanned face had a pale look. Everyone knew about the mission.

Everyone knew that Matt had disappeared off the grid for a number of years after that. No one had known if he was dead or alive. Not until he'd turned up two years ago in Chicago with a suspected smallpox outbreak. After a rocky start he'd hit it off with Callie Turner, the doctor who'd led the investigation team. They were married now, with a toddler son, and Sawyer was working with the DPA again on the lecturing circuit.

Donovan looked uncomfortable. 'That was my first fieldwork assignment.'

'You were there when she died?'

He took a hesitant breath. 'Yes…it was awful. He held her in his arms for hours. There was absolutely nothing we could do. Nothing at all. I watched him fall to pieces. All because his wife had been on that fieldwork assignment with him.'

She lifted her hands, conscious that her thin towel was edging downwards. 'But that was a one-off. Nothing like that has happened since. Matt's moved on now. He's married with a kid. So are his sister Violet and Evan Hunter. They met at work too. Why do you think it's such an issue?'

'Because I was there, Grace. I saw someone who was one of the best doctors I'd ever worked with unravel at the seams. And look at your examples. Callie doesn't work for the DPA any more and neither does Violet. They all realised that having an emotional attachment at work means you can't always do the job you should.'

She took a few steps towards him. She was feeling more and more at ease in his company. It wasn't that any other guy had ever threatened her. But since the attack, being alone in one place with a guy was a big deal for her. Particularly in the fast-fading light.

Being around Donovan wasn't uncomfortable. Maybe she was still aware of the touch of his skin, the feel of his lips. Maybe it was the satisfaction of the electricity that seemed to sizzle in the air between them. Whatever it was, it was the first time in a long time she'd been totally at ease—even in her current state of undress.

'I don't agree, Donovan.' She laid her hand on his forearm. 'I only know what I've heard through the grapevine. I heard that Callie Turner hadn't really wanted to work in this line anyway. And Violet? She's moved to specialise in foetal alcohol syndrome. I'm not sure the change of jobs was anything to do with working with their husbands.'

He frowned. 'Do you think you could have a relationship at work and be impartial to the job? Do you really think you could be unemotionally attached if something happened to someone you loved?'

She shrugged her shoulders. 'I don't know. I've never thought about it.' She met his gaze. 'I've never had reason to.' She paused for a second, not believing she'd just said that out loud.

'That's why you don't date anyone from work? Really?' She shook her head and leaned against the wall. 'I love my job, Donovan. I do. I've no idea which part of the DPA I'll end up in. But I do know that I would love my partner to share my enthusiasm and commitment to the job. It's hard to explain to someone else that you have to fly away at a moment's notice and you can't give any indication of when you'll be back. How do you get someone—who doesn't understand our work—to understand that?'

He was watching her closely and as his face softened she wondered if it sounded as if she was trying to persuade him he should be dating her. Her words might have implied that and the thought made her cringe. She didn't want to have to persuade someone to be interested in her. That was embarrassing.

There was the tiniest shake of his head. The muscles in his body tensed. But his voice was quiet. Resolute. 'I don't date colleagues, Grace.'

There was no doubt where that was aimed. But instead of hurting her, it only made her indignant.

This time she didn't reach out gently and touch his forearm. This time she stepped right up to his chest, her head directly underneath his. 'So you just kiss them, then?'

It was the fewest of words. With everything implied.

She had no idea what was going on his head or hers. She'd been swept away when he'd kissed her. They couldn't deny the attraction between them any more—not when they'd both acted on it.

Kissing the boss was never an ideal situation. And she didn't want people to second-guess why she'd got the job.

But part of her was curious about her feelings towards Donovan. She'd never felt a buzz like this before. But in the last few months she'd never met anyone she felt safe around either. Donovan was both.

The dim light cast a shadow over his face. For a few seconds she didn't know whether he was angry or sad. She could almost read his scrambled thoughts as he tried to make sense of her reasoning.

His fingers clenched around the door handle behind him. He was going to leave. He was going to walk away.

But he didn't. He dropped his lips to hers as her towel slipped to the floor and all rational thought left the building.

* * *

Her lips tasted even sweeter than before, the feel of her naked body next to his igniting all his senses. One hand circled his back, her palm stroking up and down the length of his spine. The other lifted to the side of his cheek and her fingers scraped against the feel of his stubble.

Remember why you're here. The words echoed in his brain as his scrambled senses tried to make order of what he was doing. Grace was beautiful. Utterly delectable.

She was making him lose focus. Making him lose sight of his goals. He was here to do a good job. To get to the bottom of the Marburg virus outbreak. People were already talking. Grace was already under the microscope.

It would hardly ingratiate him or her to the director if he suspected anything had happened between them.

He pulled away, breaking their kiss suddenly. Her lips were reddened and full, her breathing heavy. She was startled and it was hardly surprising. She was standing naked in front of him and if he stayed there a minute longer he would never leave.

He put his hand back on the doorhandle. 'I'm sorry, Grace. I have to go. This can't happen between us.'

He yanked the door open and strode out into the warm Florida air before he changed his mind.

CHAPTER SEVEN

SHE WAS WALKING down the corridor towards him in a purple wraparound dress, flat shoes and her white coat. But in Donovan's head she was wearing that orange bikini again and walking out from the sun-kissed ocean with water streaming from her body.

'Donovan? Did you hear me?' A pointed elbow stuck into his ribs.

'Hey!' He turned. John was looking at him with an amused expression on his face. His eyes drifted off towards Grace, who'd stopped to speak to one of the nurses in the corridor.

John raised his eyebrows. 'If I could manage to keep your attention, even for a few minutes, that would be great.'

He felt a rush of colour to his cheeks. When was the last time he'd actually blushed? Embarrassment wasn't the norm for him. Then again, he'd always been completely focused on the job before. After the events of last night he was wondering if he'd ever be able to focus on the job again.

He'd been right. This was why getting involved with someone at work was a bad idea. A really bad idea.

He pulled himself back into professional mode. 'What's up, John?'

John held out the paperwork in his hands towards him. 'After fighting for two days, I've finally managed to secure us entry to the national park.'

Donovan smiled and nodded. 'You mean after two days of careful negotiations.'

John let out a stream of colourful language. 'No. I mean fighting.'

'So we're in?'

'We're in. You can collect the samples this afternoon.'

The words flowed over him and every sense on his body went on full alert. 'Aren't you collecting the samples?'

John shook his head. 'Callum asked if I could help out in the lab once the case histories were investigated. The samples are practically meeting David at the door right now.'

Donovan bit the inside of his cheek. Darn it. He wasn't going to countermand an order given by Callum. He might have been the first team leader on the job, but now Callum was here the final decisions would really be made by him.

He cleared his throat. Maybe this wouldn't be as bad as he was expecting. 'Where exactly are we collecting the samples from?'

John checked his reference sheets. 'The fruit bats have some nests in the surrounding tree trunks, but their primary habitat is in the limestone caves. There is a tour of the caves and the entrance and walkways are lit up. Unfortunately, there's no lighting further inside where the bats roost.'

The horrible creeping sensation he'd been expecting

washed over his body. He didn't care about lights. What he did care about was an open exit route.

'How far into the caves do we need to go?'

John shook his head. 'I'm not sure. I think it might be around eight hundred metres. I can check if you want?'

'No. That's fine.'

Eight hundred metres. Half a mile. Well away from any visible entrance point. Tracks in caves didn't go in nice straight lines. Not like Roman roads. No, they would follow every twist and turn of the mountain they were worn into.

John looked back down the corridor and smiled. It was obvious he was oblivious to the thoughts currently crowding Donovan's head. 'I take it you'll want to take our newest recruit on the sample-collecting expedition?'

His head jerked round. Did John know something had gone on between them? How could he?

He bit back the snappy reply that was about to form on his lips. He'd worked with this guy for three years. John was older, and maybe a whole lot wiser. It was obvious he was just yanking his chain. And he had nobody to blame but himself. John had obviously noticed the way he was looking at Grace.

That would have to stop.

'Grace!' he shouted down the corridor, his tone a bit sharper than he'd actually meant it to be.

She started and turned round. For a second her eyes widened as she caught the expression on his face, then she obviously realised John was by his side. Her feet moved quickly down the corridor and he willed himself not to watch the swing of her hips in that confounded dress. Her clothes—or lack of them—were going to be the death of him.

'I've reviewed most of the patients,' she started quickly. 'There are a few who need some further attention, but most are stable for the moment.'

She was doing exactly what he would expect her to do. Getting on with the job. But even the way she said those words crept under his skin. The quick talking was obviously a self-defence mechanism. He recognised it, because he was in that place himself.

John seemed oblivious. 'Looks like you've got a state park to visit.'

He held the paperwork up to her and her eyes scanned the page. Her fingers automatically moved to her hair, grabbing a little strand and twisting it round one index finger. He noticed the tiniest, subtlest widening of her eyes. 'I'm going to collect the samples?' Was that the smallest tremor in her voice?

John kept smiling. He didn't notice all the little nuances in Grace's behaviour that Donovan did. 'Yeah, you and Donovan are going this afternoon.'

'Can't you go?' Her voice had risen in pitch and her eyes were fixed on John, almost as if she didn't want to look at Donovan in case he questioned her reaction. She hunched and then shrugged her shoulders, as if something had just irritated them.

Her scar. He hadn't asked her about the scar last night—even though he'd wanted to.

The smile had vanished from John's face. He reached up and touched Grace's arm. 'It's part of the initiation when you join a fieldwork team. You try out all roles in the team to see where you fit best. Would you prefer not to do it, Grace? Is there a problem?'

His voice was serious, questioning with a little hint of concern. It was important that every member of the team was able to function fully—filling in for each other in case of emergency. Grace had proved herself more than capable of dealing with the clinical cases, but the DPA fulfilled many more roles than that.

She was hesitating. The look on her face told him she was searching her brain for an appropriate answer. She fixed a smile on her face. 'No, John, it's fine.' Her eyes skimmed the information in front of her. 'We'll have guides, won't we? And the caves are lit?' There was an anxious tone to her voice, along with an edge of hopefulness.

Donovan was curious. She was asking the same kind of questions that he had. He hadn't noticed her having any kind of reaction in the isolation chamber back at the DPA. Enclosed spaces hadn't seemed to be an issue for her. So why the reluctance?

John's eyes were flicking between them both. He was obviously looking for a steer from Donovan. He spoke smoothly. 'I was just telling Donovan, the caves are quite deep and the fruit bats supposedly roost near the back of the caves. That's where you'll be collecting samples. The front part of the caves are lit for visitors, but not the back.'

She baulked. There was no other word for it.

John tried to fill the silence. 'They're supposed to be quite atmospheric. You know, with stalactites, stalagmites and lots of fossils. The cave tours are really popular.'

It was all sounding a bit desperado now. Donovan had no idea what her issue was. But he had issues of his own.

He lifted the paperwork from John's hands. 'Thanks for this. Grace, I'll meet you at the front entrance at one p.m.'

The abrupt words made her flinch. And the hurt expression on her face made him flinch in turn.

He couldn't afford to give her special treatment. He couldn't afford to make obvious allowances for her. She was expected to do a job. Just like he was.

He turned on his heel and walked away.

Right now she needed a good old-fashioned shot of midazolam. Something to sedate her and calm her down to a mild panic.

Florida, in summer, in a hazmat suit was not a good place. The suit was airtight, with a one-piece jumpsuit underneath and an outer suit impermeable to most chemicals. The sealed hood with its viewport was stifling, even though she had her own air supply, and the protective gloves made her feel like she had no dexterity at all.

The suits were a necessary evil. The route of exposure of the Marburg virus from the fruit bats had never been discovered. They knew how the virus passed from human to human, but how the virus had got into humans in the first place was still open to debate. It could be airborne, through contact with body fluids from the bats, or from surfaces in the caves. Therefore all staff had to wear protective, airtight suits. Nothing else was an option. They couldn't risk any more people being exposed to the virus.

She turned. There was no point moving just her head as the hood stayed in place and she ended up looking at the inside. She had to move her whole body round by shuffling her feet in the protective boots. Sweat was already beginning to pool on her forehead and she wasn't sure if it was the fact that the environment within the suit could be up to twenty or thirty degrees hotter than the temperature outside, or if it was the thought of going into those dark, imposing caves. As soon as the suit was sealed the humidity went up to one hundred per cent within a few minutes—not comfortable for any human.

People were assembling around her. The box for transporting the samples they would retrieve from the caves was sitting in front of her. She could hear Donovan talking through the speaker in the hood to those around about him.

The words were the slightest bit distorted, coming through the hood. But was that a trace of anxiety she could hear?

Grace tried some deep breathing. Long, slow breaths in and out. Her skin was prickling at the deep, blackness at the back of those caves. There was some lighting around the front, but the tourist part only lay in the front part of the caves. Where they were going was *waaaaayyy* back.

She shifted on her feet. She wanted to get this over and done with. If she'd known Donovan would keep talking for so long she would never have let them seal her suit. It was time for some definitive action. She picked up the kit box. 'Are we ready?'

Donovan's eyes met hers. There was something about wearing these suits. Lumbering around as if they were about to take a space-walk. There was layer upon layer within these suits and it almost felt as if they were separated by miles instead of inches.

The sun was reflecting off the faceplate of his sealed hood, making it hard to pick up any visual cues. But Donovan wasn't acting the way he normally did. He was saying twenty words when four would do.

It was almost as if he was stalling.

But why?

He'd looked at the plans for these caves. Four hundred metres in and they would have to turn a corner, following the natural line of the cave. Four hundred metres in and he would lose sight of the exit. He didn't care about how dark it was. He didn't care about how deep they went.

He just wished the way out was always visible. Always in his line of sight. If it was, he would be fine. He could do this. But the map had already told them that wouldn't be possible.

Which was why he was currently using every delaying tactic under the sun. He hated this. He hated it that he felt like this.

This was the first time his childhood phobia was actually going to cause a problem for his job.

Over the last few years he'd always managed to hide his fear, control it even. The isolation chamber had been tough, but in his head he had always imagined the exit route. But the caves were unfamiliar. They weren't so easy to visualise.

The state ranger was beginning to look annoyed. And no wonder. A few beads of perspiration were already winding down his back—and he was used to wearing a hazmat suit. The poor guy must feel as if he were boiling alive.

He glanced over at the dark caves once again. It was almost as if they were mocking him, laughing at him and his juvenile fears.

This wasn't a sealed-in elevator with a door that might never open. Prickles started along his arms, running down to the palms of his hands. It was like a million little centipedes stamping over his skin. He kept talking to himself. Willing himself to stay calm.

He had control. He was choosing to walk in there. He was the team leader. He had to collect these samples and establish if this was the cause of the outbreak. He had responsibilities, to himself and to his team.

And to Grace. She was shuffling around next to him as if someone had put itching powder in her suit. She'd never done this before. He had to set a good example for her.

He had to do this. The quicker he went in there the quicker he got out.

There. He'd convinced himself.

Grace had picked up the sample box and was hovering.

'Let's go, people.' He moved quickly before he changed his mind, walking as best he could in the uncomfortable suit. Grace and the state ranger quickly followed, but he was so focused, so intent on his goal that he barely noticed.

In and out. In and out. If he kept saying it, he might believe it.

Grace was doing her breathing exercises. She was clutching the sample box as if her life depended on it. What she really wanted to do was turn on her heel and run but, perhaps thankfully, her clumsy suit didn't allow for that.

She felt as if the blackness from the caves was reaching out towards her like a giant black hand, crossing over the pathways drenched in Florida sunlight and trying to envelop her and suck her in. It put her nerves on edge.

There was a bright white spotlight near the cave entrance, with another few lighting up some of the internal walkways. Her steps slowed as she neared the entry point. Her throat was dry and scratchy even though she'd taken a drink just before she'd been sealed into the suit. Any more liquid could result in other problems. What went in had to come out and she had no idea how long they would be in these caves.

She swallowed. The lights were fine, but they only focused on the front area. The state ranger was already heading through the first cave. Why did the fruit bats have to roost so far into the caves? Sadistic little critters.

She squeezed her eyes shut for a second—it was easier not to look—and walked straight into the back of Donovan. The face plate bashed against her nose. 'Ouch!'

Donovan turned round. He had the strangest expression on his face. 'What's wrong?' His voice was snappy and sounded even stranger as it came through the speaker and echoed around the cave.

'I...I...' Her brain wouldn't work. She couldn't figure out the words she wanted to say. The last thing she wanted to do was tell Donovan she was scared of the dark. It made her sound like a five-year-old.

Already the hairs were standing up on the back of her neck. The lights didn't reach around the corner they were about to turn and the shadows around her were disappearing rapidly.

It took a few minutes to realise that Donovan hadn't moved. His feet seemed just as stuck to the floor as hers.

'Hey!' The call came from the state ranger, who hadn't wasted any time reaching the back area of the caves. 'Are you two coming?'

She gulped. Was she? Her hand reached up automatically to catch a lock of her hair and wind it around her finger. Impossible. Layer and layers were in the way.

Donovan's face changed. Was that a hint of a smile? Followed by a nervous laugh?

Her shoulder was itching uncontrollably. She had absolutely no chance of being able to scratch. She turned her back to the wall of the cave and pressed herself against it, trying to avoid the lumpy oxygen supply strapped inside her suit, while rubbing gently on the wall.

He was looking at her oddly.

She took a deep breath. 'I'm not good with caves.' Her eyes skirted around her surroundings. She was trying not to let her feelings envelop her. 'I'm not good with being in the dark. I was attacked a few years ago in a dark parking lot. Ever since then I've slept with the light on.' The words rushed out of her mouth before she could stop them. She didn't want to look at him. She didn't want to see the disappointment on his face.

Silence. All she could hear was her own breathing. Then one word came out of the darkness. The one she least expected.

'Snap.'

This was the worst feeling in the world. He'd never felt so exposed as he did right now.

Trouble was, Grace's expression was pretty much mirroring his own right now—and it wasn't because she was reflecting off his plastic hood.

He reached out and touched her shoulder. 'Do you want to leave, Grace?'

He was the team leader. He had to ask the question.

He had to look out for his staff member. To be honest, if she said she wanted to leave right now it would give him an excuse to leave too.

The thought of having a panic attack around his colleagues was more than he could bear. But the prickling feeling on his skin, thudding heartbeats and rapid breathing couldn't really be anything else.

But he couldn't think about himself right now. His own sensations of panic were being overtaken by a whole load of rage. 'Is that what the scar is on your shoulder?'

He flicked on the torch he had in his other hand. The darkness hadn't bothered him at all. He'd had the flashlight but just hadn't flicked the switch. He'd been too busy focusing on the entrance to the caves that was about to disappear from his line of sight.

The cave around them was illuminated in the light from the torch. There was a tear rolling down her cheek. His hand lifted to her visor. Too many layers, too many things in the way. All he wanted to do right now was wipe away her tear with his finger.

'You were stabbed in the attack?'

She nodded. He wanted to hold her. He wanted to wrap his arms around her and pull her close to his chest. The feelings were overwhelming. He'd known from the second he'd seen the angry scar that there must be a story behind it. He just hadn't banked on his reaction to that story.

He bent his knees so he was face to face with her. 'What were you doing in a dark parking lot at night, Grace? And why didn't you just give them your bag? It was only a bag. Things can be replaced. You can't.'

As he said the words he almost felt a hand around

his heart, squeezing tightly. He hated the thought of someone doing that to her. He couldn't stand the fact she'd been attacked, let alone what outcome there could have been.

Her voice was shaky. 'I was working, Donovan. It was my last shift at Atlanta Park Hospital. I stayed a bit later to make sure my charts were up to date and by the time I got outside the lights were out in the parking lot.' She shook her head. 'I didn't fight him. I'm not that stupid. But he didn't care. He made a grab for my bag and just stabbed me anyway.'

He could see her whole body trembling inside the thick suit. 'That's why I don't like the dark. I get nervous. I have trouble dating now. I hate being alone with a man. It brings back a whole lot of memories I can't deal with. It doesn't matter that it's irrational. I know that. They're just still there.'

The dating stuff started circling around his brain. Grace was nervous around men? Why hadn't he noticed? He'd kissed her, for goodness' sake!

But it was the other words that struck a chord. The irrational fears. They resounded around his head. 'I can relate to that, Grace.'

She looked confused. 'But you're Donovan. You're not scared of anything. You managed to tackle a guy with a gun.'

He took a deep breath. He'd never revealed this part of himself to anyone. He hadn't wanted to. He didn't want gossip circulating about him that could affect his position at the DPA. He'd never been prepared to take that risk.

But this was Grace. Someone he felt a connection to. And she'd just put herself on the line for him. He had to be honest with her. He had to let her know that she wasn't alone. He could ask her about the dating stuff later.

'Irrational fears are a funny thing. You're right. Apart from a few jittery nerves, I wasn't that scared of the guy with the gun. I knew if the timing was right, I could overpower him.'

'Then I don't get it. What are you scared of?'

He pointed to the light streaming in from the entry point. Even saying the words made the little hairs stand up on his body. 'I need to know I can get out of places. I had a bad experience as a kid. I was trapped in an elevator for hours. As long as I can see the way out, I'm fine. And in most circumstances I can. Take the exit route out of my line of sight and a whole host of things start churning around in my head.'

She looked horrified. 'That must have been awful. What age were you?'

'Six.'

'And how long were you in the elevator?'

He gave a big sigh. Talking about it brought it all back to him. The feeling of abandonment. The silver walls all around him. Needing to pee so badly it hurt. Crying so hard it made his chest sore. Wondering if he would ever see his mother again.

'Six hours.'

'Six hours? For a six-year-old?' The pitch of her voice rose in obvious shock. This was why he didn't tell people. He didn't want sympathy. He didn't want to relive the horror. He just wanted to put this all in a box and forget about it. Too bad his subconscious wouldn't let him.

'So how do you expect to collect samples at the back

of a cave, hundreds of feet away from the exit?' It was the obvious question.

'The same way you expect to collect samples in a cave with no lighting,' he countered.

They looked at each other. For the first time it seemed okay to admit to a fear. They were on an equal footing. One fear overlapped the other.

The temperature in his suit was rising—and it wasn't just down to the suffocating Florida heat. It wasn't quite so stifling in the caves. The air was damper, more humid, but those were probably contributing factors to the spread of the virus.

No. The temperature was rising in his suit purely because of the way Grace was looking at him and the inappropriate thoughts that were clouding his brain. This was what he'd feared. Romantic entanglements with a colleague meant your mind wasn't on the job. And right now his certainly wasn't.

He wanted to run his hands through the tangled waves of her hair. He wanted to feel her skin beneath the palms of his hand. He wanted to feel the warm curves of her body pressed against his.

The hazmat suits made them look like spacemen on an Apollo mission. Nothing sexy. Nothing revealing. And yellow probably wasn't his colour. But Grace? She made anything look good.

She was still staring at him. There were the tiniest beads of sweat along her brow. It just made him want to touch her all the more. Last time she'd had water on her brow had been in the sea, in that orange bikini.

And then she did it. She ran her tongue along her dry lips. It was almost the end of him. He let out a moan that resembled a little growl. Thank goodness there was no one near them. He shook his head inside the hood. 'Grace, don't.'

She lifted her hand, palm open, and held it up facing him. She ran her tongue along her lips again. 'Why, what am I doing?'

She knew. She knew how ridiculous this was. But the buzz of electricity was giving them both the distraction that they needed. Who knew hazmat suits and bat caves could be sexy?

She moved her hand again. 'Okay, Mr Team Leader. We can do this. Together.'

He took a deep breath, willing his body to stop reacting to her every move. For a few seconds at least his childhood fears had been forgotten. He lifted his gloved hand to press against hers. 'Together.' He smiled. 'Wanna hold hands?'

She leaned forward, lowering her voice. 'That's not really what I want to hold. But let's just get this over and done with, okay?'

No. His body was definitely not playing fair. Thank goodness for padded body suits.

He pulled his shoulders back. He had a job to do. Irrational and unreasonable fears be damned.

As for the sexy distracting chat—they could talk about that later. Alone. Naked. Undisturbed. And Grace could hold any part of his body she wanted.

He took long strides towards the back of the cave, turning and following the path far away from the entrance. He didn't think about it. He had a clear way out behind him. He had a torch in his hand to show him the way.

He sensed a little movement at his back. The light pressure of a hand resting on his suit. Grace was

matching him step for step. She was just holding on
for the ride.

A flicker in front of him showed him where the
ranger had stopped. He pointed his torch in the direction of the bats roosting on the curved roof. The ranger's brow was furrowed. 'What kept you? Did you two
get lost?'

Donovan didn't answer. He swung round and held a
hand out to Grace. 'I'll collect some samples from the
cave floor. You swab the sides of the cave.'

The ranger swung his torch to one corner, lighting up
the corpse of a dead bat lying on the cave floor. 'What
about that? Do you want to take a specimen?'

Donovan nodded. 'I'll bag it and seal it.' It didn't
really matter what had caused the death of the fruit bat.
David would still be able to test it and see if it carried the
virus. He turned and handed his torch to Grace, waving
his arm towards the ranger. 'Can you light up the area
for her while she collects samples?'

She shot him a grateful glance. He didn't mind fum-
bling around in the dark. It only took a few minutes to
collect the samples of bat droppings he required for the
lab and to bag and seal the dead bat. Who said this job
wasn't glamorous?

'All right, Grace?'

Her hood, lit up by the torch next to it, was casting
an impressive range of shadows around the cave. Her
outline looked like a monster from a kid's book. The
stalagmites and stalactites were all over the deep part
of the cave here. In any other circumstances it would
be a perfect setting for a horror movie.

She glanced at him. 'What is it?' Her voice wasn't
trembling any more. She didn't seem so rattled.

He smiled. He was trying not to think about how he couldn't see the way out from here. It was much easier just to look into Grace's eyes and think about a whole host of other things.

'I was just imagining you in one of those kids' story-books. You know, the monster in the caves kind of thing?'

'You're just all charm, aren't you?' she shot back. She gave him a little wink. 'I'll make you pay for that later.' His distraction techniques were working.

He stood up and pushed the double-bagged bat into the sample case. 'Are we done?'

She breathed an obvious sigh of relief and nodded. 'Let's get out of here.'

He turned back towards the way they'd entered and gave a little start. Darkness. Nothing in front of him. No obvious way out. Sealed in a million tonnes of rock along with some deadly bats.

He squeezed his eyes shut for a second. He was Donovan Reid. He couldn't do this. In any other lifetime this would be described as a wobble. He couldn't let that happen.

Then he felt Grace lay her hand on his arm. She held out the torch in front of her. He could see she was taking some long, slow breaths. She glanced sideways at him, aware that the ranger was watching them both. 'Let's go.'

She walked first, letting the thin torch beam ahead of her be the beacon lighting the way out. She moved briskly, without talking, until they reached the bend in the cave that revealed the entrance ahead.

He felt all the pent-up air rush out of his lungs. He hadn't even realised he had been holding it. As they neared the entrance his phone beeped loudly. It was inside his suit, it would have to wait.

It took a few minutes to reach the outside of the caves. The decontamination unit was set up outside and they all stripped off their gear and headed for the showers. This time there was no sharing of cubicles. No untoward views of a naked Grace. It was almost disappointing.

He towelled off his hair and picked up the phone. The screen was steamed up and he wiped it clean and stepped outside.

No.

'What is it?' Grace appeared beside him, towel-drying her hair too.

He held up the phone. 'Just what we don't want to hear. Two adult fatalities in the last hour. One at our hospital, another, a late diagnosis, at a hospital in Mexico. He visited the caves last Thursday. John found him during the visitor follow-ups. We need to step up a gear.'

'But what else can we do?'

His eyes skimmed over her body. She was wearing simple clothes. A T-shirt and a pair of fitted trousers. All he could think about was what lay beneath.

It couldn't happen. He couldn't do this.

This was exactly what he'd feared. People depended on him to stop this outbreak. He couldn't do that while his head was full of Grace.

She was watching him with her green eyes. Trusting him because of what they'd just shared.

He kept his tone sharp as he walked away from her. 'Get those samples to David at the labs. I'm going to speak to whoever is in charge of the park. I'm going to get the whole area cordoned off.'

He couldn't turn round. He *wouldn't* turn round.

Because he didn't want to see the expression on her face.

CHAPTER EIGHT

WHAT WAS WRONG with him?

He'd barely spoken to her in the last few days. She was getting more conversation out of Mara from the kitchen than she was from Donovan.

Oh, he mentioned patients and gave instructions. The caves had been confirmed as the site of the virus. The Jamaican fruit bats had been rounded up and taken away while some scientist worked out how the virus had travelled between African and Jamaican bats.

She'd waited the last two nights to see if he would knock on her door. She'd even hesitated outside his door the other night, not even knowing if he had actually been there or not. Then she'd sat in her room, pulled the doors back and stared out at the beach to see if she could spot him running.

It was ridiculous.

Callum Ferguson, in the meantime, was charm himself. He spoke to her for an hour at every handover, praising her work, answering any questions and giving her a few hints about things she was unsure of. She was finally starting to shake off the bad feelings that Frank Parker had initiated. Was finally starting to feel like a valuable member of the team.

But Donovan was doing nothing to help that.

He was sitting at one of the nurses' stations, working on a computer. She wasn't going to avoid him. She hadn't done anything wrong. So she flopped into the seat next to him and picked up the phone.

'Hi, it's Dr Grace Barclay from the DPA team in Florida. I'm just phoning to check on the condition of the kids we sent to you a few days ago.'

She listened carefully, taking a few notes. They had five kids now in other ICUs. Two still very serious and three who seemed to making small improvements.

She replaced the receiver with a sigh. She didn't even care what kind of mood Donovan was in right now. 'Tyler Bates, the five-year-old we resuscitated? He's still not doing great. They've transfused him three times and are giving him extra clotting factors. He's still haemorrhaging.'

Donovan turned his head slightly. 'And the other kids?'

'Obi, Sarah and Mario have made slight improvements. Jenny is still serious.'

He nodded and turned back to his screen.

'Aren't you going to say anything else?' The stats for the Marburg virus were circulating around her head. Anything between a twenty-three and a ninety per cent death rate. They had treated more than thirty kids so far. She couldn't bear the thought of having to deal with a child death. She'd never had to do that before. She was getting angry with Donovan's deafening silence. She stood up, sending the wheeled chair skidding behind her. Her voice rose. 'Do you know that his mom's pregnant? They've forbidden her to enter the isolation room. The risk to the baby is too great. She can't even hold her little boy's hand.'

'Sit down, Grace.' His words were quiet and they just infuriated her all the more.

'No, I won't sit down. I don't want to sit down. I want you to talk to me.'

He raised his eyebrow. 'I am talking to you.'

'No, you're not. Not really.'

One of the nurses hurried past, her eyes flicking from one to the other. She picked up a prescription chart and disappeared into another room.

Donovan took his hands from the keyboard and leaned back in his chair. 'Grace, it's late. We have to hand over to Callum in an hour. I've got another three suspected cases in sites around the world. I'm trying to organise a way to get their samples checked in labs that have no idea what Marburg virus looks like. What do you want me to do? Ignore the work I'm supposed to be doing, to deal with your temper tantrum?'

She stopped dead. 'My what?'

'Your temper tantrum.' He waved his arm at her in exasperation. 'That's clearly what's going on here.'

She was holding back sobs. She walked to the other side of the desk. It was safer. She couldn't punch him from there.

She leaned over towards him, 'What I'm doing, Donovan, is offloading to my team leader. I'm juggling more than twenty paediatric patients right now—an area I don't specialise in. We only have one paediatrician and he's on the other team. I've got another two kids that should ideally be transferred to another ICU, but there are no available beds at Panama Health Care, and if I send them to another facility I'll have to authorise another DPA team to attend.' She drummed her fingers on the desk.

'My brain won't stop reminding me of the death rate for Marburg.' She waved her arm down the corridor. 'We've lost five adult patients now. How long will it be before we lose a child? And will I be left to deal with that too? Because, quite frankly, Donovan, I don't know if I can.' She ground her heels into the floor. 'So, no, Dr Reid, this isn't a temper tantrum. This is a frustrated colleague wondering if she's cut out to be on a field-work team. Believe me, if I was having a temper tantrum, you would know it.'

There was a fire in her eyes he'd only glimpsed on occasion before. A fire that made her seem more beautiful than ever. Even after five days here, staying in a backwater motel, her dark hair was glossy and her skin glowing. Grace looked as if she should be on the cover of a magazine.

All of a sudden he couldn't stand it. He couldn't stand it a second longer. His brain seemed to have lost its *don't-say-that* clause. The kind that made you adjust what you really wanted to say to the words that formed on your lips. 'Grace, what's going on here?'

She pulled back. She seemed surprised by his forthright question.

Her brow wrinkled. 'What do you mean?'

He waved his hand. 'This. Us. What is this?' He was confused. It was strange for him, because clarity of thought was one of his great strengths. He just couldn't make sense of this any more.

For a second she said nothing. Her mouth wasn't hanging open, but it was obvious words were stuck in her throat. She sighed and put her head on the desk.

Not the best sign he'd ever seen.

'I've no idea. I can't work it out myself.' Her words were mumbled into the top of the nurses' station and under her waves of shiny hair. She lifted her head, her green eyes fixing on his. For a few seconds he actually felt clear-headed. 'This is you, Donovan. This is your fault. You kissed me. You touched me.'

He half smiled. 'You weren't complaining. In fact, I'm not entirely sure if I did initiate that kiss. It felt pretty mutual.'

'It did. Didn't it?' She thumped her head back down in exasperation then held out her hands. 'Why is this so wrong? Why can't this just be a simple boy-meets-girl?'

'Why do people like Frank Parker exist?' His eyebrows rose automatically. He still felt murky. The lights seemed unnaturally bright. But being around Grace just felt so natural.

She sighed. 'Frank Parker. I hate that. I hate that whether or not I can date someone depends on what some lowlife said on Twitter.'

'Who said anything about dating?'

She looked a little shocked. He hadn't quite meant it to come out like that. It was almost as if someone had taken the safety filters off his brain and mouth. 'Well, no. Of course. I didn't mean that...'

He stood up and put his hand over hers. *Zing.* There it was. Every time they touched. For a second he felt a little light-headed. Had he swayed? Just as well there was a barrier between them, because right now he just wanted to take delectable Grace in his arms and pull her close to him. It was like this whenever they were around each other. As if some invisible force just pulled them together.

'I don't just want to date, Grace.'

There. He'd said it out loud. It went against every one of his principles. It went against every instinct to protect her from gossip. It went against his deep-rooted fear about not being on the ball at work because he was too busy thinking about a colleague. But he just couldn't help it. He had to say it out loud.

His sensibilities didn't seem to be in place today. He was thinking with his heart and not his head.

His heart. His brain was definitely stuffed with cotton wool today because he never thought things like that.

But how else could he describe it? Grace had lighted up his world these last few days. Every smile, every flick of her hair, every sway of her hips. All he could think was that he didn't want this to stop.

He didn't want to go home to an empty apartment every night and a dog who looked at him as if he'd been abandoned. Because that was just it, it didn't really feel like a home. Even Casey wasn't filling the gap that was there.

Was this what love felt like? Donovan wasn't sure that he knew. Attraction to the opposite sex had never been a problem. Raging hormones had never been a problem. But this was a whole lot more than that.

He didn't just want to have sex with Grace. He wanted to have a relationship with her. He wanted to make her smile. He wanted to make her happy.

He'd never even tried anything like this before. Maybe that's why part of his brain kept screaming no. He didn't want to do anything to hurt Grace. He didn't want to do anything to make her vulnerable. If anything, he wanted to protect her.

He could feel heat rising in his skin. It felt stranger

than before. Different from the usual effect of being around Grace.

There was a flicker of something in her eyes. He squeezed his shut for a second. The lights in here seemed even brighter than before. It was relief. Relief that he'd acknowledged the obvious attraction.

Kissing seemed like the obvious way to acknowledge it, but saying it out loud made it real.

'I don't know what it is about you, Donovan Reid,' she said softly, looking at his warm hand over hers. She shook her head slightly. 'I just know that in the last few days I can sense whenever you're around, whenever you're near me.' The edges of her lips turned up by the tiniest margins. 'This has to be real. Donovan. I don't do this. I don't feel like this around men. Not in a long time.'

Something clicked inside his brain. 'Since the attack?' His hand subconsciously squeezed hers.

'Especially since the attack. I haven't really felt safe around any man since then.'

'And around me?'

'It's different. You're different. We're different.' It was almost as if she couldn't meet his gaze again. They were in the middle of a ward. Other staff were wandering around. 'What happened in the caves...' Her voice tailed off.

'You've never told anyone that before?'

She shook her head. 'No.'

'Neither have I. A team leader who doesn't like not having a clear exit route? It isn't exactly ideal. Who knows where we could end up? It makes me feel like a liability rather than a valuable member of staff.'

Words. Words he'd never thought he'd say out loud. What was wrong with him?

She nodded in acknowledgement. 'We make an unlikely pair.' She drew in a deep, haltering breath. This time she did meet his gaze. Voices were starting to echo round about him. Noises increasing in volume then fading just as quickly. 'I know you have reservations, Donovan. But you've just admitted you feel exactly the way that I do. We're not Sawyer and his first wife. What happened to her was terrible, but that doesn't mean it's ever going to happen again. The DPA has made provisions for that. We could give this a chance if we wanted to.'

He could almost hear her holding her breath—waiting for his response.

But he couldn't think clearly. It was easy to focus on Grace and the overwhelming feelings he had towards her. But he was losing perspective all around him. This couldn't work. It just couldn't. She was still waiting for his answer. The expression on her face was pained. He blinked. It was almost as if she was surrounded by fog.

Things were starting to feel unreal. Like some weird dream. He had to try and take some sense of control again. His vision was blurring. Was this what not eating did to you? Made you feel so muggy and unfocused?

He tried to straighten his thoughts. He wanted to tell Grace how he really felt about her. He wanted to tell her how much he hadn't wanted to leave her room the other night, how all he'd really wanted to do had been to push her back onto the bed and feel the softness of her skin on the palms of his hands.

But the words just couldn't form on his lips. Grace was a wonderful doctor. The last thing she needed on her first fieldwork trip was distractions. She needed a chance to make her mark on the team in her own right. Not with whispers and rumours surrounding her. He had to step back. He had to step away from her. He had to protect her.

'No, we can't. We can't give this a chance, Grace. It has to stop here. It has to stop now. From this moment on it has to be a strictly professional relationship. Nothing else.' She was shifting in his gaze, coming into focus then blurring. He had to be clear as he possibly could. 'I don't want anything else.'

Her face crumpled and she spun on her heel and strode down the corridor as fast as her legs would carry her. If she stayed a second longer she couldn't be held responsible for her actions.

It was the way he'd just looked at her. As if nothing had ever happened between them. As if he'd never run his fingers over her skin, never felt his lips on hers.

He'd looked at her as if she were just a regular team worker he'd had no connection with at all.

And it cut her to the bone.

She'd been the one to walk away. She'd said at the beach that it had been a mistake. But he'd been the one to come to her motel room. He'd been the one that had kissed her as if he never wanted to leave.

Then, after what had happened at the caves...

She knew now. She knew him. And there wasn't another person on the team who knew what she did about Donovan. Likewise, he was the only person to know about her inbuilt fear, the one she was trying so hard to get past.

Whether he liked it or not, they were connected. And

she felt it. Every single time she was around him. No matter how much he ignored her.

How could he not be feeling it too? Because this didn't feel like a passing fling. This didn't feel like some silly one-night kiss. This went deeper than she'd ever experienced before, running through her veins, tugging completely at her heartstrings. Every time she saw him her heart gave a little leap, her skin went on fire and her senses on red alert.

It was like a constant adrenaline surge. She couldn't eat. She couldn't sleep. She just thanked God she was still doing a good job. Because right now it was the only thing that was working in her favour.

Donovan felt like crap. His head ached, his muscles were sore and he felt as sick as a dog. He glanced at his watch again. Callum was due in a few minutes. Thank goodness. Right now every minute felt like an hour.

Grace was mad at him. And to be honest, he probably deserved it. When she'd snapped at him he just hadn't had the patience. But she was right. About everything.

He should have been supporting her more. He knew this was her first fieldwork assignment and she'd more than proved her capabilities already. Dealing with sick children was always more difficult for any team member. Dealing with kids who had a virus with a potentially high death rate was another thing entirely.

He should have taken the time to have a private discussion with her about what had happened between them. He could have done this so much better.

He should go after her. But then he might say something inappropriate like he loved her. He couldn't do that. He couldn't risk her position on the team. And right now he just didn't think he could get his body to move. His legs felt like lead and he rubbed his eyes as the words on the computer screen seemed to dance around him.

'Donovan? Donovan?' The voice grew sharper.

He felt fuzzy. He definitely needed to sleep. Or maybe he needed to eat? When was the last time he'd eaten? But his stomach was churning. He couldn't face the thought of food right now.

'Donovan.'

The voice was right in front of him. David thumped into the chair next to him and shook him by the shoulders. 'What's wrong with you?'

David leaned forward, then immediately pulled back again. 'Are you sick?'

'Just tired. I need to sleep.'

'No. It's more than that. What are your symptoms?' The voice was direct and intense. David might work in the lab but he was a fieldwork member could fill any role on the team. He wouldn't hesitate to take any actions he needed to.

Donovan stretched out his back, trying to loosen his sore muscles, and went for his natural automatic response. 'I don't have symptoms. I'm fine.'

Or maybe he did? His brain started to straighten out. What were his symptoms?

It was as if a thousand little caterpillars started marching over his skin with ice-cold feet.

He couldn't have contracted the virus—could he?

No. He'd been wearing protective gear since he'd got here. Any patient contact he'd had he'd been fully covered. As for the caves, he'd worn the full hazmat suit. Nothing got through that.

The chills continued. The resus case. He hadn't been wearing full protective clothing for that. He'd pulled on a pair of gloves but that had been it. A child hadn't been breathing, and he'd prioritised.

He'd had to maintain Tyler's airway and the little boy had already been haemorrhaging. Truth was he'd probably been exposed to all kind of body fluids.

'I want to draw your blood.' David's voice had never sounded so firm.

Grace. He needed to talk to Grace. He needed to apologise and give her more support. He didn't have time for this.

David was walking around now, in and out of treatment rooms, collecting supplies. Before Donovan could argue, a tourniquet had been tightened around his upper arm and David was tapping the skin in his inner elbow.

'Stop it. What you are doing?'

David ignored him. 'Do you feel sick, nauseous? Have you had any diarrhoea? Sore head, scratchy throat? Any chills or a rash?'

He slid the needle under Donovan's skin with the ease of long experience then started slotting on the collection bottles for the various samples of blood.

Donovan didn't know whether to be mad or grateful. And that told him everything he needed to know.

'When do you think you could have been exposed? We've been here just over five days. You must have been exposed at the beginning.'

His head was pounding. He had to stop thinking like a doctor. For once in his life he had to play the part of a patient. 'No sickness, no diarrhoea. Yes, I have a headache, a sore throat and some chills. But that could be a hundred other things.'

He opened his eyes to face David's grey ones and the mask covering his face. It gave him a jolt. His colleague was taking no chances.

'The resus,' he finally said. 'I could have been exposed at the kid's resus. It was five days ago. Maybe a little bit more.'

David finished collecting the samples and pressed a cotton-wool ball into the crook of Donovan's elbow. 'Hold this.' He glanced up and down the corridor. There were approaching footsteps.

'Callum, I've just taken a sample from Donovan. He's having some symptoms. Can you arrange for him to be put in an isolation room until I get some results?'

The air turned blue with Callum's Scottish expletives. He didn't hesitate and moved straight over to Donovan. David thrust a gown and gloves towards him and was met with another outburst of words.

Donovan was fine. He was absolutely fine. But any second now he was going to be sick all over his shoes. And this fuzzy headache made him feel as if he was surrounded by a huge cloud of cotton wool. Words and pictures were disorientating him. Like any person, he'd had sickness bugs before in the past, but this didn't feel like a normal bug.

Callum's loud voice carried up the corridor as he sorted out a bed. Among all the voices and confusion there was only one clear thought in Donovan's head. Only one thing he could focus on. Grace.

He wanted to talk to her. He wanted to touch her skin and run his fingers through her hair. He wanted to sit down face to face with her. He wanted to tell her that everything about her confused him. He'd never been so distracted by a woman in his life.

He'd never had that gut-clenching feeling about a woman before. She could make him smile just by walking into the room. She played in his thoughts every day and every night. And no matter how much his gut told him that dating someone in the team was a bad idea, every other part of his body disagreed.

He squeezed his eyes shut and he could see her walking out of the sea in her orange bikini with the water streaming from her body; he could see her striding across the concourse at the airport with her wraparound dress and newly found confidence.

He could see the hurt and fire flash in her eyes when she'd been mad at him earlier. Why hadn't he spoken to her? Why hadn't he gone after her?

'This way, Dr Reid. We have a room ready for you.' One of the nurses was at his elbow. Totally gowned, gloved and masked. Infection-control procedures were in place.

Oh, no.

He'd kissed Grace. He'd definitely swapped body fluids with her while he'd been incubating the disease. He'd put Grace at risk. He felt a sharp pain in his chest as if someone had just grabbed hold of his heart and squeezed tightly.

No. Not Grace. Anyone but Grace.

'Callum!' He had no idea where Callum was but he had to tell him. The nurse at his elbow jumped as she tried to lead him down the corridor. Panic seized him. This was what he'd dreaded. This was what he'd always feared. And he'd been right.

He was finding it difficult to focus, difficult to concentrate. Grace was the one solid picture in his mind. His head was thumping, it felt as though the pulsing blood supply was echoing around his brain. This wasn't normal. It wasn't right.

Thumping footsteps and a heavy hand on his arm. 'Donovan, what is it?'

'I kissed Grace. I kissed her.' He couldn't hide the desperate tone in his voice. Neither could he make out Callum's reply. The world around him was swimming, hazy lights merging and blackening, the strangest feeling flooding through his body as all energy seemed to leave him, turning his legs to jelly.

Then everything went dark.

She was eating the greasiest, unhealthiest pizza in the world. She'd been so mad she'd left the hospital without eating and had found out to her peril that Saucer Boys Pizzas was the only option near the motel. The bad punctuation should have told her everything she needed to know.

The grease wasn't helping the horrible feeling in the pit of her stomach.

The horrible feeling that she'd made a terrible mistake.

She pulled open the doors to the beach, drinking in the ocean view and releasing some of the odour of toxic pizza.

The plastic white chair on the tiny balcony was designed to be uncomfortable. What she'd really like to be doing right now was sitting with a glass of wine in hand, watching the sunset on the horizon. But she wasn't in that Zen-like kind of place.

She was too worried about the kids. She was too

worried about doing her absolute best on her twelve-hour shift tomorrow. She was too worried she might miss something important.

She was too worried about Donovan and her actions around him.

There. She'd let that thought into her crowded brain. It almost felt like some of the other thoughts were there deliberately, trying to push him into the background and pretend he wasn't important, when the truth was he was centre stage in her brain all the time.

Donovan didn't want to be involved with someone at work. End. Of.

It didn't matter that he'd told her he was attracted to her. It didn't matter the way his body reacted when they kissed. It didn't matter that the man could glance at her from the other side of the room and set her skin on fire.

This wasn't going to happen.

The long and short of it? Donovan was right.

She was too busy thinking about him to focus on her job. Her cheeks flushed with embarrassment and her eyes felt wet instantly.

She had a horrible sinking realisation. She was in that first flush of love. The kind that made you dizzy and lose focus.

Shouldn't love make you shout from the rooftops and sing to the world? Wasn't love supposed to make you happy and view the world through rose-tinted glasses?

Not when the person who held your heart in their hands had just told you there was no chance for you.

She buried her face in the pillow on the bed. It didn't offer any comfort as it was hard and impossibly lumpy. She had a horrible feeling of dread. As if there was something else—something more—and she just didn't know what.

The sooner she got out of there the better.

The door knock sounded sharply. She jumped and glanced at her watch. Then her heart started to flutter. Donovan. It had to be Donovan.

She stood and crossed the room quicker than she'd thought possible. Her hand hesitated at the doorhandle. This was it. This was where she had to admit to exactly how she felt about him. This was where she had to put her hand on her heart and tell him that he was right.

Dating the boss was never going to work. She was beyond distracted. She wanted to love everything about this fieldwork post, but all she could think about was Donovan.

Until she'd been in this position she could never have imagined how it felt.

Maybe there would be a chance to join another team. Maybe if she could wait it out a little longer, she would have opportunity to decide where she wanted to specialise and move to another department.

That could work. It would be time limited. They could have a no-touch policy for a few weeks—or, at worst, a few months. Surely they could last that out?

Her heart gave a little surge. It wasn't hopeless. It wasn't. This could work.

She pulled open the door. 'Donovan, I was just thinking that—'

Except it wasn't Donovan. It was Callum Ferguson. His large frame filled the doorway. Thank goodness she was appropriately dressed.

He leaned against the doorjamb, folded his arms and

gave her a crooked, knowing smile. 'So, Dr Barclay. You kissed Donovan Reid.'

'What…? Who told you that?' She wasn't quite sure how to respond. Her first reaction was to deny it. But Callum was already looking at her as if he could read her mind.

She couldn't quite get over the fact that Callum was standing on her doorstep. He was the last person she'd expected to see.

But there was something else. The usual twinkle in his eyes wasn't there. Was he mad? She felt a little shiver go down her spine. Callum didn't look mad. This was something else entirely.

'What is it?'

He sighed and ran his fingers through his grey hair. *What wasn't he telling her?* 'Donovan had to tell me he kissed you, Grace.'

'Donovan told you? But why?' Her mouth started working before her brain. Why on earth would he try and get them both into trouble? That made no sense. No sense at all. Unless…

'Oh, no.' Her hand flew up to her mouth. Unless Callum needed to contact trace. Her public-health head could put the pieces together a whole lot quicker than her Donovan-filled brain.

'What's wrong? What's wrong with Donovan?'

Callum's firm hand rested on her upper arm. 'Grace, calm down. I know you only finished work a few hours ago but I think it would be best if you come back to the hospital.'

There was serious edge to his voice and she was ominously aware that he hadn't yet told her what was wrong with Donovan.

'Of course.' She crossed the room quickly, slipping her feet into her shoes and picking up her jacket and bag. 'Let's go.'

It was only a five-minute drive back to the hospital. Her brain was in overload. She was trying not to acknowledge the fact that Callum had obviously left the hospital to come and get her. They'd been getting one of the hospital maintenance staff to pick them up and drop them off before this.

She was trying too hard to keep control. The fact that Callum knew she'd been kissing Donovan seemed irrelevant. The initial embarrassment had only taken a few seconds to disintegrate into the wind with the thought that something was really wrong.

She'd been feeling a little melancholy before. Realising the strength of her feelings for Donovan, and his attitude, which had seemed unreasonable before, was probably for the best.

The car pulled up next to the ambulance bay of the hospital, a little cloud of dust rising around them as it screeched to a halt.

She jumped out and waited at the door for Callum. He didn't waste any time, striding down the corridor and heading towards the lab. 'Come with me,' he called over his shoulder.

She bit her lip. 'Where's Donovan?' But he didn't reply and she sucked in a breath so quickly it hurt.

She hurried after his disappearing frame. For a big man, Callum could move quickly. He lifted the phone outside the laboratory entrance and buzzed the staff inside, putting them on speakerphone. Everyone was wearing a hazmat suit, and there were three staff. Was Donovan in there?

All three heads turned. David, John and Lucas from the other team. No Donovan. She winced. 'Is anyone going to tell me what's going on?' She was starting to feel desperate. As if there was some unspoken rule that no one could tell her what was wrong. There was still the horrible feeling in the pit of her stomach. The reason that Donovan would have to reveal personal information to Callum, to allow the public-health duty of contact tracing to take place. But why wouldn't someone just put her out of her misery and tell her?

David looked up from his microscope, his eyes darting past her and fixing quickly on Callum. The man she'd shared a few jokes with earlier now couldn't look her in the eye. 'I can't find any evidence of Marburg virus in his sample. No shepherd's crook. Even if it was in the early stages there would still be some evidence in the sample.'

Callum nodded. 'Best guess?'

John walked over to the glass panel. 'While you've been gone I've been up and taken a lumbar puncture. I think we've got a meningitis case. Give me an hour.'

Callum nodded. 'I'll start him on some IV antibiotics in the meantime. I'm not going to wait on the results.'

He touched her elbow. She felt numb. Numb with shock. She'd thought Donovan had been off with her earlier. She'd had no idea he was ill. What kind of a doctor was she if she couldn't pick up symptoms in a colleague?

'Grace? Do you want to come back upstairs with me?'

She nodded and followed him to the stairwell. Donovan must be seriously unwell if they'd first suspected Marburg virus. Meningitis was every bit as serious and some of the symptoms were similar to Marburg. The headache, sore neck and throat, temperature and nausea.

Her legs were moving quicker and quicker. She couldn't help it. More than anything in the world she wanted to see Donovan. She wanted to know that he'd be all right.

As soon as they exited the stairwell she could see a flurry of activity at one of the rooms at the end of the corridor. She couldn't stop herself and started to run.

Callum matched her step for step. 'What is it?' he asked the nurse inside the room.

Her face was pale. 'A rash. It's started to appear across his abdomen.'

Her eyes met Callum's. They didn't need to say a word. Both of them knew that in some cases of meningitis, by the time the rash appeared it was too late for the patient.

Donovan was lying on the bed, his face coated in a sheen of sweat, his eyes closed. His chest was bare, the definition of his toned arms clear. She walked over to the side of the bed and touched his damp hair. His skin was burning. 'Donovan? It's Grace. Why didn't you tell me you were feeling unwell?'

He didn't move. He didn't respond. Not even a flicker of acknowledgment. She turned to the nurse. 'How are his observations?'

The nurse frowned. 'His level of consciousness has deteriorated quite quickly. I've put him on neuro obs. His blood pressure is dropping and he's pyrexial.'

Callum walked over to the nearby trolley. The nurse had already just brought out some antibiotic supplies. He pulled up a bolus of cephalosporin into a syringe, looked at the clock on the nearby wall and started administering it directly into the venflon on Donovan's hand.

Grace couldn't help herself. She pulled the thin sheet

back from Donovan's chest. The tiny red and purple-
hued petechial spots seemed to be materialising before
her eyes. She knew exactly how serious this was. She
grabbed his hand. It was colder than the rest of his body.
He didn't even flinch when she squeezed his hand. Her
eyes went to the clock as she watched Callum slowly
push the first dose of antibiotics into Donovan's vein.
She was trying to do some calculations in her head.
This seemed to be a very rapid onset. Was it some kind
of bacterial meningitis? She could only pray that he
didn't become septicaemic, with all the complications
that could ensue.

She looked around her and pulled up a chair. She
didn't care what else was going on. She was going to
stay here by Donovan's side.

She met Callum's gaze and stared hard. She would
say the words out loud if she had to. She didn't care
who heard.

He finished administering the antibiotic and reached
across the bed, putting a hand on her shoulder. His Scottish accent was heavy, the way it always became when
he got emotional. 'I've contacted the DPA. A replacement team is on their way.' He looked down at his colleague. 'He needs a CT scan. There isn't one available
here. He's also going to need ITU facilities.'

She nodded as a single tear snaked its way down her
cheek. She couldn't bear the way his hand didn't feel
the way it had the last time it had touched her body. It
was clammy, cold. It didn't feel like Donovan's hand.
Not the warm hand that had stroked her skin. The lack
of response from him was more than disturbing.

She picked up his chart. 'Can we give him some ste-
roids before we arrange the transfer?'

Callum nodded as he picked up another glass vial and started pulling the liquid into a syringe. 'On it.' He hesitated. 'Grace, do you want to go on the transfer?'

'Yes.' She didn't falter for a second.

She didn't care what anyone thought. Although it helped matters greatly that none of the team had commented at all. In fact, most of them seemed quietly supportive. She didn't doubt that Callum had shared the information about them kissing. He'd had to. If they'd first suspected Marburg virus, they had to know Donovan's every contact.

Would there be repercussions now their kiss was out in the open? They were two consenting adults, it was hardly criminal behaviour. But she already knew relationships between team members weren't really approved of. If she was going to be allowed to remain in fieldwork she would be transferred to another team. That had become the norm after Sawyer had lost his wife.

Callum injected the steroid slowly. It would be hours before they had an official diagnosis. But in suspected cases it was always the case of treat first, ask questions later. Cases of meningitis had been known to kill in twelve hours.

It didn't matter that it would probably be a helicopter transfer and she'd never been on one before. She didn't care that even the sound of helicopter rotors made her nervous beyond belief. All she could focus on was the man lying on the bed next to her and the fact the last words she'd said to him had been in anger.

The phone rang shrilly outside. One of the nurses darted out to answer it. The other came and fastened the blood-pressure cuff around Donovan's arm.

Grace gave her a smile. 'Don't worry. I'll do his observations. I'm going to be here anyway.'

'Dr Ferguson, that's Panama Health Care about the transfer to ICU.'

He paused in the door way and gave her a resigned sort of smile. 'Don't worry, Grace. Donovan will be fine.'

She could only pray he was right.

CHAPTER NINE

ONE FRANTIC HELICOPTER transfer later Grace was beginning to lose hope.

Donovan's blood results had gotten steadily worse, edging closer and closer towards septicaemia. His blood pressure had bottomed out, his temperature had shot sky high and he'd needed assistance with his breathing. His body was in shutdown and she didn't need anyone to tell her that.

Not the nurses that hovered around his bed, not the machines that alarmed at all times of the day and night, not even the admin assistant who'd told her where she could find some clean scrubs and a shower.

She didn't want to leave his side. She *couldn't* leave his side.

Callum was always phoning the ICU. Another team had arrived to assist in Florida and things were under control at the hospital. She was glad. Because right now she couldn't focus on anything but Donovan.

Was there really a huge difference between Callum Ferguson, the Granddad of Disease, not being able to focus on his job and her? He might not be sitting by her side, but he seemed to know every one of the staff members on the unit on a first-name basis.

She shifted in her seat again. The worst part of all of this was that sinking feeling in the pit of her stomach that Donovan had been right all along.

When the worst had happened, she'd fallen to pieces. She hadn't been able to function. She'd been unable to focus. There was no way they could work on the same team in the future. No matter what happened between them. She couldn't go through this again.

His hand twitched and she was on her feet immediately. He'd had a few involuntary muscle spasms in his legs but nothing like this.

The accessory muscles around his chest started to move and his eyes flickered open. Panic. He was sensing the ventilator and starting to panic.

'Nurse!' she shouted. 'He's waking up.'

The nurse was at her side in an instant, obviously used to dealing with the clinical situation. She adjusted some dials on the machine and leaned over Donovan, speaking softly.

'Hey, Dr Reid. I'm Marcie, one of the nurses here. You have a little tube down your throat to help you breathe and some medicines to try and assist you. How would you feel about getting that tube out? Can you blink for me or give my hand a squeeze?'

Donovan blinked as if his life depended on it and the nurse called over a colleague. They sounded his chest, whilst Grace waited impatiently at the side. His sedation, which was already minimal, was stopped, the ventilator disconnected. And after a few painful coughs from Donovan the tube was removed.

Grace shifted nervously as the nurse blocked her view. She was still talking quietly to Donovan as she adjusted his position on the bed and gave him a few tiny sips of water to help his throat.

After the longest five minutes of her life she finally moved and gave Grace a smile. 'We'll be doing fifteen-minute obs and one of our medics will come and check Dr Reid over. Would you like me to give Dr Ferguson a call?'

Callum. Of course. The old devil had charmed all the nurses in here with his thick Scottish accent. 'That would be great, thanks.'

She pulled her chair closer to the bed and sat down next to Donovan, waiting for the nurse to be out of ear-shot before she spoke.

Feelings of pure relief were washing through her. He was awake. He was conscious. His temperature was coming down and he'd been extubated. A few hours ago she'd feared the worst.

She took a deep breath and tried to appear casual. 'Well, you certainly know how to cause a commotion.'

He leaned forward and lifted his arm, taking a sip of water through the straw on the table placed in front of him. His voice was dry and throaty. 'It's a special skill.'

He sagged back against his pillows. Just taking that drink had looked like a gargantuan effort.

She smiled. It was definitely Donovan. He was back. There was a slight tremor in his hands and he was defi-nitely pale and thinner, but she'd never seen someone look so good.

'Are you going to tell me what happened?' His voice was strained.

She waved her arm out, 'Welcome to Panama Health-care ICU, Donovan. It seems that taking over the kids ICU wasn't enough for us.'

Deep furrows lined his brow. 'I had Marburg?'

She wondered how much he would remember. Meningitis could have lasting effects—sometimes even brain damage. But Donovan appeared to have all his faculties and was just trying to orientate himself.

She shook her head. 'No. You didn't have Marburg—though they did suspect it at first. You had meningococcal meningitis.'

'Me?' He looked incredulous. That was a danger of working in a fieldwork team. After a while the team members—no matter how good their training—started to think they were impervious to certain diseases.

'You.'

'What type?'

There were lots of different strains of meningitis. 'W135.'

'But I've been vaccinated against that.' He rubbed his hands over his face as if trying to make sense of all the facts. The staff at the DPA were vaccinated against everything they could be.

'And that's probably why you're still here. You and I know that vaccination isn't infallible. If you hadn't been vaccinated things could be a whole lot different.' She couldn't hide the shiver down her spine. She was trying to talk like a fellow professional, giving him the information he needed to fill in the gaps in his head, but her body was reacting in a much more personal way.

'But where on earth could I have caught that?'

He was thinking out loud. She could tell straight away. He really didn't need a response. 'Do you want me to write you a list, Dr Reid?'

His eyes met hers. There was still an element of confusion in them. His muscles would ache from lying in that bed and his throat would be sore for days. She felt his eyes drift up and down the length of her body.

Her hands went to her hair self-consciously. She hadn't washed it in three days. She'd barely washed her face. Any trace of make-up was absolutely gone. She'd had to steal some deodorant from one of the nurses on duty and this was her third set of scrubs. Navy blue was certainly not her colour.

'Grace, how long have you been here?' He looked around him. 'How long have I been in here?'

Wow. She must look bad.

She took a deep breath and plastered a smile on her face. 'Three days.'

'Three days?' His voice echoed around the unit and every head turned in the direction of his exclamation.

She put her finger to her lips. 'Shh. Yes, three days.'

'But what about the Marburg? What about the patients? Who is looking after them? Are there enough staff? Why aren't you there?' The words came tumbling out of his mouth with no pause to take a breath.

There was a tiny sinking feeling of dread in her stomach. His questions were entirely natural. He wanted to make sure everyone was okay. But the last one was hurtful. The last one made her think that he saw her as nothing more than a colleague.

Maybe he hadn't remembered what had happened between them. Maybe she'd imagined that first twinkle in his eye when he'd woken up.

She bit her lip and tried to answer as methodically as possible. 'They flew in another team. David and John are still working with Callum. There's been another adult fatality but no child fatalities from the Marburg virus in the last few days. Two new cases have been identified elsewhere.' Her voice faltered a little and she wondered if he noticed. She was trying to take into account the fact he'd just woken up after being really ill. She was trying to remember that his body would be exhausted, having fought off meningitis for three days. She really should leave him alone to rest and sleep.

But she couldn't. She hadn't had anything to think about these last three days but him. No matter how she examined her feelings about him, or her reactions to him, it all came down the same thing. Donovan had been right. This couldn't work.

She met his gaze. He still looked pretty dazed. 'Why do think I'm here, Donovan?'

She left the question hanging in the air between him. It took a few seconds for him to react. Almost as if the little jigsaw pieces were fitting into place in his brain.

His eyes widened. 'I told Callum. I told him about us.'

'You did.'

His head started shaking. 'I had to. I had no idea what was wrong. I just couldn't think straight. I could have hurt you. I could have infected you with something.'

She gave the slightest shake of her head and pointed to a plastic container of meds on his bedside locker. 'I've been given antibiotic cover.' It was normal for close contacts of patients with meningitis.

She licked her lips. She'd already made her decision. She knew what she had to do. All she had to do was press Send on the email.

She couldn't keep working with Donovan. If anything like this happened again, she'd never be able to concentrate on the job they were there to do. It wasn't fair to the patients and it wasn't fair to the other staff members. Watching his chest rise and fall for the last three days had brought that home to her.

Being attracted to someone was one thing. Acting on it another. Feeling as if your life would end if theirs did was something else entirely.

She'd cried every time his blood pressure had dropped or temperature rose. Not doctor-like responses, not professional responses, but from-the-heart responses.

He closed his eyes for a second and rested back against his pillows. It was obvious his body was exhausted. It would be another few days until he would be well enough to be discharged. 'I'm sorry, Grace. I never meant for this to happen. I never meant to put you in harm's way.'

'You didn't. I'm a big girl. I did that myself.'

He opened his eyes. 'What do you mean?'

'I kissed you right back.'

She saw the flicker behind his eyes. But it didn't seem like emotion, it looked like regret.

'You were right, Donovan. You said people who work together shouldn't be emotionally involved. And I didn't get it. I didn't get it until Callum turned up at my door and told me you'd collapsed and were unconscious.' Now she'd started she couldn't stop. 'I felt as if someone had reached into my chest and squeezed my heart with both hands. I've spent the last three days and nights worrying myself sick over you. I've even fielded calls from your dogsitter.' She shook her head.

'But you were right. I can't work like this.' She waved her hand towards him. 'We can't work together. It's no good. I need the chance to see what a fieldwork team is like without complications like this.'

Was she connecting with him? She just couldn't tell. And the wave of hurt washing over her was getting stronger by the second. She had to get out of there.

He was safe. She knew he was safe. It was time to walk away before she embarrassed herself.

She stood up and reached out and touched his hand. It was a mistake, and she knew that instantly. The zing shot up her arm and she pulled it back to her chest.

'I've requested a transfer to another team. I think, under the circumstances, the director will approve it. I hope you feel better soon.' Tears were pooling in her eyes, the heat in the room clawing at her chest. She needed to get out of there.

He moved, his hand reaching towards her. Every part of him looked exhausted. The best thing she could do right now was let him rest. He started to speak, 'Grace, I...'

But she wasn't listening. She needed to get away. She didn't want platitudes, she didn't want to add excuses to the mix. She would chalk this up to experience.

She picked up the bag at her feet and headed to the door. The wash of cool air was an instant relief. The doors in the distance took her to the outside and her feet powered down the corridor.

Out of the hospital. Away from the claustrophobia of the unit. Away from the pain in her heart.

Donovan's befuddled brain definitely wasn't working. He threw back the thin sheet on the bed and tried to move his legs. It was like having the body of an eighty-year-old. They edged towards the side of the bed in slow motion. One of the nurses appeared at his side. 'What do you think you're doing?'

He pointed in the direction of the door. 'Going after her.'

The nurse looked at the swinging door and sighed. 'What did you say to upset her? She's sat here for the last three days and nights, breaking her heart. If that's not a sign of a woman in love, I don't know what is.'

His heated skin felt chilled. Everything about this was going so wrong. When his eyes had flickered open and Grace had been sitting at his side, everything had felt right in the world. Even in the midst of his confusion, as he'd tried to make sense of things around him, knowing Grace was right next to him had grounded him.

She was his anchor. His place in this world. She was the last thing he'd thought about when he'd been ill, and the first person he'd seen when he'd woken up.

But he'd hurt her. Without even trying to. His brain and mouth didn't seem to want to engage together.

But all of a sudden it was as if a symphony of light appeared around him. 'It's what I didn't say.'

The nurse raised her eyebrows. 'Say what?' He tried to stand and she pushed him back firmly. 'No way. Tell me what you need to say to her. I'll catch her in the corridor.'

He shook his head and gave her a rueful smile. 'I need to tell her that I love her.'

The nurse blinked then waved her finger. 'Oh, no. That you have to do yourself. Give me a sec.' She disappeared behind the nurses' station and came back with a phone in her hand. 'What's her number?'

He must have looked blank. 'Her number. I know she has a mobile phone because she charged it at the station.

'Oh, right.' He racked his brain before hesitantly reciting out the digits of what he hoped was Grace's number. The nurse pressed them in and held the phone to her ear for a second. She held it out towards him. 'It's ringing. Go on, then, Dr Reid. Just call me Cupid.'

The sun was blisteringly hot. Her three-day-old clothes were scrunched up in a plastic bag at her feet and long beyond redemption. She hadn't given much thought to walking about outside the hospital in scrubs. It was hardly ideal.

The bag on her shoulder gave a little buzz. It took her a second to realise it was her phone. She'd turned the ringer off while she was inside the ICU.

She fumbled around and pulled it out. Unrecognised number. She pressed the button and held it her ear. 'Dr Grace Barclay.'

'You didn't let me finish.'

A deep throaty voice. Donovan. Where on earth had he gotten a phone? 'There isn't anything else to say.' Her breath was caught in her throat and her heart fluttering in her chest. How could he have this effect on her?

'Yes, there is. I love you, Grace. I don't want you to walk away like this. I want to talk.'

She felt herself sag against the wall. 'But…'

'But nothing.' His voice was raspy. It must be paining him with every word.

'I love you, Grace Barclay. I get what you say about the work thing. My first thought when I realised something was wrong was that I might have infected you too. I couldn't live like that, Grace. And I might be right, but I'm wrong too. I can't just walk away. I can't pretend that

I don't think about you every minute of the day. You're what I want, Grace. You.

'I don't care about gossip. I don't care about talk. I want to protect you. I want you to love working at the DPA. I want you to grow and flourish and for everyone else to see what Callum and I already have—that you're a great doctor. I don't want to get in the way of that We can find a way to make this work. There's always a way to make things work.'

Her brain was whirring, trying to absorb his words. The three little words she'd wanted to hear. The three little words she'd admitted to herself but not said out loud.

'Grace? Say something. Please. Anything?'

Her heart was fluttering in her chest, the corners of her mouth creeping upwards. He'd said it. He felt it too.

The barriers were down. All bets were off. This was about him and her.

'I love you too, Donovan.'

There was a cheer in the background from the phone. 'Who was that?'

'The nurses. Now, can you come back so I can kiss you?'

'I think I can manage that.'

EPILOGUE

One year later

THE DREAM HAD turned a little strange. The waves lapping up on the beach weren't clear blue water any more but something kind of rough and soggy.

'Casey!' She sat up in bed and pulled her hand back from where Casey had been licking it.

She turned but the bed was empty, a hollow in the mattress showing Donovan had only just got up.

Things had worked out perfectly. Grace was now a member of Callum's team. No drama, no gossip. With the director's blessing she'd simply done a swap with another member of staff.

Casey jumped up onto the bed, trying to burrow in beside her. It was his new favourite trick. 'Get off.' She laughed as she pushed him away, noticing his collar had been replaced by a big red bow.

'What on earth…?'

She pulled Casey onto her lap. He tilted his head to the side, staring at her with his big brown eyes. After a few months of tiptoeing around her, with some disdainful doggy stares and some huffs, he'd finally accepted Grace into the family.

'Well, who looks very pretty?' She looked around either side of Casey's head, her fingers catching on something attached to the ribbon. There was a tag.

She snapped it off and read the card.

Will you be my new mommy?

Her breath caught in her throat as her fingers felt something else attached to the ribbon. Something with a bit of sparkle.

'Donovan?'

He appeared around the door with a tray in his hands.

'Casey! You were supposed to wait for me.'

He laid the tray at the end of the bed. 'I think I'm supposed to be in this position when I ask this.' He moved down onto one knee next to her side of the bed, his grin stretching from ear to ear as one hand moved over and rubbed Casey's ear.

He unfastened the red ribbon and laid the ring in the palm of his hand. 'Grace Barclay, I love you with my whole heart. You're the woman who can always show me an exit route, and you definitely hold the key to my heart. Will you marry us?'

She leaned forward and wrapped her arms around his neck, 'Will you say that in our wedding vows?'

'That you always show me the exit route?'

She nodded and placed her hand on his chest. 'And you always light up the dark for me.'

'I like the sound of those vows. Is that a yes?'

'That's definitely a yes.' And Casey gave a yelp as the two of them rolled over on the bed and landed on top of him.

* * * * *

HIS GIRL
FROM NOWHERE

BY
TINA BECKETT

MILLS
BOON

Published in Great Britain 2014
by Mills & Boon, an imprint of Harlequin (UK) Limited,
Eton House, 18-24 Paradise Road, Richmond, Surrey, TW9 1SR

© 2014 Tina Beckett

ISBN: 978-0-263-90781-0

Harlequin (UK) Limited's policy is to use papers that are natural,
renewable and recyclable products and made from wood grown in
sustainable forests. The logging and manufacturing processes conform
to the legal environmental regulations of the country of origin.

Printed and bound in Spain
by Blackprint CPI, Barcelona

Dear Reader

There have been times in my life when I've jokingly said, 'I wish I could start all over again—change my name, my location…go someplace where no one knows who I am.' That got me thinking. What if, for reasons not of my choosing, I *had* to do all those things? What if I wound up in the wrong place at the wrong time and my life was put in danger—or the lives of my loved ones? Could I do it? Give up everything and assume a new identity?

That's what hippotherapist Trisha Bolton must do when she enters a witness protection programme and finds herself in a new town with a brand-new name. She's not allowed any contact with those from her past and has learned the hard way that it's better not to trust anyone—not even neurologist Mike Dunning, whose quiet intensity puts her on guard from their very first meeting. Yes, there are sparks erupting between them, but it's better not to become too attached—because at any moment her past might just catch up with her.

Thank you for joining Trisha and Mike as they navigate the waters of trust and betrayal and learn the true meaning of new beginnings. I hope you enjoy reading about these very special characters as much as I loved writing about them.

Love

Tina Beckett

Recent titles by the same author:

THE DANGERS OF DATING DR CARVALHO†
TO PLAY WITH FIRE†
HER HARD TO RESIST HUSBAND
THE LONE WOLF'S CRAVING**
NYC ANGELS: FLIRTING WITH DANGER*
ONE NIGHT THAT CHANGED EVERYTHING
THE MAN WHO WOULDN'T MARRY
DOCTOR'S MILE-HIGH FLING
DOCTOR'S GUIDE TO DATING IN THE JUNGLE

†*Hot Brazilian Brothers!*
*NYC Angels
**Men of Honour duet with Anne Fraser

**These books are also available in eBook format
from www.millsandboon.co.uk**

CHAPTER ONE

SOMEONE WAS IN her barn.

At least, according to her horse's soft nicker there was. Balancing the bay gelding's right rear hoof on her thigh, Trisha Bolton paused, the curved metal pick in her hand coming to a halt as she listened. Great. It had taken a couple of firm nudges to get Brutus to lift that last leg so she could finish scraping the debris from the bottoms of his hooves. She didn't want to signal she was done until she actually was. Because she doubted he'd co-operate a second time—even for a chunk of carrot.

Brutus snuffed, a huge exhalation of sound, and shifted his weight. Maybe he was just impatient to be let out to graze with the other horses.

"Steady, boy." She readjusted her grip so his hoof didn't slide down her thigh and drop onto her foot. "We're almost done."

"Hello?" she called out, just in case. "I'm over in the cross ties."

No one responded.

She frowned as she caught the soft sound of footsteps at the far end of the concrete aisle between the stalls, heading her way. So there *was* someone here. The shoes were quiet, making little sound, each step planted carefully. Not rubber-soled quiet like a tennis shoe, but not the defined click of a riding boot either.

Five miles south of Dusty Hills, Nevada, her little chunk of land lay at the very end of a quarter-mile dirt track. Not the kind of place someone just happened upon. If you found her operation, it was because you came looking for it. And she didn't have a client at all today, which meant…

Oh, Lord. Roger?

She swallowed hard, then forced herself to relax. No, he'd been moved to Virginia. Would be there for a very long time, according to the courts.

Today was their third anniversary, though. It would be just like him to reach out and remind her that he was still a part of her world, no matter how many miles separated them.

Brutus would be able to see whoever was here from his position at the front of the stall. Trisha, however, still hunched over his back hoof, had her choice of two lovely views: the slatted back wall of the grooming area or her horse's muscular backside. She could take her pick.

She tried again. "Who's there? Larry?"

Her barn helper wasn't scheduled to muck out the stalls again until tomorrow morning. And Penny was out at a supply fair, hoping to score a new bareback pad for those of their patients who had better control over their motor skills. And, besides, both of her workers knew enough to make their presence known when they came through those barn doors. As did all of her clients. There was even a cheerful sign to that effect over the entry beam: *Feel free to say hello!*

Fear of what could be out there still governed so

many of her decisions. Most days she was okay, but today wasn't one of them.

There was still no answer to her greeting. And the footsteps were closer now. Still quiet. Stealthy, almost.

Brutus tossed his head, the clips attached to either side of his halter jingling in a way that didn't help her nerves. Her fingers tightened around the wooden handle of the hoof pick. She could always use the tool as a weapon, if need be, although the thought of cutting someone with it made her feel physically ill—reminded her too much of past events.

The agents had sworn her new identity was secure. That assurance, along with the many miles between her and her past, was supposed to ensure her safety. But she'd seen enough to know there were no guarantees— of anything—in this life.

Giving up on finishing her task, she took a step back and allowed Brutus's hoof to settle heavily on the ground. He shifted his weight onto it and tried to glance back at her, probably wondering what the heck was going on. Then his ears pricked forward, and he looked at something off to the right. She flattened her hand on his haunch, so he'd know where she was as she swiveled toward the front, keeping her body close to that of her horse. The earthy smells of fresh manure and warm animal faded away as she struggled to keep track of the sounds.

Should she call out again?

What if it was someone she didn't know? Or, worse, someone she did?

Get a grip, Trish, and think.

If it came down to it, an intruder would have to duck under one of the nylon ties that secured Brutus's head to either side of the grooming stall, giving her a few precious seconds to slip behind the animal and out the other side—preferably without getting kicked in the ribs in the process, if something startled her horse.

Like a gunshot?

"Easy, boy." The soft quaver in her voice made Brutus's moist coat twitch beneath her fingertips. He could sense her growing fear.

Why she'd decided to keep her rifle locked in a safe in the house was beyond her. No, it wasn't. She'd rather risk her own safety than that of her young patients.

She slid her hand back a few inches, tangling her fingers in the long silky strands of Brutus's tail. There were no true pain receptors in the hairs, so he wouldn't feel a thing if she had to use it to give herself some momentum to swing behind him.

If *they'd* found her, they'd target her and not her horse. At least, that was her hope.

There! A man came into view on Brutus's left, silently facing her from the other side of the aisle with dark narrowed eyes. His shoes were black. Shiny. Leather bottoms. A professional's shoes. Thick dark hair was swept back from his face, and his hands were buried in the pockets of his gray slacks. If her heart hadn't been thundering in her chest like that of a racehorse headed for the finish line, she might think the stranger was dangerously handsome.

As it was, he just looked dangerous. Hard carved lines made up his jawline. And a muscle tensed and released repeatedly in his cheek.

Terror swept over her as he withdrew a hand—empty, thank God—and motioned her out of the stall without a word.

She stayed put.

"C-can I help you?" The hand in Brutus's tail tightened into a fist as she prepared to bolt. She held the pick slightly away from her body, hoping to draw the man's attention to it and make him think twice about coming in after her. The memory of blood—too much blood—made bile rise in her throat. Could she really slash him with it?

Yes. She'd already proven she was capable of things she'd never dreamed possible.

He motioned to her again, his frown deepening as his eyes moved to the horse and then back to her.

Why didn't he say something?

If you think I'm coming out of this stall, without knowing exactly—

Her horse had had enough of the thickening tension. He pinned his ears and shied to the right, hindquarters shimmying in an arc away from her. The abrupt movement caused her to lose her grip on his tail just as he let out a shrill whinny.

It was as if a bomb had gone off. Trisha found herself flying through the air, steel bands around either arm as she tumbled through space and landed in a heap on the hard concrete outside the stall.

Scratch that. It wasn't concrete. It was a body. The steel bands: hands, which still gripped her upper arms. His breath whooshed against her ear in rhythmic gusts.

And the words coming out of his mouth… Well, those weren't sweet nothings.

So he *could* talk.

She patted the ground in a panic, searching for her hoof pick. And then her heart stopped as she saw it. Five feet above the guy's head. Too far to reach.

Her thighs were wedged between his, and she felt every hard muscle of his torso tensed and ready, but that wasn't what she was worried about. As quick as a bunny she stroked both palms over the stranger's sides, down his lean hips, and then dragged them back up the front of his thighs, feeling for any lump that wasn't a body part. Roger had taught her exactly where to look. Had made her pat down her contact. Right before he'd aimed his gun and…

She reached the man's pelvis, fingers probing, searching.

"What the hell?" The stranger flipped her over so that he was on top—weight resting on his bent elbows, strong thighs still bracketing her legs. Only now her hands were imprisoned by his on either side of her head. "Are you seriously doing this? Now? You could have been killed."

Her brain hitched. She'd thought she *was* going to be killed. By him.

There was still one place she hadn't checked. The back of his waistband. But she couldn't move. And she was having second thoughts about who'd sent him. Especially since things were beginning to show some interest at the spot where they were joined together.

Breath still sawing in and out of her lungs, she stared up at him, trying to hold perfectly still. "Who are you? And why are you here?"

One eyebrow crept up, and his frown eased. "Maybe you should have stopped to ask that before feeling me up."

Feeling him…

"Excuse me?"

This was no killer. So who was he? She licked her

lips, praying he wasn't an estranged parent of one of her patients. If so, she'd definitely not made the best first impression. Then again, neither had he.

"Why didn't you say something, instead of just standing there? You scared me to death. Not to mention dragging me out of the…" She closed her eyes for a second before reopening them and glaring. "You never make sudden movements around a horse. Especially not that horse. You could have gotten us *both* killed."

The harsh dipping of something in his throat caught her attention. He stayed put for another second or two then rolled off her with a harsh oath and climbed to his feet. "Believe it or not, I was trying *not* to scare him into doing something crazy."

He held a hand toward her, but she ignored it and scrambled to her feet under her own power, hoping she looked more in control of herself than she felt. "Well, consider that a fail." She glanced at Brutus for proof, only to find him with his head hung low, lids half-shut. His nostrils flared as he huffed out a tired breath.

Really? Trisha rolled her eyes. *Thanks for backing me up there, bud. You could at least look a little shaken up.*

The stranger eyed the horse as well, looking more than a little wary. "I guess now's as good a time as any to ask. Are you Patricia Bolton?"

She nodded. At least he hadn't used her other name. A few more muscles came off high alert.

He continued, "Well, Ms. Bolton, despite our rather questionable introduction, it seems we share a mutual acquaintance." One of his hands shifted to the small of his back. The one place she hadn't checked.

Her brain skittered back toward panic, the blood draining from her head. "Is it Roger?" she whispered.

His gaze sharpened, and he lowered his hand, taking a step forward, only to stop when she jerked backwards. He shook his head, his eyes still focused on her face. "No, not Roger. Clara. Clara Trimble. Her mother said you were hoping to work with her. I'm Mike Dunning, the neurosurgeon who performed her operation."

Mike had seen all kinds of expressions on a woman's face as she lay beneath him—lust, need, affection, love. But never in his life had he inspired abject terror. He should have realized the hands sweeping over his body had had a quick furtive quality to them, not the slow, languorous touches he was used to. She'd been looking for something specific.

"I'm sorry I scared you." He'd been a little panicked himself when that animal had given that high-pitched shriek. His nerves had already been stretched to breaking point the second he'd set foot in the barn, and each step had made the feeling that much worse. He hadn't dared call out to her, had barely been able to push one foot in front of the other.

Mike and horses could no longer be considered friends. Not that they'd ever been particularly close. But four years and a whole lot of distance had changed nothing, it seemed. He still couldn't stand to be near them.

The woman in question gave a rough exhalation of breath, drawing the back of her hand over her brow and leaving a smudge of some dark substance that made his lips curve.

He'd tackled her to the ground, what did he expect?

"Clara," she said. "Of course. Doris said she was going to ask you to contact me. I expected a phone call, not a visit."

His brows went up, more convinced than ever that putting his patient on the back of a thousand-pound animal was a bad idea. Both the horse—and its owner—seemed strong-headed, unpredictable. He'd seen first-hand what kind of devastation that combination could cause. He curled his left hand into a loose fist, the emptiness he found there mirroring the void within his chest. "I'm not about to prescribe something for a patient I can't fully endorse."

"Oh." She bit her lip and backed up another pace or two before dropping onto a white plastic bucket against a nearby stall door. "If you had just called first…"

"I did try. I left a message on your machine a few hours ago. I had a break and decided to stop over in person, instead of waiting for you to return my call." He turned to look at the animal behind him, expecting it to break free of its ties and grab hold of his shirt at any second. He gestured at it. "And if this is your idea of safe, then I'm afraid—"

She stood in a rush. "Brutus isn't one of my therapy horses. I can assure you the horses I use with my patients are extremely gentle and love their job. Brutus is a…special case."

Special. Yes, he could see that. About as special as its name.

He glanced around the rest of the barn, but it was empty. "So where are the other horses?"

"Out in the pasture. It's their day off. Brutus was just about to join them." She crossed over to her horse, murmuring something in a low voice before wrapping an arm under the creature's neck and leaning her temple against it.

He swallowed back a ball of fear when the big animal shifted closer to her. "Could you come away from there, please?"

Instead of doing as he asked, she leaned sideways and grabbed a loop of leather off a peg on the wall and unclipped one of the ties holding the horse in place. She replaced it with a hook from the loop in her hand. Then she unsnapped the tie on the other side.

The creature was free, except for that thin cord she held.

As if knowing exactly what he was thinking, the horse snorted and bobbed its head.

"What are you doing?"

She eyed him, a slight pucker between her brows. "I told you. Brutus needs to be turned out."

To his shock, she held the length of leather out to him. "Do you mind leading him while I take the wheelbarrow out to the compost heap?"

"I'd prefer it if you just put him in a stall." He gestured to the row of empty boxes.

She bent over to pick up the curved metal instrument she'd been using when he'd arrived. For a second or two he'd wondered if she'd planned on gutting him with it, before dismissing the idea as ridiculous. She tossed the item into a wooden chest then shrugged. "Okay. I'll lead him and *you* can take the wheelbarrow. The compost heap is on the way out to the pasture. We can talk on the way and you can see the other horses." She gave a quick laugh, seeming to have recovered her composure. "You might want to watch your shoes, though. Wouldn't want to ruin them."

He glanced to the side and saw a wheelbarrow filled with a substance he recognized, and which looked suspiciously like the smudge on Ms. Bolton's forehead.

Despite the situation, he couldn't stop a smile from forming. She thought he was afraid of a little horse manure? He would have set her straight, but she was already on the move, the horse swinging out of the stall and passing within two feet of where he stood. Its hooves made a familiar clop-clop as the pair moved toward the far doors.

He rolled his eyes. The things he did for his patients.

Okay, Mike. You're a brain surgeon. You've seen a whole lot worse than this.

Yes, he had.

He curled his hands around the handles of the wheelbarrow and lifted, finding the thing surprisingly heavy. Marcy had boarded her horses at another location, heading out there in the mornings and coming home in the evenings. He'd never had much to do with her profession. Until the night she hadn't come home at all. And he'd been left to live with the aftermath.

An aftermath that still rose up to choke him at times. Like now?

Hell. The sooner he got off Patricia Bolton's property, the better.

He caught up to her within a minute, making sure to stay on her far side, away from the horse, which trudged forward like it hadn't a care in the world. You'd never know it was the same animal who'd minutes ago caused him to charge into the pen, his only thought to drag Ms. Bolton out of harm's way.

Apparently, she hadn't needed his help after all.

"So, what set him off?" He wasn't sure why he asked. Maybe to try to understand what had happened four years ago.

She glanced at him. "The way you motioned me out

of the cross ties. He's leery of arms that move in quick jerky motions. Especially if they're flicked back and then brought down in a rush."

That made him pause. "Why didn't you say something the first time I did it?" She'd just stood there and let him repeat the gesture a second time without saying a word.

"I thought you were…" She shook her head. "It's complicated. Just don't do it again."

Not much chance of that, since he'd probably never see Ms. Bolton—or Brutus—again after today. That included those deep green eyes fringed with thick dark lashes. And her cute blonde ponytail that was currently swishing back and forth with every step she took. And her extremely inviting derrière, which seemed custom made for gripping.

Tightening his fingers on the handles of the wheelbarrow and glad the metal object hid a certain wayward body part, he tried to shift his thoughts back to his patient. "So Doris Trimble thinks you can help Clara."

"I think I can too." She glanced sideways at him and then back ahead.

There was no hint of conceit or of trying to win him over to her position, just a matter-of-fact response. Did she actually expect him to take that at face value, without any substantive proof? Well, he'd just match her short response with one of his own.

"How?"

"There are studies. Testimonials—"

That word made him snort.

She drew up short and her horse halted as well, heaving a huge breath and then blowing it out with a blubber of lips, like a child irritated at being kept from his recess.

"Look, if you've already made up your mind, why are you even here?"

Good question. He could have told Clara's mother no. Or just signed off on the recommendation form that would allow insurance to cover the therapy. Or, like Patricia had said, he could have just called and had a brief conversation with her. He had tried, as he'd told her, but he couldn't bring himself to put a child in harm's way, no matter how uncomfortable coming out here might be for him. Still, she was right. He needed to extend her the same courtesy he expected to have afforded to him. He needed to hear her out.

"I want Clara to have the best treatment options, so I'm not ready to rule out anything."

"And yet when you ask me for data, you make scoffing sounds before I've said ten words."

"Fair enough. So convince me." He let the wheelbarrow's supports touch the ground and crossed his arms over his chest, waiting.

"Great." She shook her head and started back down the path without a word, the horse again moving with her.

This woman was impossible. He grabbed the handles and followed her. It was really hard to carry on an intelligent conversation while hauling a load of manure.

She held up the tip of her rope and pointed off to the left. "Dump it over there behind that wooden barricade, if you don't mind. You can leave the wheelbarrow there. Thanks."

By the time he'd done as she asked, she'd released Demon Seed—a better name than Brutus, in his opinion—into a large fenced grassy area.

Mike arrived just in time to see four other horses

making a beeline for the newcomer, tails flowing out behind them as they galloped toward the fence. There was a kind of strange powwow between the animals, accompanied by various sounds, then one of the horses wheeled around and raced away from the group. The others soon followed suit. None of them looked particularly tame.

"Those are your therapy horses?"

"Yes. Brutus is the only one not used in the program."

"How do you keep them under control?"

She glanced out at the field. "They know when it's time to work and when it's time to play. I can assure you that they take their jobs as seriously as any other kind of service animal."

Was she talking about seeing-eye dogs? "But not Brutus."

"No. Not Brutus. I told you, he's a special case. The other horses are teaching him what it means to be a…" She shrugged. "Well, a horse. Sometimes horses—and people—have to relearn what it means to be normal."

That was one thing on which they could both agree. He hadn't quite made it there yet. "So tell me about your program."

She waited for a minute then smiled. "You say you want to know about it, but every time I start to talk you shut yourself off."

"Sorry?"

Her fingers touched his left forearm, sending a jolt through him. "You cross your arms. Meaning you're not going to accept what I have to say."

He unfolded his limbs, mostly to dislodge her fingers. "Not true."

"No?"

Okay, so she was right. But he wasn't sure how to get past it. He could stand there with his arms hanging straight down, but it wouldn't mean a thing. He'd still be skeptical, and he couldn't think of anything she could do that would change the way he felt. Marcy had told him one thing and then gone and done another. How did he know Patricia wouldn't bend the truth to suit her own purposes? "I guess we're at an impasse, then."

"Not quite. I think I might have a solution."

He couldn't think of one to save his life. "I'm listening." This time he kept his arms loose at his sides, his innards knotting up instead.

"You have to experience what it's like to be one of my patients."

He thumbed through his mental schedule. "If you'll give me a specific time, I'll see if I can make it out to observe—"

"Oh, no. I don't mean you can watch. I want you to 'do.'" She leaned a curvy hip against the rail of the wooden fence next to her.

"Do?" The muscles of his chest tightened, and he realized he'd crossed his arms again. This time he let them stay put.

"I want you to go through therapy as if you were one of my patients."

"I don't understand." Actually, he did understand. He just didn't want to. Already the gears in his head were beginning to whine like one of the bone saws he used in surgery.

Her smile grew, a genuine flashing of straight white teeth, her ponytail whisking back and forth as she shook her head. "You don't have to understand, Dr. Dunning. Not yet. You just have to show up."

CHAPTER TWO

SHOW ME YOURS, and I'll show you mine.

Trisha mounted and gathered the reins in her left hand, giving Brutus a quick pat on the neck with the other hand for standing still.

The good doctor had taken up her challenge two days ago and upped the ante in a way that was juvenile and yet, oh, so effective. He'd expected her to balk. Had counted on it, if she wasn't mistaken. She'd made a quip about how safe her horses were, that her patients hadn't shed a drop of blood yet—a good thing, she'd said laughingly, since she couldn't stand the sight of blood.

He'd gotten this speculative gleam in his eye as soon as the words had passed between her lips, then had issued his ultimatum. And assured her that his profession did indeed involve blood.

Was she game?

Game? Really?

She'd been forced to stab a man—had almost killed him. So the doctor's jibe had stuck in her craw. As if she had been some sissy, shying away from a paper cut or a bloody nose. It was so much more than that.

So she'd tilted her chin, taken her aversion to blood and guts and forced it to the back of her mind, drawing the heavy drapes closed on reality and agreeing to his request. He would sit through three sessions of therapy—as in literally sitting on Crow, her gentle giant—once he'd observed three sessions with a patient. She, in turn, had to sit in the glassed-in room above the surgical suite and watch him saw through a person's skull. That wasn't exactly the way he'd put it, but it was basically the same thing.

Dr. Dunning had definitely gotten the better end of that deal. Only she could tell that he didn't see it that way. His fear of Brutus had been almost palpable.

I was trying not *to scare him.*

That thought had never crossed her mind as she'd stood in that stall, her own knees quivering with terror when he'd silently motioned her out of there. He'd been as scared as she had.

Did that mean their mutual fears canceled each other out?

Hardly.

But if he could push through his, then she needed to try to push through hers. As it was, she'd seized his words, telling him that meant he had to "see hers' first—in other words, he was going to see how *she* operated. Whether or not he'd show up for her session with Bethany Williams this afternoon was still to be seen. She was counting on him really wanting to do what was right for his patient. And since Clara's team of doctors had done almost all they could for her through surgery and the normal course of physical therapy, her mom wanted to expand their horizons. Try some other options.

Trisha had only been in Dusty Hills six months, so getting the endorsement of a local neurosurgeon seemed a good way to get her name out…to put her on the path toward making it in this small town. If he could just see Clara on a therapy horse, he'd see how much it could help her. The five-year-old had definitely responded to the way Trisha had stroked her tiny fingers over Crow's inky-black coat. Trisha just needed Dr. Dunning to sign off on treatment, both for the sake of health insurance and her own liability insurance. Which reminded her, she'd have to list the good doctor as one of her patients for a little while so he'd be covered. Just in case.

She sighed and fanned her legs, making a clucking sound as she asked Brutus to break into a slow jog. She'd already warmed him up with some circles on the longe line, so he responded to the request quickly. "Someday soon I'm going to ask you to lope, big boy. Just to show you it's safe."

Her horse had endured the wrong end of a whip in his past life, the long pale scars—devoid of hair—visible on his haunches. He still shied away from sudden movements near his head—especially if those movements were made by a man—and Trisha couldn't blame him. He was as much in need of therapy as any of her other patients. So when she'd told Dr. Dunning he was a special case, she hadn't been kidding. But the horse had come a long way over the past several months. So had she.

In his own way, Brutus was helping her recover as much as she was helping him. Guiding the gelding to the center of the indoor arena to go through a large sweeping figure eight, they changed direction from clockwise to counterclockwise, and she smiled when one of his ears swiveled back to face her, listening for any verbal cues she might give. "Good boy."

Although Brutus had shown his nerves at Dr. Dunning's presence in no uncertain terms, things could have been a whole lot worse, according to what she'd been told by the rescue organization. Trisha might have maintained her poker face a little better than her horse had, but she hadn't been unaffected. Oh, no. Especially not once she'd realized the man had not been a killer sent to deliver a personalized anniversary message, courtesy of her ex-husband. Her fear had morphed into something else entirely when he'd flipped her onto her back, his firm warm chest pressing against her breasts, his breath mingling with hers. Her thoughts had taken off in other directions. Dangerous directions.

She'd wanted to wheel away from him just like her horse had. Only she hadn't been able to, and not just because he'd had her pinned to the ground with his body, hands imprisoning hers.

Two days later she still couldn't shy away from him. No, in all likelihood, she was going to have to work with the good doctor on a regular basis. *If* she could convince him she and her horses were not a danger to him or his patients.

To do that, she was going to have to find a way to keep her job at the forefront of her mind. And since he was due at the barn in two short hours, fifteen minutes ahead of her first young patient, she would have just enough time after working Brutus to shower and dress in something a bit more professional than her standard faded jeans and halter top combo. And somehow she needed to squash her silly reaction to the surgeon's presence. Especially since she had big plans for the man. Plans that included making him shed that thick coat of control he wrapped around himself and get him to agree that she could help some of his patients.

If she could just get the man to co-operate.

Hippotherapist does sound a little bit like hypnotherapist.

Mike turned his car into the driveway leading up to Patricia's place. This could have all turned out differently had he heard Doris Trimble correctly. He'd been so sure she'd said she wanted her young daughter to visit a hypnotherapist that he hadn't even glanced up from his prescription pad, but had continued writing as he'd asked her what she thought that would accomplish. Then the word "horse' had been mentioned and his head had jerked up to attention as she'd explained about the new equine therapist in town. By the time he'd got the gist of what she'd been talking about, he'd been in too deep. He hadn't been able to just shoot the suggestion down, especially after getting a good look at the hope imprinted on her face. Clara had grinned wider than he'd ever seen as her mother had continued to make her case.

"Have you already taken her to see this person?"

"Just for a quick peek at the horses," she'd said, a fleeting look of guilt flashing through her eyes. "Clara seemed to love. She responded immediately."

Perfect. This wasn't going to be a passing idea, evidently. He was either going to have to get behind the plan and support her, or give her at least one good reason why she shouldn't let Clara anywhere near Ms. Bolton or her horses. Hopefully that reason would come today.

There was no paved parking area near the barn, so he pulled into the same spot he'd parked in the last time. Glancing to his left, he spotted two horses close to the fence. They seemed to be studying his arrival with interest. He thought one of them might be the infamous Brutus. He could swear the animal on the right gave him a look of pure dislike, lifting his head to follow Mike's movements as he got out of the car. He had to fight not to climb back into his vehicle and beat a hasty retreat.

"Well, guess what? The feeling's mutual." He tossed the words at the animal, only to stiffen when a quiet feminine voice answered him.

"What feeling is that?"

He swiveled around. Patricia Bolton had evidently come out of the barn when she'd heard his car drive up. He shrugged. "Just talking to myself."

She glanced out at the pasture, where Brutus was still staring at them. "I see."

"Ms. Bolton, look, maybe we can save ourselves both a whole lot of—"

She held up a hand to stop him. "Call me Trisha. My patients do."

His patients called him Dr. Mike, but it seemed a little presumptuous to ask her to do the same. So he said, "Okay…Trisha. Why don't you call me Mike?"

"Great. If you'll come with me, I'll show you how I prepare for my first clients of the day."

So much for leaving. She'd smoothly intercepted any pre-emptive strike he might have made and disarmed him.

Following her inside the barn to the very place he'd lain with her on the ground, the image of tangled arms and legs and of fingers running up his thighs came back with frightening clarity. He swore he could still feel her touch. He shook his head to banish the sensation.

There was a horse tethered in the same position that

Brutus had been the other day, only this time there was some sort of saddle draped over a post, along with a brightly patterned blanket. "I was just grooming him before saddling up. This is Crow."

Pitch black without the slightest trace of white, the animal's coat had a healthy gleam that made Mike think she'd gussied him up just to show him off. His mane was even braided. She needn't have bothered, though. Because just standing there near the horse made his gut contract.

"Do you want to touch him?" Trisha walked right over to the animal and stroked a hand down his neck, smoothing a misplaced braid.

"That's okay." He kept to the far side of the aisle, hoping against hope there wasn't going to be another incident like the one a couple of days ago.

"Come on. He won't hurt you. You've agreed to ride him next week, so you might as well get some of the preliminaries out of the way."

What had he been thinking, coming out here again? His wife had died handling one of these animals. Did he really want to do this? No. But something about Trisha's quiet voice and calm manner made him take a step closer. She wasn't afraid at all.

But, then, Marcy hadn't been either. And yet in the blink of an eye she'd been gone. And he'd still had to deal with her horses and clients in the midst of everything else. Thankfully, one of her close friends had helped out, going as far as buying the horse that had turned his world upside down. He'd tried to warn her off, but Gloria had insisted it was what Marcy would have wanted, that what had happened had been a tragic accident and not the horse's fault. She was probably right.

Still, he didn't want to be trapped in a confined space with one. Anything could happen. "Okay, but could we do this outside the barn?"

She blinked, but nodded. "Sure. Let me just saddle him up."

Making short work of it, she talked him through the process of swapping the animal's halter for a bridle, and then she explained the parts of the therapy saddle and showed him how to put it and the blanket on and how to tighten the strap beneath the horse's belly. Why she thought he needed to know any of this, he had no idea. Marcy had taken him at his word when he'd said he wasn't interested in riding. She'd never tried to force the issue. Maybe partly to cover up what she'd really been doing at the barn.

If he'd been with her that last day, would she still be alive?

That was something he really didn't want to think about too closely.

She gave the saddle one last check then said, "Okay, let's lead him outside."

His lips quirked. "No wheelbarrow today?"

"Nope." She grinned back at him. "You lucked out."

He wasn't sure he'd consider this lucking out, but he'd do whatever it took to get through this and head back to his own job. Where he felt secure and confident.

Like the last time he'd been here, he remained at Trisha's side as she told him that a horse should always be led from the left. "Have you ever been around horses at all?"

How to explain without…explaining? "I have, but I haven't worked with them closely."

There. Not bad.

Then she arrived at a rectangular fenced-in area that was covered with sandy-looking material. It appeared to have been freshly raked, a system of grooves running through the grains—for his benefit? She stopped and tied the reins to the middle fence post and glanced at her watch. "We still have about five minutes before Bethany arrives so why don't you introduce yourself to him? Come stand next to me."

Mike stiffened when she patted the animal on the neck. It was either explain why he had an aversion to horses or do as she asked. He moved closer as she continued stroking the animal.

"This is how I'd approach a patient who's here for the first time." She took Mike by the hand, her fingers firm against his as she lifted it and pressed his palm to the animal's coat, slowly guiding it down the length of the neck. "Isn't he smooth?"

Was he supposed to answer her? Because, no, it didn't feel smooth. All he could think about was how anything could happen. In the time it took for him to blink. And that familiar horsy smell that had clung to Marcy whenever she'd come home from the barn... It was right here, with all its terrible reminders of secret meetings and half-truths.

None of it was comforting.

And yet as Trisha continued to guide his hand in slow sweeping strokes over Crow's coat, the horse stood extremely still, as if he somehow sensed the turmoil lurking just below the surface. And slowly the textures and temperature of the animal's body began to make themselves known.

"Relax," she murmured, her voice like the softest silk. "He won't hurt you."

He couldn't bring himself to let his muscles go loose, but he did try to concentrate on things other than how huge and powerful the animal was. Like the warm grip of Trisha's hand as she held his. Like the scent of her hair and the tickle of her ponytail as it brushed his neck when she twisted her head. He concentrated on her instead of the horse. She bent a little lower, her hand guiding his down the upper portion of the horse's leg. "Crow could stand here all day and let you do this. He loves it."

He gulped. Crow wasn't the only one who could stand there all day. He was suddenly enjoying Trisha's touch a little too much, allowing his hand to rest in hers a little too heavily.

He didn't understand why his thoughts were even heading in this direction. He'd been with a couple of other woman since his wife's death, but those had been quick clinical sessions born out of physical need more than anything.

When Trisha's thumb curled into his palm as she lifted his arm to place it high on the horse's back, the friction caused a chain reaction in his body.

She wasn't purposely trying to switch on his motor, but it was cranking to life anyway. He tried to close his eyes to blot out her face, but it just heightened all of his other senses. The heat of her body next to his. The soothing little sounds she made as she murmured to the horse…to him.

"Isn't this nice?" she whispered.

Definitely not soothing.

"Trisha…" He turned his head to find her looking right at him, eyes soft and inviting.

He swallowed again.

Hell. He couldn't believe what he was thinking of

doing. Or, worse, that he might actually be getting ready to...

His free hand came up to cup the back of her head, just as a shrill childish voice sounded from behind them.

"Cwow! Cwow! I come see you!"

Crow's head went up, and Trisha's eyes jerked away from Mike's, breaking the spell. She let go of him, and he took a couple of quick steps back, though she seemed to recover her composure with ease.

"Bethany," she said. "Hello! We've gotten Crow all ready for you."

A dark-haired child in a wheelchair rolled toward them, accompanied by two women, one about Trisha's age and the other about twenty years older. The younger one came over and stood next to the horse, draping an arm over his neck as Trisha walked over to the other two. She embraced the woman and murmured something to her, then knelt in front of the child. "Are you ready for your ride? We're going to work really hard on our balance today, aren't we?"

The child nodded, her hands gripping the armrest of her chair as if she was preparing to rise. When she didn't actually leave the seat, Mike started to move forward to help, only to have Trisha meet his glance with a subtle shake of her head. He stopped in his tracks.

"Dr. Dunning, this is Bethany Williams and her mom, Gretchen. And this is my assistant, Penny."

He somehow managed to mutter out the appropriate greetings, although he was still feeling shakier than he cared to admit by what had happened a moment ago. He'd been about to kiss the woman.

Struggling to make sense of this crazy day, he watched while Trisha strapped a shiny black helmet onto the girl's head before helping her from her chair and leading her step by step to the horse. He was surprised by the headgear, but maybe things were different with kids. Marcy had certainly never used a helmet. If she had…

Mike turned his attention back to the girl to distract himself. She had a lisp, but her eyes were bright with intelligence. Her gait, though, was uneven and periodic shudders rippled through her muscles. Cerebral palsy? Possibly. She had enough control over her body that she could lift her foot toward the low stirrup with help and then between the three of them—helper on one side, Trisha and the mother on the other—they boosted her thin frame into the saddle. She immediately reached for and gripped the nylon straps on either side of the saddle for all she was worth.

She wasn't totally steady, but she wasn't afraid. Of that Mike was certain. Giddy was the term that came to mind. Once Bethany was in position, she grinned and scrubbed at the horse's shoulder with the tips of her fingers, still holding onto the straps. Her obvious joy at being there made Mike feel a little bit ridiculous about how cautious he'd been when even petting Crow. Then again, no one else had seen Brutus flip out a few days ago. And no one else had driven out to a barn four years ago to see why their wife wasn't answering his calls, only to discover her sprawled unconscious on the ground, a black horse that looked very much like this one standing over her.

But that's not what he was here for. Neither was he here to hit on the woman in charge of this horse and pony show. He was here to observe, and that's exactly what he should be doing.

* * *

"R-references?" Trisha somehow got the word past her paralyzed vocal cords, although she wasn't sure how. He'd watched her like a hawk the entire time she'd worked with Bethany. And out of the corner of her eyes she'd noticed him speak to the girl's mother. Gretchen loved bringing Bethany here. She figured of all her patients, Gretchen—a fellow horse owner—would be the most vocal about the benefits of hippotherapy. Which was why it shocked her so much to have him ask for references as soon as Bethany and her mom had left in their gray SUV.

"Yes. Mrs. Williams certainly seems to like what you do here, but I'd like to hear from a few people you no longer work with. Maybe a few clients from your last location."

So he knew she was fairly new to Dusty Hills but no way could she give him any names of people from her past. She stood next to his vehicle and thought through her possible responses. Why hadn't she realized someone could ask her this? Because everyone else had been happy to see her credentials—which were real enough. The FBI had somehow gotten them altered to show her current name, but all the classes and certifications were valid. They'd just cautioned her about using her university diplomas as actual references, or hanging any documents on the wall of her home or office, saying they wouldn't hold up if someone dug too deeply.

"I'd rather just stick with my current clients, if you don't mind."

His fingers paused on the door handle to his car. "Do you have something to hide, Ms. Bolton?"

Great, they were back to last names, evidently. She

couldn't blame him but, dammit, she was good at her job—had worked hard to get her HPCS certification. Doing what she loved was the one thing that had been non-negotiable with her relocation deal, especially after everything that had happened. The only concession she'd made had been that she'd promised not to advertise or be listed on any specific hippotherapy database. Which meant word of mouth was all she had to go by—and it was proving much tougher than she'd thought in a small town like Dusty Hills.

She tried her rehearsed explanation. "I just think there are enough clients in the area, some of whom you probably know, who would be able to answer any questions you might have. I teach straight riding lessons as well. I can give you some of those names too."

He seemed to consider that for a moment or two before he relented. "I guess that will have to do, provided some of those names are from people who are no longer with you. I don't want there to be any question of conflict of interest."

Conflict of interest? She wasn't sure what he meant by that.

Did she have any patients she no longer treated? She didn't think so. Her client list wasn't that long, and those who were on it seemed to stick around. "Let me see what I can come up with, and I'll get back to you."

"I'm not a very patient man, Ms. Bolton. Don't make me wait too long." Mike opened the door to his car and propped one foot on the floorboard.

Don't make me wait too long.

A shiver went over her as her mind headed down a very different avenue. Had he said it that way on purpose? There was no indication he had, not even an embarrassed shifting of his glance away from hers. Just a cool, calm gaze that held hers far too long. How could the man wall off what had almost happened between them before Bethany's session? She was still a mass of conflicting nerves and emotions. Her legs were shaking, and she felt like she was going to lose it at any second. Mike, on the other hand, seemed to have forgotten…or maybe he hadn't been getting ready to kiss her at all.

That thought was even more mortifying. Could her radar be that far off base?

Evidently it could. At least, with this man.

Ha! Just look at how far off base she'd been with Roger, a man capable of murdering someone in cold blood and then acting as if *he* were the injured party. Even his name had been fake.

Yeah? Well, so was hers now. Evidently aliases were all the rage.

As Mike folded his length into his car and pulled out of her lot in a cloud of dust, she gave a choked cough and noticed that Larry and Penny were both standing in the doorway of the barn, staring after the car. And Larry—the old coot—had the silliest grin imaginable on his grizzled face.

Oh, no. The last thing she needed was for them to get the wrong idea.

Because she was having enough trouble wrestling her own "ideas" back into place without giving them any more ammunition.

Ammunition.

Another shiver went through her, a little more wary this time as she remembered a few days ago—the way her fingers had clutched that hoof pick, palm sweaty, throat tight.

She'd thought she was going to die.

That's what she needed to focus on. What *could* happen, if she wasn't careful. What had already happened to the man who'd been sent to protect her a year ago. He'd died. All because of her.

Roger had almost killed her too, choking her on his desk in a jealous rage. Only her flailing hands had landed on a letter opener and she'd swung it round as hard as she could, stabbing him in the side. The FBI, alerted to the situation by their dying agent, had arrived in a hail of gunfire minutes later, arresting Roger and the rest of his minions.

Her ex had lived to stand trial, and he could still try to find her even now. He had the money and the contacts. The only thing she wasn't sure of at this point was how hot his rage still burned.

And how far those flames were able to reach.

CHAPTER THREE

"WE'RE WORKING ON IT. I want to observe a few more of Ms. Bolton's sessions before I'll feel okay recommending this particular course of treatment."

It was the best answer Mike could give Doris Trimble when she came into the office and asked again about going down the hippotherapy route. The woman nodded, the tightening of her hands in her lap showing she didn't really understand what the problem was, but she didn't try to pressure him into making a decision. She was willing to defer to his opinion, something that made his already low mood sink even lower.

He didn't want his personal history to get in the way of doing what was best for his patients. He just wasn't sure hippotherapy *was* what was best for Clara.

Then again, he was running out of options, other than saying that Clara's current condition was the best they could hope for: limited mobility and function. The swelling in her brain had subsided thanks to surgery and time, but the damage caused by the horrific car accident a year ago had not. She had burn scars on various parts of her body—the skin stretched tightly over the joints, making bending them difficult. Her mother seemed to think that riding would help stretch that skin and make it more supple. She was probably right about that. He'd watched how Bethany Williams's body had moved with the horse and though it had been subtle, her limbs and joints had followed the animal's strides, her narrow shoulders stretching out and back as she'd gripped the straps on the saddle.

Muscle did have memory, so it was possible the same rhythmic movements could help Clara improve her balance and build some core strength. But improve cognitive function? That he wasn't sure of. He promised himself he'd take some time this week to do some deeper research.

It would have all been so simple if Trisha had landed in someone else's pond. But she hadn't. She'd wound up in Dusty Hill's tiny pool, and, as much as he didn't want to, he was going to have to make a decision on how to deal with her. Because even though he practiced neurology in the next town over, he had a feeling Clara's mom wasn't the only one who was going to discover Trisha's little outfit. More people were going to ask about her and her horses.

He knew exactly how much a referral from him could help her. He could be the best thing that ever happened to her, financially speaking. But that wasn't his main concern. He knew that sooner or later some of his other patients—whether they were past, present or future—were going to come into his office, eyes shining with excitement about the possibilities of hippotherapy, asking if it could help their relative. Could he prescribe it? He needed to have a ready answer—an objective one—one backed by research and unclouded by his personal issues.

He moved his attention back to the girl in the wheelchair. "Let's see how you're doing, Clara, is that okay?"

The lolling of her head was the only answer he got, as she struggled to focus on his face. Clara was seeing a variety of specialists today, her graft team, her occupational therapist, along with her physical therapist and orthopedist. They would come together later in the day and discuss their individual findings and try to figure out where to go from here. As he lifted Clara and laid her on the exam table, he wondered how Trisha expected to keep children like this upright on that horse. Crow—was that the animal's name?—was pretty large. He hadn't paid close attention to the sizes of the other horses. And that saddle had seemed soft and flimsy, with fabric grips rather than a traditional saddle horn. How would Clara even hold on?

He hadn't thought to ask, because something had distracted him. Namely the sight and scent of a certain equine therapist. One who'd stroked his hand down a horse's neck and made him wonder what it would be like to stroke his fingers down the silky skin of her throat instead.

"Okay, Clara." He reached over to grab his reflex hammer, putting Trisha out of his mind. "You know the drill."

She still couldn't sit completely under her own power, although he thought she'd grown a little more stable over the past few months. He smoothed a couple of strands of blonde hair back from her forehead with a smile that was a little more forced than normal. "Are you ready?"

He carefully went through Clara's reflex reactions and strength, looking for any increase in weakness or spasticity on her left side. Things looked much the same as they had a month ago, something her mother found frustrating, and Mike couldn't blame her. It had to be agonizing to work so hard and see so little improvement. It was another reason she was so eager to try something new. Anything new.

He couldn't let himself be swayed by that.

Helping the five-year-old back into a sitting position and calling her mother over to help keep her stable, he studied Clara's eyes, smiling at her and watching her reaction. Her lips curled as she tried to smile back, but the left side still lagged behind the right, not lifting as high. He did a few more tests and then they bundled her back into her chair and Mike gently strapped her in. Those blue angelic eyes followed his movements and he could almost see the plea inside of her, although he knew it was probably his imagination.

Shifting his attention back to Doris, he sighed. "Give me another week to get some more background information on hippotherapy. I'll give you a call as soon as I feel I can recommend something one way or the other."

Doris smiled, then, as if unable to resist, hugged him. "Thank you. I know you'll do the right thing." As soon as the words were out she released him and brushed her fingertips beneath her eyes. Mike's gut clenched. Again.

Doing what was right wasn't always a black-and-white decision.

He accompanied the pair out to the waiting room just as his receptionist swiveled in her chair. "A Ms. Bolton called to set up your next appointment. She said she's a hippotherapist?" Her puckered brow said she had no idea what that was.

Join the crowd.

Unfortunately, Clara knew exactly who that was. "H-h-h-horsy l-lady!" The stuttered words—the first thing she'd said since arriving—came out of the five-year-old's mouth as a loud squeal, causing every head in the waiting room to swivel toward them. So much for keeping Trisha's existence quiet for now.

Rather than feeling irritated, Mike squatted down in front of the child and waited patiently until she looked at him. "Do you like the horsy lady, Clara?"

Clara's head gave that funny little roll that was meant as a nod. "N-nice. Want…h-horse."

"We'll have to see what we can do."

He glanced up at his receptionist. "Find a spot on my schedule that works for Ms. Bolton as well and pencil me in. Oh, and find my next scheduled tumor resection and ask Ms. Bolton if she can free up that time." If she was going to put his feet to the fire, then he intended to do the same. It was time for her to live up to her end of the bargain. And soon. He ignored the sharp twist inside him that said he wasn't being fair.

Of course he was. This was what they'd agreed on. Although, if he was honest with himself, he'd suggested the trade because of the way she'd shuddered at the word "blood" when she'd joked about her horses. He'd felt so sure she'd decide it wasn't worth it. That hadn't happened, making him wonder just how badly she needed new clients.

As he waved goodbye to Doris and Clara, a hard, cold lump formed in his throat. This was worst bargain he'd ever made. One that would require more delicate maneuvering than his most difficult surgery. And like most of those surgeries, the outcome was anything but sure. But first of all he wanted to see exactly *who* he was dealing with. There was something odd about Ms. Bolton…about the way she'd balked about giving him references from her previous location. He'd been lied to before. And unfortunately he'd found that some lies weren't harmless. Some of them destroyed lives.

Asking his receptionist for five minutes before sending in his next appointment, he made his way back into his office and dialed up an old friend. Swiveling away from the door, he waited through three rings then a familiar voice came on the line. "Mike. How are you?"

"Fine, Ray, and you?"

"Can't complain. Although things have been a little too quiet lately."

Mike took a deep breath before forcing himself to continue. "Well, maybe I can help you out with that. Can you do me a favor?"

The sheriff's gruff voice came back over the line. "Depends on what it is. Although I do owe you a pretty big favor."

"You don't owe me anything, Ray." His friend's mother had had an aortic aneurism, and Mike had steered them to the finest specialist in the area. The sheriff wouldn't let it go, saying he'd pay him back somehow.

"Sounds pretty serious."

It was. If only he could tell Ray why. It was a little hard as he wasn't sure of the answer to that question himself. "We have a new physical therapist in town who uses horses in her work."

"Oh, hell, Mike. Sorry, man."

His old friend knew all about Marcy. They'd all been friends once upon a time—had all grown up together in Dusty Hills. Ray even knew about the affair his wife had had with one of her fellow trainers. "It's not about her horses. I asked her for references, and she got a little squirrelly on me with her answers. Is there any way you can do a check on her?"

"I don't know, Mike. I'm assuming we're not talking about a credit check."

"No." He pushed ahead. He still had several patients to see so he needed to make this quick. "I have a patient's mother who wants to use her services, but I don't want to recommend something unless it's on the up and up."

"You think she has a record?"

Did he? No, not really, and he wasn't sure how ethical it was to ask his friend to do a background check.

"I'm not sure."

A chuckle came over the phone. "There is such a thing as the internet, you know."

Hmm…he hadn't thought of that. He typed the name Patricia Bolton into the computer on his desk and lots of suggestions came up. Too many. He wouldn't even know where to begin. "I guess I could try that."

"What's her name? I'll poke around some, but I can only dig so deep without having an iron-clad reason."

He swallowed, wondering if he was doing the right thing. This seemed a little too close to invasion of privacy for his taste. And just because Marcy had told some whoppers it didn't mean that every woman he ran across was stretching the truth. Except Trisha had definitely been evasive about giving him names of clients outside Dusty Hills.

We're talking about the welfare of a patient here.

Yes, they were. "I understand, Ray. Her name's Patricia Bolton."

"I remember her. Pretty little thing. She blew into town six months ago with a couple of men and an enormous horse trailer. The men didn't stick around more than a few hours. She, however, did."

A couple of men. That was strange. Ray or his deputy normally parked out on the main entrance to town, so it made sense that they'd see folks they didn't recognize every once in a while. Dusty Hills was a pretty close-knit community, most people lived and died in the same houses they'd grown up in, which was why his practice was in Mariston, a city many times larger than his hometown. "Maybe her husband travels or something," he mused.

The thought made a sick sensation worm its way through his gut. Especially after what had nearly happened between them—or maybe it had all been one-sided. He'd never thought to ask if she was married, although he hadn't noticed a wedding ring. Next time he saw her, he'd look a little closer.

"Maybe he does," Ray said. "I'll look in public records and see what comes up. If she has any outstanding warrants I'll let you know."

Mike scrubbed a hand across the back of his neck. He had no idea exactly what he was looking for. "Thanks. I have an appointment with her this Thursday."

"I'll give you a call on Wednesday, then. How's that?"

"Perfect."

"Oh, and, Mike?"

"Yeah?"

"You might not want to get too involved with her, just in case."

He could have set his old buddy's mind at ease about that possibility. Because he didn't plan to get involved with the woman at all.

* * *

What was he doing here?

Trisha's heart lurched as she glanced back and saw a familiar figure standing at the rail of her outdoor arena. Did he *enjoy* sneaking up on her?

It wasn't his fault that she was still jumpy this far after the trial. Or that being out of contact with her mother and brother had been weighing on her mind recently. She knew it was for their own protection, and she'd die if anything happened to either of them, but it didn't make it any easier. Watching her ex-husband gun down the man he'd accused her of sleeping with had driven home the dangers of getting too close to anyone. Roger might be in jail, but that didn't mean he didn't have friends on the outside.

Her eyes went back to the fence. She hadn't expected Mike to come to the barn until Thursday. But Monday morning found him with his forearms resting on the top rung, watching her as she coached her student over the first of the low jumps. Sweat trickled down her back—not just from the ninety-degree temperatures but in reaction to his unexpected presence. She tipped her wide-brimmed straw hat further back on her head, trying to slow her racing heart.

She'd had to supplement her hippotherapy income by giving riding lessons two days a week. This was one of those days. Mike hadn't called before coming, so she wasn't sure if he just wanted to talk to her or if he'd hoped to catch her with a patient. A kind of surprise inspection. Well, he'd surprised her all right.

She pulled her mind back to her student, calling out to her, "Don't forget to keep the reins loose as he goes over the cross rails. You need to support him but not restrict his head." She swiped at moisture on her temple with the back of her hand. "Go ahead and continue through the course."

The girl nodded her understanding and loped around the outside as she made her way toward the next jump.

Trisha glanced back at Mike, who now had a foot propped on the lowest rail of the arena. Still the same shiny uptight shoes he'd worn on his other visit. Very impractical for doing anything at her place. But maybe he'd come straight from work. If so, he was going to have to wait. She owed it to her student not to let her attention wander.

The next jump went without a hitch. Sarah sailed over the two-foot bar, letting her reins out and leaning low over the horse's neck as she went.

"Perfect! Good job. Head for the next one."

Keeping her eyes on her student, she edged toward the fence where Mike stood. At least Groucho, her gray lesson horse, was behaving perfectly. That had to be a mark in her favor.

She didn't turn her head, but once she reached him she murmured in a low voice, "Can I help you?"

He didn't say anything for a minute as if he was struggling with something. "Do you have those references I asked for?"

She blinked. He couldn't have called for that information?

"Sarah's—my student's—mom should be here in another ten minutes or so. Feel free to talk to her, if you'd like, although she's not one of my patients. The list of other references is in the house."

"You give lessons as well?" There was a harder edge to his voice that made her glance at him for a second.

There was that pulsing muscle again.

She focused back on Sarah's progress as she made it over another jump in the course and turned Groucho to head back to the starting position. "I'm fairly sure I mentioned that already. Until I have enough patients I'll need to keep the horses in shape and exercised." She shrugged. "Besides, I enjoy it. I'll probably continue even once my caseload expands."

Lord, she hoped it would. If only Mike would co-operate.

Sarah came level with them and drew to a stop, leaning over to stroke Groucho's neck.

"You did great, honey," Trisha said. "Why don't you walk him on the rail and let him cool down?"

"Okay, Ms. Bolton."

Trisha stiffened for a second then forced her muscles to relax. It still startled her to hear someone call her by that name, even after living with it for the last six months. At least the name Patricia was close enough to Patty Ann that she'd gotten used to it a little quicker. But Bolton was light years from the name Stoker, the name she'd been born with.

"You okay?"

Mike had evidently seen her reaction.

"I'm fine. It's just hot." As if to punctuate that statement, she swept the hat off her head and shoved her damp hair off her forehead, before replacing the head-gear.

"Nevada can be pretty steamy. You're not originally from here?"

STS: short tenable statement. Something the agents had drilled into her head before they'd left her in a town so far removed from the bustle of New York City that she wondered if she'd ever get used to it.

"Nope. My dad was in the military, we traveled around a lot when I was a kid."

There. That had worked with most of the other people who'd asked about her past.

"Interesting. I've lived in the same spot my entire life. What places have you been to?"

Oh, Lord. At least Sarah was headed their way again, the interruption giving her a chance to think before she answered. She gave the girl a smile as she plodded by on Groucho. "You're doing great. One more pass and then you can take him back to the barn, okay?" Hopefully Sarah's mom would arrive and rescue her from having to remember the sequence of towns she was supposed to have lived in. They'd chosen places that were as far from her mother and brother's locations as you could get.

She quirked a brow, her legs feeling shakier than usual around him. "You want the whole boring list or just the highlights? I take it this is part of the job interview."

He smiled. "Sorry. Too nosy?"

Yes! And nosiness around the wrong people can be a very bad thing.

But she didn't say that. Instead, she shrugged. "Not at all. I just haven't lived a very exciting life."

Another lie. They just kept coming. But what choice did she have?

Mike leaned just a little bit closer, so close that she could feel his breath on her overheated neck. It felt cool and wonderful, drying some of the sticky perspiration. "I doubt that very much, Ms. Bolton."

The words made her glance at him sharply as Sarah

continued around the track. She gulped. "Oh, I assure you it's true."

She put as much emphasis as she dared into the words, hoping it would derail him from asking her any more questions, then she looked back toward her student, who'd just dismounted and was leading Groucho to the gate. Trisha headed over to open it for her, relieved when Mike stayed put.

"Do you want me to put him up in his stall?" Sarah asked.

"How about if you rub him down and then let him out in the pasture. It's too hot for him to be confined." She didn't have any other students today. Besides, Groucho had earned a break for being such a good boy. She gave his neck a pat, smiling when he leaned over the fence and nudged her shoulder. "I think he agrees with me."

Trisha swung the gate open so Sarah could lead the horse through. The teen unlatched her helmet and took it off, letting it dangle over her wrist. "Do you want me to send my mom out once she gets here? The girl's eyes skated to Mike, and Trisha wondered how much she'd heard of their conversation.

Mike wasn't paying attention to them, he was scribbling something inside the hard-backed notebook he'd brought out to the arena. Whatever. She still wasn't sure what he'd hoped to accomplish by coming out here today. "Why don't you have her pop out to say hi?"

"Okay." Sarah headed for the barn, Groucho in tow. Propping her hands on her hips and watching them move away from her, Trisha delayed having to interact with Mike again for as long as possible.

When she finally glanced back at him, his eyes were on the pair. "Don't you need to go with them?"

"Sarah's been around horses her whole life. She knows what she's doing. In fact, she and her mom are off to look at a horse tomorrow. She's ready to step it up another notch."

His mouth tightened, and she thought he was going to argue with her. Instead, he walked over and handed her a sheet of paper.

"What's this?" She looked down, trying to decipher his writing.

"A conditional recommendation for treatment. I did a little research over the weekend." He slid the clip on his pen onto the notebook's thin leather cover. "I can revoke it at any time, though. And I'll still want those references."

Despite the sliver of irritation that went through her at the imperious way he spoke of revoking his recommendation, it was soon dissolved by the rush of glee that swept over her. "You'll have them by tomorrow. Does this mean you're giving me the okay to work with Clara?"

He nodded. "I want to observe you with her, though, so if you could make the sessions for late afternoon, I'd appreciate it. If those go well, I'll consider sending a few other patients your way."

She wanted to wrap her arms around his neck and hug him tight…wanted to leap into the air and do a fist pump. But she forced herself to remain still and calm.

Be professional, Patty. Oops! Make that Trisha.

"Thank you, Mike. You won't regret it."

He gave a visible swallow. "Make sure I don't."

Sarah's mom came out, and Trisha introduced the two, tensing as she waited for Mike to interrogate her. But he didn't. He simply shook the woman's hand and asked how long Sarah had been taking lessons with her and how she liked it.

"My daughter loves Trisha. I don't think you could drag her away from this barn if you tried."

He nodded. "I'm glad she uses a helmet. It's important."

"Trisha insists on them. And I'm glad of it as well."

A glimmer of what might have been relief washed through Mike's eyes as he laid his arm along the top rail of the fence beside him. "Trisha seems to be a smart lady."

Did Mike believe that? Because she'd definitely gotten the idea that he didn't trust her or her horses. Maybe things were changing. A thought occurred to her. Maybe he would even reconsider making her watch him perform surgery. Yes! She'd been half-afraid it would bring back memories of Roger clutching his side, blood pouring from the stab wound and spewing words that had only half penetrated her brain. Until the Feds had broken in and taken charge of him. Trisha's fingers crept up to her neck as if she could still feel his squeezing grip. She straightened, dropping her hand when she noted everyone's eyes on her.

Sarah's mom smiled, breaking the awkward silence, and held her hand out to Mike. "It was nice meeting you." As they shook hands again, she said to Trisha, "We'll see you next week, then? Sarah wants to compete at the horse congress this year."

"She'll be ready. She's very good. And so is that horse she's getting. Thank you for letting me go out with you to look at him."

"She was thrilled. This has been her dream since she

was a little girl, and I think she and Laredo will be a good match. She wants to train horses someday."

Mike's arm slipped off the rail, and his smile froze. Goodbyes were said, but the neurosurgeon was much stiffer than he'd been moments earlier. Why?

The man was impossible to decipher. She gripped the paper containing his recommendation a little tighter, half expecting him to wrench it from her hand and rip it to shreds.

As soon as Sarah's mom was gone, Trisha glanced up to find Mike's eyes on her. She wrapped her fingers around the warmth of the wooden rail to her right. "Did you want anything else?"

"I did, as a matter of fact. Did my receptionist call you?" His voice was soft, but there was still a thread of tension that ran through it.

"She did."

"The surgery is tomorrow afternoon. Can you make it?"

Her nose wrinkled. She'd so hoped he wouldn't make her go through with it. "What kind of surgery is it again?"

"I have to remove a tumor."

She swallowed. "But you've already agreed that I can help Clara."

"No. I've agreed that you can *treat* Clara. Under my supervision."

"You know nothing about horses."

His arms folded across his chest in a way that was becoming far too familiar. "You'd be surprised."

Surprised. How? "I thought you said you'd never really interacted with them."

"Let's just say I've seen more than I wanted to see."

Which told her exactly nothing. And far too much. Maybe she needed to ask for some references of her own.

"So you're going to let me supervise your patients and dole out advice to them as well?" As if she could remain upright long enough to watch him make his first incision. She'd probably pass out cold on the floor.

"That would be hard to do from your vantage point. You'll be in the observation suite above the operating room, remember?" Maybe the tension in her stomach came through in her face because he studied her for a minute, his own features softening. "If you want to skip the surgery, you can. We can meet in my office once I'm done and talk about your treatment methods. You can give me your references then."

She shook her head. "We had a bargain, and I'd like to stick to it."

Maybe she was crazy, but knowing the treatment area was in a separate room helped. She could close her eyes the whole time and block out what was going on below her. She relaxed a fraction. "So what time tomorrow? I have a lesson at one."

"Surgery is scheduled for four. If you're sure."

"I'll be there."

She reached up to adjust her hat, only to have him catch her hand and look at it, then slide his thumb over her ring. The act made her swallow. "What are you doing?"

"Do you always wear this?"

Licking her lips, she glanced down at where his thumb still fiddled with the fake class ring. Its purpose was to cover the pale patch of skin where her wide gold wedding band had once rested. Another suggestion from the Feds.

"Yes. Why?"

"Just wondered how safe it is for someone like you."

Her heart lurched. "S-someone like me?"

"Working with horses." He released her hand, and she let it drop to her side. "Couldn't it get caught on something?"

Oh, Lord, she needed to get a grip. "I'm careful."

At least she was trying to be, which was why she'd worn the ring in the first place.

He seemed to accept her words at face value because he went back to the previous subject. "I'll have my secretary call you with directions to the hospital. If you could get there a half hour early, that would be great. Things get hectic as it gets close to surgery time."

"I'll be there. And I'll bring the references." She wasn't sure how much longer she could keep putting it off.

Once they'd said their goodbyes and he'd left, Trisha fired up her computer to enter a reminder onto her calendar. And as her fingers hovered over the keys, she found herself typing in the good doctor's name…looking for what, she wasn't sure.

Nothing. There were a ton of Mike Dunnings in the world evidently. She narrowed the search, typing the word "Doctor' in front of his name and listing his location as Dusty Hills, Nevada.

There. A whole screen of possibilities.

Hmm…he had his own website. Interesting. She scrolled further down the list of results and found his name listed as Head of Neurology at a hospital in Mariston. And he was on various committees in Dusty Hills.

The tenth entry down made her pause, her brows coming together when she saw a picture of Mike with a woman. The black and white shot was grainy, but the couple were looking at each other and smiling. Then she looked at the title. Her eyes widened as shock rolled through her system.

She stared at it, unable to look away.

Oh, God. It explained everything. His reaction when Brutus had shied during their first meeting. His comment about not wanting to scare the horse. His dragging her bodily from the stall.

Not only had Mike been married. He had also been widowed. She read the headline one more time: *Wife of renowned local surgeon dead after tragic riding accident.*

CHAPTER FOUR

HE SHOULDN'T HAVE made her come.

He'd offered her an out at the barn yesterday, but he should have known she wouldn't take it. Mike pulled the overhead light above the operating table a little to the left to better illuminate the target area as he prepared to separate healthy tissue from diseased.

Trisha's green eyes had been feverishly bright when she'd met him in the waiting room an hour ago. At first he'd thought it was excitement, similar to what he felt each time he went into the operating room. Then he realized it was fear. Maybe even horror.

Like he felt whenever he was around horses?

Even after he'd realized she was scared, he'd still led her to the observation room. Like the ass that he was.

He could still remember touching that huge class ring on her finger yesterday and being far too glad it wasn't a simple gold band. Realistically, it would have been better if she wore a five-carat rock on that finger.

"Getting ready to dissect the tumor." He kept his voice calm as he spoke into the recorder, knowing she could hear every word he said, He may have been able to school his tone but, inside, his gut felt like a pile of scorched embers. Caused by regret?

Possibly. In fact, if he could stop the surgery right now and send her home, he would. But he was too far in at this point. He wasn't going to risk his patient's life in order to ease Trisha's discomfort. He glanced up to the window to find her seated in the front row, her eyes closed tight.

Huh. Maybe she'd gone to sleep. Maybe he was worrying for nothing.

Somehow he doubted it. More likely she was avoiding looking down at where he was working.

His insides cooled just a bit. Okay, so she wasn't forcing herself to stare down at the surgery. That should help his guilt factor. Although it was still whispering that he should do something nice for her after this. Really nice.

Like what?

Using the precise laser and paying attention to the visual readout before him, he eased his way beneath the tumor, cauterizing blood vessels as he went. Millimeter by millimeter he began the delicate process of separation—one that would hopefully give his patient a new lease on life.

If only he could use the same process on his own life, cutting away all the heartache and betrayal and leaving behind only a good set of memories. Memories that were painless and fun.

Maybe even as much fun as he sensed he could have with Trisha, if he let himself go in that direction.

Not a possibility, unfortunately. Trisha might be perfect for some other guy, but not for him. An unwilling smile came up when he remembered her directing him to that wheelbarrow full of manure. Kind of fitting, really. He felt like his whole life had been wedged deep into a steaming pile of...

He shook his thoughts free and took a breath, his glance again skating to the window above him. This time Trisha's eyes were open and watching. The way she hunched lower in her seat told him he was wrong about her being okay with this. She wasn't.

You're not the only one who can read body language, lady. I bet you have no idea what yours is telling me right now.

Finishing the line he was making with the laser, he glanced at one of the nurses who stood at the ready in case he needed her. "Gail, I hate to ask, but would you mind going up to the observation room and telling Ms. Bolton she can go home? Tell her I'll call her later about our mutual patient."

The nurse's eyes went from his to the lone figure above them then she nodded, her brows not twitching an inch, although she had to be wondering why on earth there was a stranger in the deck above them. Everyone else was probably wondering the same thing, but no one dared ask.

"Do you want me to scrub back in afterward?" she asked.

"Yes, thank you."

Finally able to put Trisha out of his mind, he got back to the surgery, lifting out one part of the tumor and dropping it into a stainless-steel collection tray. "That needs to go down to Pathology. If they can look at it while I dissect the rest of the growth, I'd appreciate it."

"Right away, Doctor." His assistant quickly labeled the specimen and headed out the door with it.

Another four-centimeter segment of tumor to remove and then he'd re-examine the area and make sure he'd gotten as much as possible before closing up.

Less than ten minutes later Gail was beside him again, murmuring, "I told her, but she said she wants to stay until the end. She said she doesn't want to be the one to renege." The woman hesitated before finishing, "She said you'd know what she meant by that."

He did. Great. So much for making himself feel better. "That's fine. I just thought she might not be feeling well."

"Well...um, she did ask me to hand her a trash can." A chuckle accompanied the remark.

What? Surely Trisha wasn't seriously going to stay if she felt like throwing up.

If she did, that was her problem at this point. His was his patient.

Forcing his mind back to the procedure once and for all, he completed the surgery a half-hour later. The pathology results came back just as he was finishing up, so there was at least one piece of good news. The tumor was benign. It might slowly grow back after a year or two and have to be removed again, but at least it wouldn't spread to the far reaches of the patient's body and invade other cells. They could always try using radiation the next time to destroy the rogue cells, if its growth got out of control.

He reattached the section of skull he'd removed and stitched the edges of the patient's scalp together as neatly as possible. Her hair would cover everything once it grew back in. "Let's wake her up."

The anesthesiologist began lightening the sedation and removed the intubation tube as soon as the patient showed signs of stirring. Mike waited around until the woman could respond to simple questions, then gave her shoulder a gentle squeeze, promising to visit her once she got settled in the recovery area. He stripped his gloves with a frown and headed for the observation room, where Trisha—true to her word—still lingered. He pushed through the doors, his gaze stopping at the white plastic-lined can at her feet and finding it empty. Well, that was one less thing to worry about. He sat down beside her, aware that he was a little less composed than he would have liked. "You really didn't have to stay."

"I did. I didn't want there to be any questions later on."

Questions? She really thought he was petty enough to use that to prevent her from treating Clara? "You don't think much of me, do you?"

She studied his face for a few seconds. "Honestly? I don't know what to think of you. I feel like you're dismissing hippotherapy's benefits without knowing anything about it. It would help if I knew why."

Would it? If he told her what had happened to Marcy, would she feel better about his reluctance? Doubtful. She'd just give him the same line Marcy's friend had. *Accidents happen.* Yes, they did. But her friend didn't know the whole story about who his wife had been meeting that day. It had been Ray Chapman who'd gotten a visit from the mystery man a week after the accident— another horse trainer—who was supposedly as torn up by grief over Marcy's death as he was. She'd been planning on asking for a divorce. And he had never guessed. How much of a fool did that make him? His own wife had lied and cheated and he'd just kissed her goodnight at the end of each day without a care in the world.

He sighed and decided to evade Trisha's request. "I don't know enough about hippotherapy to make a judgment one way or the other. Which is why I thought this would a step in the right direction." He waved a hand at the room around him. "I thought we'd take a look at each other's professions."

Her brows went up. "Really? Is that what this was about? I thought it was about seeing who had the most guts." She swallowed, her glance going to the operating room below, which was being swabbed clean. "Okay, so that didn't come out exactly right."

He leaned back. "No matter. I'd say you were pretty gutsy for not walking away when given the chance."

"Don't worry. Your turn is coming. And don't expect me to give you an out when the time comes."

"So let's do it now."

Holy... Okay, so that had to be the guilt talking, because it sure wasn't him.

"Now?" She blinked.

"Why not?" He'd wanted to do something nice for her. How about putting his own courage to the test?

"I don't have any clients scheduled for today," she said, her voice thoughtful.

"Maybe we could jump ahead a bit and get this over with. You wanted me to see what it's like to go through a therapy session, right? Let's do it."

"You want to get on a horse." She sounded dubious. Almost as dubious as he felt.

"If that's what therapy involves, I'll get on one." *Clang, clang, clang!* The warning gong went off inside his head.

She sat up a little straighter. "You'd have to do exactly what I tell you, and Penny isn't scheduled to work today."

What did her helper have to do with anything? Unless maybe Trisha thought she needed a chaperone.

After what had happened last time he'd been in her barn, maybe that wasn't such a bad idea.

"Thinking of feeling me up again?" He lifted a brow to show he was teasing.

Then his mind turned back to the task in hand and his smile instantly disappeared. "Are you planning on using Brutus?"

"With you? Oh, no."

"With who, then?" A chill ran over him. She said she didn't use Brutus in therapy. Had she kept something from him?

Her head tilted. "Well, Penny's ridden him before. And, of course, I have. So has Larry. But I'd never let someone I didn't know ride him."

"Because of his issues."

She nodded. "Because of his issues…and theirs."

"Theirs"—meaning *his*? If that was the case, he was only too happy to be excluded from the hop-on-Brutus club. "As long as we're clear on this. You wouldn't use him with Clara. Ever."

"Not ever." Her voice was emphatic enough to convince him she meant it. "If you're serious about doing a session today, we probably need to get going before it gets too dark. I like to use the outdoor arena for my sessions rather than the indoor."

Interesting. He thought about asking why, then decided it might be better if he didn't know.

"Let me just speak to my patient and let my paging service know where I'll be."

"How about I meet you back at my place, then? I need to change and get a few things ready."

Change. Get a few things ready. A flashbulb went off in his head and illuminated a whole scene he shouldn't even be imagining. But he was. Things like glowing candles and skimpy nightwear.

"Great. I'll see you back there in an hour or so." With that, he stood and headed out the door. And away from those pictures of Trisha changing into something a little more comfortable—and a whole lot more dangerous.

"Hold onto the pommel until you get your balance."

Trisha frowned at the way Mike's knuckles grew white as he gripped the saddle horn and waited for her to set Crow in motion. Did he think she was going to start the horse out at a lope? She decided to set his mind at ease. "We're only going to do a slow walk."

"Right."

His voice was as tight as his grip. Something was wrong. No one should be this afraid. "I think we should call this off."

The man's head came up at that. "I thought you weren't going to give me a chance to back out."

"Changed my mind."

His jaw tightened. "Start him up."

That made her smile. "Sure, we'll just wind up that little crank on his side and he'll be ready for action."

His expression didn't budge. This man liked to be in control. She could only imagine how he must feel, letting someone else call the shots. Then again, maybe that's exactly what he needed. So if he wanted to go… they would go.

She raised the line attached to the horse's halter to get Crow's attention. "Okay, Crow, walk."

The horse knew this drill by heart. He carefully stepped out, not even the slightest hint of a lurch as he moved into a walk that was more of a glide. A show horse in his past life, he was the epitome of slow, methodical movements. Not even a swish of the tail disturbed the steady rhythm, nothing that could put a young, disabled rider off balance. "Good job."

Mike didn't say a word. He just held on.

Maybe it would have been better if they'd waited until Penny came in tomorrow—she could have walked beside him like she did with their other patients and act as a spotter—and an encourager.

"You okay, Mike?"

"Hanging in there."

"Don't worry. We won't go any faster than this."

His posture relaxed the slightest bit. Wow, for a neurosurgeon who performed operations on a regular basis he was really uptight. Then again, she knew why, and it made her heart ache. The news article said his wife had been found beside her horse—she'd died a few days later in the hospital, never having regained consciousness. Her organs had benefitted six different people. That hurt the worst. Trisha had a feeling Mike had been the one who'd had to make the decision no one should ever have to make: when to turn off the machines. She couldn't imagine anything worse. No wonder he held a grudge against anything equine. If she'd been in his place, would she be the same?

No, because she knew horses. Knew there was always a risk, just as there was with almost any activity. Riding a bike, paddling a canoe—getting married—nothing was completely safe. And she trusted her horses a whole lot more than she trusted most men nowadays.

But should she really be making him do this, now that she knew about his wife? If she insisted they not go through with it, though, he was bound to ask why.

She doubted he'd appreciate knowing she'd looked him up online. So she let the horse do one complete circle around her and then reassessed his demeanor. Mike's form was actually not bad, except for that unyielding grip. Maybe she needed to do something about that.

"Remember, I'm controlling him with the longe line. You don't have to worry about steering him or keeping him at his current pace. Just concentrate on his rhythm. It's kind of a forward and back, push and pull motion. Feel it?"

His brows puckered as if he was concentrating, but other than that nothing changed. "I'm not sure what I'm looking for."

"Close your eyes for a minute."

He shifted his attention back to her then did as she asked, his hands tightening their grip.

"Okay, concentrate on how Crow is making your body move. Because, even at a walk, his motions are acting on you, whether you're aware of it or not. Don't fight it. Let his strides carry you—really try to feel it in your hips. Keep them loose and let them move forward and back in the saddle." She waited for a second and watched his frame to see if he understood what she was looking for. She timed her voice to match each beat that the horse took, the slow gentle movements of Mike's body in the saddle. "Push. Pull. Hips. Moving. Forward. Back. Push. Pull. Slow. Rhythm. Don't. Rush."

Mike's eyes opened, his head turning toward her, some dark emotion coming from between the narrowed lids. "Believe me. I *never* rush."

Heat swept over her as his meaning hit her. Time to switch gears. "Crow, whoa." Right on cue, the large black horse slowed to a crawl and then stopped just as smoothly as he'd started. "Good boy."

Still looking at her, one of Mike's brows lifted.

"I was talking to the horse," she said, not sure what it was about him that made her mind stray into dangerous waters. "Why don't you give him a pat on the neck for doing what he was supposed to?" Maybe she should try to focus on her job, and remember who she was working with and why. Desensitize him. Show him that his wife's tragic death had been by far the exception to the rule...just like a plane crash. Or a boat accident. There were things in life that couldn't always be controlled.

Like marrying a man named Roger Smith whose real name had turned out to be Viktor Terenovsky—head of one of the most notorious Russian mafia groups? She'd pretty much felt completely out of control ever since that fateful visit from the FBI two years after her wedding. Things had spiraled out of control after that, when they'd planted an agent at the house. Six months later, the agent had been dead, her marriage had been annulled and she was in the witness protection program. And her husband—who'd vowed to hunt her down and make her pay—was in a federal prison for the rest of his natural life. But not before he'd ruined her life as well, effectively separating her from everyone she'd ever loved. Her throat clogged, wondering how her mother and brother were doing.

"Thank him?" Mike asked, bringing her attention back to him. "You mean like pet him?"

She drew a careful breath and tried to focus. "Yes. That's exactly what I mean."

He seemed to close his eyes for a second, as if trying to wrap his head around her request, before leaning forward and pressing his palm to Crow's neck then quickly removing it. "Would you make your clients do this?"

"Absolutely. Penny would probably have to help them, but it's important for my clients to realize these horses are living creatures who are an important part of their therapy team. They need to say thank you, just like they would thank a human being who helped them."

"So I just thanked him."

"You did." She wasn't sure exactly how much Mike was expecting her to do with him. "Are you up for another round?"

"How long do you normally work with your patients?"

She shifted the long length of longe line to her other hand. "A half-hour to an hour, depending on their abilities."

"And we've been working…?"

She smiled. "Oh…about five minutes, give or take a minute."

"Crap."

There was a wealth of meaning in that single word. "You ready to quit?"

"No. If you could make it through my surgery, I can make it through your treatment."

A flash of admiration went through her, and she wondered how far he was willing to let her go. How much control was he willing to relinquish? "How was your balance that last round?"

One side of his mouth quirked. "I didn't fall off, so I guess it was fine. Why?"

She'd thought it was pretty fine herself. "I'm thinking you might be ready to advance a step. Try something just a bit harder."

"You said we were only going to do this at a walk."

"Yes. And we are."

"So by harder you mean…"

Her lips curved. "Have you ever ridden a bicycle with no hands?"

"No hands? Are you kidding me?"

"Nope. Put your hands on your thighs and just sit there for a minute."

Mike's chest inflated as he took a deep breath and held it then released it. He took one hand off the pommel and rested it just above his knee. "You're not going to start him up again, are you?"

"No. I'll let you know before I do anything."

Off came the second hand, which went to his left thigh. He sat there like an abandoned ventriloquist's puppet, not a single muscle moving.

She nodded her approval. "Good. Now put your hands back on the pommel."

Mike went back to his previous position, although his fingers weren't quite as white this time.

"Okay, we're going to walk again. Concentrate on your balance. When we come up on the halfway point, which will be at the far end of the arena, let go of the pommel one hand at a time, like you've just done, and grip your thighs. You'll still have the illusion of holding on, but your abs and leg muscles will be doing most of the work."

His frown returned. "And if he takes off?"

"He won't. Unless you kick him."

"No chance of that."

She lifted the longe line again to signal to Crow that he was going to move in a minute. "Just take it slow and easy. Ready?"

He nodded.

She gave the command, and the horse went back into his careful glide. Holding her breath, she could almost see the gears turning in Mike's brain as he tried to figure out if he was really going to do what she'd asked. Up came the halfway point and one hand came off the pommel. He stayed like that for a few beats then added the second hand.

"See if you can keep your hands there for ten strides. Count them. Out loud," she added, in case he wasn't sure.

"One...two...three...four..."

His numbers were more an afterthought than anything, because she could tell all his concentration was on keeping track of Crow's movements. Plod, plod, plod. Mike kept perfect pace with his counting, his hips moving back and forth. When he hit ten, he glanced at her in question.

"You can put your hands back on the pommel."

Once he did, she asked Crow to stop again. "Really, really good. Now thank him again."

She could have sworn his eyes gave a half-roll, but he did touch the gelding's neck again, holding the pressure for a little longer this time. "He doesn't act like he even cares."

"Oh, he cares." And so did she. She was feeling a combination of pride, elation and some other emotion she couldn't decipher. "I'm going to walk toward you. Stay in the saddle until I reach you. Then I'll tell you how to dismount."

The man actually chuckled in response.

She began looping the longe line around itself as she made her way toward the pair. "What?"

"I hadn't actually thought getting down might be a problem. Until now."

She smiled back. "We'll worry about that in a minute."

Once she reached him, she held onto Crow's halter. "Okay, reverse what you did to get up. Swing your right leg over Crow's back, then kick your left foot out of the stirrup and slide down his side…hopefully landing on your feet, if all goes well."

He followed her instructions, except as he started to slide down the horse's side, she stepped closer, reaching out with both hands to steady his descent, palms sliding up his sides. His breath hissed in at about the same time as hers whooshed out of her lungs at the contact. The second his feet touched the ground, he went very still.

Did he think she was feeling him up again?

This isn't one of your patients, Trish. She started to let go and take a step back, only to have him grab her hands and keep them in place.

"Sorry," she said. "I'm used to working with kids who aren't very steady."

"Yeah, well, I'm feeling none too steady right now myself." Still holding one of her hands, he turned round to look at her, his back to the horse. He nodded at the longe line she still held. "Do you need to put him somewhere?"

The low tone made her blink. He was still gripping one of her hands, making no effort to let her go. The scent of soap and warm horse rose between them, teasing her nose and jarring her senses. The combination was earthy and real and, oh, so sexy. "I—I can unsaddle him in a minute. I'll just unclip him so he can go over and get some water."

He released her. Trisha's hands shook as she un-snapped the line from Crow's halter and let him go. The gelding headed straight for the far corner of the outside arena, where he could see the inside of the barn and the other horses who were still in their stalls.

Why had he wanted her to let Crow go? Because the horse made him nervous? Or for some other reason?

You're being ridiculous. He's probably going to chew you out for touching him again. Or maybe he just wants to co-ordinate our schedules so he can watch Clara's first session.

Maybe he hadn't even felt that amazing jolt of elec-tricity that had passed through her as she'd touched him.

His hands went to her shoulders, and he turned her around to face him. The look in his eyes said she was very, very wrong. He'd felt it all right.

And he was about to do something about it.

CHAPTER FIVE

THIS WOMAN WAS going to be the death of him.

First she called out commands that sounded a little too close to an instructional sex video—raising disturbing images in his head. Such as what it would be like to do those things while horizontal, with a certain hippotherapist wedged beneath him. Only there'd be no "nice and easy" or "slow" about it. If they ever came together, it would be hot and intense and incredibly carnal.

Then she'd told him to grip his thighs and count out loud. More pictures had formed. Equally disturbing.

Her hands sliding up his sides as he'd gotten off the horse had added the final log to the fire—one he'd been doing his hardest to put out. It made him wonder if she'd done it all on purpose—although if she had, he had no idea why.

"Is there a problem?" Her wide green eyes held a trace of wariness along with a whole lot of something else.

"Are you *trying* to get something started here?" If she'd been attempting to rattle him, she'd done a fine job of it. He *was* rattled. And he only knew of two ways to fix the problem. One…run like hell. Or two…kiss her until he no longer cared.

Unfortunately, since he was in a sandy fenced-in arena, getting out quickly might prove a physical impossibility. Not to mention a certain part of his body was yelling for him to choose the second option, no matter what it might lead to.

"What do you mean?"

"I mean it's been a while, but I don't think my brain has completely forgotten what it's like when there's a certain amount of chemistry between two people."

"Chemistry?"

She'd injected a note of uncertainty into her voice, but the way she moistened her lips said she knew exactly what he was talking about.

"Are you saying you haven't felt a spark or two when we've been together?" Even during that first panicked meeting, something warm and molten had flowed between them.

"I don't know what you want me to say."

He took a step closer, his hands leaving her shoulders and cupping her cheeks, instead. "I don't *want* you to say anything, Trisha."

"Oh."

He couldn't hold back a smile. "Can you come up with one valid reason why I shouldn't do something incredibly stupid right now?" His thumbs strummed along her cheekbones, the skin soft and warm. "Think hard."

Her lips parted then her hands went to his forearms, sliding slowly up to his shoulders. "I'm drawing a blank."

"Hmm. Well, then, that makes two of us." He glanced to the side where the horse stood, head hung over the gate, before his arm went around her waist and reeled her in. "Think he'll stick to his side of the room?"

"Pretty sure he's not interested in anything we're doing right now."

"What about what we're *about* to do?"

With a pre-emptive "Hail Mary" or two that he hoped would see him through, Mike lowered his head and covered her mouth with his.

Her lips were every bit as soft and moist as he'd feared. Or was it hoped?

It didn't matter, because the woman wasn't just letting him kiss her. She was kissing him back, her mouth sliding over his in perfect counterpoint to the movements of his. And when he opened, so did she, to the devastation of anything rational that was left inside him. His tongue immediately surged forward, affirming his earlier thoughts that this woman did not generate anything soft and gentle in him but rather an urgency he was suddenly having trouble reining in.

When he tried to draw back, however, Trisha was right there, making sure he didn't go far. She made a little sound in her throat when he went deeper, her fingertips pressing into the skin at the back of his neck as she leveraged him even closer.

One of his hands went to the small of her back, warning her that she was playing with fire. It backfired, though, because trapping his flesh between the taut muscles of her belly and his own pelvis was a pretty good imitation of something else. The tight space made him want to do one thing and one thing only: thrust forward hard and fast. He did the next best thing and lived vicariously through his tongue, allowing it to act out his fantasies in her mouth, his hands moving to cup that luscious behind he'd admired, keeping her hard against him.

Instead of letting him have his fun and pulling free before he got beyond the point of no return, though, her fingers went to his polo shirt and yanked it up from his waistband, allowing her access to his skin. Wasting no time, she burrowed beneath the opening and splayed her hands out on his bare back, her touch sending a jolt of need racing through his system.

He left her mouth, skimming across her jaw with biting kisses he vaguely worried might be a little too rough. Until she tilted her head toward him with a low moan that sounded almost as desperate as he felt. He took his cue from her and jerked her shirt from her jeans, continuing around her waist until it hung free. He didn't head for her back, though. With his lips pressed to her neck, his fingers skated up the smooth skin of her sides and found the curves he was looking for. Her warm breasts, encased in a satiny cocoon that squeezed them together. He moved his body sideways to give him more access, while maintaining enough pressure on his erection to keep it from raging at him in despair.

Taking a second or two to breathe, he slowly allowed his fingertips to drag over her bra, bumping softly over the tight nipple at the very center of the cup and then coming back to do that again. Trisha's throat moved against his lips as she swallowed and her back arched slightly, moving into his touch.

It was then that Mike had his first doubts about how far Trisha was willing to let this go. Or how far he was willing to take it. Mike had stopped carrying a condom in his wallet the day he'd said "I do" to Marcy at the altar. After her death he hadn't been able to bring himself to go back to those old habits.

Putting Trisha or anyone else at risk was not an option.

He somehow forced the muscles in his arm to obey his thoughts and pulled it free of her shirt. His head came up, and he found Trisha's eyes already open, staring at him in some confusion.

She wasn't the only one who was confused. He hadn't gotten this carried away since…well, in a long time. With that realization came the guilt. He couldn't even remember what it had been like to feel that for Marcy, although he knew he had at one time.

He eased his hips back, allowing the dull ache of withdrawal to pull him back to earth. Back to sanity.

She was still looking at him. To blot out that view, he pressed his forehead to hers. "I don't know what I was thinking. I'm sorry."

Trisha's hands came out from beneath his shirt as well, and he felt her shrug. "I don't think either one of us was doing a lot of thinking. No need to say you're sorry."

Like hell there wasn't. But he wasn't sure if he was apologizing to Trisha or to Marcy's memory. Either way, it wasn't something he wanted to analyze right now. "Right." He completed the separation process and took a step back. "I'll just go, then."

"Okay."

She tucked her hands into the back pockets of her jeans, her T-shirt still skewed sideways and perched high enough on her left side that he could see an inch or so of creamy white flesh. She made no effort to tug it down. Her posture showed off the tight peaks of her breasts still very much in evidence. She either didn't realize it, or she didn't care. He had a feeling it might be a little bit of both.

Marcy had always been so meticulous about the way she'd dressed, even on the days she'd gone out to the barn—of course, knowing what he did now, her reasons seemed pretty obvious. His glance went to the far side of the arena, where Crow stood, saddle still in place, looking bored by the whole scene. Trisha was right. The animal didn't care about what the two strange humans had been doing.

For the first time in his life he wished he could look inside a horse's mind and borrow a little of that couldn't-care-less attitude. Because right now he did care. As he stiffened his shoulders and swung away from woman and horse, heading for the open barn door on the side of the arena where his car was parked, he could still feel her looking at him. But she didn't say anything else or give any indication that she wanted him to stay.

That had to be a good thing, right? If ever there was a woman he should stay away from, it was Trisha.

He emerged from the barn and blinked at the sun a time or two before digging his car keys from his pocket and settling into the beige leather seat of his vehicle. Putting the car into drive, he headed down the long gravel driveway. The dust kicked up by the vehicle blotted out the view in his mirror. Another very good thing.

Because if he couldn't see it, he could pretend it didn't exist. Just like a child playing peek-a-boo who hid behind his hands. If he kept the idea firmly in his head, it would become true, sooner or later.

He had a feeling it would be later, however. As in a couple of decades from now.

"Looks like horses aren't the only things that scare him, Crow." Trisha stroked the horse's neck, leaning her forehead against him, only to pull away again when it reminded her of the way Mike had pressed his forehead against hers, his breathing still rough and uneven.

She shivered.

He'd run from the scene of the crime so fast that she'd barely had time to pull her thoughts back together, much less try to convince him to move to the nearest clean stall, which was where her thoughts had been centered the second his mouth had hit hers.

She'd been looking for release. That had to be what it was. Her body was still on high alert, even now, and it had been over thirty minutes since he'd left. If he came back, she couldn't guarantee she wouldn't melt right back into his arms.

Scratch that. She *would* melt into them.

She'd forced herself to go through the motions of unsaddling Crow and giving him a good rubdown. But her eyes and ears had been watching for any sign that Mike might have changed his mind. But once the roar of his engine had faded, it hadn't come back.

What was she doing, playing around with something as serious as this? She was supposed to be living a quiet, uneventful life, not getting involved with a man she barely knew. Wasn't that what had gotten her into trouble in the first place? Roger had wined and dined her so quickly she'd barely had time to catch her breath. The truth was, he'd been obsessed about having her, and once he had he hadn't wanted anyone else near her.

The solution? He'd married her.

But what she'd once thought was old-fashioned and sweet had soon turned into a nightmare from which there'd been no escape. In the end, he hadn't been "Roger" at all, but a cold-blooded killer. The funny thing was, she was now following in his footsteps. Not the killing part but the hiding-behind-a-fake-name thing. He'd gone by a false name at the beginning of their relationship, and now she was going by one at the end of it. How turned around things had gotten once the Feds had come and revealed the scope of her husband's ruthlessness. He'd controlled a whole lot of lives, including hers.

She swallowed. Did she really want to drag Mike into all that? Feeding him phony bits of information in an attempt to keep him in the dark? Wouldn't that make her the same as Roger?

Her ex had claimed he'd done it to protect her.

Well, she was doing exactly the same thing. Lying to protect people. Only she was doing it to protect their lives, not someone's fragile sensibilities.

Besides, Mike had been hurt once already—terribly. Could she risk being the cause of him getting hurt again?

He doesn't love you. He was only interested in a quick roll in the proverbial hay.

Well, that's all she'd been interested in as well. It would have been so easy to just do it and then go their separate ways. After all, it happened all the time in the real world. Have a few drinks: wind up in bed. Meet up in a chat room: head for the nearest motel. Give a man a riding lesson: have sex in a deserted barn.

Easy.

So why, then, had he run?

She scrubbed her fingertips behind one of the gelding's ears. "Be glad you don't have to worry about anything other than food and a warm place to sleep."

The horse's left ear swiveled in her direction and he blew out a breath, as if giving a sympathetic sigh for her trials. Or maybe he was just bored.

Laughing, she took hold of his halter and snapped a

lead line onto it. "Let's put you with your buddies, okay? You can take the rest of the day off."

Trisha led him out of the arena and headed across the lot toward the pasture.

Sarah had called a few minutes ago, which was another sign that she and Mike stopping when they had was a good thing. Her student had been out to check on the horse she'd bought and asked if Trisha would come out and help trailer him for the trip home. So at least she wouldn't have to think about Mike or what had almost happened for a while. As of Thursday, though, he was scheduled to come out and watch Clara Trimble have her first physical therapy session.

No problem. She could and would face him without batting an eyelid. She had to. Somehow. She'd come down this road looking for a referral and she'd do whatever it took to get one. It would mean her new lifestyle would be safe without the Feds having to step back in and find her an alternate job, which was what they'd wanted to do in the first place. So if she could just get Mike to agree to endorse her...

Her mind slithered into uncomfortable territory as a memory of their time in the barn flooded back to her. Surely he wouldn't think she'd kissed him to have access to more of his patients. No, he'd already given her the okay to take Clara on as a client. But he might think she was hedging her bets for the future.

Maybe she should call him. And say what? *Hey, I wasn't going to have sex with you just to get my hands on your patient list—honest.* Wouldn't calling to deny a question that had never been asked amount to a confession? Or at the very least plant a seed of doubt in his mind?

Better to just act like nothing had happened.

She slid the latch to the pasture gate free and let Crow loose to graze for the rest of the afternoon. Acting like nothing had happened sounded like a good plan.

Now all she had to do was get her head and her heart to co-operate. Because right now they were still focused on her empty driveway and hoping against hope she might see that cream-colored car heading back her way.

CHAPTER SIX

MIKE WAS HALFWAY to his car after a long day at the hospital when his phone vibrated against his hip. He rolled his eyes. *Can't I get out of the parking lot first, guys?*

He'd already had a day from hell, his teeth clenching at the memories of yesterday's kiss until the muscles in his jaw ached from fatigue. Dumping his car keys back into his front pocket and grabbing his phone, he glanced at the readout.

He frowned. Not the hospital after all. It was a Dusty Hills number. Punching "Talk", he lifted the phone to his ear.

"Dunning here."

"Mike?" The low throaty voice was the one that had haunted him for the last twenty-four hours.

"Trisha? Is everything okay?" He couldn't imagine her calling him just for kicks. Besides, she sounded funny.

"No. They're bringing Sarah in. Are you at the hospital?"

"Sarah?" He racked his brain. The name was familiar but... Wait. "Is she the student I met?"

"Yes." There was the shrill sound of a siren on the

other end of the phone. "We went to get her horse and…" She said something to someone in the background.

At the word "horse", icy needles had begun pricking at his scalp in a thousand different spots. "Did something happen?"

"There's been an accident." A second or two of silence. "Are you at the hospital?"

An accident. Dammit! He reversed course. "I'm here. How far out are they?"

"Probably fifteen minutes. Her mom is in the ambulance with her." Trisha's voice was so shaky he could barely make out the words. "I need to go. I have to take care of the horse. Call me when you know something."

His jaw clenched again, his aching muscles protesting the action. "Stay away from that horse, Trisha."

"What? No, I can't. I have to help. I'll call you later." With that the line went dead.

Crap! He strode through the hospital doors, already hitting the redial button of his phone. It rang four times on the other end, and then Trisha's voice mail picked up—her pre-recorded voice sounding obscenely cheerful. A million words—none of them good—went through his head. He didn't even know where she was. Was she at her place? All Mike could picture was that huge horse she'd been grooming the first day they'd met. Had he—or Sarah's new horse—gone crazy somehow?

Getting involved with Trisha in any way, shape or form had been a mistake. As soon as he had finished assessing Sarah, he was going to call Clara's mother and tell her he was revoking his recommendation. If Trisha was boarding unsafe animals, he didn't want his patients anywhere near that place. Although, if something happened to her, it was a moot point.

He swallowed hard as he arrived at the emergency room to find Peyton Wright, one of the ER doctors, on the phone. He motioned to Mike, covering the phone with one hand. "I was just about to page you. We have a head trauma coming in."

The chilly sensation of déjà vu slithered through Mike's gut and coiled around his spine. He shut down that line of thought as soon as it started.

"Teenage girl?" he asked, even as he hoped it was someone other than Sarah.

Peyton's brows went up. "Yep, I'm on with the ambulance right now." He finished giving instructions to the emergency services crew then got off the phone. "Looks like we've got a possible concussion or skull fracture, along with a broken femur.

The horse had thrown her? "Riding accident?"

"No. Car." He paused. "Are we talking about the same case?"

Trisha had said there was a horse involved. "Do you have a name?"

"A Sarah Millner?"

Mike nodded. "You sure the injuries are from a vehicle?"

"That's what they said. The other driver was drunk. He's coming in too, but doesn't seem to be injured. He'll be headed for jail as soon as he's been assessed, from what I understand."

Maybe he'd misunderstood her. Maybe she wasn't at the scene of the accident. Maybe Sarah's mother had called her and told her. His jaw loosened fractionally. That had to be it. Her voice had been shaky so whispers from his past had hijacked his imagination, playing tricks on him.

The ambulance pulled into the bay just a few minutes later, and Mike's concentration went to his patient. As the paramedics wheeled her in, rattling off vitals and their findings in the field, the familiar blonde hair and ponytail told him it was indeed Trisha's student. Her mother ran alongside the gurney. Peyton took the lead, while Mike tried to piece together what had happened. "They said it was a car accident?"

The frantic woman dashed the back of her hand across her eyes. "Yes, we were hauling her new horse home and someone ran a red light and hit Sarah's side of the car. The police say he was drunk." Her voice dropped to a whisper. "The airbags went off, but once I realized what had happened and turned to her, her side of the car was pushed toward me, and Sarah looked…" Her voice gave way. "She looked like a broken doll."

"We're going to do all we can for her." He motioned to the nurse. "She needs to get some information from you. Is Sarah allergic to anything?"

"Codeine makes her vomit, but other than that, no." The gurney made a quick turn, leaving them behind. "I want to go with her."

"You can in just a little while. Let us check her over first, okay?" He squeezed her shoulder. "I promise I'll come out and find you as soon as I know something." A random thought went through his mind. "Was her instructor in the car with you?"

When the woman looked confused, he tried again. "Was Trisha—Ms. Bolton—there?"

"She was following us in her car." Sarah's mother looked at him a little closer. "You were at her barn the other day, right? You asked me some questions."

He nodded, knowing he needed to get back to where

Sarah was but also knowing that Peyton wouldn't hesitate to haul him back there if he needed him. "That's right. Was Trisha involved in the accident?"

Her eyes filled again. "No. Oh, God, Sarah's poor horse. She'll never forgive me if he doesn't make it. The trailer tipped over during the accident and...Laredo was thrashing and screaming. I could hear him banging against the sides of the trailer, but I had to take care of Sarah. Trisha offered to stay and help get him out."

"Of course you had to take care of your daughter." He replayed Trisha's words in his head and his gut tightened into a hard ball. She was there. At the scene. Trying to take care of an injured and frantic animal. That's why she hadn't answered his call. "I'll go and check on Sarah."

He strode down the hallway, pressing the redial button on his phone as he went. Again, it went to voice mail after a few rings. Mike had visions of Trisha injured or worse as she tried to deal with Sarah's horse. There was nothing he could do about it right now, though, he already had one patient. All he could do was pray it wouldn't soon be two.

"How is she?" Peyton was bent over Sarah, examining her.

"Pulse is strong and regular. Pupils look good. The EMTs called it: her femur is broken and it looks like she's got a concussion, judging from the contusion on her forehead." He took a step back. "You want to take a look?"

Mike examined her, paying special attention to her skull. No depressions that he could see, although she did have a huge purple knot forming where the left side of her forehead had hit something hard. "I want a CT before anything is done to her leg, just to be safe."

"You want to order it?"

He wanted to go to Trisha, but his place was here. For now, at least. "Yep." He marked her chart and made the call, going with her to the imaging area. Fifteen minutes later they had their answer. She did have a concussion, but she was already regaining consciousness. Mike accompanied her to her room, where Peyton would see about her leg, and then headed for the waiting room. Her mother had to be frantic.

As soon as she saw him she stood slowly from her chair, the terror in her eyes obvious. He flashed a quick thumbs-up sign just to put her at ease, and she sagged back into her chair, tears running down her cheeks.

"She's got a concussion and her left leg is broken, but she should be fine. They're getting her settled in, and once they do, you can go back to see her, okay?"

"Oh, my God. I was so scared. She wasn't moving, wouldn't answer me." She pushed back a strand of hair with a shaking hand. "Thank you so much."

"You're very welcome. I'll be available if you need me." He jotted down his cellphone number on the back of a business card. "Call me if you have any questions. We'll want to keep her tonight, but I think she'll be able to go home in a day or two. Nothing strenuous until that leg heals."

She nodded. "I'll make sure she rests."

"Any news on her horse?"

"Nothing. Trisha said she'd call as soon as she could."

Those pricking needles went back to work on his scalp. "Where did the accident happen?"

"On Santa Fe Road, near the big water tower."

He knew where that was. His fingers closed around his cellphone. The smart thing would be to simply try to call her again, but that's not what he wanted to do. "I'm sure they're doing all they can for...Laredo, did you say his name was?"

"Yes. I hope you're right. I don't know what I'm going to tell Sarah if she asks."

"Just tell her he's being taken care of. No need to panic her just yet."

One of the nurses appeared in the doorway. "Mrs. Millner, I can take you to see your daughter now, if you'd like."

"Yes." Sarah's mom picked up her purse and headed after the nurse, stopping for a second to thank Mike again.

As soon as she was around the corner, he knew what he was going to do: head for Santa Fe Road.

Trisha pulled her knees up to her chest as she sat on the floor of the empty horse trailer. Where the hell was that tow truck anyway? A police car still sat off to the side, the officer writing up his notes. She could probably leave the scene and let the police take care of it, but she'd promised Sarah's mom she'd stay here.

Now that Laredo was safe and in good hands, she wanted to be at the hospital, making sure Sarah was okay. Every muscle in her body ached from trying to get to the injured horse and free him from the overturned vehicle. They'd ended up having to winch the trailer back into an upright position in order to free him and coax him out.

The poor animal had been racked with tremors so strong he'd barely been able to remain upright as the veterinarian had checked him over for injuries. One knee was swelling, and he had a gash on his right hip. The doctor didn't think either was a debilitating injury, but he wouldn't know for sure until they'd gotten him back to the clinic and taken some X-rays.

The terrified sounds Laredo had made as he'd struggled to free himself would remain with her for the rest of her life. Along with the sight of that car coming through the intersection and slamming into the Millners' car— the way the trailer had wrenched sideways and flipped to the left, almost taking the car over with it. Everything had happened in slow motion as she'd skidded to a halt with a scream.

Covering her face with her hands, she took deep breaths as she struggled to contain the emotions that were tumbling over and over inside her, trying to get out. If she let go now, she doubted she'd be able to stop. She sucked air in through her nose until her lungs were full, and then forced it back out of her mouth in a slow, controlled hiss, just like a jogger headed into his tenth mile.

Find the rhythm, Trisha. Don't think about anything else. In...two, three, four. Out...two, three, four.

On her tenth breath cycle, the sound of an approaching vehicle made her lower her hands and glance up. Not the tow truck she'd been hoping for, but an expensive-looking car. Great. Instead of going past her, though, it slowed then pulled off the road.

She straightened her spine as the face inside the vehicle came into sharp focus.

Mike. What was he doing here?

Her hand went to her chest. Sarah? Had something terrible happened? Scrambling off the trailer, she practically ran to the car. Mike got out and reached for her just as she stumbled into him, pulling her close. "You okay?"

"I'm fine." She leaned back to look at his face. "Sarah? Is she—?"

"She's okay." He eased her cheek back to his shoulder, his left arm looping around her waist. "Her mom's worried about her horse. What in God's name made you promise to try to take care of it?"

Something about the way he said it made her pause.

Of course…his wife had been killed in some kind of accident involving a horse. But *she* wasn't his wife. She wasn't anything to him.

Maybe it was just the impersonal concern that one human being might have for another. "I'm fine, Mike. I had to help. Laredo was…he was terrified. Trapped. How could I just leave him there all alone? I couldn't walk away, any more than you could have walked away from one of your patients."

He didn't say anything, but something brushed lightly across the top of her head. His chin? His lips?

After a minute he asked, "How is he?"

"Banged up and bruised, but the vet thinks he'll recover."

"So he's not out at your place?"

"No."

The warm solidity of his chest beneath her cheek calmed her like nothing else could, the slight lingering scent of his aftershave flooding her senses with each breath. He'd come here to find her. Why? To check on Laredo? Because Sarah's mom was worried about him?

Somehow she didn't think that was it. Why, then?

Maybe it was better not to know. Maybe she should

just enjoy his presence as she waited for the tow truck to arrive.

"You feel a little shaky. Do you want me to take you home?"

She started to shake her head then realized he couldn't see it the way they were standing. "A tow truck is coming for the trailer. And I have my own vehicle."

The last thing she wanted to do was drive, though. Witnessing that accident…seeing an animal in that condition who'd trusted them to keep him safe was one of the worst things she'd ever gone through—almost worse even than finding out who her husband really was. Worse than having to live the rest of her life in hiding. At least she'd had some power over her own destiny, could understand what was going on. Unlike Laredo. Would he ever allow himself to be loaded into a trailer again after this?

The officer evidently wondered what was going on, because he was suddenly there, asking Mike who he was. Mike explained he was a friend, and that he'd come out to check to see if Trisha was okay.

A friend. Huh. She couldn't remember a friend ever kissing her the way he'd kissed her.

He hadn't mentioned Sarah or her mother when he'd addressed the cop. Or even identified himself as a doctor. Had he really just come out to check on her? As if to verify that, his arm tightened around her and she let her eyes shut as she settled closer, glad not to have to deal with any of this for a few precious seconds. The officer didn't ask anything else, so he must have gone back to his car. They stood that way for a little while, and she'd have been content to stay there for the rest of her life. But she couldn't. Even as she thought it, she heard the wheezing sound of an engine in the distance. This time it was the tow truck, she knew that without even having to look.

She took a deep breath and went to take a step back, only to have Mike grip her a little tighter. "Why don't you sit in my car and I'll take care of this?"

"I'm okay. I need to drive to the hospital as soon as the truck leaves. I want to make sure Sarah is okay."

"She is. I promise. The doctor treating her is a friend. I told him to call me if there was any change."

He didn't insist she get into the car, but stood there with her as she spoke to the driver and got the name of the auto body shop they were taking the truck to. The policeman left as soon as the truck did, the officer giving them a half-wave as he pulled back onto the road.

She wasn't sure what she was supposed to do at this point. "Thanks for coming out. I'll let you get back to whatever you were doing."

"I'll follow you to the house."

Tugging free, she looked up at him. "I'm sure you have other responsibilities."

"I was just coming off my shift when I got your call, so I'm free for the rest of the day." He gave a small smile. "I have to admit, when you said there'd been an accident I thought Brutus might have gone berserk again."

That's why he'd sounded strained on the phone. "I don't let my students or patients ride him. I told you that."

"Accidents don't always happen while riding."

The tight words weren't referring to Brutus, or to anything involving her.

"No, they don't." She kept her voice soft, hoping he would volunteer more information, but when he dug his hand into his pants pocket and came out with his car keys, she realized he wasn't going to volunteer anything further. "I'll take you up on that offer to follow me home. I'll even make us some coffee, if you'd like some. Besides, I really do want to hear how Sarah is doing, if you don't mind calling the hospital."

"I don't."

He waited for her to climb into her car and start it up before he moved back to his own vehicle. The ride to her little ranch seemed to take forever, but it probably only lasted fifteen minutes. She pulled in beside the barn, suddenly needing to check on her own little herd and make sure they were okay.

"I'll just be a minute," she called, when Mike powered down his window, his brows raised in question.

She slid the door to the barn open, and went in, checking each stall and rubbing Crow's nose when he leaned his head over the door of his stall in greeting. She breathed in the familiar scents that surrounded her, letting them calm her nerves. It was okay. Sarah was going to be fine. Laredo was in good hands. Her own horses were safe. Reaching up, she circled Crow's neck, horrified to find her eyes had filled to overflowing. "It's going to be okay." The words weren't meant for him, they were meant to reassure herself.

Crow's head went up just as a pair of hands landed on her shoulders. She stiffened for a split second then realized it had to be Mike. Allowing her head to lean back against his chest, she scrubbed her palms beneath her eyes. His arms went around her waist, his chin coming to rest on her right shoulder. She felt surrounded and cared for in a way she hadn't for many, many months. This man had no deep dark secrets. Well, he did have one, but she was pretty sure the rest of the town knew about it. She didn't blame him for not wanting to announce it to every newcomer who wandered into Dusty Hills. Her heart ached for him.

"Are you okay?"

She twisted in his arms until she faced him, splaying her hands on his chest. "I will be. I just had to make sure my guys were safe."

A low chuckle rumbled in his chest. "Your guys, huh?"

She smiled back, her world slowly going back into its right orbit. "What? You didn't know I was surrounded by a horde of hungry admirers—emphasis on the hungry part?"

"Oh, I have no doubts you have plenty of male admirers fighting for your attention."

"Not so many." Most of the men she knew weren't her biggest fans. Not any more. But, then, Mike didn't need to know that. "I lead a pretty boring life, in fact."

"I would have to disagree with you there." One of his hands came up, his fingers sliding into the hair at her nape. "Most of my encounters with you have been anything but boring."

True. And most of those encounters had ended up with her falling into his arms. Literally, at times. And once it had ended up with him kissing her.

The memory of that frantic session in the barn washed over her. She wanted that again…wanted his lips on hers, wanted to forget about the horrors of this afternoon, even if just for a few minutes.

As if he'd read her mind, he tilted her head back until their eyes met. He stared at her for several long seconds as if seeking confirmation of something. Then slowly, far too slowly, his head lowered until his lips touched hers. A shard of longing went through her. This was how it was supposed to be between a man and woman: attraction that built until there was no denying it on either side. At least, not on hers. She was attracted. Had been from almost the moment she'd set eyes on him.

His mouth increased its pressure, the hand in her hair holding her in place, not that she had any intention of moving. To emphasize that point, her hands slid up his chest, and she went up on tiptoe to meet him halfway.

Crow had evidently gotten tired of them, because the sound of munching hay came from somewhere behind her. Or maybe that was her horse's way of grabbing a bowl of popcorn and settling in to watch the show.

And she hoped there would be something to see this time.

If she had anything to do with it, the man was not going to run out on her again. No, he was going to stay right here and make her forget that anything else existed but him, and his mouth on hers. But more than that, she wanted him to finish what he'd started yesterday.

CHAPTER SEVEN

Now wasn't the time for this.

Even as the thought went through his head, his hand tightened in Trisha's hair as if his body was declaring mutiny on all things rational.

She's just had a bad scare, you idiot. You need to back off.

Trisha's fingers, which had been resting on his shoulders, suddenly curled around the back of his neck, gripping tight as if she, too, sensed his thoughts.

Not the actions of a woman who wanted him to take a step or two back.

To test that theory, he changed the angle of his mouth, his body soaking up each new sensation. Her lips were soft, sweet…clinging in all the right ways. Ways that made moving back difficult, if not impossible. Ways that made his body harden and his hands itch to explore. For now, though, he focused his attention on that central point of contact, knowing that it could end at any moment.

Maybe he'd be saved by the bell. But the phone at his hip remained silent, no warning chirp or vibration coming to the rescue.

Trisha's body pressed closer, breasts flattening

against his chest, belly coaxing dangerous reactions from a certain part of his anatomy.

To hell with this.

His arm swept around the small of her back, hauling her fully against him, and the intent of the kiss changed—going from hesitant and exploratory to hard and demanding in an instant. His tongue pierced the space between her lips, delving straight and deep, letting her wet heat bathe him, the quick scrape of her teeth only adding to the sharp pleasure.

A small sound came from her throat. Not a panicked squeak at his sudden invasion, but a low hum that urged him to continue. Asked for more.

A request he was only too happy to grant. Using his body, he backed her against the nearest plank wall and crowded her tight against it, never taking his mouth from hers.

Better. Much better. He no longer had to use his hands to bind her to him, and could send them to other places.

Like her breasts.

His fingertips trailed up her waist until he reached the outer swell, gauging her reaction as he reached the uppermost part. He didn't know about hers, but his body's response was instantaneous at even the hint that he might get to hold the weight of those generous curves. His hips angled in closer, the ache inside growing stronger. He forced his hands to continue higher, strumming along the sides of her neck, her whimper and her slight lift onto tiptoe signaling that she wanted his hands back where they had been.

He mentally sought out his wallet…found it in his back pocket, cursing himself for slipping a little something in there after their last encounter. He'd mentally flogged himself for doing so, but had worried about what might happen if things ever got more out of hand. That lack of protection had saved him the last time, but he'd worried about the next. Except that meant that he was even less likely to call a halt to things now.

As if testifying to that fact, he took one step back. Not to stop what he was doing but to do more. His mouth came off hers as his hands retraced their steps with aching slowness. He reached her breasts, but instead of continuing down the sides and heading back to his starting point he took a detour, fingers sliding toward the middle, encountering nipples that were already tight with need.

Trisha's eyelids fluttered shut and her head fell back against the barn wall behind her. She moaned when he allowed his thumbs to linger, passing back and forth over the center of her breasts. She had a bra on, he'd bumped over the edges of it a few seconds earlier, but it was evidently thin, because he could feel everything: the soft fullness; the warmth; that tempting pebbled nipple. In fact, he could go just like this… He curved his right hand, and she filled it to overflowing, arching her back and pressing herself into his touch.

Yes. He squeezed, his other thumb never stopping its sweeping motions.

Her teeth dug into her lower lip, then her eyes opened and she gave a fair imitation of a glare as she settled back against the wall beside Crow's stall. "If you run away again, I'll chase you down and make you finish this."

Run away?

Oh, when he'd left last time.

He gave her a slow smile that he hoped got across his

meaning. "I wasn't prepared last time. This time I've got everything I need."

"I'll say." Her brows went up, and her hips rotated forward until she found him.

She wasn't some shrinking violet, he'd say that for her. And that made him even hotter.

He bent, pressing his lips to her neck and biting his way down to her shoulder. She squirmed against him and her fingers curled into his hair, gripping as he continued his quest. Then he was there, wet mouth meeting dry T-shirt-covered nipple and sucking it.

"Ah!" Her handhold on his hair tightened as she arched into his mouth, and he imagined the sensation arrowing straight to her center. Which, if it felt anything like his needy flesh did right now, was kicking up a racket about being ignored. And he did have one free hand...

The waistband of her jeans was snug, but not so tight that he couldn't ease beneath it...like so. Or so tight that he couldn't make his way over the front of her panties— lace, if the texture was anything to go by.

What color?

He bit down on her nipple, hearing her pant near his ear as he held it prisoner, laving his tongue over it. His fingers reached the heat at the juncture of her thighs and everything in his mind scrambled, like a brain suddenly bombarded with too many electrical impulses. The woman's panties were already moist. Wet, in fact. If they were both naked, he could just thrust into that slick channel...and be squeezed into oblivion.

But he might not even make it that far, if he didn't shut down that line of thought.

He allowed himself the luxury of sliding his fingers

over her panties, absorbing the gentle bumps and dips that went along with being a woman.

A sharp pain went through his scalp as Trisha suddenly yanked his hair, pulling his head up. "If you don't get this show on the road, I promise you it's going to come crashing to a halt."

Crashing to a halt?

One hand down her pants and the other still on her breast, he blinked at the hint of warning in her tone. He took in her flushed cheeks. Dilated pupils. Uneven breaths.

Maybe she didn't mean crashing to a halt as in she was going to stop him. Maybe she meant crashing as in…exploding.

To test his hypothesis, he rippled his fingertips lightly over the surface of her panties. Her hips jerked forward in response, and she gasped. "Mike, please. You're going to be sorry in a few seconds if you don't stop. I need to get your clothes off."

Her hands left his hair and gripped handfuls of his shirt, tugging, trying to haul it out of his slacks.

Entranced by her frantic movements, he decided to be the devil that realized her worst fear. And he could guarantee he wouldn't be sorry. Not in a million years. Not if the world crashed down on top of him in the next couple of minutes.

Taking his hand from her breast, he caught one of her wrists and then the other, jerking them both away from his shirt and carrying them up over her head. He held them there, his lips curving up in a smile.

"Wh-what are you doing?"

He leaned forward and whispered against her ear. "What do you think I'm doing?" His middle finger trailed along the elastic edge of her panties then ducked beneath it. Her skin was softer than he could have believed. He moved along her folds, getting closer.

"No!" She struggled. "I want you inside me."

His erection jumped at the offer. One he had to refuse. For now.

"Oh, honey, don't worry, I will be. Right about…" his finger pushed inside her in a smooth gliding motion "…now."

She clamped down on him the second he entered her, just like he'd known she would.

"That's not what I meant." Her throaty moan hit his ears, just as her legs parted and she pushed herself further onto him, her body at war with her words.

"Didn't anyone ever tell you you should always say what you mean?" He added another finger, his thumb circling up to find her clit. "Or you could get into deep trouble."

Just like he was. He struggled to hang back from the edge of a steep cliff, even as he worked to push her over it. He wanted to enjoy her climax. Wanted to watch her break apart, holding his own need in check.

Maybe Trisha realized she wasn't going to get her way, or maybe she was just too far gone to care, but her hips rocked forward and back in time with the rhythm of his fingers. It was heady to see her there, fully clothed, arms pinned over her head…a prisoner of his hands and her own passions.

God, she was gorgeous.

He leaned in and bit her lip, before backing away to watch her again. Her eyes were shut tight. Mouth slightly open. Head tipped back against the wall. He doubted she'd even felt that love bite he'd just given her. Well, he bet she'd feel this.

He quickened the pace of his thumb.

Five seconds later he had his answer when her body stiffened, hips moving, moving, moving into his touch. A sharp cried rang out, a horse whinnying in response from one of the stalls, then the walls surrounding his fingers squeezed impossibly tight before releasing again, setting off a series of contractions that had him praying for mercy as he thought about what was in store for him.

His mouth watered, taking in every gasped breath, every muttered word as he continued to move his fingers, slowing the pace as he eased her back down to earth. She finally slumped forward and he released her wrists, his arm coming around her back to support her.

"Oh, God." The whispered words passed over his neck, the warm air no match for the inferno currently raging within his body. She kissed the skin just below his ear. "I told you you'd be sorry."

Was she serious?

"Oh, I'm not sorry. Don't think I am, not even for a second." He smiled, and held her in his arms. "But you may be, as soon as you point me toward the nearest horizontal surface that's not covered in muck."

She laughed, a low throaty sound that went straight to his groin. "What's the matter, cowboy? Do you have something against vertical surfaces? Or are you just vertically challenged?"

With that, she wrapped her fingers around his arms and turned him, until it was him with his back against the warm plank wall she'd just occupied. And then she slowly sank to her knees in front of him.

* * *

She was about to exact her revenge. She'd cursed and railed at him inside her head when he'd gotten hold of her hands, and she'd realized what he was about to do. Seconds later, she hadn't much cared, as long as he made those delicious sensations continue. Now she was replete and satisfied and wanted to give back to him. But she wanted to make him suffer. Just a little.

"Trisha—"

"Shh." Her fingers went to the button on his slacks, and she peered up at him as she popped it open. "I may not be strong enough to hold your hands together, like you did mine, but I have a whole lot of leather in this barn. I bet I can find something that would work." The image of a pair of thin supple reins wrapped round and round Mike's wrists, suspending his arms high over his head as she had her way with him flashed through her mind.

To block it out, she eased his zipper down. She'd wanted him inside her, well, now was her chance. It wasn't quite the way she'd envisioned the scene, but sometimes you had to work with what you had, and what she had was...

Her eyes widened at what she found in front of her, and her glance flew up to meet Mike's, noting the quick beat of a muscle in his cheek, the molten look of pure lust. She tugged and pulled on his slacks until they slid down around his ankles. Then slowly she reached up and peeled down his underwear.

Oh, man.

"Trisha." This time there was some kind of desperate plea in his voice. One she recognized. She'd felt the same desperation a few minutes ago.

Opening her mouth, she let her tongue slide slowly over him, letting the taste of his skin wash over her and fill her senses. She'd barely started before a pair of hands dragged her to her feet.

Hard eyes burned into hers. "That's not how this is going to go down."

Keeping hold of her arm, he kicked off his shoes, stepped out of his clothes and reached down to scoop up his pants. Shaking his wallet loose from his back pocket, he flipped it open.

"Condom."

"Let me go, and you can get it."

He shook his head. "I don't trust you for a second. Reach in and get it out."

That whisper at the back of her head was getting louder. Telling her that maybe she hadn't missed out after all. That maybe he'd been right, because the way she was feeling, she might just be capable of pulling a rabbit out of a hat.

Or at least a condom out of a wallet.

She peeked into the main section and caught sight of a foil packet, right next to a hundred-dollar bill—there was a small wad of bills, in fact. A trickle of something went down her spine before it drifted away again. She grabbed the condom, and Mike let the wallet fall to the ground, some of those bills spilling from it. All hundreds.

Right now she didn't care how much money the man did or didn't have. She only wanted one thing.

This time he did let go of her, and she opened the packet—on her first try!—and started to hand it to him. Only to have him shake his head and curve both hands over her breasts and squeeze gently. A familiar shaft of need bloomed in her belly and spread outward. Downward.

"My hands are full," he murmured.

And hers were now shaking, but somehow she managed to get it out of the package and roll it over him.

The second it was on, he used his grip on her breasts to reverse their positions—she was back against the wall. Mike yanked off his shirt and then reached for hers, pulling it off in one smooth move. Her pants and boots followed, leaving her standing there in her bra and underwear.

"Red. Very nice. I expected something plain and simple."

She glanced down, noting he was staring at her bra and underwear. Both lacy and red, neither doing much to conceal her from his view. "You'd prefer granny panties?"

"Honey, right now I'd take you in long johns. But I am going to take you."

The intensity behind his voice set off a firestorm of want. All over again.

"I thought you wanted a horizontal surface," she said, the breathiness in her voice sounding strange and alien.

"And I remember you questioning my abilities with regard to vertical ones." With that, he slid his hands down her hips and grasped the back of each of her thighs, just below her butt, and hauled her up. "So wrap your legs around me and get ready to hold on tight."

She tightened her legs and he walked a step or two, until the planks were at her back again. He pulled aside the elastic of her panties, until she felt him at her entrance. He then bit back a short curse—or maybe it was a prayer?—and burst into her in a single powerful thrust.

The impact of their bodies colliding sent the air whistling from her lungs as he entered her again and again. Her position gave her no control over the depth or speed, and it drove her wild to have him finally take what he wanted from her. And he wanted it deep. Mind-shatteringly deep.

He stopped suddenly, still inside her, one hand beneath her right thigh. He planted the other flat against the wall next to her shoulder. Her calves tightened when he continued to stand there motionless.

"Are—are you done?"

Oh, Lord, she hoped not.

"Are you serious?" He surged forward as if to show her exactly how wrong she was. "But I forgot about the wood. Is it hurting your back?"

"Are *you* serious?" Okay, yes, she was probably going to have some serious abrasions and maybe a splinter or two, but all she knew was that he was mashing just the right spot. She wiggled on his length, contracting her muscles and letting the hot sensation of fullness wash over her.

He let out another groaned curse. "Now that that's settled..." He planted his mouth on hers and thrust his tongue into her mouth, then he followed it with his body, a kind of echo and response that had her closing her eyes and doing as he'd suggested—holding on tight.

Again and again, his pelvic bone hitting that bud of sensitive tissue with each pass. Mouth...pelvis... mouth...pelvis. Between the two of them something was always in motion, leaving her no time to snatch a breath or pause to recover. Instead, the whine of tension inside her grew more shrill with each dueling cadence until it reached the top rung of the scale and held like an

opera singer on that final shrieking note of the climax.
Her fingernails dug into Mike's shoulders harder than
she could have dreamed possible as an explosion from
inside her body obliterated all sound. In a vacuum of
silence she fell and fell, even as Mike's mouth left hers
and she sensed him shouting, the veins standing out in
his neck even as she continued her rapid descent.

A few seconds passed before a few vague sounds
filtered back through her eardrums. Then a forehead
pressed to hers. Their breathing wasn't in sync, but random snatches of air said he was as affected as she was.

Lord. That was…that was…

There were no words.

She flattened her fingers on his shoulders, hoping
she hadn't broken the skin.

Mike took a step back, still holding her, and allowed
her legs to slide back to the earth as he eased from her.

Swallowing, she tried to recover her scattered
thoughts, just as Mike's low voice intruded. "Are you
okay?"

Was she?

She had no idea. Although she suspected that if his
arm wasn't behind her back, supporting her, she'd probably fall down in a heap.

She hoped she hadn't broken something.

That "something' now included more than the skin
on his shoulders.

She sincerely hoped she hadn't just broken her
own heart.

CHAPTER EIGHT

MIKE DISLIKED TWO things in life: lies…and horses.

He leaned back in his chair and tossed his pencil onto the desk.

He could swear that brute horse of hers had glared at him yesterday as he'd exited the barn post haste. But the glassy-eyed look Trisha had given him as he'd asked her if she was okay had spooked him. Or had it been the sex?

Yeah, that's what it was. The two women he'd been with in the weeks after his wife's death had seemed happy with quick animalistic mating sessions. Sessions that had left him unmoved. A tiny part of him wondered if the sex had been his way of getting revenge on his wife for what she'd done behind his back. Cheating on her memory, the way she'd cheated on him. That fact had upped the guilt he'd felt afterwards, because she was no longer there to debate the issue, or tell her side of the story.

His time with Trisha hadn't been about revenge. Not at all. In fact, it had been…

Something else. Something he didn't want to examine. And most certainly something he didn't want to repeat.

She'd pulled back from him quickly, grabbing her

clothes and yanking them on. Her shirt had been inside out when she'd finished, but he hadn't been about to tell her that, and Trisha hadn't seemed to notice. She'd given him a quick smile and asked if he'd be there for Clara's session on Thursday. When he'd stepped forward with an outstretched hand to touch her, she'd taken a quick step back and waved him away. "I've got to get back to work."

As if what they'd done hadn't left her legs shaking like it had his.

Vertical spaces should be outlawed.

Because never had he lifted a woman onto his hips and slammed her against a wall, thinking about nothing but getting as close as he could—until about halfway through, when a flash of something rational had made him wonder if he was peeling the skin off her back with each thrust.

She had assured him he wasn't.

He dragged a hand through his hair before tipping his head back and staring at the ceiling. In all his thirty-four years he couldn't remember feeling this bone-rattling need for a woman.

Not even Marcy.

That first kiss in the arena had built this whole thing up in his mind until it had become a train wreck, just waiting for the opportunity to career into the nearest... wall.

He laughed. He had to stop thinking about that barn wall. And slamming into it again and again.

He blew out a rough breath and turned his attention back to his desk, seeing the framed photo he kept there as a reminder. Marcy and her horse. Another train wreck waiting to happen. Why couldn't the local hippotherapist's name be Raul, or Beefy Bones Bart.

Why the hell had it been Trisha who'd landed on his doorstep, with her smile and her saucy comments?

Maybe this time would be different.

Different how? He'd known Marcy his whole life, yet in the end he'd found he hadn't known her at all.

He didn't even know where Trisha was from. In fact, she'd been evasive about everything from her references—which she never had given him, like she'd promised—to where she'd lived in the past. He couldn't help but feel she was hiding something. She hadn't volunteered one scrap of information that he hadn't asked for, and even then her answers had been purposely vague. Or was he just being paranoid because of Marcy?

Just as he was about to get up to go on another set of rounds, his phone rang.

If that was her…

Nope, his readout said R. Chapman. Ray. Nothing to do with Trisha. He frowned. Unless there'd been another accident.

His heart started pounding, despite the ridiculousness of the idea. "Hi, Ray, what's up?"

"Just checking in, like I said I would. Your hippotherapist doesn't have any open warrants. Or any convictions that I could find."

Mike was lost for a second, before he remembered he'd asked the sheriff to check on Trisha. The whole thing seemed preposterous and paranoid now. Kind of like this constant gnawing worry. Then his friend's tone came through. It was off somehow.

"What is it?"

"Nothing. I didn't find anything of concern."

A wave of foreboding rolled through him. "Come on, Ray. These are my patients we're talking about. If you know something and one of them gets hurt because you held out on me, you and I are going to have a serious problem."

There was a pause, and Mike could imagine his friend struggling with all the ethical ramifications of his job. "I'm only telling you this because you could find the same information online, if you looked. Her certifications don't hold up. At least, not under the name Patricia Bolton."

"What?" The realization hit his stomach with a sickening thud. "Maybe she's listed under Trisha."

"There are a few Boltons, but the addresses don't match. Do you know where she lived before Dusty Hills?"

No. Because she'd refused to give him any references that weren't from her current location. He'd sensed something was wrong from the moment he'd asked. The memory of her fear during their first meeting came back…the way she'd held that curved tool. "No idea. Can you give me some numbers to call?"

"I can, but you won't find anything. It's as if she's a ghost. You can follow her trail for a while. It'll even lead you on a merry little chase, over a few hills, around a few curves, but after a while it just peters out cold. Her plates come up, but they list an address in Reno—only that address doesn't exist. Same thing with her driver's license."

"What the hell?" He only realized the words came out as a shout when his door opened and his receptionist peeked inside the office. He waved her away with what he hoped was a reassuring smile but which felt more like a snarling twist of lips. As soon as the door closed again, he focused on what Ray was saying. "What does it mean?"

"I have no idea. Could be she's a felon on the run who changed her name. Or a battered wife hiding from her husband. Maybe those guys who came to town with her that day were helping her get away from something."

Crap. He had just had sex with a possible felon? Perfect. Only Trisha didn't feel like a criminal.

As if you would know. Then again, four years ago he would have sworn his wife was faithful and true.

He didn't know anything right now. Like whether he should let his old friend know he'd been consorting with her.

Consorting. He let out an audible snort.

"What?" Ray had evidently heard him. "Something I should know?"

What if Trisha really was married? The horse trainer who'd had an affair with his wife hadn't known she'd had a husband—he'd been as shocked as Mike had been to find out the truth. A creeping sense of nausea wove through his gut.

Was Trisha pulling one over on him? She had a class ring on that finger, but what if she wore it to hide the mark left by a gold band? "You didn't happen to find out if she was married, did you?"

"Nope." There was a pause. "Mike. Tell me you didn't. I told you not to get involved with her."

He wanted to tell his friend he hadn't. But he'd gone out there with a condom in his wallet. If that wasn't premeditation, he didn't know what was. As much as he might try to rationalize this thing, the evidence was there. He'd known there was a possibility he might sleep with her.

But what if she'd lied to him? About more than just her marital status?

It made the flip playfulness that he'd thought was so hot take on a more sinister tone. Like a taunt from the serpent in the garden.

Are you vertically challenged?

"Mike. You there?"

"Yeah." He shifted away from his friend's original question. "Just a little shocked. She wanted to treat some of my patients, so now I don't know what to think. Thanks for letting me know. I think I need to have a long talk with the lady in question."

"Don't do anything stupid."

Too late for that. But he could start playing this thing a whole lot smarter from here on out.

"I'll keep that in mind, Ray."

As soon as he got off the phone, his gaze fell on his wife's picture. Reaching for it, stared at it…ran his fingers over the cold glass covering Marcy's face. He'd loved her, no matter what she'd done.

Maybe it had been up to him to talk to her, to make sure she was happy. But he'd been so busy with his work back then, he'd barely had time to stop and breathe, let alone sit down and really listen to his wife.

Would you have told me, if I'd asked?

Whether the telepathic question reached her or not, he had no way of knowing. All he knew was that there was a fierce burning in his chest that had nothing to do with lust right now. He knew what he had to do tomorrow at Clara Trimble's hippotherapy session.

He was going to ask, and hope he received answers to a few very important questions.

And if he didn't like what he heard?

His jaw tightened until it was a mass of tense ligaments and hard muscle. If she lied to him again, he was going to withdraw his recommendation for Clara's treatment. And then he was going to make sure everyone in town knew that Patricia Bolton was a liar and a fraud.

"How are you feeling, honey?" Trisha tucked back a strand of Sarah's hair, glancing again at the door to her student's hospital room and praying Mike didn't come sweeping in. She still didn't know how she was going to face him after what they'd done yesterday. Trisha had once considered herself a happy person who liked to laugh and have fun. That had all changed when she'd discovered who her husband was. His accusations about her sleeping with the hired help…her shock when Roger had shot the man in cold blood.

In fact, she hadn't felt happy in a long, long time. Until yesterday.

She'd just started letting her hair down in Dusty Hills after six long months of being vigilant—of fearing for the safety of her family. But nothing had happened in the days following her husband's conviction. Maybe it was time for her to stop being so afraid and finally start living her life again.

But did she really have to start out by having wild sex in the barn? Her teeth came together, grinding a time or two as she remembered those heated moments. Had she really called him vertically challenged?

Yeah. She had. And it was pretty much the best thing

she'd ever done in her life. Her jaws relaxed, and her mouth curved.

"I'm doing okay," Sarah said, bringing her back to the present. "Still hurts quite a bit." She struggled to shift higher in her bed, and Trisha hurried to help her get comfortable. "Have you heard anything about how Laredo's doing?"

She'd meant to check on him yesterday, but had wound up in Mike's arms instead. She'd ended up calling the vet that morning. "He's a little banged up, just like you. But you'll both be fine before you know it."

At least, she hoped so. Once Laredo was strong enough to be loaded into a trailer without being tranquilized, like he had at the scene of the accident, would he do so willingly?

Maybe he'd bounce right back, like she seemed to be doing lately. She hadn't thought of her ex and what he might or might not do for the last week or so. How convenient that it was right about the time she'd started getting to know a certain sexy neurosurgeon. From whom she hadn't heard a peep. Not since their encounter. She glanced again at the door.

Maybe he was feeling as awkward as she was and wasn't sure what to say to her.

She couldn't imagine Mike having random bouts of shyness. Not after what he'd done to her—after what he'd said.

Then again, she'd said some pretty wild things herself. She'd die if he ever repeated them to anyone.

He won't. He's not the kind to kiss and tell.

As if she were an expert on what the man would or wouldn't say—or any man, for that matter. Everything about Roger-slash-Viktor had been a lie.

Just like your life here in Dusty Hills.

Except she wasn't a killer.

But she was a liar. *Only out of necessity.*

The door behind her opened, and Trisha turned, expecting to see Sarah's mom, who'd stepped out to call a few relatives and give them an update. Instead, it was the last person she wanted to see right now.

Heat flooded her face and she opened her mouth to greet him, only to find that nothing came out. She snapped her jaws shut and settled for nodding to him instead.

He didn't say anything to her at first, just chatted with Sarah about how she was doing. Still not looking Trisha's way, he flipped through his patient's chart, asking questions as he perused whatever was written there.

He finally turned toward her. "Ms. Bolton, I didn't expect to see you here today."

Uh-oh. Last name. Not a good sign. Maybe because it was a public place, and he wanted to maintain an appearance of professionalism. That was a possibility... except for the heavy layer of frost she now sensed in the room. "Sarah's my student, and I care about her. Where else would I be?"

A beat or two passed as he studied her, eyes narrowed. "I wouldn't know, actually."

What was that supposed to mean?

She shook herself. Time to stop second-guessing every word that came out of his mouth. He was probably doing exactly the same thing with her. Maybe she should try to ease the awkwardness. Or lay the reason for it on the table and see what he did. "So what did you do yesterday? Anything interesting?"

Holding her breath, she watched his reaction. Right

on cue, a dark wave of red washed up his neck and into his face. But not even that made him break into a smile. "I did all kinds of things. Made a few phone calls… learned some things I didn't know."

Things about her? The frost in the room seeped into her soul. "What kinds of things?"

He shrugged. "Things that are best left for a later discussion. Know this: my patients' well-being is very important to me." Pointedly glancing in Sarah's direction, Trisha noted that, despite her pain medication, she was looking at them with open curiosity.

He was right. This wasn't the time to discuss what had happened. But why was he warning her about his patients? Did he think she would do something to compromise that?

Or worse, did he think she'd had sex with him expecting to receive those referrals in return? The thoughts she'd had after that first kiss came back to haunt her.

Surely not! But the sooner she cleared that up, the better. She stood and crossed over to Sarah, kissing her on the cheek. "I need to go back to the barn and take care of the horses, and I have another student this afternoon. But I'll be back in the morning, okay?"

Sarah nodded and gave a huge yawn. Poor thing. The teenager had to be exhausted, and here she was having to listen to her and Mike lobbing obscure comments back and forth.

She walked out of the room, not looking behind her. Mike had evidently followed her, because her name rang out above the noise of the busy hospital floor. "Hold up for a second."

Halting in her spot, she waited for him to continue. He did better than that, however, he circled in front of her. "We do need to talk about a few things, and I have some questions."

"I can stop off for some coffee at the cafeteria, if you want to join me."

A cool smile met her invitation. "I don't think you want anyone overhearing this particular conversation."

Oh, God, it *was* about their encounter yesterday. That was the only discussion she could think of that he'd want to keep quiet. He either regretted what they'd done—*really* regretted it—or she was right on her more paranoid imaginings that he thought she was after something and was using sex to get it.

She *had* been after something. His body. Nothing more.

A faint whisper wove through the back of her skull. She ignored it, drawing herself upright. "Okay. So where do you want to discuss this—whatever *this* is?"

"How about after Clara Trimble's session? I'd like to observe her."

"Fine. I don't have any more patients scheduled afterward."

A glimmer of something that might have been anger went through his eyes. "Speaking of patients, how is your client list looking these days?"

She gulped down a ball of dismay.

Stall, Trisha, until you know what this is about. "It's about where I'd expect it to be for someone who's only been here for six months."

A couple of blips sounded from his phone. He glanced at the readout, then back up at her. "There's an emergency. I need to go. I'll see you at Clara's session."

She murmured a goodbye and watched him stride

down the hallway. Then she turned and headed toward the nearest exit, stepping into the hot Nevada sunshine.

But even the bright day couldn't chase away the storm clouds that rolled around inside her, clouds that were growing blacker by the minute. She had a feeling that things between her and Mike were about to take a drastic turn.

Scratch that. From the look on his face as they'd stood outside of Sarah's room, they already had.

The only question was why.

"What have we got?"

The gurney stopped just long enough for Mike to peer beneath one eyelid of the unconscious accident victim and then the other, before they continued to move quickly toward the surgical suite. Pupils were equal and reactive, but there was an obvious knot on the left side of the victim's skull.

"Ten-year-old male with a fractured pelvis and right wrist, as well as possible ruptured spleen. That's a pretty nasty lump on his head, so we're probably looking at a concussion as well," Peyton recited. "Fell while trying to retrieve a kite from a tree. Met a few branches on the way down. His mother's on her way."

Crap. Kids always thought they were impervious to harm, venturing further and further into the danger zone until it was too late.

Yeah, well, he might as well point that finger right back at himself. He'd ventured into dangerous territory several times recently. It looked like it had finally caught up with him. Trisha had gazed at him with those big green eyes as if she didn't have a clue what he was talking about.

Good try, lady. He couldn't wait to see her face when she realized she'd gotten caught in a web of lies.

If they really were lies. Maybe Ray had been wrong. Maybe she was who she said she was but simply hadn't shown up on his friend's databases.

The day of their first meeting came back to him. Maybe it really was an abusive ex. In which case his anger was totally off base.

He couldn't help but think it was more than that, however.

"Want me to scrub up for surgery?" he asked Peyton.

"We need to get the internal bleeding under control first, but stay close to the hospital for the next couple of hours."

"I'm on duty until eleven. Just give me a yell as soon as you're ready for my evaluation."

The other doctor took hold of the side of the bed and quickened his pace. "Will do. I'll keep you in the loop."

Two hours later Mike was back at the patient's bedside in Recovery, going over the results of the CT scan. Dexter Barkley had a linear skull fracture about three centimeters long as well as a concussion, but there were no active brain bleeds and the swelling was under control with meds. Sporting a cast on his wrist, the kid had been lucky in that his fractured pelvis had been stable enough to be managed without surgery, although it had taken a couple of hours in the ER to repair the damage to his spleen and wrist.

Poor kid. The next several weeks weren't going to be a picnic. The funny thing was, if he hadn't known what to look for, he'd have sworn Dexter had escaped with just a bump on the noggin and a little arm cast. But, as these things often were, there had been a lot more going on just below the surface, in places you couldn't see without specialized equipment.

Like Trisha? She looked perfectly normal on the surface. But what was beneath that playful, sexy facade?

He tried to shake free of that thought. He'd thought of the hippotherapist far too often this afternoon. He could only hope Clara's session brought some answers. Ones that could put his mind at ease.

And if it turned out to be a false alarm, what then? Was he going to go on as if nothing had ever happened between them?

A little voice inside of him said that's exactly what he should do. Rewind the clock and start over—make sure she knew that he wasn't interested in a relationship or anything else…horizontal or vertical.

He rolled his eyes, because as soon as he'd gotten home from the barn yesterday he'd retrieved a box from his medicine cabinet and plucked out a foil-wrapped packet. Into his wallet it had gone. He was aware of its presence with every step he took—and every time he took money out to pay for something. There it was, winking up at him like an omen of things to come.

Oh, yeah. The genie was not only out of the bottle, he was currently vacationing on a sunny little beach in the Bahamas with no return date in sight.

That left Mike with a big problem. He wanted Trisha again. Seeing her that morning had driven a fist to his gut and left him winded. He still couldn't quite catch his breath. He could always say "one more time" and hope that would be the end of it, but he knew better. As soon as he'd had her, he'd want her again. And again.

Despite what she might or might not be hiding.

CHAPTER NINE

TRISHA'S PALMS MOISTENED for the hundredth time as she slowly led Crow around the outside edge of the round pen.

Pressing her left hand against the soft fabric of her worn jeans to blot it, she prayed Mike didn't notice how nervous she was. So far the therapy session had gone without a hitch. Clara hadn't cried or been frightened as they'd placed her on the horse's back. And right now, with Penny walking alongside the child and murmuring encouraging words, it looked like any other successful treatment program.

Except for the man standing on the other side of the fence, watching them with brooding eyes. He'd briefly spoken to Clara's mom, but they now stood on opposite sides of the pen, not because Doris had moved away but because Mike had.

As they neared his location, Trisha's heart rate sped up, as it had every other time they'd passed him. This was ridiculous. It wasn't as if this man could make or break her business. Even if he refused to refer any more patients to her, she'd just go to someone else. Someone in one of the other nearby towns. Surely there were doctors who'd worked with equine therapists before.

Mike wasn't the only neurologist on the block.

She drew to a halt alongside him and forced her voice into what she hoped was a calm but confident tone. "Any questions so far?" She glanced at Penny, who was currently showing Clara how to thank the large animal.

"None that I can think of. At least, none that involve Clara." He gave a small wave to the child, who was now grinning widely at him. "Nice to see you really do make everyone say thank you. I thought I was a special case."

He *was* a special case. And he made her chest ache in a way she didn't understand. But she needed to keep this as casual as possible. The man still hadn't thawed completely. But he'd at least lightened up a little bit. That had to be something, right?

"Like I told you, everyone deserves a thank-you every once in a while." She smiled at her assistant. "Do you want to trade places?"

Penny shook her head. "I'm fine. Besides, Clara's my new buddy." The child reached up with her good arm and patted her black riding helmet, her tiny hand making a slapping sound. Penny guided her fingers back to the straps attached to the front of the saddle. "Don't forget to hold on. Crow's going to start walking in a minute."

A soft cluck to let the horse know they were ready, and the team moved away, stopping on the other side of the ring to speak with Clara's mother, who seemed delighted with how active a role her child was taking. "I've haven't seen her this interested in anything in months. Remind me to thank Dr. Dunning for giving us the okay."

A half-hour later Trisha and Penny lifted Clara from the special saddle and set her on the ground next to the horse, supporting her between the two of them. Crow's head swept down and around, blowing softly through his nostrils when Clara held out her hand. Mike watched from a distance, his hands gripping the rail of the fence. Soon Penny led Crow away to get his well-deserved rub-down and a flake of hay and the barn emptied out as Doris loaded her daughter into the van and pulled out of the driveway. Larry came out of one of the stalls and, after glancing their way, made himself scarce, maybe sensing something was up.

And it was. Mike had evidently not forgotten what-ever it was he wanted to discuss with her, because he said, "Let's walk."

"Okay. We can go to the house. I have some lemon-ade made, if you want some." She was not above ply-ing him with drink, even if it was the sans alcohol kind.

"Thanks. That sounds good."

As they headed out of the barn, she tried once again to assess his mood, but the man was locked tight. He wasn't quite as icy as he'd been at the hospital, but there was still a tension in his neck and shoulders that made her nervous. Her uneasiness increased when she invited him inside the house and he opted to remain on the porch instead, hands shoved deep in his pockets, while she went to fetch the lemonade.

Afraid of being alone with her?

Well, Penny and Larry would be leaving soon so, inside the house or outside, they would still be on their own. Maybe it was better to get whatever was on his mind out in the open.

Setting the tray with their drinks on a white wicker table flanked by a couple of matching chairs, she eased into the one across from him. "So," she said, picking up one of the glasses and taking a quick sip, "what did you think of the session?"

"Impressive. But that's not what I want to talk to you about."

"Okay. Let's hear it." If he apologized for their time together, he might just end up wearing his lemonade instead of drinking it.

Mike leaned back in his chair and took a long pull from his glass, swallowing with powerful movements of his throat. He then set the remainder on the table and leaned forward, planting his elbows on his knees. His eyes held hers without blinking. "Who are you?"

The words were soft. Even. With no hint of anger or irritation behind them.

"Excuse me?" Her mind scrambled away from the question, looking for a logical explanation that didn't mean what she thought it did. She'd assumed he wanted to talk to her about what had happened between them in the barn. Instead, it might be about something worse. Much worse.

His gaze never wavered. "You heard me. Who are you?"

She licked her lips, deciding to set her own drink down before she dropped it. A tremor went through her. She'd assumed she was safe. Had Roger somehow contacted him—or someone who worked for him? "I—I don't know what you mean."

"Let's start with your full name."

Oh, God, it *was* what she thought it was. "You already know my name."

"No. I know the name you gave me. And I remember asking for references from your past. You made excuses, if I remember right."

The Feds had warned her about keeping the same job. But it would have been the same no matter what profession she chose. Somewhere along the line someone would want to know where she'd lived, what she'd done, who she'd worked for in her past. What was she going to do? She could call her contacts and ask them to move her again pronto.

And the next time this happened? Was she going to call them every time she got spooked, or each time someone got a little too close to the truth? Was she going to run like a criminal for the rest of her life?

If that's what it took to keep her family safe. Yes.

"I have your references in the house. Let me get them." But this time she couldn't quite meet his eyes when she said it.

"I *trusted* you with my patients' lives."

That stung. And he was right. He'd trusted her to be who she'd said she was.

"I promise you, I am a licensed physical therapist and hippotherapist."

"So you've said. But there's no record of a Patricia Bolton on any of those registries."

He hadn't raised his voice. Not once. And yet every word licked at her flesh like a cat-o'-nine-tails.

"Y-you checked?"

He shifted in his chair. "Can you blame me?"

"No." If she could slip between the wooden planks on her porch she would. No matter what the Feds said, she'd lied to this man. Had put his patients in danger, for all he knew…although he'd let her go ahead with Clara's session, so he must have some doubts about what he was accusing her of.

"When we first talked, something didn't quite seem

right, so I asked Sheriff Chapman to do a quick background check. Turns out your name is—"

"You know what it is?" Panic flushed through her system in a torrent, robbing her lungs of air, her brain of thought. When she finally remembered to breathe, it came in with an awful wheezing gasp that she couldn't seem to control. Mike's face zoomed out and then back in.

"Hey." He was crouched beside her in an instant, pushing her head down between her knees. "Take slow breaths…in…out…"

He kept murmuring, but she couldn't focus on anything except what she needed to do. Who had the sheriff told? Who had he asked? Had the information traveled back to the prison in Virginia? Not even her mom or her brother knew where she was.

"Trisha." His hands cupped her cheeks and he made her look at him. "You need to slow your breathing or you're going to pass out."

She realized she was still pulling in air at an alarming rate and her whole body was trembling. The last thing she wanted to do was wind up in a hospital bed where anyone could get to her. Meeting Mike's eyes, she allowed him to direct her when to breathe, even though her chest was burning and the panic inside her threatened to swallow her whole. She blanked everything out except the sound of his voice. The world slowly came back into focus.

Blinking, she found his worried gaze on her. "Welcome back," he said.

She drew a careful breath. "Sorry. I don't know what happened."

"What the hell is going on, Trisha? Did someone threaten you? Hurt you?"

Yes. Her husband. In more ways than one. It dawned on her that Mike hadn't exactly said he knew what her name was. She'd just blurted out the question before he'd even finished his sentence. It would be so easy to say yes, that someone had beat her time and time again until she'd finally run away. But she couldn't bring herself to add one more lie onto the heap.

"No." She squeezed his hands then let go. "I'm okay, thank you."

She waited until he got back into his seat before asking, "What did the sheriff say?"

"That your identity is a little thin." He hesitated. "Are you running from the law?"

That got a laugh out of her. No, she was running *because* of the law. Because someone else had done some very bad stuff, and she'd been forced into hiding. The price to pay for making a huge mistake and trusting someone you shouldn't.

I trusted you with my patients' lives.

No wonder he'd checked up on her. If she'd done the same thing before getting involved with Roger, she'd have probably saved herself and the people around her a whole lot of heartache. And she never would have met Mike, or Sarah, or Clara, or any of the other people she was coming to love— *Yikes!* To care for.

Care. For.

While she did love Sarah and Clara and her other clients, she didn't love Mike. Not even close.

She brought herself back to his question. "No, I'm not running from the law."

"Are you married?"

She swallowed. "No."

Not any more.

As if reading her thoughts, he asked, "*Were* you married?"

Her thumb went to her finger to make sure her fake class ring was still in place, then she stood up in a hurry. "I'm not married. I never would have spent that time with you in the barn if I were."

Something dark passed through his eyes. "That doesn't always stop people."

Her chin went up. "Well, it would stop me."

"Maybe, but that still doesn't answer my original question." He stood as well, hands on the table. "So I'll ask it again. Who are you?"

She closed her eyes, the tight lines of suspicion on his face making her heart ache and her stomach churn.

I want to tell you, Mike. Please, believe me.

It was on the tip of her tongue, in fact, to say it. *I'm in the witness protection program.* But he'd already talked to the sheriff about her. All it would take was a single phone call to start an avalanche that could bury not only her…but him. Literally. Along with her mom. Her brother.

Roger had already killed once because of her. He'd love nothing better than to crush her under his heel, along with anyone close to her. In fact, it might give him more pleasure to hurt someone she cared about and make her live with the knowledge that she was the cause. Even if she told Mike the truth, Sheriff Chapman was sure to come back with either more information or to ask Mike some hard questions. Did she want Mike to have to lie for her?

No. That was her burden and hers alone.

She opened her eyes and took a fortifying breath. "I can't tell you." The words came out as a whisper.

Using her tongue to moisten her lips, she held her hands out from her sides. "Please. Oh, God, Mike, please, believe me. *This* is me. The person standing before you. The person in the barn. All me. The person who worked with Clara…and Sarah." She put every ounce of sincerity she possessed into her words. "I kissed you. Me. *Me!* And I'd do it all over again… I would. I only wish…" The cracking of her voice on that last word prevented her from going any further.

It evidently spurred Mike into action. He rounded the table and grabbed her, his eyes boring into hers for what seemed like an eternity before his mouth came crashing down, covering hers in a searing kiss that snatched away any last thoughts of saving herself. Of telling him to get off her property and take his precious referrals with him.

Because she didn't want him to go. She wanted him to stay. Wanted *this*.

The hard wooden railing of the wraparound porch was at her back, digging into her flesh, as Mike continued to kiss her as if he couldn't get enough. Well, neither could she. His arm went around her and he was lifting her up until she was sitting on the railing, legs splayed with him between them, pressing hard.

She arched back as he hit just the right spot, her hands scrambling to hang onto the post next to her as he gripped her hips, holding tight as he ground against her again.

Penny and Larry knew to leave when they were done. They wouldn't come round to this side of the house. And, God, she needed him. Needed him so badly she was shaking. On the verge of coming right then and there.

"Please."

As if he knew exactly what she was talking about, he hauled her back off the rail and set her on the ground. He ripped open the button on her jeans and shoved her pants and bikini panties down her hips. Too late, she realized they wouldn't come off without her boots.

Mike didn't try to remove them, however, he just spun her around until the rail was against her belly, and she heard the tell-tale zip of his jeans. The quick ripping of a packet. Then he was bending her over the banister. Thrusting inside. The breath left her lungs, and she saw stars. Mike's hands went to the rail on either side of her rib cage as he entered her again and again in a frenzy that matched everything she felt inside. He didn't try to touch her. There was no foreplay. No sweet nothings. No sounds at all, other than their breathing. But she was burning up inside. She parted her legs as much as she was able, gripping the wooden balusters below, needing him deeper. Harder.

He obliged, withdrawing almost completely and then suddenly lunging forward, hitting something inside her and sending a mixture of pleasure and pain rocketing through her belly.

God, yes!

Again. She wanted that again.

He reared back, then entered her with another powerful stroke of his hips. This time she cried out, but didn't try to stop him. Couldn't. Her toes curled inside her boots as she held on.

A third time. Deep. Hard.

Shattering.

Her eyes slammed closed, she stiffened and…*There! Oh!* Her body went off, a guttural moan forced up from deep inside as she contracted down tight and then spasmed open again and again, sharp pleasure washing over her as he strained inside her, keeping firm pressure on that tender spot. He must have climaxed as well, because he was no longer moving.

A minute or two later, he released the tension, his hands sliding down her arms, kissing the back of her neck.

Lord. She'd never felt so utterly satisfied in all her life.

Mike's fingers linked with hers and he squeezed gently, the act pushing her digits together and sending an ache through her ring finger.

What was he thinking? Was he still hung up on her identity? He'd said nothing as he'd taken her, and it was the way she'd wanted it. But now…

The last thing she wanted to do was lie to him. But she also didn't want to put him in danger by telling him the truth.

"Mike—"

"Shh. It's okay." He pressed his lips to her ear. "Did I hurt you?"

She smiled, relief washing through her when his voice came through warm and mellow. Not a trace of frost remained. "No. Couldn't you tell?"

"I'm glad." He chuckled. "Well that's *two* verticals."

"Mmm." She let her breath out in a sigh. "I'd call that a modified vertical."

"Would you?" His teeth nipped her earlobe. "Your people aren't going to come up on us anytime soon, are they?"

"No. They normally leave straight from the barn."

Mike eased back and slid free, and Trisha immediately missed the closeness. But it wasn't like they could just stay there forever.

"I have to get back to the office."

The regret in his voice made her smile widen. "So who's keeping you?"

"Witch." He slapped her bare butt with enough force to make her yelp. "So now that we've proved I'm not vertically challenged, I say we move on to something else."

"Like?" Her feeling of relief grew, making her feel slightly giddy, although she had a feeling that would fade soon enough. Once reality crept back in. But for now, she held it at bay with a single shake of her fist.

"I was thinking of doing something horizontal." He hauled her to a standing position and turned her around.

Her gaze went straight to the heart of the matter and then back to his face. "Now?"

He leaned in and kissed her before zipping himself back in with a pained groan. Then he reached down and tugged her clothes back up around her hips, sliding up the zipper and fastening her button. "Work, remember? Think 'delayed gratification.'" But know this, Trisha—or whatever your name may be. The next time I have you it's going to be on a nice soft bed." His voice sank to a silky drawl that made her stomach tighten. "I definitely want the bed. It's going to last all night. And those clothes are going to finally come off that delectable body. One piece at a time."

CHAPTER TEN

"I'D LIKE YOU to meet with Clara's treatment team."

Mike's voice came over the phone, the clipped words bearing no resemblance to the velvety promise he'd left her with two days ago. Just as well, since she'd pretty much decided there was no need to adjust the vertical or the horizontal. There would be no repeat performance, even if the thought of what they'd done made her mouth water and her stomach quiver. She'd never craved a man like she craved Mike. Nor had she ever before enjoyed pushing her own sexual boundaries like she did with him.

Having sex in the open…on her porch? That had been stupid. And exciting. And…stupid. The fingers of her free hand went to her nose and pinched hard in an effort to jerk herself back to the present.

As heady as sex with Mike was, how could she even consider getting involved with him when she had to hide things from her past? It was one thing when he'd thought she was who she said she was. It was another thing entirely when he knew her identity was fake. When he knew *she* was fake.

One lapse in judgment could be considered a mistake. Two lapses…temporary insanity. But if she made it to three? That was being *involved*.

"Why do you want me there?"

"I could give you all kinds of reasons."

Her breath caught. But try as she might, she caught no hint of double meaning behind his words. "Name one."

"You're working with Clara. I'd say that makes you part of her team. I want you to explain your philosophy and objectives to the rest of the group. As time goes on, we can appraise whether your line of treatment is yielding results." He paused. "Besides, I've seen you in action. I think you might be on to something."

She straightened next to the stall she'd been mucking. He'd implied she'd no longer be working with his patients if she didn't 'fess up to her real identity. She had to wonder why he'd suddenly decided to include her in his inner circle. Trying to keep an eye on her?

He said he thought she might be on to something though. A warm feeling spread through her stomach.

"When are they meeting?"

"Tomorrow afternoon."

She went through her schedule. "I have a lesson from one to two."

"The team meets at three-thirty. Can you make it here by then?"

"I suppose." Did she really want to do this?

No, but if she planned on sticking around, she needed to show she was a team player. Maybe this was Mike's way of admitting her work had merit.

Or maybe it had something to do with what had happened between them.

Did she really want to ask him?

"Good. We'll be meeting in my office. If you ask

at the information desk, they'll help you find it. See you tomorrow."

With that, he was gone. Shoving her cell phone into the back pocket of her jeans, she picked up her pitchfork and began cleaning the stalls again, forking up a clump of manure and depositing it into the wheelbarrow parked in the doorway of the stall.

This was actually Larry's job. The man's brows had lifted when he saw her scooping the waste from Brutus's straw, but he'd let her continue. She'd needed time to think this morning. No better way to do that than to engage in a mindless task that worked her muscles while letting her brain sort through various problems. Like why she'd washed her sheets this morning and had been sorely disappointed when Mike made no mention of coming out to the barn. Or the way her heart had pounded in her chest when she'd looked at the screen of her phone the second it rang and she saw his name displayed in large block letters.

Sex with Mike was wild and dangerous. He wasn't afraid to play a little bit rough, and she found she liked it, which was a revelation. A kind of scary one, in fact. Sex with Roger had been polished and sophisticated. She'd been fine with it at the time. Mike, however... Well as urbane as he might appear on the surface, or even on the phone a few minutes earlier, she'd glimpsed what the man was capable of. And oh was he capable.

Wrap your legs around me and get ready to hold on tight. Those growled word still had the power to make her insides turn moist and needy.

Sweat gathered on her brow as she hefted another scoop onto the growing pile. She stabbed the pitchfork into the heap and wiped her forehead with the back of her hand. She didn't want to leave Dusty Hills. She liked it here. She liked the people, loved her clients. But what if Mike kept digging or wanted the sheriff to ask a few more questions. The Feds had warned her about revealing anything, or letting anyone get too close to the truth. She was supposed to call them immediately if things got out of hand.

So why wasn't she on the phone already? She should leave—knew it in her soul of souls, but she couldn't bring herself to make that call.

It wasn't because of Mike.

His face swam in her subconscious. The memory of what they'd done together on the porch.

Okay, it *was* because of him. The way he'd gone from angry to worried in the space of a few gasped breaths. The way he smiled at her. Murmured things no one had ever murmured to her in her life.

Lord. What was she doing? She was playing with fire, and she knew it. Falling in love with him would be an even bigger mistake than sleeping with him. She was already inches away and creeping closer by the second. But she couldn't seem to make herself stop, no matter what the cost.

If she wasn't careful, she might find that price suddenly skyrocketing to devastating proportions. And then who exactly would end up paying for the choices she made? Her?

Or Mike?

Trisha explained her theories with grace and skill, using the large pad and easel at the front of the conference room, while three of Mike's colleagues took notes. Bringing her here could very well be a mistake, but something in her face when she'd declared that she was the person he saw in front of him made him believe her. As had the way she'd twisted that class ring at the mention of marriage. She had been married at one time, he was pretty sure, but she didn't want him or anyone else to know.

Why?

The thought had struck him that whoever it was had done something to her. Something so awful she didn't want to discuss it. Or maybe it was that she didn't want her former husband finding her.

That made his hands draw up into tight fists as she talked about muscle memory and its importance in stimulating a damaged brain. Theories he knew from his own studies, but had never related to horses.

That she worked with them still made him uneasy, but that worry had calmed somewhat. Her animals were gentle enough to work with children. He'd been on one of them himself. There'd been no hint of the animal doing anything unexpected. And she wasn't a trainer by profession, so she wasn't working with untried or unruly mounts like Marcy had done on a regular basis. And Trisha had people helping her around the barn, while Marcy had preferred to train and ride when no one else was there—maybe to hide her affair from prying eyes. That habit had contributed to her death. There'd been no one around when the worst had happened. No one to hold her—not even her lover—as her higher brain function slowly receded into nothingness.

Swallowing, he leaned back in his chair just as Trisha swiveled toward them, her eyes finding his. A tiny frown puckered the smooth flesh between her brows, and he forced his own expression to slide back to neutral, afraid she'd seen some of his thoughts.

What was the big deal? They'd had sex a couple of times. He wasn't after a lasting relationship, and he got the feeling he wasn't the only one who wanted to keep it that way. She didn't deem it important that he know the truth about who she was, so why couldn't he just leave it at that? Her presentation this afternoon was proof that she knew what she was talking about. That's all he cared about. They could have a little fun together, keep things from getting too serious. A win/win situation, if ever he saw one.

So why did that plan create a sense of discomfort, like a pebble in a pair of running shoes that jabbed at his insole with each step he took? No matter which direction he went…no matter how fast or slow he went, it was still there.

Well, he could go for a pretty long time with that rock in his shoe before he finally had to reach down and get rid of it. He could deal with it later. In the meantime, she seemed to like sex with him—he definitely liked it with her.

No problemo, right?

Right.

In fact, the less he knew about her the better. If she wasn't spilling any deep dark secrets, it meant she didn't see him as permanent companionship material. Even better. He could keep his heart out of it, just like he had with the other two women he'd been with.

With that plan in mind, he settled in to listen to the rest of Trisha's presentation. And did a few quick calculations on what his next move should be.

Because he definitely wanted to make a move. Especially now that he was sure it was safe.

A half-hour later, though, he found himself heading

for a veterinary clinic halfway across town. He'd asked if Trisha had had anything to eat, since it was after five. She hadn't—she'd been too busy getting her presentation together to do anything but work. Something that sent a stab of guilt through him. He hadn't given her much time to get ready, but then again, he hadn't given himself much time to prepare for seeing her again. His decision had been impulsive, needing to invent a reason to be around her.

Of course, she hadn't known that and had pulled together an impressive body of work that one of the other doctors had asked to be sent to him for future reference. And the man had leaned forward in his chair as he asked her a question or two, nodding as she'd answered him. Mike's spine had stiffened, and he'd given his colleague a measured glance, but had seen nothing in him but professional interest. Trisha had colored when another doctor had praised her for being so thorough. She had every right to be proud. She'd done a great job.

As soon as the room cleared out, he'd asked her out to dinner. She'd accepted. He didn't know whether to be thrilled or wary. He decided there was room for both.

Then she'd mentioned the vet visit.

"Laredo is due to be released today, and I want to make sure he trailers okay before they get to the ranch, since we'll be working with him as soon as Sarah is recovered and ready to ride again. I'll exercise him myself so he stays in shape."

"You won't work with him until you're sure it's safe, though, right?"

She glanced at him, then a funny expression passed across her face and was gone. "Nothing in life is ever perfectly safe."

He was being ridiculous. Trisha had never given any indication that she took safety for granted. All her students wore helmets. Hell, she'd made *him* wear a helmet when she put him on that stocky black horse. Marcy had grown up around horses, didn't feel the need to use them. His chest tightened.

The touch of her fingers on his arm had him looking at her again. "Mike, I promise I won't take unnecessary chances, okay? I just want to see his reaction to being loaded this first time. It might not be a problem. But if it is, I want to know it before I get into a situation that could put Sarah in danger."

His jaw relaxed again. She was being careful. Not taking unnecessary chances. He forced a note of unconcern in his voice. "Glad to hear it."

A thought came to him. Maybe if he told her about his wife, she'd take even more care. Why that was suddenly so important, he wasn't going to examine at the moment.

A man in a lab coat came out of the back. "Hey Trisha, you about ready to help us move that big boy?"

A knot formed in Mike's gut. Help? He'd thought they were just there to observe.

Trisha took her hand off his arm. "I want to stand back and watch his reactions, if that's okay?"

"Really? You've always insisted on being hands on with Brute Boy."

She shifted beside him and a beat or two passed. What was the problem?

"I only insist because he gets nervous around strangers."

"Nervous. That's one way to put it." The man shrugged. "Okay, so you're going to observe. Well, we've got him out back ready to see what happens. I'll call one of my other assistants to help."

Mike didn't want to be here. Didn't want to watch a jittery horse in action, putting everyone around it in danger, especially knowing that Trisha would normally have been right in the thick of things, if the vet's words were anything to go by. It was just another reminder of how his wife had died. Trisha had reassured him for a second or two, but this man's playful comments had brought his thoughts simmering back up where they frothed and circled like bubbles in a pan, waiting for the slightest increase in temperature to flare up and boil over.

They followed the vet to the back and Trisha murmured in a slow voice. "He's joking. I only help when I think it will put Brutus at ease."

So she only helped when the animal was agitated. Dangerous. Her words did nothing to calm him. Especially after hearing the vet refer to Brutus as Brute Boy. He'd done something to deserve that reputation.

Tell her about Marcy. Tonight. Over dinner.

They got to the back area of the clinic, where the horse—not as big as Crow or Brutus, with bones that looked finer—stood in a dirt yard, a horse trailer parked about fifty feet in front of it. There was already a man standing next to the animal, a rope attached to its halter. Even as they stood there, Laredo put his head down and snorted. He glanced at the people around the animal. No one seemed to pay much attention to the sound. Except him. He gritted his teeth and tried to push past the worry.

Another assistant came through the doors. With one person holding the rope, one person on the other side and one person beside the horse's right flank, the vet clucked to him. The animal tossed his head and pranced to the side as he eyed the trailer in front of him.

Wasn't going to happen.

The group tried again, this time the man with the rope jiggled it while the other two clucked to the animal, trying to get it to move forward. Still nothing.

Trisha touched his arm again. "I'll be right back."

His stomach lurched. He knew she'd end up rushing in there. But other than demand she stay next to him, he was powerless to stop her. She didn't owe him anything.

Moving over to a nearby bale of hay, she grabbed a handful and caught the vet's eye by waving it. The man nodded at her and said, "Back into the trailer and see if he'll follow you in."

Get in the trailer? She'd be trapped in there, if something happened. But these people were all professionals. Surely they wouldn't let her do something they weren't confident she could do.

Trisha moved to the horse's head and let him sniff the bunch of hay. He pulled a section off, munching as if he hadn't a care in the world. But when he reached for another mouthful, Trisha backed up a step. He stretched out his neck, only to find the food just out of reach again. Step went his left front foot. Then his right. Trisha moved the bundle back and forth, making it look enticing. The horse moved forward again, heading right for the darkened opening of the trailer. She glanced backward as she neared the vehicle, keeping up the movements with her hand. She went up the ramp until she was standing just inside the doorway.

Laredo hesitated, but Trisha crooned to him in a coaxing voice, "Come up and get it, boy. There's more inside." She moved back, until she was covered in shadow out of sight. The man with the rope handed it to Trisha who must have taken it, although he couldn't tell exactly what she was doing. The vet and the guy who was behind the horse moved out of the way when a feminine cluck came from inside the trailer. The horse moved up the ramp without hesitation, this time, and disappeared inside.

The men applauded, all except Mike whose whole being was focused on that trailer and the back opening. When Trisha appeared on the right side of the vehicle, he blinked in surprise until he noted another door at the front. So that's how they did it. She was soon at his side, looking up into his face.

"Hey, you okay?"

"Yep." A lie, but she didn't need to know that.

She smiled. "He did well, better than I thought he would."

Was she kidding? He'd had visions of the horse rearing, taking out several people as he struggled, not the least of them Trisha.

"I hate to think what 'bad' would have looked like."

Her smile faded. "We wouldn't have forced him into the trailer, if that's what you're thinking. It would only make things worse. We'd have given him more time. Gone slowly. Or given him something to calm him. But he didn't need it." She stepped closer. "Horses don't think like people do. He doesn't necessarily associate what happened to him with the trailer itself. And he wasn't trapped inside of the other one for long, we got him out pretty quickly and on his feet."

Mike reached out and touched her cheek. She believed what she was saying. It was there in those beautiful green eyes, which closed at his touch, leaning into his fingers.

"Trisha?" The vet's voice broke in, breaking the spell between them. "You want us to drive Laredo right back to your place?"

"Do you mind?" Trisha moved a few feet away. "Larry is at the barn, he's expecting you. I don't think Laredo will give you any problems unloading."

The vet glanced inside the trailer, where the horse was still chewing a mouthful of hay. "He's more interested in eating than in what's going on around him, so I think we're good." The other man met Mike's eye. "Are you two off?"

Mike answered before Trisha could. "We're headed out to get a bite to eat."

Admitting they were doing it together surprised him, but he held the vet's gaze without blinking. The other man nodded. "Choose somewhere good. She's worth it."

Trisha stepped next to the vet and kissed the guy's cheek. "Thanks. Take care of Laredo for me."

"Will do. Take care of yourself." With one last look at Mike, the vet turned around and headed back for the trailer. That left him alone with Trisha, and an aching sense that like Laredo and his obsession with his hay, Mike was far too interested in the woman in front of him to notice anything else around him. Like the fact that he was falling for her, despite his best efforts. And between her profession and whatever deep dark secret she was harboring, it made the prospect of falling in love with her dangerous on a whole lot of levels.

CHAPTER ELEVEN

"THE TEAM WAS impressed with your presentation."

Trisha glanced up from her plate of chicken fried steak as the low words hung between them. With the bite of meat still on her fork, she couldn't help but stare for a second or two. She'd been trying to convince him of the merits of hippotherapy from their first meeting so this hundred-and-eighty-degree turn seemed a bit sudden. Wait. He'd said the *team* was impressed, not him. "How could you tell?"

He quirked one side of his mouth in a rueful grin. "By the amount of notes they were taking. I've never seen them scribbling so fast. And I'm supposed to be the team leader on this particular case."

"It's just something new for them. Not because what I do is anything special."

"I'm beginning to think it is. Very special."

Wow. Maybe he *was* including himself in that impressed bunch. The thought was heady, making her insides do a quick twirl before settling back into place. "Thank you, Mike. That means a lot to me. Especially since I know you're not overly fond of horses."

"It's not that I'm not fond of them. It's that…" He waved away whatever he'd been going to say and picked up his glass of iced tea, taking a hefty sip and making her wonder if he was about to mention his late wife. "I was surprised you'd want to come to a mom and pop joint like Aunt Sadie's. We do have a couple of nice places in Mariston that serve sushi or some such."

The slight look of distaste on his face at the word "sushi' made her forget about her curiosity over his wife's death. She grinned instead. "Believe me, I've had enough sushi to last me a lifetime. But I've never really gotten to eat in a place like this." She glanced around the interior of the simple diner that served massive portions of country-fried steak, chicken, pork, liver…well, just about anything that could be battered and fried.

"Really? I'd think with the amount of traveling you did as a kid, you'd have eaten in a greasy spoon a time or two in your life." His eyes had turned sharp and watchful.

Crap. Being with Mike made her forget she should be pretending to be something she wasn't: a military brat who'd lived in a thousand different places. Not the New York City native she was, who'd eaten sushi, caviar, and other exotic dishes during her marriage to Roger.

She averted her eyes and cursed herself for having to lie yet again. But it was for his own good. And for hers. "My mom was picky about where she ate. She liked nice restaurants."

"I see." But he didn't. She could see it in his eyes—a kind of disappointment that went beyond types of food and childhood backgrounds. He knew she was making this up as she went, and it hurt much more than it should have to keep up the ruse. Maybe she could tell him. Maybe she could ask him to promise to keep it a secret. He'd kept their little rendezvous on the porch quiet, as far as she could tell.

But the sheriff was going to want to know if Mike had talked to her. What she'd said. He was a law enforcement officer first. Mike would have to lie to avoid telling the truth. Did she really want to make him an accessory? He was an honest, hard-working man. A good man. He had integrity. Cared deeply about his patients. No, he hadn't volunteered information about his wife, but why would he? It was none of her business. And his wife's death didn't call into question his credibility as a neurosurgeon. Her falsified background, however, would make any doctor in his right mind ask some hard questions and expect straight answers. Answers she couldn't give.

Unless…she told him.

You can't, Trisha. This isn't just about your safety. It's about Mike's…your mom's, your brother's. And what about her contacts with the Feds? She'd already watched one of them die right in front of her. Would her carelessness endanger others? Or would it encourage the bad guys to keep looking for ways to compromise the program…make people to afraid to testify, if something happened to her or someone close to her?

To keep herself from temptation, she finally popped the bite of steak into her mouth and forced herself to chew. It was cold now, though, and pretty much tasted like cardboard, a far different reaction than she'd had a few minutes ago.

Plastering a smile on her face that felt as fake as her whole screwed-up life, she kept up a stream of small talk in between bites of food. When her mouth wasn't chewing, it was spilling out a load of nonsense. She figured if she controlled the conversation, he couldn't ask her any other questions. Questions that might require less than honest answers. Because the last thing Trisha wanted to do was lie to this man any more than she already had. So she talked, and talked, and talked.

They headed out to the car as soon as the meal was over, and she kept on ripping through subjects that ranged from diseases of a horse's hooves to the most effective composting methods for manure. Fitting really, since she seemed to be shoveling the stuff as fast as she could.

Mike opened the car door for her just as a middle-aged woman, hair in a bun, appeared at the entrance to the restaurant, waving frantically. "Dr. Mike, I hate to call you back, but Reginald has done some kind of fool thing to his arm. He's bleeding bad."

Trisha's stomach turned over, a familiar queasiness creeping up her throat.

"Stay here," Mike said, leaving the car door open as he swung back toward the restaurant and hurried to the woman, asking for details as he went.

As much as she hated blood, Mike might need her help if it was something serious, so she slammed the door and went after the pair, catching up with them in the entryway. He threw her a glance that held the merest hint of a frown but didn't try to order her back to the car.

As if that would work.

"He's in the kitchen. He wanted to just wrap it with a bandage, but it bled right through, and he refuses to go to the hospital."

Mike's steps quickened, his long strides eating up the distance through the dining area, where several patrons were on their feet. She soon heard why. The sounds of profanity and threats reached her ears at about the same time as her companion pushed through the double doors that led to the diner's food-prep area.

Her eyes went wide when she saw a crimson arc that covered a six-foot section of white tile floor. Blood. The shouting continued as an older man in a white T-shirt and matching slacks held his arm over the sink, a dark red cloth wrapped around and around it. Trisha didn't think bandages came in fashion colors, which meant that had to be...more blood. Especially since the bandage was dripping the same-colored substance into the large stainless-steel sink. The hand holding the bandage in place was also dripping blood.

"Oh, no."

The nausea in her throat sloshed higher, but she forced it back with a swallow.

Mike didn't waste any time. "Call 911 and tell them to get an ambulance out here." Moving next to the man, he took hold of the arm, despite Reginald trying to jerk it away again.

"It's just a little cut. Sadie, why'd you have to call him back here?"

The woman snapped back a curt response.

Mike cut through the squabbling. "What happened?"

"The knife drawer got stuck, and I reached in to see if something was blocking it." Reginald glared around them. "Who was the idiot who put a knife in the drawer cutting side up?"

Trisha cringed as she remembered exactly how much force was required to puncture human skin and how it had felt to have hot blood spill over her hand as she'd pulled free of her attacker. Mike glanced back at her, unaware of her internal struggles. "You up to helping?"

She would have to be. This man's life was at stake. "Yes."

He started quickly unwrapping the bandage, still ignoring Reginald's ranting. Trisha crossed over to him, blocking out everything except Mike's face and the sound of his voice. "As soon as I get this off, I need to find out whether we're dealing with a vein or an artery and apply pressure."

"Just tell me what to do."

The bandage fell away and a bright red stream of blood spurted into the sink from a large gash on the man's inner arm, near his elbow. Mike quickly pressed his thumb to an area just above the injury, muttering an oath of his own. The blood flow slowed, but didn't stop completely. Trisha didn't know the difference between a vein and an artery, but she had a feeling from Mike's reaction that it was the worst option of the two. He glanced up at Sadie, the lines of his face hard and tight. "I need a couple of cloth napkins, preferably ones that have just come out of the dryer, they'll be cleaner."

"Right away, Dr. Mike." The woman hurried to do as he'd asked. The other three employees stood back, their faces various shades of green and gray. Mike asked them to go out and see if they could clear out the restaurant and watch for the ambulance. She had a feeling the suggestion had more to do with getting them out of the kitchen than anything else. The injured man was looking a little ill himself, pale faced, bracing his arms on the edges of the sink now to hold himself up.

She remembered Roger screaming at her, clutching

his side as he'd backed away from her…the way she'd gasped in a couple of breaths and had rolled off the desk, gripping the bloodstained letter opener between shaking fingers, ready to strike again if need be. Her hand went to her stomach.

"Trisha!" Mike's voice yanked her back to the situation at hand. "I need you to grab a couple of pairs of gloves from that box over on the counter. A pair for me and a pair for you." She glanced over to where he was looking and saw a large cardboard box with the words "Gloves for Food Handlers" written on the side. Hurrying over, she ripped four gloves from the inside and spied a pump bottle of hand sanitizer next to it. She squirted some onto her hands and rubbed them together before donning one pair of gloves. She carried the bottle and the other pair to Mike, glad to have something to do.

"Perfect."

Reginald was no longer swearing. He was sweating, despite the chill of the air-conditioner, and his arm was still dripping blood at a steady rate. But at least it wasn't shooting into the sink any more. "What do you want me to do?"

"I'm going to need you to put your thumb just behind mine and press as hard as you can, so I can get my gloves on, okay?"

Trisha gulped. "Okay."

Just as she set the gloves and sanitizer on a clean section of counter, Sadie arrived with a handful of white napkins.

"Thanks," he said.

She could do this. She could.

Sliding next to him, she placed her gloved thumb on the spot on the man's arm, just behind where Mike's was.

"Harder," he said.

Huffing in a quick breath, she pressed down with all her might, wrapping her fingers beneath the man's arm for more leverage. "Like that?"

"Yes. Now hold it." With that, he released his grip. Trisha's own pulse pounded in her ears when she realized that if she let go, Reginald could bleed to death.

Where was that ambulance?

Mike sanitized his hands, then took two of the napkins from Sadie and tied the ends together to form a longer length of cloth. She was surprised he hadn't just ripped off his belt and used it as a tourniquet, like you saw on television. He knew what he was doing, though. He'd pressed on exactly the right spot to get the bleeding to slow down.

Her hand was starting to cramp from holding on so tight and she'd only been here for a minute or two. Still, she held on.

He shoved his hands into his gloves and grabbed the napkin again. "You okay?" he asked her.

"Yes." She'd keep the pressure on no matter how long it took.

Mike took the tied napkins and looped them around the man's arm, lining up the place he'd knotted with the spot he'd held earlier. Then he tied it tight. "The knot should press on the artery until the ambulance gets here." He nodded at her. "Release some of the pressure and see if it works."

Sadie's voice came from behind them. "He'll be okay, won't he?"

"He's going to be fine."

In the distance, Trisha could hear the tell-tale shriek of a siren.

Finally.

Mike tapped her thumb. "Take off some of the pressure."

She hesitated, then eased her thumb back slowly, braced to press again if the blood flowed too fast. Nothing happened. The wound still dripped, but it wasn't gushing.

The sound of the siren grew to ear-shattering levels and then abruptly shut off.

Trisha had avoided looking at the gash until now, but she could see it was ugly, the cut deep and clean, the surrounding skin stained dark with blood. She was no doctor, but she was pretty sure he'd need surgery to repair the damage.

The rattle of a gurney behind her signaled the presence of the EMS team, and she took a couple of quick steps back so they could get to the man. Mike stayed where he was, giving the two men in blue uniforms a rundown on what they had and what he wanted done.

Wow. The man really did like being in charge. Then again, he *was* the doctor, and he'd probably just saved Reginald's life.

The two emergency services workers obviously knew who Mike was, because they treated him with a kind of awed deference as they jumped to do what he asked, taking Reginald's vitals, hooking him up to an IV and getting him on the gurney. They ignored their patient's muttered threats, just like Mike had, although the tirade was much less vehement now than it had been earlier, as the man realized how serious his situation was.

When the emergency technicians whisked the gurney

out of the kitchen toward the waiting ambulance, with Sadie trotting alongside it, she was surprised when Mike hung back. Especially after the way he'd directed the treatment. "Aren't you going with them to the hospital?"

"No, I'll just be in the way at this point. Stu and Gary know what they're doing."

So he did know them. Not surprising, since he'd probably worked with a lot of the local ambulance services. And he evidently could give up control when he trusted the other party to do their job.

Like when he'd ridden Crow, his hands braced on those strong thighs? Had he trusted her to do her job?

Not the time, Trisha.

Mike stripped his gloves off and nodded that she could do the same, while he explained to the restaurant staff that they'd need to close the place for at least the rest of the day. He asked for volunteers to stay and help clean up. Not surprisingly, every hand went up. Mike really did have an impressive array of talents.

As they walked through the door, he gave a soft chuckle. "Not exactly the way I envisioned spending our time after dinner."

He'd thought about them spending more time together after dinner? Doing what?

Mike opened the car door for her and she slid in, her breath sticking in her lungs as he went around to the other side and climbed behind the wheel. Had he been thinking about that promised horizontal? For some reason, the thought of having him on a bed, pressing her into the mattress, seemed even more intimate than what they'd already done, if that was possible. It was better not to jump to conclusions, however. Maybe he just meant to take her straight home, drop her off, and then be on his way.

Fifteen minutes later she had her answer when he turned into the long driveway that led to her house.

"Anyone here besides the horses?" he asked when he pulled to a halt. Neither Penny nor Larry's vehicles were there, and there was no sign of the vet's trailer, so Laredo had already been settled into his stall for the evening.

"No." She wanted to ask him in. Wanted to cash in that rain check, but what if she was wrong? What if the last thing on his mind after having to treat an unexpected emergency was sex?

It shouldn't even be on *her* mind, but it was. They'd saved a life. Both of them. They'd worked together, and she'd faced down her memories without passing out. Thanks to Mike.

It was exhilarating. Life-affirming. And she wanted to celebrate it. In Mike's arms, no matter how stupid or unwise that might be. The world hadn't collapsed the last two times they'd been together, so it probably wouldn't fall apart this time either.

If she was worried about being pressed against him skin to skin, limbs entwined together as they made love, maybe she could figure out a way to get what she wanted while not giving up too much of herself in the process.

Hmm…what if, like on Crow, he let her call the shots for once. She could just put him in a chair and lower herself…

She gulped, just thinking about it.

Still, what if he didn't want her? She threaded her fingers through each other and squeezed them together. Should she just open the door and get out?

Her hand went to the latch then Mike's low, gravelly

tones swirled through the shadows in the car. "Are you going to ask me in?"

"Do you *want* to come in? F-for coffee, I mean?"

He reached across and gently gripped her chin, turning her toward him. "I want to come in," he confirmed. "But not for coffee."

No coffee! That meant...

She smiled and leaned back in her seat, the tension draining out of her shoulders. "I'm all out of coffee anyway."

Returning her grin, he leaned over and dropped a kiss on her mouth, letting it linger for a second or two. Her pulse rate shot up, punching a hole right through the roof of the car and galloping away.

"Good thing I'm not here for the coffee, then, isn't it?"

With that, the door clicked open and Mike Dunning, his intentions plain for all to see, got out of the car and circled the hood. When he reached a hand out to her, she allowed him to help her from the vehicle, her legs trembling harder than they had during the rescue efforts at the restaurant.

As if he knew she was in danger of sinking to the ground in a heap, he swept her into his arms and started toward her front porch, where he took the four wooden steps with an ease that made her mouth water. "Well, Ms. Bolton, now that I have you back in my clutches, I think it's time I fulfill a certain promise."

CHAPTER TWELVE

STILL HOLDING HER in his arms, Mike waited for her to unlock her front door before pushing through it and leaning against it to close it.

"Horizontal surface?" He glanced around, spying a plush beige sofa with a large cushioned ottoman in front of it—both horizontal. A little further in there was a long plank farm table that made his mouth water—also horizontal.

Hmm…countertops. He didn't remember promising *he'd* be horizontal. She could sprawl out on that dining room table—all curves and hollows readily available, while he remained standing, sampling, licking…And, yep, there went his body, right on cue.

Trisha bit her lip then looped her arms around his neck. "I know you want to wind up flat on your back." She raised a brow at him when he started to protest. "You said 'horizontal,' but you never mentioned who exactly was going to be on top."

"Me." He tightened his fingers around her.

"You have a hard time giving up control, don't you?"

Was she kidding him? The last two times they'd been together he'd hung onto his control by a thread. Which was why he wanted to be in the driver's seat. "That's me. Mr. Control Freak."

She laughed. "I think you are, actually. I only know of one time that you relinquished that control. When you were sitting on Crow."

And what exactly did that horse have to do with anything? "I'm not following you."

"Easy. I think it's time for lesson number two."

Now? Hardly. "I think you've misread my intentions." He cocked his head. "Although I get the feeling that might be deliberate."

"I know exactly what you want." She slid a hand into the thick hair at the back of his head and curled her fingers around it, tightening just enough to let his scalp know she was there. Then she tugged, forcing his head back an inch before she leaned forward and ran her tongue up the side of his neck.

He almost dropped her, his fingers going boneless as a wave of pure pleasure sloshed into his gut. "Trisha."

She was at his ear now. "Give up a little of that control, Doctor. I'll make it worth your while. Promise." She nipped his earlobe. "You let me call the shots once. I know you can do it again."

That was the whole problem. He wouldn't be able to *do it* again. At least not right away. But the thought of what she might do if he handed her the reins made all the synapses in his brain start firing at once. Suddenly he wanted it. Wanted to see her lean over him as she lowered herself onto him. He could lie on the bed and watch each change of expression on that lovely face.

He kissed the thought of the dining-room table goodbye. At least for now.

Did it matter that he still knew practically nothing

about her? Yes, it did. Did it matter right this second? Hell, no.

"Okay," he agreed. "Lesson number two. Where's your bedroom?"

"I was thinking dining room."

The table swung back into his line of sight. Sounded good to him. More than good, actually. He started toward it, while she held on. When they reached the table he set her down on it, only to have her slide off and pull one of the chairs out, turning it so that the seat faced out. Then she sat, slowly, and his heart ricocheted around in his chest cavity for a few seconds when she reached out and grabbed the fabric of his slacks and urged him toward her.

Wow.

She undid his belt buckle. Then her nimble fingers went to the button on his pants and released it, followed by the quick snick of his zipper going down. "Remember when you were on Crow and I asked you to put your hands on your thighs and leave them there?"

Did he remember? His brain wasn't quite firing correctly at the moment, but somehow he managed to bite out "Yes" in response.

"In a minute I'm going to switch places with you and you're going to do that again." Her palms traveled around his hips and smoothed over his butt, giving a quick squeeze that had him tensing up. "Do you have something in this wallet?"

She eased it from his pocket and held it up.

"In one of the pockets on the right-hand side."

Leaving him standing there for a second, she flipped it open, hesitating for a second as she looked at something he couldn't see, then found the condom, plucking it from its hiding place. He briefly wondered what she'd looked at. She flicked the wallet onto the table and set the condom down next to it.

All thoughts of that fled when she reached for him again, tucking her fingers into the waistband of his pants and tugging them and his briefs down with one quick pull. Then he was bare, and there was the evidence that this woman affected him in a million different ways. He was so hard he could feel the blood pulsing in time with his heartbeat.

Trisha scooted forward on her chair, parting her legs so that her thighs were on either side of his knees.

And her mouth...

Her mouth was millimeters from the head of his erection. So close that the warmth of her breath washed over him each time she exhaled.

Her eyes flickered up to his. "Do you want me to?"

He didn't need to ask what she meant. Instead, a million different responses flooded his head: *Yes. No. Not yet. Please.*

None of them made it past his lips.

She smiled and wrapped a hand around him, sliding it all the way to the base. "I think we'll leave this until a little later." Then she let go and stood, the heady sensation of her body scraping slowly up his swollen flesh making him hiss in a breath and hold it until she was all the way up, pressed tight against him, feet still splayed on either side of his.

Her head tipped back. "Ready?"

She gripped his arms and pivoted, turning them both until his back was to the chair. "Now sit."

The command was softened with another smile, but her hands went to his shoulders and pushed. And hell if his legs didn't bend immediately, until his naked butt was parked on the chair, slacks and briefs around his ankles.

She knelt and took care of that, pulling them the rest of the way off and draping them over another chair.

He knew Trisha had a bossy streak, but this was unbelievably erotic, having her manipulate him, using her hands and voice to tell him exactly what she wanted him to do.

And he was going to do it. All of it. If she could play, then so could he. In fact, this game might just become one of his favorites.

She stood again. "Okay, Doctor, hands on your thighs, just like you did with Crow. Only this time you won't be riding him." Her lips curved in a saucy look that was pure sex. "In fact, you won't be the one doing the riding at all."

His flesh jerked at that thought.

As if she knew exactly what he was thinking, she parted her legs and moved to stand over his knees, putting her hips just at eye level. All he wanted to do was reach out and grab them and yank her closer. His palms went to the backs of her thighs, and she immediately took a step back, brows up. "Uh-uh, Mike. Not allowed. Hands on your own thighs."

Gritting his teeth in frustration, he did as she asked. She was right. He liked control. Because right now all he wanted to do was grab the woman, toss her onto that table beside them and thrust into her hard and deep.

He fought back the impulse. She wanted this, so who was he to take that from her?

Planting his hands on his legs, he waited for her to move back into place. It killed him to sit here like a lump when everything in him wanted to touch…to taste… to possess.

As soon as Trisha had stepped forward again, she set her hands on his shoulders and slowly lowered herself until she was sitting on his legs, her thighs resting on top of his hands. He couldn't move them now, even if he wanted to. Maybe that's what she had in mind.

She leaned in and kissed him. He wanted to bury his fingers in her hair and hold her in place, but of course he couldn't. Instead, she molded her hands to his head, her lips playing peek-a-boo with his, light touches that aroused him to a fever pitch but didn't satisfy.

Using her own hands as leverage, he pressed his mouth hard to hers, his lips parting hers and holding them wide open as he plunged his tongue deep into her. *Yes! This!*

She didn't push him away this time, just pulled him closer and let him do exactly to her mouth what he planned on doing to her body as soon as his hands were free. She was right. He wanted control, and if he couldn't get it one way, he was going to get it another.

A minute later she hauled herself up and off his lap, tearing her mouth from his. Breathing heavily, she pressed the back of her hand to her lips, looking a little less sure of herself than she had a second ago. She stared at him as if seeing him for the first time, then her eyes lowered to his lap and came back up. He watched her swallow.

He was more than ready to find that horizontal surface.

"Ready to hand the reins back?" One eyebrow cocked, daring her to say she hadn't liked what he'd just done.

"I…" She blinked a couple of times then seemed to pull herself back together. "No. Not yet."

Her fingers went to the bottom of her T-shirt and hauled the thing up and over her head. His throat dried up. "Not yet," she repeated, her voice firming up again. "I want you to sit right there while I take my clothes off, one piece at a time."

He'd almost made her lose her place. Almost made her give in and let him carry her off to her bedroom. His kiss had made her crave him in a way that she never would have dreamed possible six months ago.

That's what had knocked her back to reality…and back to her plan. She wanted him—merciful heavens, she wanted him—but it had to be on her terms or she was lost.

Keep up the saucy act, Trisha. Men are supposed to love it when women take over and drive them wild. Right? So why did Mike make it seem like torture? Like he wanted nothing more than to pin her arms over her head and take her?

She was the one being tortured. She wanted him to rip all her clothes off and have his wicked way with her.

Unzipping her pants, she forced her eyes to stay steady on his. At least one of his body parts wasn't complaining about what she was doing. That part stood hard and firm, willing her to get down there and pay it some attention.

Oh, she would. Very soon. Then he would forget all about her bed. They'd stay right here and make love on that chair. And they would both get what they wanted, of that Trisha would make sure.

Off came her pants. And then her bra.

"Come here."

His voice was soft. Coaxing. And she wanted nothing more than to do its bidding.

"When I'm ready." She hooked her thumbs in the waistband of her black bikini panties, noting that his fingers were now digging into the flesh of his thighs, as if forcing them to remain in place.

Her panties slid over her hips and down her thighs before she stepped out of them.

"Let go of the reins, Trisha."

Soon. She just needed him too far gone before handing them over. "Not yet."

Up came his eyes, pupils so large they threatened to swallow her whole. "You are going to be sorry you ever ventured down this particular road, woman. Because two can play at this game. And believe me when I say you are going to remember this night. Every time you sit on one of those horses, every time you slide into your bed, you are going to feel me. Right. There."

Her lips parted, her heart hammering in her chest as something deep and profound swept through her, a heat blooming in her belly and encasing her heart. She wanted him. Wanted him on his terms. Wanted him however she could get him.

She opened her hand, a symbolic gesture that meant nothing and everything. "Take them."

He didn't hesitate, coming off the chair and grabbing her up into his arms, his lips coming down onto hers and taking them. On his terms. Needy. Powerful. This time she didn't try to get away, just let him have his fill, finding herself burying her fingers into his hair and trying to force their mouths even closer.

When he finally lifted his head, she had to keep holding on to prevent herself from falling down. He kicked off his shoes, and reached over to snatch up the condom. "Bed. Now."

"Okay."

What else could she say? If he didn't take her soon, she might actually explode into a thousand pieces right here in the living room...before he even touched her. She was in danger of it even now.

He hauled his shirt over his head, baring his shoulders and torso. Not that he gave her much time to admire him because he had her by the hand, dragging her with him as he strode down the hallway and led her toward her own personal version of ecstasy...and agony.

Trisha slowly pushed her way toward the light, eyes cracking open enough to realize the light wasn't just in her imagination. It was all around her. Morning. She rolled onto her back, groaning as a languid soreness flowed through each bundle of muscles.

He hadn't been kidding. She was going to remember last night for the next several days.

Even as she thought it, her nipples tightened, remembered pleasure washing over her.

When she'd handed over the reins, he'd taken them and showed her what real control was all about. And that man was the master of his own body...and hers.

Lordy!

Flinging her hand to the side, she was disappointed when it landed on cool sheets instead of a warm, firm body. He'd left? Without saying goodbye?

She sat up with a frown then heard the sounds of water running in the adjoining bathroom. Okay, he was in the shower.

And he hadn't asked her about her past. Not once. Not before, during or after their lovemaking session. A renewed sense of hope swept through her. Yes, being in bed with him had been incredibly intimate, but it had also been freeing. And wonderful. Maybe things weren't as dire as she'd made them out to be.

After all, Dusty Hills was kind of in its own little bubble. They had contact with other towns, but the residents all knew and cared about each other…in fact, most of them had been born and raised here, except for a few outsiders who'd married residents of Dusty Hills and had come back to live with that person. It wasn't like any of them knew people from New York City or were likely to travel there and blab about the stranger who'd moved to their town. She had a pretty solid identity—well, maybe the sheriff had seen some holes but he'd evidently not gone digging any further. And Mike seemed okay with letting go of the subject.

Visions of her and Mike doing a lot more of the stuff they'd done last night danced round and round like a music-box figure that never stopped. Why couldn't she have a normal life? Find someone to love…

She swallowed. Find someone to love. Mike?

It would seem so.

But did he feel the same way? He'd never said anything about it, but the way he'd touched her…it had been personal. Much more personal than Roger's practiced lovemaking, which had been why she'd been so leery of winding up in bed with Mike. But it had been fine. More than fine.

The world hadn't ended. Neither had it paused for even a brief second when their bodies had finally tangled together in a heady mixture of tender lovemaking and wild sex that had made her cry out more than once.

She slid her feet off the bed and shrugged into an over-sized T-shirt, letting it slide off one of her shoulders. Maybe she could intercept him in the shower and have a little more of that together time.

Padding to the door, she tested the handle and found it unlocked. She entered the space on silent feet, hoping to surprise him. The steamy bathroom smelled of raspberry shampoo, which made her smile. He was evidently secure enough in his masculinity that he didn't mind using her frou-frou bath products.

She took off her earrings and her class ring, something she'd forgotten to do last night, and quickly brushed her teeth. Before she could finish, the water was switched off and in a panic she turned to see him emerge from her minuscule shower stall, a towel wrapped around his waist.

He smiled. "I didn't realize you were in here or I would have waited."

With the toothbrush dangling from her mouth and a glob of foam swirling around her tongue, she stared at him. For a neurosurgeon, he was surprisingly firm, the hint of muscles playing beneath the skin of his chest, the curve of biceps as he tucked the ends of his towel in around his waist. Long, lean fingers that could…

She turned and spit as gracefully as she could manage into the sink and turned on the water to rinse the residue down the drain. A pair of strong arms curled around her waist, and his chin came to rest on her bare shoulder. He smelled heavenly—of her soap, shampoo and a warm earthy musk that marked him as Mike Dunning…super-stud.

"I was trying to surprise you."

"Hmm." His teeth nipped where his chin had rested. "You've been just full of surprises over the last eight hours or so."

Her face heated. Only because he gave her sexuality a shot of confidence every time he laid those heated brown eyes on her.

Curling her right hand around the back of his neck to hold him against her, she used her other hand to toss her toothbrush back into the holder next to the sink. The fan in the bathroom had made short work of the steam, clearing the mirror and giving her a good view of him. He frowned for a second and then his hand reached out to capture her left one, his thumb sliding over her ring finger.

Her breath caught in her throat as he explored the naked skin, praying he wouldn't notice that there were two different indentations there. A wide strip from the class ring she now wore, but beneath it a deeper, narrower furrow, gouged out by a too-tight wedding band. The rasp of his skin against hers sent a shiver over her, and she glanced in the mirror, to find him studying her hand.

Please, don't ask. Not now.

He let go of her and looped his arms back around her middle, regarding her in the reflection with an expression that was both soft and sad. About her ring? No, she didn't think so. That had been curiosity, but to his credit he hadn't asked. She relaxed again.

"What is it?" she asked.

"I was married once. To a horse trainer."

Her stomach knotted into a tight ball that became more and more dense. She'd wanted to know. But suddenly she was terrified of him saying another word. She had no choice, though, unless she asked him to stop.

"Marcy died four years ago in a riding accident. The horse she was on was her favorite, one she had raised from a colt and trained herself."

"I'm so sorry, Mike."

He tightened his grip. "I wanted you to know why I'm so wary around horses….and women." Dropping a kiss on her shoulder, he went on. "I found out after her death she was having an affair…had lied repeatedly about where she was going and who she was with. It was like I didn't even know her at the end."

A heavy load of guilt settled on Trisha's shoulders. She'd lied to Mike too. Time and time again.

"Anyway, she was going into the outdoor arena and her horse evidently spooked—they found a dead rattler a few feet away. Marcy hit her head, breaking a vertebra in her neck. There was no hope. No brain activity. She was kept alive on machines for three days before her parents and I made the decision to donate her organs." His voice turned to rough gravel that ground her soul and made her eyes prick with tears. "I'm a neurosurgeon—went to school for twelve damn years—and I couldn't help my own wife."

Twisting round in his arms, Trisha pressed her cheek against his skin, hearing the fierce beating of his heart, drawing his warm scent deep into her lungs. This man had known such pain. Such betrayal. How could his wife have cheated on him? "You loved her, despite what she did."

"Yes. Very much. But it's also made me a wary man." His fingers came up to stroke her hair. They trailed along her left arm, following the line to where her hand lay flat against his chest. His thumb brushed over her ring finger, tracing just above the joint…the circle where her ring had lain. Just like he'd done earlier.

A chill went over her. That's why he was confiding in her. He wanted her to do the same. To tell him the truth about who she was. To prove she wouldn't hurt him the way his wife had.

She couldn't give him what he wanted. Not now. Not five years from now. Probably not ever.

Right on cue, a strange sense of expectancy began building in the air as he waited for her response.

That's what relationships were all about: sharing confidences; growing together through past experiences; being honest with each other. She'd hoped he'd be content to just be with her without any of that.

Maybe he still would. Maybe she'd give him silence as an answer, and he'd accept it as enough.

She took a step back, pulling her hand away and letting it drop to the counter next to her hip. Then she poured all the sincerity she could muster into her next words. "I'm sorry, Mike. So sorry. About everything."

Sorry she couldn't tell him the truth. Sorry she couldn't share key aspects of her life with him. Sorry that everything with her seemed to be one-sided, with Mike giving so much more than she ever could.

He could live in the light while she was forced to lurk in the shadows, a place where truth and fiction merged into an image that made her insides twist and numbed all but the most basic emotions.

Still, maybe that would be enough for him.

He studied her for a few seconds, a muscle working in his jaw. Then his eyes slowly slid back to her finger. And she knew it wouldn't be. He wouldn't stop until he knew the truth. Until he'd unmasked her and laid her bare.

She'd said she didn't want him in danger. Had wanted to draw a line in the sand and stay on her side of it. Did she really want to drag him over it and make him a part of her world? Make him lose sleep at night, wondering when her past would catch up to both of them?

No. She stuck her toe in the sand and redrew that line…deeper this time, keeping it firmly between her and Mike. She knew what she had to do.

Taking a deep breath and trying to ignore the pain in her heart, she chose her words carefully. "Thank you for last night. I had a good time."

A frown appeared. Not the response he'd expected. "So did I."

"I need to get out to the barn and start my day. The horses will be hungry." It was the only way she could think of to get him out of the house. No need to tell him that Larry normally did the morning chores. In fact, her barn helper was probably already out there.

His glance tracked over her loose shirt and bare legs.

Right. It was obvious she was dressed for a day at the barn, especially since she'd come into the bathroom to find him. She tried again. "I'll shower first, of course."

"Of course."

She slid out from between him and the counter, reaching for her class ring and screwing it back onto her finger—covering the truth with a lie. She faced him and waited, praying he wouldn't try to kiss her, because she'd do one of two things: burst into tears, or cling to him and never let him go.

Neither of those things would help her find the courage to take the next step. The only step. The Feds had said it would only take a single phone call.

Mike's jaw tightened, but he nodded. "I'll see myself out, then."

"Thanks."

As the bathroom door clicked behind him, she leaned her butt against the counter and closed her eyes.

One step at a time, Trisha. That's all you can do.

Even if those steps would carry her far away from Dusty Hills, Nevada. Far away from a man who, despite her best efforts, she now loved with all her heart.

CHAPTER THIRTEEN

"It'll take us a week or so to iron out the details. Do you want to sit tight? Safe houses are reserved for worst-case scenarios. Unless there's something you're not telling us." Clyde, her FBI contact, didn't sound irritated. Or even flustered. It was as if this was all in a day's work for him.

Well, for him, maybe it was. But for her, it was her life. Her family's lives.

Pressing the phone to her ear, she contemplated her little piece of earth. How many times would she need to do this?

She wouldn't be doing it this time if she'd kept her heart under control. She'd have to be more careful in the future.

That was something she wouldn't have to worry about for a long, long time. She had a feeling her heart would still be feeling these wounds next month and the one after that. Maybe even for years.

"No, it's nothing urgent. Someone asked the sheriff to look into my past, and I don't think he's going to let it go."

"You want me to put in a friendly call to this sheriff

and explain a thing or two to him? Let him know his questions are not welcomed?"

Leave it to Clyde to give the word "friendly' a sinister edge. He'd never blamed her for his colleague's death. Not once. In fact, he'd assured her that any one of them would have willingly taken that bullet. It came with the job. Maybe so, but that didn't make it any easier to accept. Someone had died trying to protect her. She vowed she would never again be the reason someone got hurt.

"No, I think that'll just make it worse. This is small-town Nevada after all."

This time her contact laughed. "You were the one who chose the venue."

Yes, she was. So she had no one to blame but herself. "I think I'll let you guys choose this time, how's that sound?"

"I've got a few ideas. You up for some cold weather?"

Trisha could almost see the man's smile. With an attitude that matched the bristly gray hairs sprouting from his head, Clyde seemed to have developed a soft spot for her. She wasn't sure that was a good thing. The man was almost scarier than her ex.

"As long as it's somewhere my horses can live comfortably, it'll be perfect."

There was a brief moment of silence. Then he came back. "Those animals are a liability. We can't be responsible if—"

"I've already heard the spiel." How someone might be able to track her through her movements with the horse trailer. "The horses come with me. It was my one condition for testifying."

"Let's stick to approved language, okay?" This time there was a thread of irritation running through his voice.

Right. She'd forgotten. The wrong word to the wrong person could prove deadly, something that had been drilled into her head. She'd followed those rules to a *T* and look where that had gotten her. "Sorry. You'll call before you come?"

"Yes. Just remember that each contact carries a risk of compromise. Be judicious with these calls. And with what you say over the next couple of days."

"I will. Can you do me a favor and send someone to check on my mom and brother? Make sure they're all right?"

"I'll see to it. Remember what I said about talking to anyone."

"I will. Thank you." She wasn't supposed to contact her family directly. Or leave any forwarding addresses. And she was supposed to tell as few people as possible that she was moving. But she had to tell Larry and Penny as well as her clients that she wouldn't be sticking around. But beyond that she wouldn't tell a soul. Not even Mike.

She was leaving.

Word traveled fast in a small town.

Mike hadn't heard from Trisha in the last two days. He'd been trying to give her some space after opening up to her about Marcy's death. He'd hoped she might tell him a little about herself as well. She hadn't. He thought if he waited for a week, maybe two, she'd start to trust him. That he'd gently press her again for information. If she was a battered wife, maybe she was afraid the bastard would find her.

He'd decided to give her time. They had plenty of it.

He certainly hadn't expected to hear she was pulling up stakes and moving on. He'd gotten four phone calls this morning. The first one had been from Clara's mother, frantic that her daughter would no longer have access to an equine therapist, and could he see if there was another one within a hundred miles? As soon as his mind had stopped reeling, he'd promised to look into it. The next three calls had been from colleagues, who'd also heard the news, wondering if Trisha could send them those reports they'd asked for before she left.

His hands drew into tight fists on his desk. She hadn't bothered to call him and let him know she was going. Had she already been thinking about it when they'd spent the night together?

His head thumped out an angry rhythm and his stomach burned from the acid pouring into it. She didn't owe him an explanation.

But he sure wanted one.

Ignoring the warning signals that urged him to calm down and think this through before doing something rash, he grabbed up the phone and dialed her number.

"Hello?" Larry's voice came over the phone, his harried tone obvious. This was one unhappy man.

"This is Dr. Dunning. Is Trisha there?"

"She's here. Wait." Curt and to the point. He'd bet Trisha had gotten an earful about something. Good. At least he wasn't the only one taken by surprise. It was pretty obvious that Larry must know, especially if Trisha was telling her clients.

A few seconds later she was there, her greeting sounding wary and tired.

"What the hell's going on, Trisha?"

"I'm going away for a while."

"A while." The thumping in his head grew stronger.

"Don't you mean you're moving? For good? That's what you told Clara's mother."

"Okay. I'm moving."

No other explanation was offered. That was okay, because he wasn't afraid to ask. "Why? Is this because of me?"

Silence met his question for several long seconds. Then her voice came back. "Yes."

Yes. He'd expected her to give him some song and dance about how it wasn't anything personal, that she'd been called away on an emergency, or that she had a sick mother to take care of. A lie. And as stupid as it was, he was mad that he hadn't gotten one—that she'd given him a brutal dose of the truth instead.

"I see. When will you leave?"

Another pause. "As soon as all the arrangements are made."

That made him sit up. It was a strange way to word things. Not "in a week." Not "tomorrow morning". But "as soon as all the arrangements are made", as if someone else was pulling all the strings. Were they? Had something happened?

"Are you in some kind of trouble, Trisha?" He went back to what the sheriff had said about her background. Maybe she really was running from something. Or someone. "Is this about your husband?"

"Please, don't, Mike. I'm leaving. That's the end of it."

Tell her you love her and see if it changes things.

Where the hell had that come from?

He wasn't sure, but it was the truth. He'd known it for the last week, maybe longer. He'd just been in denial. Until now. When it was too late.

If this was about him—about what they'd done to-gether—wouldn't it be easier just to say, "Hey, sorry, but I really don't want to get involved. Let's be friends"? Why go to all the expense of moving? It just didn't add up. And yet she'd said it was because of him.

She was moving. Because of him.

It was the craziest thing he'd ever heard. "What about your horses? Laredo?"

Sarah was still recovering from the accident and wouldn't be able to ride for a while. But he couldn't see Trisha leaving them all behind.

"Laredo's being moved to another boarding facility." Her voice cooled. "As for my horses, what I do with them is my business."

She wouldn't sell them. Especially not Brutus. She and that grouchy horse seemed joined at the hip. But whatever her plans were, she wasn't going to share them with him. He could take a hint—especially when it came in the form of a two-by-four upside the head.

"Are you coming by the hospital before you go?"

"I—I don't think that would be wise."

So he didn't even merit a formal goodbye. So be it. Mike had never believed in chasing after someone who didn't want to be caught. So he wasn't even going to try.

"Okay. Well, have a good trip."

"Thanks. Goodbye."

Mike had to force the words past the sudden knot in his throat. "Goodbye, Trisha."

With that, he hung up the phone and dragged various file folders in front of him. It was time to put this chapter in his life firmly behind him. What better way to do that than to fill it with work. Lots and lots of work.

* * *

Two days later he was still going strong. Just coming out of surgery, he popped his phone off his belt and checked for messages.

Ray Chapman had texted him. Twice. Since when did the sheriff text rather than leave a voice mail? Pressing a button, he retrieved the messages. They were identical.

Inf on hippo.Call. Imprtnt.

Inf on hippo?

What on earth…? Maybe the man should step away from the keypad. Or get a better set of glasses.

The air caught in his chest as he reread the message. Hippo. Hippotherapist.

He checked the time. The sheriff had left the second text almost forty-five minutes ago.

He hit the dial button on his phone and headed for his office. Maybe the sheriff had discovered whatever Trisha was hiding. It was a little too late, though, since she was leaving. Whatever it was, it no longer mattered. He'd wanted the information to safeguard his patients. That was no longer a concern as far as the hippothera-pist went, since she wouldn't be working with them any more. Still, he needed to call his friend and tell him to forget about it.

"I was wondering when you were going to get back to me." His friend's gruff voice came through, not wast-ing time on niceties. Kind of par for the course where Ray was concerned.

"I was in surgery. About Trisha. Don't bother doing any more research because—"

"She's leaving. Yeah, yeah, yeah. I kind of gathered that from the number of cars out at her place."

"Cars?" What was he talking about?

"You remember those vehicles I told you about?"

Mike searched his memory banks. "I'm drawing a blank here."

"There were a couple of dark cars that rolled into town with her. I didn't think anything of it until you asked me to check for warrants. Well, those same cars are back."

"What do you mean, back?"

The sheriff gave an irritated snort. "Just what I said. I was parked on Miller Road at the entrance to town when these two sedans drove past me, keeping a careful eye on their speed. Government issue, if you ask me. I followed 'em, and they led me straight to the hippotherapist's place. I didn't take down license plates last time, but I'm pretty sure they're the same two men, down to the government-issue haircuts." He paused. "I'm guessing they're here to take her in. She had to have been involved in something pretty big to warrant the big dogs."

Mike's heart seized. Take her in? She was either being arrested or...

I can't tell you. Her words from a week ago rang in his ears, and the significance finally struck him.

She hadn't said "I don't want to tell you" or "I won't" but "I *can't.*"

She'd also said she wasn't running from the law. So if she wasn't being arrested...why were there strange vehicles at her place?

As soon as the arrangements are made.

She wasn't being arrested. She was being moved.

"Thanks, Ray. Keep an eye on her place for me. I'm on my way."

He hit the parking lot at a sprint and climbed into his car, flooring the gas pedal as soon as he found an open stretch of road. For the first time he cursed the hospital's location and the time it took to travel back and forth. Fifteen minutes later he passed Sheriff Chapman's car and sped on by, taking the first right. A cloud of dust spewed from beneath his vehicle as he skidded onto the dirt road. He saw the sheriff pull in behind him then switch on his lights and siren and swerve into the next lane before moving past him. Instead of busting him for speeding, Ray appeared to be leading the way.

Three minutes later he'd spun into Trisha's driveway. Mike pulled in beside his friend and braked in a hurry. There were indeed two sleek black SUVs parked in the gravel lot beside the barn, as well as a horse trailer hooked up to Trisha's big truck. That's not what captured his attention, however. It was the two men in dark suits...guns drawn.

Pointed straight at his windshield.

The sheriff was already out of the car, holding up his badge and demanding to see some ID.

The men ignored him, although they put their guns back into the holsters strapped across their chests. One of them, a big guy with close-cut gray hair, moved over to talk to his friend. Mike stepped out of the car, keeping his eyes trained on the second man, who looked a little trigger happy to him.

Trisha came bursting from the house at a run, feet bare, a long white skirt flowing out behind her. "It's okay. I know them."

Mike wasn't sure if she was talking to the men or to

him and the sheriff. It didn't matter. Seeing her again crushed the air from his lungs and set his heart racing.

It seemed all that work he'd been doing hadn't helped after all.

She hurried over to him. "Mike, what's going on?"

"I could ask you the same thing."

She gave a visible swallow, then her chin lifted, and she crossed her arms over her chest. "I already told you. I'm leaving."

"Are you in trouble with the authorities?"

Her head swung in a slow arc to the left and to the right.

Her eyes—puffy and red—held his. Despite her defiant posture, she didn't seem angry. She seemed composed. Resigned, even.

"You're not being arrested?"

She shook her head again. And he knew. Knew why she couldn't tell him. Knew why the men had drawn their guns the second they'd seen the sheriff and him barreling toward them. They expected someone to come for Trisha. To try to hurt her. Maybe even kill her.

Damn. He should have known. Should have figured it out.

He moved toward her, only to have her hold out her hand when he was about five feet away. "Mike, please, don't. It's better for everyone this way. I—I don't want anyone to get hurt because of who I am."

The burly guy with the crew cut swung round and strode toward Trisha, pointing a finger right at her chest. "Hey. Not another word. We talked about this."

Mike saw red. He grabbed the guy's arm, only to find himself flat on his back, his jaw feeling like it had been hit by a fifty-pound bag of cement.

Trisha was on her knees beside him in a second, cradling his head and waving off the man who stood over him with clenched fists. Her eyes filled with tears, spilling over and running down her cheeks. "I'm so sorry. I never meant for any of this to happen. You're right. My name isn't Trisha Bolton. It's—"

"No." He stopped her. "He's right. You shouldn't say anything else."

A flash of hurt went through her eyes, but she reached up and dashed the tears from her cheeks.

He took a deep breath. "I don't care who you are. All I know is that if you're leaving, I'm going with you."

Silence met his declaration. Even the oaf who'd just sucker-punched him seemed dumbfounded.

Mike wasn't sure where the words had come from, but he knew he meant them.

"You can't," Trisha whispered. "You'd have to give up everything you love—your career, your home, your life."

She hadn't said she didn't want him to go with her. She'd said he'd have to give up everything he loved.

"No, Trisha, I wouldn't." He lifted a hand to her face, ignoring the tightening of the guy's hands in front of him.

"Yes, you would." She seemed steadier now. Trying to firm up her resolve maybe. "And I can't allow that."

He smiled and slid his fingers down her throat. "You're operating under the false assumption that I love any of those things. I don't. The only thing I love is…you."

Her eyes widened. "What?"

The sheriff, who had been hanging back, now moved toward them, his hand on his own gun. "You want to press charges, Mike?"

The burly guy gave a harsh laugh. "You've got to be kidding me."

"I never kid about assault, son." Ray's eyes were cool, his mouth tight.

Crap, he wasn't joking. Mike got to his feet, even though he wanted nothing better than to stay in Trisha's lap and have her stare into his eyes. But he really wanted to do this out of the public spotlight. He reached down and helped her up as well. Turning to his friend, he placed a hand on his shoulder. "No harm done. I think we both want the same thing: to make sure Trisha's safe." He glanced at the man he guessed was a federal agent. "Is that right?"

The guy's jaw shifted from one side to the other before he answered. "That's right."

Mike kept hold of Trisha's hand. "I'm going to take her over to the barn for a few minutes so we can talk in private. If you all don't mind waiting here. I'd appreciate it."

The agent stepped in front of them. "Ms. Bolton?"

"It's okay. I'll go."

She allowed him to haul her to the barn, but once they ducked through the door she tugged her hand free. "You love me?"

"I was hoping to take things slow the other day, hoped that by telling you about Marcy you'd realize I wanted to deepen things between us. But then you panicked, and I realized I'd screwed things up. I didn't know how much until you said you were leaving."

"I was scared. Terrified. If I told you who I was I could put you—as well as my family—in danger. Roger could try to find me through you. Or he could hurt you just to get back at me." She must have seen his confusion, because she licked her lips. "You were right. I was married at one time. My ex-husband was with the Russian mob, although I didn't know that when I married him. Long story short, I testified against him, and they put me into witness protection. The only thing real about me are my horses. Everything else is made up."

"Not everything. I fell in love with you. Not your alias." He realized something. "You haven't said how you feel."

She reached up and looped her arms around his neck. "I was willing to give it all up. This town, my patients. For you. Does that give you some idea?"

It did. But he didn't want any misunderstandings. "It's not only women who need the words, Trisha."

She laughed and kissed his jaw. "Okay, then. I love you. Better?"

"Better." His heart swelled, telling moisture gathering behind his eyes. He clenched his jaw, forcing the tide back. "So where are we off to? Mexico? The Dominican Republic? I kind of like the idea of you sprawled on a beach in a tiny bikini."

"How about staying right here?"

"Won't you be safer elsewhere?"

She shook her head. "I wasn't worried about me in the first place. I was worried about you. About my family."

"You have parents? Do you talk with them?"

"My father's dead, but I have a mother and a brother. No, I don't talk to them. They know I'm safe, but they don't know where I am or my new name. Someday maybe that will change, but for now I'm okay with it as long as they're not in any danger."

A horse neighed in the distance. Trisha's head turned in that direction. "I need to know something. Are you going to be okay with my profession, and about keeping secrets from people? I know with your wife…is it going to bother you?"

Mike thought through that for a second. Tried to piece together his jumbled emotions about Marcy and their last few months together. "I think I still need to work though some things. When what I felt for you became greater than my fears about the past, I knew I was in trouble."

"Maybe we should talk to someone about it. Because I plan to stick around for a long time."

He gathered her hair into a ponytail and tipped her head back to look in her eyes. "That sounds like a plan, because I'm going to hold you to sticking around. I might even let you give me some more lessons."

"That sounds perfect."

"So we're all in this together? The Feds and the horses and the secret agent lifestyle?"

"Definitely together. That's the only way I want to do this."

One of the horses' noses appeared over the door of a stall and regarded them before he cocked his head and let out a long shrill whinny that echoed throughout the barn.

Trisha laughed. "I think Brutus might just agree."

EPILOGUE

"ARE YOU SURE?"

Mike, coffee cup halfway to his mouth, stopped to consider her question. She held up a finger to let him know she'd be with him in a minute.

Her contact at the FBI was on the phone, letting her know that Roger, aka Viktor Terenovsky, had attempted to escape while being transferred to another prison and had been killed by police officers at the scene. "We're sure. It's over, Trisha."

Over. She glanced at her husband and then at the new high chair that was parked beneath the kitchen table. Happy hands were busy smearing morning oatmeal over the white plastic tray and a dot of the stuff clung to long dark lashes that looked very much like her daddy's. The tiny blob bounced up and down with every blink of her eyes. Abigail Cardoso Dunning had been born in the middle of a snowstorm—a rarity in these parts. Luckily her dad was a brain surgeon and had been able to figure out how to deliver her at home, even if his hands shook as he held his baby girl for the first time. She motioned to Mike tapping her own finger to her eyelashes and then pointing at Abby.

Mike grinned and set down his coffee and grabbed

a napkin, attempting to wipe off the offending spot. Only Abby acted as if the square of paper were some terrible monster, twisting her head to and fro to avoid being touched by it.

No, sweetheart, it's not a monster. The real bad guy will never be able to knock on your door...or pose a threat to you.

"I hate to say I'm relieved he's dead," she told Clyde. "But I am."

That got Mike's attention. He stared at her with enough force that she covered the handset with her palm. "Roger was killed last night while trying to escape."

"Wow. After five years. I thought his ghost would always be hanging around our doorstep."

The Feds had been pretty unhappy about Trisha staying in Dusty Hills and spilling the details of the situation to Mike, but she'd refused to keep any more secrets from this man. Once it had been out, the two agents had had no choice but to accept her decision to stay. They'd even promised to check in on her mom and brother periodically. And Ray had assured them that the town was pretty protective of its residents. No one else needed to know but them, and he'd keep a personal watch over the place. If someone so much as cruised past Trisha's driveway, he'd make the call himself. No one ever had. The two of them—three now, with Abby—had stayed put, and Trisha finally felt like she could safely put down roots. Maybe now she'd even be able to call her mom and introduce her to her granddaughter.

Trisha thanked the agent, knowing this was probably the last time she'd ever hear from him. "I appreciate everything you've done for me."

"You know," Clyde said, "you can probably even go back to using your old name if you want."

Patty Ann Stoker. That name seemed to come from another era, belonging to another woman. Her life was far removed from her upper-crust roots back in New York City.

She glanced at Mike, who'd finally succeeded in wiping the oatmeal from Abby's mouth and eyelashes. She smiled. "I happen to love the name I have." *And the man who had given it to her.* "I think I'm going to keep it."

* * * * *